CRYSTAL CROWNED

BOOK FIVE OF AIR AWAKENS

CRYSTAL CROWNED

BOOK FIVE OF AIR AWAKENS

ELISE KOVA

Silver Wing Press

Published by Silver Wing Press
Copyright © 2016 by Elise Kova

Cover Artwork by Merilliza Chan
Editing by Monica Wanat

ISBN (paperback): 9781619844780
ISBN (hardcover): 9781619844773
eISBN: 9781619844797

Library of Congress Control Number: 2016906373

Printed in the U.S.A

*For those who dare
to write their own love story*

TABLE OF CONTENTS

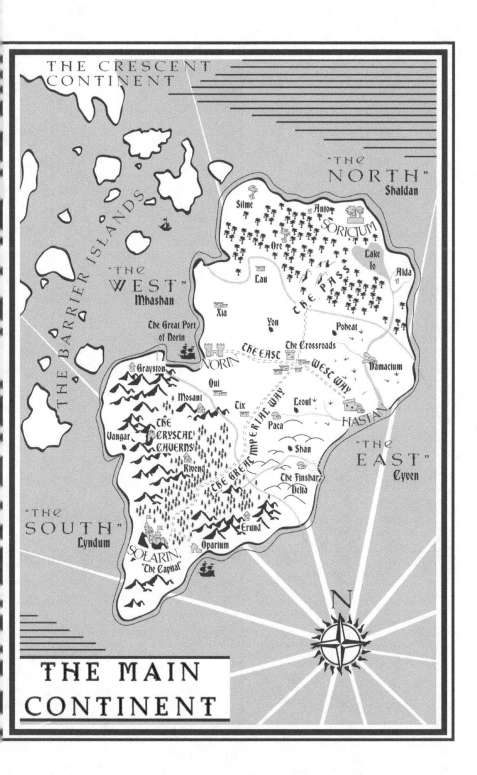

CHAPTER 1

FRIGID AIR CLAWED its way under the pelts piled atop Vhalla Yarl, hunting out her warmth to herd it away as only winter could. She rolled over, jarred awake by a searing pain in her shoulder. Wincing inwardly, she eased off the wound, her hand instinctually reaching to rub it. It throbbed and itched worse with each passing day. Elecia was doing all she could to heal it, but healing supplies were severely limited. Even for a sorcerer of the woman's caliber, there was only so much that could be done to quicken the healing process.

Vhalla rubbed her eyes and pushed herself to a seated position. Her companions rested where they had finally collapsed the day prior, the after effects of mental exhaustion. Fritz breathed heavily to her left, huddled against Elecia. Jax lay to Vhalla's right. The Northern princess and her guard curled in on each other, slumbering in the corner.

Her eyes met the Westerner's, and Vhalla inquisitively searched his gaze. Jax understood her silent question, snaking a hand out from under the blankets and pointing to the doorway. Vhalla stared at the vacant space to her immediate right, the vacancy that had let the cold in. *One of her companions was not as she had left them.*

Easing herself slowly up, Vhalla crept out of the bedroom,

pulling a heavy blanket around her shoulders. The main room was empty. Fire smoldered in the recesses of the hearth, offering little to ward off the chill. It was easy to take stock of the Charem family home; there was the room in which the guests slept, the loft above that held Fritz's family, and the main room in which she now stood. Her eyes fell on the boots lined up by the door, and her gaze noted the empty space between two pairs.

Booted and bundled, Vhalla ventured into the early twilight morning. The moon and stars still offered as much light as the early tendrils of dawn. The world of heavy snow and skeleton trees was void of color. It seemed as if it was withholding life until those horrors that had been unleashed upon the land were sorted out.

A line of footprints led away from the front door. Vhalla struggled through the deep snowdrifts on her short legs. She followed the tracks up a short ridge toward a sitting figure looking over the small quick-moving stream that the Charems used as their primary source of water.

The Emperor of Solaris sat as still as a statue. He was cut from midnight shadows and moonlight. The light dusting of snow looked like stars upon a night sky against the dark blanket over his shoulders. His skin was carved from alabaster, not even reddening by the cold. Vhalla wondered if a man with fire in his veins even felt the chill as she did.

She eased down next to him, their sides touching. She followed his line of sight, trying to see what so captivated his attention beyond the early morning's horizon. She slowly took his hand in hers, lacing her fingers against his.

There was no lightning to his touch now, only heat. But even without the Bond, she knew how his mind worked. She felt his emotions like a phantom limb—a hollow and strange sensation of what should be there, of what her heart knew was there, but wasn't. Vhalla finally drew her eyes to study his profile.

She had yet to find words to say to him. After the group's proclamation that he was their true Emperor, he had announced that he was retiring early. Vhalla had gone with him, letting him draw whatever support he could from her presence. He had clung to her throughout the night, but withdrew before the sun rose.

She wanted to find the right words. She wanted to say something to give him strength, to remind him of all he still had. She wanted to say something that wouldn't echo as a false display of support. But it would all be empty solutions to a problem that they both knew couldn't be fixed. What did one say to a man who had lost everything but gained the world?

"Aldrik," she began weakly.

"We need to move." His voice was stronger than she expected, and it gave her pause. "You said there was a messenger."

Vhalla nodded, though she wasn't sure how he saw the motion. His eyes still had yet to leave that distant point on the horizon.

"There will be others, many others. Victor is clearly trying to make a quick claim for the Empire, before any have an opportunity to group against him," he spoke mechanically, emotionlessly. His mind was moving faster than the wind, but his heart seemed like it had stopped altogether.

"Aldrik," Vhalla tried again, a little stronger.

He continued without giving her his attention, "We need to unite the people faster than he can, under the banner which they have been fighting for—the Solaris banner. We must protect them."

"Aldrik."

She tugged firmly on his hand, and his head finally swung to her. His eyes were listless, only the hint of red at the edges betrayed that a piece of his heart had survived the latest blow.

A heart that had been shattered with the death of his brother no more than days before.

A weak condolence stopped before it could pass her lips. Vhalla swallowed it down. She pressed her mouth into a firm line, giving him a nod. "We will protect your people."

The knot in his neck bobbed as he swallowed hard. Her arms slipped out from under the blanket, wrapping tightly around his shoulders and pulling him to her. His hands found life again and tugged her toward him and onto his lap, swaddling her under his blanket against his warmth.

The pads of his fingers dug into her side and shoulder. It felt as though they were trying to meld back into one mind and one body, as they had once before with the Bond. Aldrik's face buried in the side of her neck, and Vhalla stared at nothing as his breath seeped through her layers to her skin.

"*Our* people."

They remained until the sun crested the horizon, tucked against each other, the silence speaking louder than any words could. Aldrik hoisted her, carrying her halfway back to the Charem home, a happy trail of smoke emitting plumes from the chimney. Vhalla saw it only as a beacon. If Victor's tainted monsters had any sentience left at all, they would know to come in this direction soon.

Or, far more likely, Victor would drive them in logical directions. The creature had demanded people kneel so the new king could see their loyalty. Clearly, the crystals created a magical connection between Victor and his abominations.

Back inside the house, no one said anything about the return of the Emperor and the woman who was once the Windwalker. Cass, the eldest Charem daughter, kept the conversation going throughout breakfast. But it wasn't nearly as lively as Vhalla's first meal with the brood. Reona sat listlessly, moving food around her plate as though the face of the tainted monster they'd witnessed in town was beneath it and she wanted to keep it hidden. Elecia alternated between concerned glances at Aldrik and hushed whispers with Jax. Fritz tried to remain his bubbly self, but even that seemed hollow. There was a deeper, somber current that tore its way across the world, and the table had been swept up in it.

When the food was mostly finished, Aldrik cleared his throat lightly, more to prepare himself to speak than to gain the attention of anyone. "I require a word."

There was no confusion as to who he required a word with and, shortly thereafter, the seven of them were crammed into the smaller back room. The Firebearers conjured thin motes of fire to hover harmlessly in the corners, warming the room to a comfortable temperature—but their efforts did little to warm Vhalla. She sat next to Aldrik, so close they were touching.

"We will leave tonight," Aldrik announced the moment his unorthodox council was settled.

"Tonight?" Fritz was reluctant to even consider the notion. "It will be absolutely freezing. Cass said she saw the makings of a storm on the horizon when she was getting wood this morning."

"All the better. The moonlight will guide us; it's full enough, and the storm will hide our tracks."

Had Aldrik been looking at the horizon for storms? Had he woken so early to see if they could make headway in the darkness? Vhalla wondered in surprise. She had no doubt as to the sincerity of the grief that piled on his shoulders. But her prince—*no, Emperor*, she corrected mentally—remained ever focused. In the end, his nature and upbringing won over his grief.

"Fritz," Vhalla interrupted her friend before he could protest again. "We need to go. We're a danger to your family if we stay."

"What?" The blonde's expression changed dramatically.

"Victor is announcing that the whole of the Solaris family is dead, that I am dead. His monster demanded that all kneel before their new king so Victor could bear witness to their loyalty. Those who did not met a horrible fate. A fate I would never want to see brought upon your family." She spoke gently, but she wasn't going to spare Fritz the truth. He had been to war, he knew horrors, and he needed to know that it would be at this doorstep if they didn't leave.

"But . . ."

"She's right," Elecia interjected. "If—when—Victor finds out Aldrik is still alive, it will turn into a manhunt. What do you think will happen to anyone who is known to harbor or help us?"

Fritz slumped.

"You can stay." Vhalla reached out, lightly touching her friend's knee. "We have to go, but you don't have to. They're not hunting you, Fritz, and you can lie about your involvement. I will understand if you stay."

"Don't be stupid, Vhal." Fritz squeezed her hand. "The Charems aren't a bunch of weak flowers. We can protect ourselves. By the Mother, Cass can be more frightening than anything I've ever seen Victor create."

Vhalla tried to maintain an appropriate expression in the face of Fritz's determined smile, but she was certain she fell short. Her friend hadn't seen what Victor had created. He couldn't comprehend what type of magic the former Minister of Sorcery was capable of now.

"If I leave you now," he continued, "Larel will come back from the dead and haunt me 'til my dying breath."

She squeezed his hand in reply. Vhalla felt genuinely guilty about taking her friend from his home when he had just returned, especially when the world was so uncertain. But she also felt relief that he would remain by her side. Fritz was a man;

he could make his own choices, and, as his friend, she had to let him.

"Now that that's settled," Elecia gave Fritz an approving nod, happy as well that he'd be joining them, "the fastest route to Norin from here would be the old roads. But if we took the Great Southern Way through the—"

"We're not going to Norin," Aldrik stated, reclaiming the conversation.

"What?" Elecia asked in confusion that mirrored Vhalla's.

"My uncle will raise the banners at the first word of what Victor has done, with or without me."

"Mhashan will never support a tyrant who has murdered their prince and seeks to oppress them." Jax gave Aldrik an approving nod.

"However, the East is not so simple." Aldrik's eyes fell on Vhalla. She straightened, trying to grow into the role he was not so subtly placing upon her. "The East is uninterested in war. They'll side with the victor—" Aldrik grimaced at the word, realizing the brutal irony at the same time as everyone else, "—with the *winner*, if they think it means preserving the peace and government for their people."

"Bleeding heart Easterners." Elecia rolled her eyes.

"Stay your tongue," Aldrik warned his cousin. "They are part of this Empire, and we need them for our army." He turned his attention to the silent Northerners in the room. "We will need your people as well."

"As long as our deal remains, you shall have them." Sehra, princess of Shaldan, Child of Yargen, gave an affirmative motion.

Vhalla's stomach clenched, but her expression betrayed nothing of her uncertainty at those words. *If* she and Aldrik wed and she bore him an heir, their child would be sent to the North as a gesture of good faith and a promise to look after the people in the recently conquered land. Sehra met her eyes, as if trying to root out Vhalla's turmoil at the thought.

"Your deal remains," Vhalla spoke on behalf of her and Aldrik. She would say the words that they needed—that she knew he wasn't prepared to speak again.

"Come north with us until the Eastern cutoff." There was a cooling hostility between Aldrik and the Northern women. It was almost tangible in the way he had changed his speech patterns toward them. Now that he was no longer in a forced engagement with the princess, things were more relaxed between them. The deal for his child aside, there were signs of hope for the future negotiations between the Northern clans and their new ruler. "We will all be safer in a group."

"I protect Sehra," Za proclaimed in her broken Southern common.

"You will," Aldrik agreed with a graceful nod of his head, "but it will be easier when you have extra eyes to keep watch at night so that you may rest." This seemed to satisfy Za, so Aldrik continued, "When we arrive in Hastan, I will send word regarding plans to regroup in Norin."

"So we *are* going to Norin then?" Elecia couldn't hide her eagerness at the idea of returning home.

Aldrik nodded as he confirmed, "We must. If there are no further questions, then we should spend the day prepar—"

"There is something else," Elecia spoke over Aldrik, eliciting an arch of a dark eyebrow from her Emperor. Her eyes turned to Vhalla. "She should stay here."

"No." Vhalla wasn't sure who said it first, her or Aldrik.

"You can stay hidden among the Charem girls." Elecia was now appealing to Vhalla. "If Southerners passed for you on the march, you could pass—"

"No." Aldrik wasn't hearing another word.

"Aldrik." Elecia's attention shifted. "I know you want her to come. But you also want her alive, don't you? She can't protect herself."

"This is not up for discussion."

"She cannot come!" Elecia finally snapped. "If she does, you are a reckless fool, and your life is worth far more than hers!"

"Don't you dare," Aldrik snarled at his kin. Magic flashed dangerously around a clenched fist, red sparking to orange fire.

Elecia remained unfazed and didn't back down. "If you die, who will the banners rally behind? If she comes, you will throw your life away for hers the first time she needs protecting. And such a need *will* arise, especially since she's just a Commons."

"Elecia, I am your Emperor now—"

Vhalla's heart stopped at those words said aloud.

"Then act like it!" Elecia clearly was not struck by the same awe. "Think of the people you are responsible for. They need *you*, Aldrik. They need their Emperor. No one will stand to challenge Victor if not you. No one can unite the banners like you can."

"Do not assume for a moment that I do not know how many lives I am responsible for." Aldrik's voice deepened. "This is not your choice."

"And it's not yours either, Aldrik." Vhalla finally spoke up, silencing the group. "It's mine."

"Vhalla . . ."

Her lover's eyes searched her desperately. Anger quickly turned into fear that she would agree with Elecia. That she would leave him. Vhalla knew that logic defined it as the "right" choice. But what they were, everything she and Aldrik had ever been, defied logic.

"I will go."

"Are you mad or just selfish?" Elecia snapped viciously.

Aldrik ignored his cousin and gave Vhalla a slow, relieved smile.

"If I stay," Vhalla began, tearing her eyes from the quiet joy that a smile on Aldrik's lips gave her to look at the seething Western woman. "What will happen the first time Aldrik thinks me in trouble?"

The woman had no response.

"How will constant worry about my wellbeing impact his focus?"

Elecia still said nothing.

"Who will push him when he needs to be pushed?" Vhalla stole a glance at Aldrik, hoping he didn't take offense to her words. "Who else is unafraid to say what needs to be said, when it must be said, to him of all people?"

She met Elecia's disbelief with a challenge. Aldrik and Vhalla had wrapped their lives around the "appropriate" decisions as dictated by the world. They'd hidden their wants and pushed aside what they had known to be true. *What had it earned them?* A world of death. She'd had enough of doing what the world wanted.

"I am not helpless," Vhalla insisted. She had been training for weeks with Daniel. "Give me a sword, and I can defend myself."

"Damn you both." Elecia wasn't giving up gracefully. "You'll get yourselves killed, and that's the end of that."

"Nothing will happen to either of us."

"You can't honestly believe that, Aldrik."

"Oh, enough," Jax groaned. "If you're that worried, I'll do it."

"What?" the three said in unison.

" 'Cia is right, Aldrik." Vhalla had never heard anyone other than Aldrik use Elecia's childhood nickname, but Elecia made no objection to it being uttered by Jax's lips. "You must live, and you know it. But me? My life means nothing. So I'll be her sworn defender."

"Your life isn't nothing," Vhalla couldn't stop herself from objecting.

Jax tilted his head back with laughter. "You still don't really know much about me, do you?"

Vhalla pressed her lips together in frustrated thought. She searched for a way to object, and yet she couldn't, which was all the more aggravating.

"Why?" Aldrik seemed more curious than disbelieving.

"For Baldair."

Vhalla inhaled a sharp breath, the name like an ice dagger to her gut. She remembered what Victor had said about the late prince, about quartering his body and feeding it to the dogs. Her hand rose up to massage the angry scar that covered her shoulder to chest.

"The last order I received from him was to protect her—"

"Fine job you did of it," Aldrik remarked curtly.

Jax faltered a moment, a wounded expression overcoming his face.

"It wasn't his fault," Vhalla insisted, equally sharp. "What happened is on my shoulders." She wasn't going to let Jax take Aldrik's ire for it.

"Let me have another chance." Jax was relentless. "I am owned by the crown. It's a fitting duty."

Elecia averted her eyes at the reminder, as though she could un-hear the truth that spilled from Jax's lips. Vhalla knew his situation had been similar to her previous enslavement, but she had no idea how it had come to pass. It was now something she desperately wanted to know.

"That leash now transfers to you, my Emperor." Aldrik seemed more bothered by what Jax was saying than Jax himself.

The conversation was moving too fast for Vhalla to inquire about what leash.

"Order me to do it, and I'll defend her to my dying breath. I'll treat her life as my own. I'll do it for Baldair and for you, my sovereign."

Aldrik considered it, much to Vhalla's shock.

"Come now, I'm not the hero type. Let me have this moment as we go out and save the world." Jax gave a toothy grin as easily as if he was talking about the weather.

"Jax, I am not in the mood for levity." Aldrik pinched the bridge of his nose with a sigh. "Very well."

"Excuse me?" Vhalla finally entered the conversation, *sharply*. "I get no say in this? I said I can take care of myself."

"Then use me only for those times when you can't take care of yourself," Jax countered easily. Sensing her continuing objection, he added, "Don't take Baldair's last order from me."

It was part threat, part anger, part sorrow, and all determination. Vhalla bowed her head, frustrated. He was tugging on just the right heartstring to get what he wanted, and she hated him for it.

"All right," she agreed weakly. "But find me a sword the first moment we can."

"Well, if there is nothing else." Aldrik cast a wary eye toward Elecia. "We leave at sundown."

They followed their Emperor's decrees, every last one of them. They tacked the horses and filled their bellies with the last hot meal they were likely to get for the foreseeable future. The Charem family swore their secret loyalty even as Aldrik ordered them to bend knee in body—but not in heart—to Victor. After the moon had begun its journey into the sky, they rode out swathed in the darkest cloaks the Charems owned.

The Emperor Solaris led his loyal few into the uncertain darkness.

Chapter 2

THEY HAD UNDERESTIMATED Victor, specifically the speed at which his abominations could be created and moved. Those forced to follow his will were going to be subjected to death by ten thousand cuts from witnessing those they loved being turned into horrors. And this would be before Victor began mobilizing an actual structured army to take the continent. That is if any survived to object to Victor's rule.

As the Emperor and his loyalists arrived at the first tiny town beyond Fritz's home, they discovered it painted red with blood.

Half frozen bodies, glistening crimson, littered the ground in the mid-morning sun. Men, women, children—the young and old—were reduced to shades of former life. Vhalla stared on tiredly. It shouldn't hurt any longer, but pain sat rooted in her chest. She had seen this before. She had lived this blood-stained life recently, now more real than when she had filed books away in the Imperial Library.

Vhalla unfurled the vise-like grip she held on her reins and raised a hand to her shoulder, soaked through to the skin from the heavily falling snow. Her fingers massaged the angry scar tissue. It ached and stung all the way down her arm. The physical pain was a mask for the visceral guilt that tore its way through her.

This was her fault.

"He didn't spare anyone, did he?" Elecia whispered. Whatever had caused the carnage was long gone, but she still kept her voice low, in homage to the dead surrounding them.

"Why didn't they kneel?" Aldrik's brows knotted together, deep lines appearing between them. He asked the question they all were thinking.

"They never would've." Fritz swayed in the breeze, nearly falling out of his saddle. Vhalla wondered if he'd known people in this town like she'd known people in the neighboring town to Leoul. "For centuries, the eldest in every family went to serve in the Imperial guard, back to when the South was just Lyndum." The Southerner shook his head. "They'd never accept someone who wasn't a Solaris on the throne."

Aldrik's lips pressed together into a scowl. Vhalla struggled to find something to relieve his pain, but there was nothing she could say when her guilt was just as heavy.

"We'll rest here until sunset," Aldrik decided, pointing to a small tavern.

The seven housed their mounts in the attached stables, alongside a tired-looking pony and a spooked mare. It was expectedly empty inside, void of both corpses and survivors.

"Well, they still have ale," Jax revealed from his inspection from behind the bar.

"Leave it," Aldrik ordered.

"Just because you—"

Aldrik silenced Jax with a pointed look that he quickly abandoned when he pinched the bridge of his nose with a sigh. "I will have no drunken stupors on this journey."

"One drink does not a stupor make." Jax crossed his arms

over his chest; it hid the slight tremble Vhalla had noticed in his hands when he had run them along the bar.

Aldrik sighed heavily. "Do what you will. We move again at sundown. You should enjoy the beds while we have them."

Taking his own advice, Aldrik dragged his feet up the small stairs that presumably led to the inn's rooms. Concern lined Jax's forehead as his eyes followed the Emperor's departure. Vhalla caught his look and gave a nod in affirmation, following on Aldrik's heels.

His cloak was already hanging to dry when she poked her nose in the crack of the doorway. Aldrik turned quickly at the sound, nearly crumpling from exhaustion when he saw it was only her. Vhalla eased the door shut behind her and rested her back against it.

"These people served my family for centuries." Aldrik started a small fire with a look, and Vhalla was relieved to see that, despite his mood, it did not flare out of control. "A whole town of them, sons and daughters, loyal to the Solaris name until their end. And I-I was never made aware."

"We will honor them."

"How? With what?" Aldrik's voice had bite, but his expression was tired and his eyes searching.

"Until this is over, we will have to carry their memory with us. But when we have fixed all this, we can do more," she vowed, as much to him as to herself.

"This is something that cannot be fixed."

Vhalla bit her lip thoughtfully. "For those face-first in the snow? No." She squeezed her eyes closed with a soft sigh. Baldair was behind her eyes as the ghost who rode with them all, the man they'd had no time to properly mourn but were reminded of at every turn. "He seeks to turn the continent into this desolation, Aldrik. It is not too late for everyone still breathing.

We fight for them. We honor the dead with a commitment to the living."

When Vhalla opened her eyes again, he stood before her. Aldrik considered her for a long moment. His long fingers rose to the ties of her cloak at her neck, and Vhalla let him slip the fabric off her shoulders. She let the warmth of his hands seep as deeply as it could into the icy brambles that had vined around her heart.

"You're soaking wet," he breathed. "Aren't you cold?"

"Freezing," she whispered in reply.

"Fortunately for you, your *future husband* happens to command fire with his hands." Aldrik watched her as his declaration settled onto her shoulders.

"Truly?" It was hard to believe, even now, with the world as it was.

"If you do not wish it, now would be the time to tell me." The words could've been a jest, but they carried a serious note.

Vhalla raised a hand to the watch at her neck. Its chain had barely missed being severed by Victor's axe, the only pity fate had taken upon her. Aldrik followed her motion to the token he had given her the first time he had asked for her future to be spent at his side.

"My love," he sighed in relief, resting his forehead against hers.

Their noses brushed against each other, and Vhalla pressed an exhausted kiss into his mouth. The day would permit no further affection than that, but she allowed herself to melt into it. Her lord, friend, and lover—if she didn't ground her heart in something, it wasn't going to survive the rest of their journey.

They left promptly at sundown as Aldrik had instructed. Vhalla knew the man had hardly slept at all, but she was in no place to scold him for it, as she had spent most of the hours awake as well, haunted by the town's stillness. On their departure, Vhalla held them up, insistently searching the town and bodies for a useable sword. When she found one, it was small, and not nearly as fine as anything she had used when training with Daniel, but the cold steel felt reassuring on her hip.

The next afternoon, they stayed in the woods, which was far less comfortable than sleeping in one of the abandoned rooms of an inn, but it was easier mentally. Periodically throughout the day, Fritz used his Waterrunner abilities to command the snow to shift and hide their tracks, including the last hour or so before they broke camp. They rotated watches and slept huddled against each other.

One night, they slept against a fallen tree, then in a cave, then out in the open. They passed abandoned homes, slaughtered towns, and places where the people were so silent and still they could have been dead. They walked parallel to the Great Imperial Way, which appeared and disappeared in the distance, through the trees and snowdrifts. But for all of their concerns and careful progress, they never saw another wandering soul.

As the days and distance slipped by, silence became their primary companion. At first, they didn't speak out of necessity and nerves, then out of respect for the dead, then out of fear of discovery. But it finally became the way of things, the world too much to be expressed with language. Vhalla began to yearn for Aldrik's nightly whispers affirming his adoration when he took her into his arms so they could sleep hunched together. It was one of the few things that kept her strong.

Vhalla lost track of the days. It could have been a week. It could have been a year.

When they came across a small hunter's hovel, she wanted to cry with relief. Abandoned, it offered an opportunity for them to get out of the cold and to dry out their boots. The front had mostly collapsed, but the remaining walls supported a pitched roof that stood in defiance of the snow.

"I'll give it a look." Jax swung down off his horse, quickly inspecting the structure and deeming it stable enough for them to spend the night.

"Is it too close to the road?" Elecia glanced nervously at the Imperial Way, barely visible through the trees.

"We haven't seen anyone for days," Fritz groaned. "I want a roof."

"It's not going to be any warmer than sleeping outside; half the front is missing," Elecia pointed out.

"If we hang up our cloaks to dry on the walls, it could block the light from a small fire and keep us warm enough." Jax turned to Aldrik, who remained mounted at Vhalla's left. "What do you say?"

Aldrik glanced back to the road, clearly weighing the options. "If we don't get out of the cold, one of us will fall ill, and that would be worse," he decided.

They dismounted and tied their horses to the closest tree. Fritz led the charge for "making house" and quickly demanded everyone's cloak. Elecia helped alongside Jax. Though the Western man never let Vhalla out of his sight for very long— her new shadow.

"I'll take the first watch," Vhalla offered with a yawn.

"Are you sure?" Aldrik asked.

"I've been getting the most sleep; it's my turn to watch."

"Yes, but—"

"I'm fine." Vhalla rubbed her shoulder for emphasis. It was still tender, but the skin grew stronger by the day. She knew the ache she felt would always be there. It would be there until Victor died, and it would be there every moment afterward. "Rest, Aldrik."

Her Emperor conceded, disappearing under the cloak Jax

was using to close up the gaping hole in the building's front. Vhalla's attention shifted to the two who remained in the snow.

Sehra walked to a tree and placed both her palms on it. She did this every day, regardless of when they stopped, dawn or sunset. Vhalla watched as the young woman brought her forehead to the icy bark and remained still and reverent.

None of the group had questioned or stopped the Northerners. Vhalla looked on, curiosity finally getting the better of her.

"What are you doing?" she asked when the two women headed toward their sleeping place for the night.

Za and Sehra looked at each other, momentarily startled. Sehra studied Vhalla for a tense moment. Whatever test she had been silently administering, Vhalla passed.

"I'm looking for traces of crystal magic," she answered.

"You can do that?" Vhalla blurted in surprise.

Za snorted.

Momentarily wearing a small satisfied smile, Sehra answered, "I can."

"How?"

"You doubt Sehra?" Za asked defensively.

"She doesn't," Sehra answered before Vhalla could. "She just doesn't understand. Crystal magic is much like the old magic. Similar, but different. Like light and darkness, two halves to a whole. One knows of the other, even if they cannot command it."

The princess's explanation could've been condescending but wasn't, Vhalla noted. She considered this for a long moment. She understood what the princess said, but she still had no concept of what made crystal magic and "old magic" different.

"And you can do this because you are a Child of Yargen?"

The smile Sehra gave then was certainly genuine. The young woman had been schooled in diplomacy and it showed. But her youth also betrayed her in moments when she felt as though she could relax. Vhalla filed this information away in case she needed to capitalize on it in the future, and hated herself for doing so.

"That is so," Sehra affirmed.

"What does that mean?"

"It means that I am chosen to wield Yargen's power and be an overseer of fate." The way Sehra spoke showed she believed every word of what she was saying, no matter how fantastical it sounded.

"Like a God?" Vhalla tried to confirm she knew what Sehra was claiming before she passed judgment on it.

Za laughed at the question. "Only Gods are Gods."

"More like an agent of the Gods," Sehra elaborated. "You have much interest?"

"I do." Vhalla swallowed, easing the next words between her lips with as much grace and strength as she possessed. "I want to know more about where my first born will spend his or her childhood, should it all come to pass."

The wind agreed gustily with Vhalla's words, whipping snow and hair across her face. Sehra remained so still that Vhalla wondered if she'd thought, rather than spoken, the words.

"Do not fear so deeply, Vhalla Yarl." Sehra made a fist with her right hand, clasping the left over it. The gesture meant nothing to Vhalla, but she understood enough meaning—that there was peace, strength, and respect ahead for them all—from the princess's expression. "The path you chose to walk with me is not easy. But it is right."

Deeming the conversation finished, Za and Sehra disappeared. Vhalla felt like she'd ended up with more questions than answers. She paced around, racking her brain for everything she'd read on the North, but it was precious little. Vhalla felt frustrated with herself. She could name almost all the Southern kings in order, but not one of the Northern Head Clans.

The crunching of snow and the whinny of a horse cut through her thoughts. Vhalla turned away from the structure where the mounts were tethered. Something spooked the horse: a snow hare, a fox creeping from its den. Her fingers closed around the hilt of her sword, debating whether to draw it. Would the sound alert any potential threat? Would it give up a potential advantage she had?

She briefly thought about waking Jax or Elecia or Aldrik, but the soft glow of the firelight winking through the gaps in the hung cloaks had just faded. *They had only just fallen asleep, and she wouldn't wake them for what was likely nothing.*

Vhalla held her breath as she rounded the corner of the structure where the horses were tethered. She saw nothing. Just when she was about to relax, the snow crunched to her right.

She swung the sword on instinct. Vhalla caught sight of Imperial armor, a palace guard. The world slowed as she arced her sword down into the man's shoulder. It rang out against his plate, alerting the rest of her group.

The sword hummed as it fell from Vhalla's hands. She stared in shock at the ghost who confronted her. *It couldn't be.*

"What the—?" Jax was the fastest to rouse, bursting through the hanging cloak and skidding to a stop as he rounded the corner.

The man gripped her without hesitation. Spinning her in place, Vhalla was compressed against a familiar chest, and he held her head against his shoulder with a palm over her mouth. A dagger was at her throat in an instant.

Aldrik was fast on Jax's heels, his eyes were aflame with rage the moment they landed on the blade pressing into her throat.

"Don't move," a rough masculine voice demanded. "If you don't want her to die, don't move."

CHAPTER 3

"I'M GOING TO take one of your horses," the man continued. "You'll let me or she dies."

"You don't know who you've picked a fight with, friend." Jax shook his head with a laugh. He stepped forward into the snow and froze. Vhalla watched as his eyes alighted with comprehension. Jax heard what she had heard. He saw what had made her willingly disarm herself. "Daniel?"

Vhalla closed her eyes in relief.

"Wh-who-what?" Daniel's grip loosened some. "No, *no* impossible. It's not possible." With a growl, Daniel jerked her back toward him, tightening his hold. "Don't lie to me, specter."

"Daniel." Jax held up his hands in a motion that was meant to show harmlessness. Vhalla briefly appreciated its irony, coming from a man who could summon flame with a thought. "It's me, Jax. The woman you are holding is Vhalla."

The man holding her, the person who spoke with Daniel's voice and wore enough of Daniel's image to convince Jax, let out a rasp that was nearly inhuman in its craze. He cackled, and it squelched the small bud of hope that had bloomed in Vhalla's stomach.

"I don't know who you are, but I know you're a liar. The Lady Vhalla Yarl is dead."

She wished he'd loosen his grip over her mouth long enough for her to get a word in.

"Daniel," Fritz spoke softly, taking a step from behind Jax. "She's not dead, she's right—"

"Don't tell me she's alive! I watched her die on the Sunlit Stage! I watched him force her to kneel as he let his monsters tear her apart limb from limb." He was nearly shouting, and Vhalla hoped that Sehra had been correct in there being no crystal magic, and therefore no abominations, nearby.

Who had died in the public execution?

"Next." Daniel laughed again, the blade biting into her throat from his trembling hand. "Next you'll be telling me that-that the man standing there is . . ."

The words faded into the wind. Aldrik's eyes were alight with rage, his posture rigid. But his focus had shifted off Vhalla and onto Daniel, presumably meeting his eyes.

"I am the Emperor Solaris," Aldrik finished, dangerously quiet.

"Supreme King Anzbel, he . . ." More raspy laughing. "Enough, I don't know who or what you really are, but I am getting that horse and I am going. I don't care if I have to kill her for it!"

"You would shame Baldair's memory?" Jax exclaimed. No one moved. "Daniel, he gave you an order. He asked you to protect the woman you are threatening to kill, to protect her until your dying breath."

"Stop . . ." Daniel whispered.

"No! You swore an oath to the guard. As long as your heart beats, you are to honor it," Jax pressed. The knife at her throat quivered, and Vhalla ignored the pain. "Brother." The world turned on Jax's singular word. "Let her go."

Suddenly, the knife was gone, and his grip went slack. For all of Jax's words, he clearly didn't completely trust his brother-in-arms in his present state; he closed the gap between them, grabbing for Vhalla and spinning her half behind him.

Now freed, she could assess the man everyone else had seen all along. The man she was thankful she hadn't killed. Daniel was haggard. His armor was crusted with blood, and yellow bandages were wrapped around his forearm where a gauntlet was missing. His hair was slick with sweat and grime. The makings of a proper beard crossed his chin.

None of this scared Vhalla. A body could be washed, injuries tended to. It was Daniel's eyes that broke something in her. There was something deeply wrong down to his very soul, something that no potion or salve could cure.

"Daniel, it's me." She finally lowered her hood, studying his expression for some trace of the man whom she had marched with and learned from.

"I-I cut you," he stammered.

Vhalla raised a hand to her neck. "So you did. Don't worry, it doesn't hurt."

"I was supposed to protect you." He swayed. "And then, I watched you die."

"I'm fine." Vhalla took a step forward. Jax shot her a warning look, and Vhalla replied with a glare. The Western man didn't stop her, but he stayed near her shoulder as she crossed the gap to Daniel. The man was like a stylized painting, from far away he may be passible for a man, but the moment she was up close she could see every frayed brushstroke and wavering line. Vhalla boldly took his hands, and he nearly jumped out of his skin at the touch. "See, I'm fine. You, however, are not. Come inside and sit. Get out of the cold."

Za volunteered that she and Sehra keep watch, casting a leery eye toward Daniel. Even after the Northerners left, it was cramped with the six of them in the small structure. Daniel was jumpy with the proximity to people, his eyes darting wildly.

"Elecia, will you please look at his wounds?" Vhalla asked.

The Western woman looked to Jax and Aldrik, who both gave nods of silent approval. She radiated uncertainty but did her duty as a cleric. Daniel jerked away violently the second Elecia's hands landed on his forearm.

"No!" He scrambled away. "Don't-don't touch me."

"Daniel, we can't heal you if—"

"I killed them!" He lunged forward, grabbing Vhalla's upper arms to the point of bruising. "Don't fix me, I'm broken." Daniel shook her, and Vhalla hissed at the pain it caused in her right shoulder.

"Brother, stop." Jax intervened. "You're hurting her again."

Daniel stared in utter horror, then nearly threw Vhalla aside and scrambled away. She stared, heartbroken, as the man brought his knees to his chest, clutching his head.

"I killed, they died, they died, they died, and I killed them, it was—"

Vhalla wrapped her arms around his rocking shoulders. This time he tensed but didn't lash out at the touch. "Stop," she breathed. "Let Elecia check you."

Daniel whimpered and squirmed, but as long as Vhalla held him to her, he let Elecia perform what ministrations she could. It was awkward having to work around Vhalla's arms, but Elecia had more tact than to point this out.

When Elecia finished, Vhalla loosened her grip and asked, "Why are you here?"

"I-I ran." Daniel choked on his words, letting out a pained, strangled noise.

"What happened?" Jax pried.

Daniel held his temples and stared at nothing. He cried, rivulets streaking through the blood and grime on his cheeks.

"Daniel—"

"No! No!"

"Soldier." Aldrik forcefully stepped into the conversation with a single sharp word. Daniel froze. "This is an order from your Emperor: report."

Vhalla wanted to scold him for taking such a tone, but Aldrik had seen and heard something she hadn't. The command snapped something back into place, and Daniel's breathing slowed, his eyes regaining some sanity.

"It-it was only him. He walked right in, and no one even thought of stopping him until the first group of guards died." No one needed to ask who "he" was. "It should've been easy, there was only one man. But every time one fell, he took their eye and turned it into one of those rocks—those *crystals*."

Vhalla's mostly empty stomach churned at the memory of the guard who had walked into the village closest to Fritz's home.

"They rose. They fought for him. They were dead but kept walking until that awful, awful blue-green light faded." Daniel turned to her, almost pleading. "What could we have done?"

"My father?" Aldrik asked, but by the look on Daniel's face, Vhalla wished he hadn't.

"His death was only the beginning." Daniel turned to Jax. "It's just us now, brother."

"What happened to the guard?" A dark severity overcame Jax's words.

"Raylynn tried to keep Baldair's body from him. To keep him from disgracing it as he did. You know how those two were. Never anything, always something. She died defending him." Daniel hiccupped. "The Supreme King shattered both Erion's legs, stripped, and saddled him, then sent him back to the West. There's no way he made it in this cold."

"And Craig?" Jax asked after a long pause.

"Craig and me . . ." He was suddenly talking too fast, the words avalanching out. "Erion told us to bend knee. That we couldn't help anyone if we died, too. Erion was better suited as a message to the West but—Victor kept us for his monsters."

"Monsters?" Vhalla whispered.

"Those who displeased him went into the rooms. They were exposed to the taint . . . At first they were fine, but then, their screams, their flesh. It changed, *they changed*. By the Mother, their screams—their screams as they ripped open skin to make rooms for talons and wings and horns and scales and—"

He was crying again.

"Enough, that's enough," Vhalla tried to soothe.

"Don't touch me!" The man seemed to be on reset. Alternating between disbelief, violence, and soul crushing sadness. "I killed them. The feedings began. Blood, they need to develop a taste for blood, the King said. They need fresh meat, the King said.

"Craig and I, it was us. We knew it would be one of us next. Craig told me, he gave me this chance. He offered himself to that monster knowing I would be the one to feed him to it— knowing it would give me the chance to run. He screamed for me as they ate him. He screamed for me as I ran."

Vhalla sat in numb horror. Struggling to find words in the wake of everything Daniel was pouring forth and splaying at their feet.

"If he finds me, I will be food. Or he will turn me into a monster." Daniel looked to Jax. "Don't give me to them. Don't give me to his revels for his blood guard, drunk on gore and control. Don't let his court of sorcerers have me."

"Brother, you're fine now," Jax lied.

Nothing about Daniel was fine. Nothing about their situation or the world was fine.

"We will take you home," Vhalla vowed. "We're going East now."

This was her fault. She had helped Victor and unleashed this force. Beyond that, if she had kept Daniel closer and had been a better friend to him, maybe he would have been with them before now. Maybe Jax would have thought to get him before charging into that dark night for the Crystal Caverns. She had made so many mistakes. *How many people she loved would pay for them?*

"He'll slow us down." Elecia couldn't keep her thoughts to herself.

"He needs our help." Even Fritz was surprised at her cold assessment.

"We need our own help." Elecia firmly gripped her convictions. "He's going to slow us down; he's beyond halfway to madness. Not to mention, we endanger him as well, now that he knows we're alive."

Vhalla stopped to consider this. It was the reason they had left the Charems. But the Charems were capable of being clever. Daniel was a child lost in the woods.

"This is not up for discussion." Daniel was their responsibility now, and Vhalla would see him home. Her mind was made up.

"What right do you have?" Elecia snorted.

"My right as your future Empress!" Vhalla shot back so fast the words nearly gave her whiplash.

Everyone held their breath, and Vhalla's heart slowed. *Their future Empress.*

Aldrik didn't say or do anything to contradict her claim.

"Fine," Elecia huffed. The woman seemed almost satisfied at Vhalla's proclamation, despite being on the receiving end of her ire.

"You're really going to help me?" Daniel looked up at her.

"We will."

"Why? Thank you. But why?" He shook his head violently. "I am worthless. I can't—I am pathetic, less than a maggot. I killed my brother and survived off his death. I deserve to be a monster." Daniel wailed, "Don't let me become one!"

"Hush, enough," Vhalla soothed, running her hand through his oily hair. "It's decided. Now, put some food in you and rest. We'll move at sunlight."

Daniel choked down a tiny portion of their rations, the act calming him some. The rest of them used the opportunity to settle down, hoping Daniel would follow their example. He did, curling into a ball near where Vhalla was tucked against Aldrik. Jax positioned himself in the corner between them. The flutter of his eyelashes betrayed him. As long as Daniel was unstable and near her, Jax was going to sleep with one eye open.

Aldrik's touch, his warmth, his breath, washed away some of her nerves as Vhalla bundled under his cloak. Her eyes settled on Daniel, and Vhalla instinctually shifted closer to Aldrik, feeling him passing judgment on them both. Daniel had known almost as long as Vhalla and Aldrik had been aware that they were more than prince and subject. But this was the first time he'd truly seen them together.

"You will be Empress?" he whispered.

"She will be," Aldrik answered this time.

Daniel cackled. "No, no, you won't be. There is no throne for either of you any longer. Only blood."

She watched as the shell of her friend, the man who could've been her lover, settled back after his decree. Daniel studied them with a wild glint to his eyes. A secret look that spoke of horrors only he knew.

CHAPTER 4

V HALLA'S SHOULDER WAS so stiff the next morning that it was practically immobile. She hadn't thought about how she had slept—pressed against Aldrik, scrunched up all night. She massaged it gingerly.

"What will we do about the horses?" Fritz asked with a glance at Daniel.

"We need to stop somewhere for supplies today," Vhalla mused aloud. "We'll see if we can find another."

"Horses are rare," Daniel spoke. "With everyone trying to flee the South. It's why I-I was going to . . ." His eyes looked at the faint red line at her neck, and Daniel swayed, stumbling a half step away. "I'm sorry, Vhalla."

"It's fine, Daniel." She gave him a brave smile and set the example for everyone. A silent reminder that he was part of the group. "We'll ride to the next village. There's one near the cut off for the East. We'll look for supplies and horses there."

"Until then?" Fritz rephrased his prior question.

"Vhalla and I will share," Aldrik announced. "We will use Lightning." He motioned to the horse that Vhalla had been riding, the one she'd ridden on to the end of the continent during the march. "Give Daniel your cloak, Vhalla. You can sit under mine."

"This, it, it's too much. I don't deserve it." Daniel's shaking fingers hesitantly accepted the cloak she pressed into his hands. "Thank you. I'm sorry. Thank you."

"Take the help, brother," Jax encouraged.

Aldrik swung up into Lightning's saddle, scooting forward and removing his foot from the stirrup so Vhalla could also mount. She shifted, figuring out how they needed to sit so that they could both fit comfortably.

"Get under my cloak," Aldrik reminded her.

"But then I can't see."

"You are already shivering. And you're not holding the reins anyway."

Vhalla gave a silent farewell to her friends and lifted the edge of his cloak to bring it over her head. It completely covered her as she sat flush against him, her arms around his waist. Vhalla rested her cheek flat on his back. He was as warm as ever, her personal pyre, and it was almost comfortable under the heavy fabric. The world vanished into his slow and steady breathing, the sound eroded away her tension in the same fashion as waves on a shore. As Lightning began moving, Vhalla closed her eyes and pretended that they were not on the run, that they were headed off for a grand adventure.

She'd had enough adventures. Vhalla sighed softly. Perhaps they were headed simply to visit her father.

"Will Lightning be all right?" she asked, tilting her head up. The horse wasn't accustomed to carrying two riders.

"Yes." Aldrik barely spoke as he lifted his hood. With her ear on his back, Vhalla heard the deep rumble of his voice with perfect clarity. "He's from the same line as Baston. He's a strong horse. One generation away from a purebred War Strider."

"What?" Vhalla was surprised.

"When I knew you would be riding to war, I wanted to trust your horse. It was impossible for me to acquire a proper War

Strider on such short notice, especially without question. But Lightning was lithe and fast; he seemed better suited to you, anyway."

"Why didn't you tell me?" she asked.

"When we first marched I couldn't find the words to tell you. How would it have looked? Crafting your armor? Choosing your horse? I had no interest in being called puppet master again."

Vhalla huffed softly in amusement, hearing her words from his mouth. She nuzzled his back gently and felt the small breath of air that started from his stomach and carried a smile up to his lips.

"You're silly," she breathed. "Thank you for it. And for your help today with Daniel."

There was a long pause. "I know he means something to you."

"He does." Vhalla didn't deny it.

"You and him . . ." Aldrik paused, uncertain if he wanted to continue down that line of inquiry.

Vhalla never wanted her love to be insecure, but there was something almost reassuring of the reminder that he was mortal and felt hesitation and jealousy.

"We were nothing," she reassured her engaged. "We could've been, but we weren't. I had promised my heart to you."

A hand released the reins to weave its long fingers against hers. Vhalla sighed contentedly. His fingers traced shapes around her wrist as the rocking of the horse lulled her into a hazy state.

"I will never make you regret that decision. Never again," Aldrik vowed.

"I promise the same."

Their trek to the Eastern cutoff was blissfully uneventful. They came across another mostly abandoned town where Fritz, the only Southerner of the group, took the risk to barter for supplies. There wasn't enough food for any of them and hollow stomachs now tested patience. What helped, however, was Vhalla taking the watches at night. Jax protested vehemently after her being nearly killed by Daniel, but Vhalla was insistent. She'd willingly dropped her sword for Daniel. There weren't many other people who could elicit such a response.

She spent days sleeping against Aldrik's back; as a result, she was the most well-rested of the group. Which made taking watches so everyone else could sleep the most logical task. They hadn't encountered another shelter and were forced to spend more cold nights on the ground.

Not long into travelling together, Daniel began thrashing violently in his sleep. Arms and legs were thrown everywhere as he whimpered and cried to himself. She was reminded of her days following the Night of Fire and Wind and, instead of waking the man abruptly, she settled herself at his side.

Daniel threw a right hook that she narrowly dodged as her palm flattened against his sweat dotted brow. His eyes gained clarity as he realized who she was. Vhalla said nothing, making a soft *shh'ing* sound and beseeching him with her eyes to go back to sleep. His lower lip quivered, and he stared at her fearfully as she tenderly stroked away the sweat slicked hair from his forehead.

She didn't lie to him. She didn't tell him it would all be all right. She simply sat in solidarity, understanding his pain.

The next morning, he had a rough edge. Throughout the day, Vhalla made every effort to remind him of who he was, who she was, where he was going, that he escaped Victor's clutches. It helped, for a bit, until the whole process repeated itself. Yet, despite all this, Vhalla hadn't really understood the depth of Daniel's terror until one late afternoon, a few hours into her watch.

That afternoon, a flash of light in the distance caught her eye.

Vhalla stopped as she squinted across the bright snow toward the Great Imperial Way. Raising a hand to shade her eyes, three figures slowly came into focus. Two guards and a beast that crawled on all fours between them. The monster was worse than anything she had ever dreamed, could ever imagine.

A long black tongue lolled from its gaping jowls. Teeth too large to fit in its mouth jutted out at odd angles, razor sharp; inky black saliva oozed between them and dripped onto the road. Talons scraped through the snow, whispering on the stones of the road underneath.

She stood, transfixed with horror, before spinning into motion.

"Fritz," she breathed, shaking her friend's shoulder.

"Vhal—"

Vhalla clamped a hand over his groan. She raised her other finger to her lips, whispering hastily behind it, "We need an illusion."

As she pulled her hand away, Vhalla pointed to the patrolling horrors. Fritz stared with disbelieving horror.

"Fritz, *now!*" she hissed

"Right." He crouched down, waving his hands through the air. Vhalla saw the tell-tale shimmer of magic, like heat off stones on a summer's day, between them and the road.

She woke Aldrik next. "Patrol."

His dark eyes were immediately alert and awake. They darted to Fritz, who remained transfixed on his illusion.

They slowly woke the rest of the group. Sehra scowled the second her eyes opened, though Vhalla knew from the way her gaze instantly scanned the horizon, that her expression wasn't because she'd been woken prematurely. Her focus settled on the horror, and she took a sharp intake of air through her nose.

"Sehra," Za hissed. The archer unslung her bow from across

her chest, pulling an arrow from the quiver at the small of her back.

"Hold," Vhalla beseeched. Za scowled at the order. "Illusion."

They both looked to Fritz before exchanging another glance. Sehra gave a small nod.

Vhalla turned back to the road. The crystal monsters were almost directly across from the group and showed no indication they had any idea of the travelers bedding themselves into the snow a good stone's throw away. Everyone seemed to hold their breath.

Then Daniel woke.

Vhalla didn't know if he woke on his own or if he sensed the tension in the air. Or if Jax had chosen to wake him in case they needed to run. Whatever the case, the result was the same.

The moment Daniel's eyes caught sight of the patrol he began to shake violently. Vhalla tried to move in the same instant as Jax. She was farther away, he was slower.

A cry of sheer terror rose from Daniel's throat. Jax's hand clamped over his mouth so hard he pushed the other man down into the snow. It was cut short, but it seemed to echo through the still forest into eternity.

The beast's pointed ears perked up, turning in their direction. Daniel remained thrashing on the ground, Jax trying to get him under control. They rolled in the snow.

"They've come for me!" Daniel wailed in horror, which made it true.

The beast and walking horrors began running toward the sound. Fritz looked back, panicked.

"Fritz, camouflage Aldrik as anyone else. Aldrik, Jax, Elecia, handle the soldiers. Za, Sehra, the beast. I'll handle Daniel," Vhalla ordered in quick succession, praying that the crunching snow under the fast approaching enemy hid her use of names. She didn't know what connection they had with Victor, but she remembered how the reanimated solider had demanded people to kneel so Victor could *see* their loyalty.

Jax rolled off Daniel, and Vhalla jumped onto the panicked man. She wrestled with the flailing Easterner and focused on keeping him in one spot while the rest of the group set into motion.

Ice crackled as Fritz abandoned his illusion. Wickedly sharp spears blocked the creatures' way, stalling them a moment. Za notched an arrow while Sehra raised a hand as Vhalla had seen her do in the Crystal Caverns. A flash of light and the arrow flew like a sunbeam, straight and true at the beast. It struck between the eyes, and the creature dropped dead.

Sehra slumped, panting heavily. Za took a half step in front of her charge, sending another arrow flying. It was followed by fire. Vhalla had never seen Aldrik char something so completely. It was as if he unleashed all his rage in one singular burst. The soldier was blackened.

"Don't let them take me!" Daniel wailed. "I left the king, the one true king! Don't let them take me."

"Stop!" Vhalla cried. The man had somehow turned into an octopus, seeming to sprout limbs by which to throw Vhalla off. She took an elbow to the face and a knee to the gut but held fast. "No one is taking you; you're going home."

"They will feed on me! They will eat me!" he screamed.

"Stop!" Vhalla scrambled, pinning him down by sitting on his chest and holding down his arms with her knees. "Look at me." He didn't stop thrashing, shaking his head back and forth. "Look at me!" she cried, gripping his cheeks. Spit bubbled out of his mouth from his sobs. "No one is taking you! No one. You're free! You're going to Paca, where you will eat candied nuts until you're old and fat."

Daniel exhaled white puffs of air as he slowly regained control of himself.

"I won't let them take you," she whispered. "I promise."

He choked on the reply, and Vhalla could only give him part of an encouraging smile before she was heaved off.

Jax tossed Vhalla aside and practically lifted Daniel from the ground. "Do you want to get us killed?"

Vhalla had missed the last soldier falling, but the three attacking monsters seemed dead. *Then again, they'd been dead to begin with.*

"Stop it, Jax." Vhalla stood, rubbing her shoulder. "You know he didn't mean it."

Jax scowled and sighed. "I know, I know."

"I'm sorry," Daniel blubbered. "I-I almost got you killed. I almost. Baldair asked me to protect you, and I almost got you killed."

"Daniel, it's all right," she tried to soothe.

"No. No." Daniel fell to his knees. "I killed them, I killed them."

His eyes lost clarity as he fumbled around in his armor. Vhalla recognized the blade he drew as the one he'd held against her throat. But this time, he didn't turn it on anyone else.

"I will only hurt you again. I will only kill again. I have failed Baldair. I have failed my oath to you."

Vhalla barely had time to think "no" as Daniel turned the blade on himself. She saw what was happening a second too late.

But it didn't puncture skin.

Aldrik and the Easterner tumbled head over heels. The Emperor was far more coordinated and faster than the crazed and deranged soldier. In a second, he'd wrenched the blade from Daniel's grasp and punched him clear across the face with the other hand.

Anger and relief flashed across Vhalla's chest.

"You idiot!" Aldrik shouted. He grabbed Daniel's collar with a hand, shaking him like a ragdoll. "You are better than this."

Daniel wanted to object, but Aldrik wouldn't let him.

"You don't think so? Then you further shame my brother and that foolish Golden Guard of his. You prove that he picked weak men, easily broken," Aldrik snarled. "You selfish fool. She's trying to save you, and you would hurt her with this?"

Both men looked at the discarded knife, the rest of the group forgotten.

Aldrik sighed heavily, and his shoulders slumped with an invisible weight he'd been bearing for a decade. His grip slackened. "I know," he was half talking to himself. "I have been there. It feels like there is no other choice. That the world is too heavy, too horrible to ever lessen. I know that you will hate me, hate us, hate her, for not letting you sit here and die.

"But someday, when you are happy and content—and I know you will not believe me when I tell you that you will someday be happy and content again—you will thank us. You will thank us for not letting you leave this mortal coil without a fight because you have more to give."

"Aldrik . . ." Elecia breathed. Her fingertips were pressed against her lips, and Vhalla watched recognition widen her emerald eyes. The woman understood something about her cousin that she had never been told and could suddenly see a cornerstone of the cage of guilt he'd constructed for himself.

"Promise me you will stay alive," Aldrik demanded. "Promise me that you will fight that man's darkness. That you will stand with me in the sun."

Daniel swallowed in shock, in horror. And something moved back into place. Something shifted in his eyes in the right direction. He nodded.

"I give you my word, my lord."

CHAPTER 5

ANIEL'S HORRORS, HIS broken mind, could not be fixed with a word. But there was something magical about his agreement with Aldrik. As they travelled on, he had longer moments of clarity. He spoke in short, clipped sentences with Jax. He broke down less.

He still thrashed in his sleep and avoided Vhalla as though it brought him physical pain to look upon her or the bruised eye she sported. But he remained—mostly—stable. As stable as one in his condition could be.

They finally reached the cutoff to the East. Once more, Vhalla saw a patrol in the distance during her watch. But Fritz's illusion kept them secret, and this time Daniel kept his breakdown to muttering and rocking.

"We go North," Za announced as they slowed. It stirred Vhalla from sleep, and she roused from under Aldrik's cloak.

Sehra held Vhalla's eyes for a long moment. Vhalla nodded in affirmation. "Our deal will stand."

"I know it will." The Child of Yargen did something then that Vhalla had not seen once from her. Her mouth curled into the makings of an exhausted, but sincere smile. "My eyes have seen the truth. You will protect this land."

"I will." The vow was redundant and unnecessary, but Vhalla

said it all the same. She would release that vow into the world as many times as needed until it became true.

Sehra turned to Aldrik. "Entrusting your heart to this woman may be the smartest choice you've made, Aldrik Solaris."

"I would not disagree." The Emperor gave a small nod of his head. "I will send word when we arrive in Hastan. I hope you will find safer travels in the West."

"I keep Sehra safe." Za sat straighter in her saddle. Sehra gave her handler an appreciative look.

"Shaldan has good stock. We will be fine. I will await your word."

The two Northerners continued parallel to the Great Imperial Way as the six others went along the Eastern cutoff. Vhalla watched until the thinning forest and glare of the sun off a light dusting of snow obscured them from view.

"Do you think they'll keep their word?" Aldrik whispered uncertainly the moment she was under his cloak once more.

"I do," Vhalla affirmed with a nod. "The enemy of our enemy is our friend." She paused, thinking over her next words. "And those friends may have more to give and teach us than we know."

"If only that relationship hadn't stared at sword point," Aldrik mumbled.

Vhalla squeezed him lightly. "An Emperor for peace can focus on healing those wounds."

"At the cost of the first fourteen years of my firstborn's life."

"Wards are not so uncommon," she tried to soothe. "I left my home at seven."

"Don't pretend that this sits easily for you."

She had no response to his bitter statement, so Vhalla simply pressed her cheek to his back and closed her eyes.

The forest continued to thin over the coming days. The snow began to melt and disappear until it was just cold, brown grass being crushed beneath the horses' hooves. The weather warmed the farther they headed, north and the coastal breezes, unbroken by mountains, kept the ominous gray snow clouds in the south.

The first sight of the East nearly brought tears to Vhalla's eyes. Hills rolled upon themselves like sails in the breeze. There was an earthy smell that lingered on the nose, rising up from the fertile ground.

They rode away from the road and tree coverage lessened. Should one of Victor's patrols be in the area, they would stick out above the tall grasses. But there weren't any further patrols. There weren't many people at all, and that fact began to deeply worry Vhalla. The road was vacant of carts carrying winter harvests to market. Fields were empty. The first abandoned town they rode through made Vhalla realize the foolishness of her notion that Victor had only permeated the South. The man wanted to rule the world.

She chose to ignore the fear in the back of her mind, thoughts that gnawed on her more each day. She feared that Daniel's family would not be where he had left them. It was not a far spiral for Vhalla to become worried about her own father. Aldrik sensed her concerns and broached them once while riding, but Vhalla didn't want to speak of it. It was as though saying the words out loud would only increase their likelihood of being real.

Fate cast a small smile upon her. As they pushed on into the heart of the East, signs of Victor's tyrannical hold began to lessen. The people had a certain edge to them that Vhalla wasn't accustomed to seeing. But they still went about their days. They still tended to their fields, and the smell of baking bread hovered every time they passed a farmhouse.

Vhalla no longer hid under Aldrik's cloak. Her amber-hued skin and nut-colored hair blended in with the shades of the

East. She was fairer than most of her people, but that came from spending most of her time in libraries and not out in the fields.

The sights and sounds healed Daniel to the point that he actually took the lead. It helped when people began to recognize him. An old man stopped as he was going about his business. A woman called from a nearby field.

Daniel's voice sounded stronger with every word he spoke, and Vhalla allowed herself a smile. If a random acquaintance could help him that much, she dared hope for what returning to his family could do. *Taking him home had been the right decision*, she assured herself.

"My home isn't far now," he informed the group. "I can go from here."

"Well, if you insist." Elecia shrugged.

Vhalla shot her a small glare of frustration. "We will take you there," Vhalla insisted.

"I-I've cause you all enough trouble. Even on foot, it'll only—"

"No, Daniel," she interrupted gently. "We will see you to your door."

All the empty towns and blood-stained homes appeared in her mind. The villagers had told them that they didn't expect to see any of the guards returning. That the walking horrors had made it this deep into the East and informed the men and women of Victor's decrees. Vhalla wasn't going to let Daniel head into the unknown. *What if his family had been killed fighting in the memory of a son they believed dead?*

The thought remained with Vhalla for the rest of the afternoon as she watched the houses and fields pass. Egmun's words returned. She had been the key, something to be used, and he had known it from the second he knew what she was. Vhalla massaged her shoulder. Ten lifetimes would not be enough to fix everything for the world she had so wronged.

Daniel's home was just outside of Paca, right where he said it would be. It betrayed no signs of turmoil; there was no hint of malice or foul play. Vhalla held her breath as the small home grew larger and larger until they were right upon it, close enough to hear the metallic clang of hearth tools.

He dismounted slowly, and Vhalla did the same, remaining a hesitant step behind him. None of them spoke. The peaceful hum of daily life and the soft clanking of stirrups filled the air. Daniel raised a hand to knock, and the wooden door swung open from within.

A middle-aged woman wearing an apron, flour up to her elbows, stared up at the soldier at her doorstep. The confusion on her face made Vhalla worry that perhaps in Daniel's current mental state he had brought them to the wrong home. All her concerns were shattered when the woman let out a wail of shock, followed quickly by tears.

"Danny, my boy!" the woman cried, throwing her arms around Daniel's shoulders.

"Danny boy?" an older man blubbered as he appeared, blinking at the travelers on his doorstep. As soon as his eyes fell on the two embracing family members, he reached out and took them in his arms.

"Ma, Pa," Daniel let out in a voice that Vhalla had never heard from him before. "I-I deserted my post. I—"

"Shh, my darling child, quiet." The woman stroked the hair of her son as he clung to her tightly.

"I-I k-killed—"

"Only the people he had to so that he could return home to you," Vhalla interrupted.

Her interjection into the conversation broke the moment, and all three turned to look at her. Daniel rubbed his nose with the back of his hand, the one that was missing his gauntlet. Vhalla gave him an encouraging smile. The blood would never wash off his hands; she was all too familiar with that. But he could begin to put it behind him. He could let himself be home.

"Who are your friends?" his mother finally asked.

"They are . . ." Clearly uncertain at how to respond, Daniel wavered.

"My name is Vhalla Yarl," she answered for him once more.

"Don't use your real name!" Elecia hissed in disagreement.

"Fritznangle Charem, of the noble Charem clan!" Fritz announced cheerfully, pulling back his hood.

"Elecia, of the actual noble house Ci'Dan," Elecia sighed in resignation.

"Jax," the Western man spoke simply.

All eyes landed on Aldrik expectantly. With the smallest of sighs, he released his reins and reached up for the sides of his hood. His hair hung limply around his face, an equal mess to the grime that covered them all. But it didn't matter. His commanding presence was never powered by his adornments, despite what Vhalla may have thought at one point or another. The very skin of the man before her was fire, he burned with something stronger than all his carefully cut clothes and imposing black armor.

"Emperor Aldrik Ci'Dan Solaris."

"What?" The woman glanced among them at the odd proclamations. "Daniel, these people, surely you must know what's happened at the capital."

"I do." Daniel jerked away from his mother's touch. "I know very well what's happened in the capital." He sighed heavily, letting out the sharpness in his voice. "But I also know that they are who they say they are. And if it wasn't for them, I wouldn't be alive."

"Then, my lord," the woman addressed Aldrik. "Thank you for returning my son home safely to us."

"Do not thank me." Aldrik motioned to Vhalla. "Thank my lady."

Whatever gratitude the woman was heaping upon her was momentarily overshadowed as Vhalla stared up at Aldrik. *His lady*, those words, so publically spoken. They no longer hid their love for the other—they embraced it for all to see.

"Let us give you dinner, somewhere to stay for the night," the woman offered.

"We can find arrangements in town," Aldrik said definitively. "I would not want to put your family at further risk with our presence. But my thanks for your offer of hospitality."

"Anything for the true Emperor." The woman smiled, and it looked as though her face hadn't worn that expression in far too long. "And the people who brought Daniel home to us."

"Will you put an end to this nonsense about the Supreme King?" Daniel's father asked.

"We will." There was no hesitation about Aldrik.

"Vhalla . . ." Daniel turned to her.

She looked up at him and staring back was the tired shell of a man she once knew. Coming home had done him good, and the rough edges were already smoothing out around him. But he had been so horribly broken that Vhalla knew his mental shape would forever be altered.

Were it not for her, he would not be in this state. He would still be that man with whom she had sat on a rooftop at the Crossroads. A man who would have been hers if the stars constellated a different design for her heart.

"I'm sorry." Vhalla struggled to find any volume to her words. "I'm sorry for what I have done."

"Vhalla?" He was understandably confused.

"I know you don't understand." She swallowed the lump in her throat. "And that's okay, you don't have to. But I want you to hear me and take my promise that I will fix this. I will put an end to the caverns once and for all."

"I believe you." With that simple agreement, he added fuel to her purpose. His belief in her was more than she deserved, and she would treasure it forever.

Vhalla hugged him gently, a creature that she knew would spook if she moved too quickly or held too tightly. "Stay safe, and be happy."

Jax was waiting behind her when she released Daniel. Vhalla hadn't even heard him dismount, and the man was still as a statue. The two Golden Guards, likely the last two living members, assessed each other.

"Soldier," Jax took a long pause to gather both words and emotions. "You're dismissed from your post."

It was something Vhalla would've never thought to say, but the profound impact it had on Daniel was instantaneous. Tears glistened in his eyes, overflowing at the corners. He reached for Jax, and the two men embraced.

"Baldair would want you to know that." Jax rested a palm on the top of his head. "You have been honorably dismissed from the guard."

Jax drew his hood as soon as he broke away from Daniel. They all did as they rode out and away from Daniel's home. Elecia and Fritz talked lightly between themselves, the distance from the South finally beginning to lighten the mood between them all. But one of them still had a dark cloud hanging over his head. Jax kept his head down, and his hood drawn tightly around his face, all the way into Paca.

The small Eastern town was just as Vhalla remembered it. A worn town hall was the largest building, a small stage for announcements and elections at its front. It was also where the band would play during the Festival of the Sun. She paused, smiling fondly.

"Is this your home town, Vhal?" Fritz stopped as well.

"No." She shook her head. "But my family would often come here to trade in the market or for important events. Leoul is even smaller than this, not much there."

"How far is your home from here?"

Vhalla hummed in thought. "Perhaps a day's ride northwest?"

"Not in the direction we're headed then," Fritz sighed on her behalf.

"No, it's not." Vhalla couldn't keep the wistful longing out of her voice.

"We should go," Aldrik said definitively.

"To Leoul?"

"To your home," he clarified.

"But it's a day's ride out of the way, and we're in a hurry," Vhalla protested weakly.

"I think we should go as well." Elecia was the last person Vhalla expected to voice her support. She elaborated at Vhalla's inquisitive stare, "Family is incredibly important. I would want to make sure my father was safe."

"We will stay here for the night, get a good night's sleep, and ride to your home tomorrow."

The Emperor had spoken, and a weird mess of contradictions waged war in Vhalla's chest. She was excited to go home. She missed her father desperately after all that had happened. But she was terrified of what she may find. Her origins were no secret. What if Victor had sent a monster out for her father? And even if her father was safe, what if he wanted nothing to do with her? So much had changed since she was last home. *Would he be proud of the woman she had become?*

Luckily, Vhalla knew the route to the inn well enough that she didn't have to dedicate much of her cluttered mind to it. There wasn't any risk of the inn being filled, given the circumstances of the world, so they didn't have to fight for stables. An old man, bald at the top and white on the sides, was asleep on the counter.

"Geral?" Vhalla blinked at how little had changed. Between her speaking and the door closing behind Fritz, the portly man stirred, adjusting his suspenders.

"W-welcome!" He coughed away the sleep that was stuck in his throat. "Not many travelers these days! How can I help you?"

"Geral, is it really you?"

"Well, I don't know who else I'd be," he chuckled. "And who is really you, miss?"

Vhalla lowered her hood, and he stared at her face blankly. She knew her hair was a mess and she was caked in dirt. Crossing the gap to let him get a better look, Vhalla rested her hands on the countertop that she had been barely tall enough to see over the last time she'd touched it. Geral squinted at her from the other side.

"I . . ." Disappointment hit her harder than she expected when he was unable to place her. "I was just a girl the last time I was here. It makes sense you don't remember me. I would always come with my mother and father for the Festival of the Sun and . . ." She daydreamed away for a long moment. "Sorry, we'll need a room for the night."

"Two," Aldrik corrected.

"Three silver." The man turned to fetch keys that hung on hooks behind the desk as Aldrik placed the money on the counter.

"So, ladies' room and gents' room?" Elecia inquired as they headed up the stairs. Aldrik shot her a look that explained such was not the case, eliciting a sharp gasp. "Don't make me sleep with *them*!"

"You've been sleeping with them the whole time." Aldrik rolled his eyes and thrust one key into Elecia's hand.

"That's different! There was no alternative. This is so improper."

"Be improper with me, Lady Ci'Dan." Jax waggled his eyebrows.

"Don't give the lady trouble," Aldrik scolded.

"I'm never trouble!" Fritz pouted.

Jax smirked proudly. "I'm always trouble."

"Cousin, you are lucky I love you." Elecia's sharp glare didn't have weight behind it, and Aldrik smiled tiredly. "And I get first choice of bed."

"Second!" Fritz bounded into their room behind her.

Jax didn't move. "I'd like to stand guard outside your chambers."

Vhalla blinked in surprise, realizing he was addressing her. She'd almost forgotten that he had been her close shadow on the ride, not only because they were traveling in a pack, but also because he had somehow become her sworn guard.

"Jax, go rest." The Westerner folded his arms on his chest at Aldrik's demand. "If something happens to her while she's tucked in my arms, it will never be blamed on you."

"Happy to serve." Jax bowed, pausing before the still open door Elecia and Fritz had disappeared within. "Oh, and if you two need a third, be sure to let me know!" With a wink and a laugh, he popped into the room.

Aldrik shook his head. "That man."

"Never a dull moment," Vhalla agreed.

The room was small and tidy. A single rope bed, a small table at its side. The window was drawn to keep out the cool nighttime breezes.

"What is it?" Aldrik asked, closing the door behind him.

"They didn't have glass the last time I was here." Vhalla rested her hand on the pane. "But not much else has changed."

Two warm palms fell on her hips, and Vhalla felt the length of his body behind her. The perpetual heat that radiated off him was a contrast to everything else in the harsh world. She leaned back into that warmth, letting his hands slide around her front to hold her tightly to him.

"You've changed," his breath moved her hair as he spoke.

"I have," she whispered in reply. If nothing else, that one fact was certainly true. When last in the East, she had been a girl without purpose. Now she had an inkling of what the weight of the world felt like. She knew how the title of nobility fit her shoulders and the greater role she had to play. She wouldn't return to her father an unaware girl.

He rounded to face her. "And I love the woman you have become, deeply and completely."

"I love you, Aldrik." Vhalla savored his touch as he palmed her face. "And I fear I always will."

"Ah, Vhalla." He chuckled, pausing just before his lips came into contact with hers. "That is the one thing I do not fear."

CHAPTER 6

THE EMPEROR HAD certainly been fearless that night when it came to heaping his adoration upon his lady. He had reminded her of the fire that lived in his veins. He immolated her passion at the altar of their mutual vows. The early rays of dawn peeking through the glass of the window found them still tangled.

A banging on the door interrupted their otherwise peaceful morning, pulling them from slumber. Vhalla groaned and rolled over. Two arms enveloped her, stronger than they looked.

"Aldrik." She pressed her face into his bare chest. They had found a basic washroom the night previously and, while he didn't have access to his usual eucalyptus scented soap, he still held the aroma of smoke and steel, a scent all his own.

"What is it?"

"You're here." Given the madness that had passed, something about waking up in his arms, skin on skin, was wonderfully impossible. It affirmed that not only had last night been real, but it had been the tiny glimpse of a future they fought for.

"Where else would I be?" He chuckled deeply, laying a sweet kiss upon her.

"Nowhere else, never again."

"Are you both up yet?" Jax called through the door. "Let me know if you're naked so I can come in."

"Jax." Elecia's voice was sharp as the daggers her eyes likely were throwing him. "Do not make me think anything of the sort about my cousin, *please*."

"We all know what happened. It's not like they were quiet," Jax shot back.

Elecia began singing a Western song, loudly, over her companion's words.

"What did we do, forcing those two together?" Vhalla laughed as she sat up. She didn't feel the least bit guilty for her passions; there wasn't even a ghost of a blush on her cheeks.

"Elecia could survive loosening up a bit." Aldrik stood.

Now, there was a sight that would put color on her face.

Jax began rambling, "Oh my liege, the day has begun, let us start the fun, the time of the sun, has indeed come, so won't you please—"

"Oh, Mother, don't talk in rhymes," Aldrik groaned through the door. "It's the only thing worse than your sense of humor. We'll be down in a moment."

Their illusion of peace dissipated like the morning's fog over a field. Soon enough, clothes were back on their rightful frames and cloaks were thrown over their shoulders. Vhalla considered Aldrik as they walked down the stairs to join the group. *The Emperor was going to be in her home.*

"You lot are up early," Geral observed, a steaming cup of wheat tea between his hands.

Vhalla returned the keys with a smile. "So are you."

"True enough." The man paused, his expression sobering. "Dodging the Inquisitors?"

"Inquisitors?" She looked to her comrades to see if they knew of what Geral spoke, but the group looked just as confused as Vhalla.

"I thought you would've heard . . ."

"There's been a lot to hear," Vhalla encouraged delicately.

"It's all the Supreme King's doing," Geral began.

"Do you support the regime change?" They should've found that information before staying under the man's roof.

"Do I look like a man who would support senseless violence?"

"You don't." Vhalla gave a breath of relief. "So, what is the Supreme King doing with Inquisitors?"

"They are sweeping the continent, but their presence has been especially felt here in the East. They have a way to use crystals to see if someone has the powers of a Windwalker."

Vhalla was instantly reminded of Victor's ledger. He knew there would be more. Not many, but they would be out there. A Windwalker could be the only possible opposition to his powers. The information was as useful as it was terrifying for the people who were confirmed to have the ability.

Geral continued, "A group of strange travelers, like yourselves, may want to know information like that."

"Thank you," Vhalla said sincerely, raising her hood to leave.

"I think it's funny," Geral added. "I only ever heard of one Windwalker in all my years. The first one to leave the East's nest and fly. That was the girl named Vhalla Yarl." He rested his elbows on the table leaning forward. "Though, I suppose she wouldn't be a girl any longer. You know, she would stay with her parents at my inn during the Festival of the Sun. And when I heard the tales of all that was happening to her—the good, the bad—I cheered for her alongside the rest of the East."

Vhalla's hand went up to her shoulder, gripping it just above the scar.

"She's the pride of the East. A beacon of a new future where people may start seeing Cyven as more than just some pastures and crops between North and South." Geral sipped his cup once more. "What happened to her was a crime. But, then again, I hear she had a good record of dodging death itself. The truth could be right under our noses."

"Things have a strange way of working out." Vhalla's words were laden with shock.

"They do indeed." The man shifted his hands and turned the mug; upon it was the blazing sun of Solaris. "Now go, before the Inquisitor begins his rounds through the town."

Vhalla took one last look at Geral before the door closed behind them. His warm words had restored her—and terrified her. These were her people, and they stood behind her. She had betrayed them, and now she had to do whatever was necessary to save them.

"How much did we pay him?" Elecia broke the silence as they were checking their saddlebags.

"Three silver," Aldrik answered.

Elecia and Fritz shared a look. "Fritz and I went down when you two were being slow. The man said we had given too much on accident." She held out her hand to Aldrik, three shining coins in its center.

He had returned the money.

The thunder of horses interrupted Vhalla's thoughts. Five men rode boldly into the center of town, up to the small stage she had admired fondly the day before. Each echo of their footfalls upon the wood sounded like a dagger to her childhood.

"By the order of Supreme King Anzbel, we have been sent to inquire as to the magical merit of this town." All five wore black cloaks with a silver wyrm stitched upon the back. People seemed to shrink into their homes as he spoke. "All towns in the East will be searched. The searches will be random and continue in perpetuity. All those presently in the town are asked to report now."

"We should go," Elecia whispered. "While they're distracted by the initial bulk of people."

"We should," Fritz seconded.

Vhalla didn't move. She watched as the people of Paca, *her people,* walked forward to the center of town. Diligent and dutiful to orders set forth by those in positions of leadership, the Easterners lined up.

The leader gave a nod to two of his men, who began making a quick sweep of the town, starting on the opposite end.

"Those who are known sorcerers, please report to my assistants and you will be asked to demonstrate your gift from the Gods and bypass the test." He motioned to the two men at his side. Vhalla noticed none of them were Eastern. "Everyone else, the test is simple. You will hold a crystal. Should it shine, our righteous and Supreme King has demanded you shall be put to death for possessing the accursed powers of the wind."

Vhalla couldn't breathe. He'd said he wanted to make a world for all sorcerers. He'd lied. Victor was King Jadar born again.

"Victor is afraid," she forced her mind to keep moving past her anger. "He's afraid of Windwalkers. We can still stop him."

"He can't honestly think that there are more Windwalkers." Aldrik shook his head.

"There are." Vhalla didn't even look back to see the confounded stare on the Emperor's face. "There have been more. They've all been kept hidden or killed."

The leader produced a crystal from his bag and, one by one, he moved through the line of people, passing it from person to person. Vhalla wondered how long it would be before the Inquisitor began showing signs of the taint. She remembered Daniel's stories of monsters and wondered if it was all some greater part of Victor's machinations.

For nearly everyone the crystal did nothing. Vhalla held her breath, glancing at the other two Inquisitors slowly making their way from where they hid in the shade of the stables toward the crowd.

"Vhalla, we need to leave," Jax urged, as she was the only one of them not mounted.

She took a step back toward Lightning. She couldn't do anything. She couldn't stop this.

And then she heard a scream.

The boy was maybe twelve, not far from his coming of age ceremony, barely old enough to have fuzz on his chin. He looked around in panic as everyone gaped at him—even the Inquisitors seemed surprised. The crystal glowed faintly from between his clutched fingers.

"No!" A woman, presumably his mother, swatted the stone away like the bad omen it was. "No, it-it's a mistake!"

"I am truly sorry." The Inquisitor did not sound sorry in the slightest, he sounded almost giddy. "But our Supreme King made these crystals with his divinely given magic; they cannot be wrong."

The man in all black grabbed the boy's arm. His mother grabbed the other.

"Please, please, he . . . I will raise him right; I will raise him to love the Supreme King. We will not let his magic show." The woman began to sob.

"The law is clear." The Inquisitor ripped the boy away as the town looked on in horror.

Vhalla realized it didn't matter if Victor could find all the Windwalkers. Displays like this would ensure that none of them would ever expose themselves to the world. Magic would become legally outlawed again in the East; it would be even worse than the Burning Times. Victor was clever, and he was sending a clear message for anyone who'd dare expose their powers.

"No!" the woman screamed. "No, no!"

"He's just a boy!" another brave soul protested.

"No," Vhalla took another step toward Lightning.

"You lot! You must report!" One of the Inquisitors making their round of the town had finally caught sight of them.

"He's my boy!" Other members of the town had begun to restrain the woman for her own sake as the Inquisitor dragged the lad up the line.

"Stop!" Vhalla cried and dug her heels into Lightning. "Stop this!"

"What?" The leader looked honestly puzzled for the briefest of moments as she raced down the small street through the center of town. He pushed the boy to the ground defiantly. "You will be next for going against the Supreme King's decree!"

"Fine, but let him go," Vhalla spat back fearlessly. "You don't want him. I'm the one you want." She threw down her hood. "I am Vhalla Yarl, Duchess of the West, Lady of the Southern Court, and the one whom you call the Windwalker."

The Mother, hanging high in the sky above, must have looked fondly upon Vhalla's otherwise foolish act because, at that moment, a gale swept through the town. It pushed her cloak about her form from behind, as though an invisible hand was placed upon her. Everyone held their breath.

"She lies!" one of the assistants cried. "Do not hesitate!"

The assistant threw out his hand and a spear of ice impaled the boy through his center. A cough of blood, a gurgled cry, and the mask of death was upon him.

With an anguished scream, Vhalla charged. She didn't care if she no longer had her wind. She would rip the man limb from limb with her own two hands.

Vaulting off Lightning, she tackled the leader head first. He reared back to punch her and Vhalla dodged, bringing her knee up hard between his legs. The wind left him, and Vhalla pushed him off her. He stumbled off the stage with a menacing groan and a string of colorful words. She drew her sword fearlessly.

The crackle of ice lit up the air and Vhalla turned. But where the assistant had been was now nothing more than a charred mark on the ground, the temperature of the square rising by several degrees.

"Move and die!" Fritz shouted, holding out a hand to one of the remaining two Inquisitors. Jax was poised, ready to attack the other.

"Wh-who are you?" The leader scrambled away, looking between Vhalla and the Firebearer on the horse.

"The Fire Lord." Aldrik threw down his hood, staring down the man who suddenly looked like nothing more than an ant beneath a mountain. He held out a hand and fire crackled off his finger, setting the leader ablaze.

Vhalla was expecting some further retaliation, but the remaining assistant by the stage fell to his knees and brought his face to the dusty ground. No one seemed to be able to process this reaction.

"My lord, my lord," the man wailed. He turned his face upward, looking to Aldrik as though he were a god. "You have returned from the Father's halls to save us."

"Are you really who you say you are?" An elderly man moved away from the mother grieving over her fallen son.

"I am." Vhalla looked on at the broken family in sorrow, wishing she could reverse the clock. "We are."

"We can't believe them," snarled one of the Inquisitors, a blonde Southerner who viciously stared down Fritz.

"She is Vhalla Yarl," Geral spoke up. "I would know that mess of hair from anyone."

"You live," the other Inquisitor Jax was threatening spoke with awe. "It's true, the Prince of Mhashan lives." The Westerner dropped to her knees as well.

"Vhalla Yarl," the mother hiccupped her name softly. Everyone turned. "Will you end this?"

"I will," she vowed without hesitation. Her people looked to her, and Vhalla would never fail them again. Vhalla jumped back onto the stage, addressing Paca. "The fires of Solaris, the fires of justice, burn bright and hot. The sun is rising, and it will cast this darkness from the earth. We will end the Supreme King.

"We ride to Hastan." She barely noticed that Aldrik gave her an odd look from the corners of his eyes, but Vhalla was too focused on reassuring those gathered to give it much heed. "We will ensure the East stands with us, with the West, and the North! And we will end this."

"So stand with Solaris, or die with the false king," Aldrik decreed.

"The West harbors no love for the false king," the nearest Inquisitor assistant spoke. "I am glad to kneel with my Emperor."

"You're pardoning them?" the grieving mother shrieked.

Vhalla looked between her and Aldrik uncertainly.

The Emperor took a long and slow breath through his nose. "Why did you serve the false king?"

"My daughter was in the Tower," the man answered. Vhalla noticed the other Westerner shift, bowing her head. The family resemblance was suddenly apparent. "The King said she would remain safe if her family answered his call for Inquisitors."

"And you?" Aldrik had noticed the apparent familial connection between the two Westerners and he turned to the Southerner.

"I-I-" the man stuttered. "There was no other choice. This or die."

The Westerner to Vhalla's left narrowed his eyes some, but he didn't say anything. Vhalla keenly remembered Daniel's description of the state of the capital. She understood many likely couldn't understand what the Inquisitors had faced.

"Are your hearts loyal to Solaris?" Aldrik asked.

The three gave their affirmation.

"Then I will pardon you."

"On one condition!" Vhalla knew that grieving mother could whip Paca into an angry mob if there wasn't a condition added. Some form of punishment was due for the people to rest at night.

Aldrik turned to Vhalla. He gave her a long stare, but didn't object. The singular act spoke volumes about the authority he had already given her.

Vhalla took a deep breath, praying she had formulated a good enough idea so quickly. "If you run off or oppose Victor, he will take your lives and the lives of those you love. Your deaths will help no one. There are patrols, I assume you are meant to report in, and he has the power to find you beyond all that. You do not want to be examples for that maniac."

No one objected.

"Loyalty at the cost of innocent blood is not the foundation for a throne." She stared into the eyes of the Easterners, pleading with them to understand what she was saying. "Two wrongs do not make a right. And killing those who have only fought for their freedom, killing them for the sake of vengeance does not make us any better than that which we are fighting against."

"So you may keep your lives, *if* you use them to help your brothers and sisters here in the East. Go as you were told. Use the crystal to find Windwalkers. But for every one you find, tell them to hide. Turn that wretched *thing* that Victor has saddled you with as a gift. Be not the harbingers of death but the devotees of life. Tell the Windwalkers to flee, to perpetuate the belief that there are and will be no more in the East, for now."

Vhalla would not let go of her secret dream that one day Windwalkers could study safely alongside other sorcerers.

"Spread this word to other Inquisitors who do not want to take children from their mothers. Do this and you will have earned your pardon."

The Inquisitors looked from Aldrik to Vhalla, trying to decipher if she truly had the ability to make such a decree.

The Western man finally spoke. "At least if I am to die, then it would be as someone I can look in the mirror." He stood. "If it would please our lord?"

Aldrik took a deep breath and gave Vhalla a look that she couldn't quite decipher. His eyes were sad, but bright with passion. His shoulders were limp and heavy, but the corners of his mouth tugged upward ever so slightly in the smallest of smiles.

"It would please me greatly. As it is the first decree of your future Empress."

CHAPTER 7

VHALLA WOULD FOREVER remember the reaction of the people in Paca to Aldrik's announcement that Vhalla would be their future Empress. The people embracing her, celebrating her, replayed over in her mind during their ride out of the small town. It played over until a different nagging thought crept up from the back of her brain, until this new thought spoke so loudly that she had no other choice but to address it.

"I'm sorry," Vhalla said guiltily. "For running off as I did towards the Inquisitors."

Her four companions looked at her in surprise.

"You don't need to apologize, Vhal," Fritz said cheerfully.

Vhalla shook her head. "It was reckless of me, and it put you all at risk as well. I'll be more careful in the future."

"Well, be sure you do," Elecia said in a haughty tone. Vhalla shared a small smile with the woman before she turned her focus back to the road.

"Vhalla," Aldrik summoned her attention quietly. "I would also be careful about letting people know our movements."

She thought a moment. "You mean saying we were headed to Hastan."

"We're fairly easy targets right now. The more people who know we're alive, the more people who will be hunting us."

"I'll be more careful," she vowed. Vhalla wouldn't apologize again. Apologies meant nothing, and they weren't going to help them. She simply had to be better than she had ever been before. It was a journey she had been on for some time now, and Vhalla was discovering that the path to being the person she wanted to be had no end point. There would always be room for her to adapt, to change, and to improve.

"Well." Aldrik shifted in his saddle, casting off the weight of the morning. "You were never in any real danger. Those scraps of sorcerers can't stand up to me."

Vhalla laughed for the first time in weeks. "I forgot I rode with the Fire Lord."

"Fire Lord," Elecia snorted. "What a ridiculous title."

"We could think of a title for you as well, 'Cia." Aldrik paused a moment. "Stone-Skinned Lady?"

"More like Stone-Hearted," Jax sniggered.

"There is only one title I'm interested in," Elecia spoke only once she was assured she had stalled long enough for everyone's attention. "The Lady of the West."

"We'll see about that," Aldrik chuckled. "Does your grandfather know you're vying to overthrow him?"

"I'd never," Elecia gasped.

"It's nice to see you smile," Fritz remarked to Vhalla from her left. "I haven't seen it in I don't remember how long."

Vhalla shrugged. "There haven't been many things to smile about."

"There are, though. Don't you think?" Fritz wore a small expression of joy himself. It was small, but it was there. "We're all alive, aren't we?"

"That we are."

"I think we'll likely give your father cause to smile as well, with his daughter coming back from the grave." Fritz combed his fingers through his steadily lengthening hair.

That was something Vhalla hadn't thought about. They had known in Paca of Victor's claims of her death. Fear gripped her. *What if her father thought her dead and had left to flee Victor's slow encroachment north?*

Vhalla looked ahead. This far into the middle of the continent, the hills by the southern mountains had begun to flatten, and there was at most a small slope to the land. She could see a far distance, but her home was still well out of sight.

They rode the day with the wind on her cheeks. There was no spark, no magic calling to her in it. Once in a while, she'd clench her hands into fists, foolishly thinking that her magic would return simply by being in the East. But her magic would not return to her unless there was enough to restore the flow to her Channel.

They saw an old road sign that was the first marker of Leoul. The dusty road and worn fences, which penned in livestock and pastures, began to look familiar to her. It all began to connect like a puzzle of memories, and Vhalla could suddenly recall obscure details like how many trees one farmer had in their field, or how many windows another home had.

A child-like squeal rose up in her throat as Vhalla shot out her finger, pointing at a lone tree in the distance. "My farm!" She clutched the reins tightly. "Can we go faster?"

"Works for me!" Fritz cheered and kicked his horse into a lively trot.

The rest of them did the same. The old gnarled oak still stood tall and laden with leaves, even during the winter months. It sat between two large fields that looked a lot smaller than she remembered. Her home came into view.

And Vhalla's heart stopped.

It was exactly as she'd left it. The thatched roof that looked thinner by the year. The barn with the broken door that had never been fixed. The weeds determined to crawl up the flagstone. Her eyes had seen horror and blood, but somehow they could still look upon the structure that had given her eleven happy years without it spontaneously combusting from being under her stare.

Smoke rose cheerfully from the chimney. The smell of bread wafted in the air as they drew closer. Vhalla glanced over her shoulders, making sure everyone was still with her. The logical part of her brain warned her that this could be a trap. That it could all be a plot to ensnare them.

Vhalla dismounted quickly and paused for a breath at the door, listening to the shuffling within. Her tensions broke, and she knocked feverishly.

"Father!" she called, keeping her voice barely under control. There was a clamor from within. "Papa!"

Casting aside her hesitations and fears, Vhalla pushed open the door, only to have it pulled the rest of the way.

Her father stood on the other side. Of average height and muscled even in age, the rich tone of his skin betrayed every hour he spent in the field. Hair that matched hers in color and tone spilled down in a mess to the bottom of his ears.

"Vhalla?" He blinked, as though she was about to disappear.

"Papa!" The child within her was unleashed, that little girl who desperately wanted her father to hold her and say everything was all right. The girl who had been thrust into the world fearful and unknown. That girl finally won for the first time in months, and tears spilled onto Vhalla's cheeks. "Papa, Papa, Papa . . ."

Her knees lost all their strength, they were suddenly world weary and exhausted. Her father gripped her upper arms, following her to the ground. They stared at each other in awe, the rest of the world utterly forgotten.

"You're okay."

"I should say that to you, little bird." He pulled her in for a tight embrace.

"I'm sorry. I should have come home sooner. I should've been here. I became a lady. I sent coin. Did you get it?" It all spilled out, uncontrollable. "I wanted to come home, Father, but I did so many things. I didn't even know who I was. I didn't know what I wanted. But I know now, I know."

"Hush." Her father held her cheeks and smoothed away her tears. "You're working yourself into a frenzy for no reason."

Vhalla swallowed and nodded, the last of her tears escaping on a laugh. "I'm so happy to see you." Worry had given birth to grief, which shattered in the face of joy.

"I am happy to see you." He pulled her in for another tight hug. "Are you all right?"

"I am."

"I heard so many stories, tall tales all focused on my little bird. I was worried, but I was proud."

Vhalla sat back on her heels, rubbing her face. She felt foolish for crying so much when nothing was wrong. But, if anything, she cried because it was right and perfect and everything she hadn't dared let herself hope for.

"Now." Her father stood. "I am sure you have much to tell me, but let's start with your companions."

"Right." Vhalla stood as well, having completely lost herself in her father being alive and well. "Well . . ." Her eyes scanned their rag-tag lot. It was actually a humorous sight. The disgraced lord, the Southern Sorcerer, the Western noble, and the Emperor.

"Fritz is my dear friend; we met in the Tower of Sorcerers." Vhalla introduced her friends to her father in the order they dismounted. "He's helped me countless times and is a really gifted Waterrunner."

"Elecia is also my dear friend." The woman in question

looked startled that Vhalla would call her such. "She doesn't let me get away with anything, Papa. She's really gifted and strong, also."

"Jax is—"

"Her personal guard," the Western man finished.

Vhalla squinted at him, about to correct him that he, too, was a precious person to her.

But her father interjected, "Thank you for protecting my girl."

"She's pretty good at protecting herself." Jax placed his hands on his hips, assessing her thoughtfully. "Just as good as she is at getting into trouble."

"I can hear you, you know," Vhalla remarked dryly.

"Oh, I know." Jax grinned madly.

"You have certainly found interesting company to keep." Her father chuckled and turned to the last remaining man in question. "And you are?"

Her chest tightened. Her Emperor? Her lord? Her prince? Her friend? Her lover? Her betrothed? Any of those titles could've fallen from Aldrik's lips.

"My name is Aldrik," he said simply.

Vhalla stilled, even Elecia looked surprised at Aldrik's casual introduction.

"M-my lord." Her father dropped to a knee in surprise.

Aldrik stared down at him for a long moment, before kneeling as well, so he could speak at eye-level. "Just Aldrik is fine."

"No-no, I couldn't," her father protested. He had served in the military for years. Vhalla knew how engrained respect for nobility was in his mind. How he knew his place before his leaders and sovereigns. He knew it so well that he had been the one to teach it to her.

"I'm asking, please, simply Aldrik." He spoke in a casual cadence and actually smiled.

"Papa, it's okay." Vhalla tugged on her father's arm, urging him to stand. Her father looked greatly uncertain still. "Aldrik is, well, I'm going to marry him."

Her father looked between Vhalla and Aldrik, clearly struggling to process this.

Even Aldrik looked at her in surprise, but he collected himself quickly. "That is, sir, if you have no objections."

The Emperor looked even more surprised when the Eastern man before him burst out laughing. "It's Vhalla's choice, not mine. I'm not the one you're asking to wed. If she is happy, then I am happy." He held out a hand to Aldrik. "Rex Yarl."

"A pleasure to finally meet you, Rex." Aldrik clasped hands with her father, and Vhalla had to remind herself that she wasn't in some dream land. The Emperor was really shaking hands with her father.

"Where should we tie up the horses?" Jax asked.

"Oh, right. There should be enough space in and around the barn." Vhalla looked up at the sky. "Doesn't look like rain, so they should be fine on an outdoor tie."

Elecia, Jax, and Fritz took the horses to tie, tactfully giving Vhalla, Aldrik, and her father some time alone.

She slipped her hand in the Emperor's, his fingers folding against hers. "Let me show you my home."

Her father still seemed nervous by Aldrik's presence. He walked calmly enough at her left side, but he kept making occasional glances at Aldrik. Vhalla tried to gauge his expression from the corners of her eyes, which proved difficult. Just because she knew what she wanted and didn't need her father's approval, well, that didn't mean she didn't want it.

"These are the strawberry bushes Mama and I planted when I was little." It was almost spring, and they already had tiny fruits nestled between their leaves.

"One spring, Vhalla ate them all in one afternoon," her father spoke to Aldrik, looking at the plants fondly.

"I had such a stomach ache!" Vhalla laughed, remembering exactly the time her father spoke of.

Rex smiled at his daughter. "Your mother had no sympathy for you either."

"She was so cross."

"As was I. I wanted one of her berry tarts." There was still a note of sorrow when he spoke of his deceased wife.

"She did make the best tarts," Vhalla sighed wistfully.

Vhalla picked three of the fruits for each of them to try. They were tiny and somewhat bitter from not having ripened enough. But, for Vhalla, they tasted of springs long past, seasoned sweetly by reminiscing.

Walking around the flagstone, they came across a tree that Vhalla had planted from an off-shoot of the old oak. She remembered it as nothing more than a tiny sapling, but it was now almost taller than she was.

There was the outdoor soaking barrel, where she and her mother had spent many an afternoon bathing. It wasn't far from the outhouse. But they passed all these and headed for a low rectangular stone with a dish-like dip in the center of the top. Vhalla looked at the empty bowl thoughtfully.

"Mama." Vhalla dusted the dirt around the edges, careful not to touch the inside of the dip. "You're dirty; tell the Mother to send a good rain."

"The plants could use it, too." Her father slung an arm around Vhalla's shoulder.

"Do you still miss her?" Vhalla asked one of their ritual questions.

"Of course, little bird. Every single day." His longing was as palpable as his heavy sigh.

For the first time, Vhalla realized that she understood her father's pain. She'd always thought she knew before, but she never had until now. Losing her mother was an exceptionally great pain, but of a different sort than losing the person who held the other part of her soul. Vhalla looked up at Aldrik.

"What was her name?" Aldrik asked.

"Dia," Rex answered.

"Dia. That is a lovely name." Aldrik turned back to the marker. "Dia, I realize you are aware, but your daughter has grown into one astounding woman, and I would be lost without her."

"I'm sure she knows." Rex squeezed Vhalla lovingly. "Just as I do."

"We should get dinner started," Vhalla tried to keep her words light, not wanting to betray the sudden ache of her heart. She remembered how she had sat for the first few hours following her mother's Rite of Sunset, watching the wind slowly blow away the ashes from the shallow basin at the top of the marker. This was the font of her mother's winds, so said Eastern lore.

Shortly after, Vhalla found herself side by side with Fritz preparing dinner. Jax and Elecia squabbled around the tall table by the countertop, and Aldrik and her father chatted quietly by the hearth. She kept glancing over her shoulder, trying to pick up what they were saying, but even in the tiny, one-room house, she could only make out every couple words.

"You all right, Vhal?" Fritz asked. He was busy cutting some smoked and salted pork.

"Actually, I couldn't be better." She smiled, giving up trying to figure out what her father and Aldrik were whispering about. "Have I cut these right?"

"Yes, yes. Put them in the pot," Fritz instructed. "I would've thought you were a better cook."

"My mother only taught me the basics," Vhalla confessed.

"Oh, right, sorry."

"Don't be," Vhalla eased her friend's mind. "I really do like thinking of her; I remember all the things she taught me. Cooking just wasn't one of them."

"Who knows, Vhalla Yarl," Elecia joined their conversation. "Perhaps you do have a trace of nobility in you yet, for being more accustomed to others preparing food for you."

Vhalla rolled her eyes. "Well, Lady Ci'Dan, I, at least, am willing to dirty my hands enough to prepare the food that I am to eat," Vhalla jabbed lightly.

Getting the rise out of Elecia that she sought, soon the other woman was cutting root vegetables at Fritz's instruction and giving Vhalla free hands to start on the bread.

"Would you look at that." Jax leaned against the table. "Elecia Ci'Dan, on a dirt floor, cutting vegetables."

"Enjoy it while you can." Elecia didn't even turn around.

"You know I will." Jax's eyes moved up and down Elecia's form a few times.

"You letch." Vhalla nudged him.

"Can you blame me?"

"Jax." Elecia paused, flipping the knife in her palm deftly. "Is now really when you want to try to get cheeky with me."

"Knife throwing only excites me more."

Fritz and Vhalla roared with laughter.

"It's good to have the house so lively again," Rex said as he and Aldrik rejoined the conversation. "Your presence has been missed."

"Speaking of missing, Mother's spices are also gone." Vhalla pointed to the empty windowsill.

"There was a bad drought a year ago. I couldn't spare water for even them."

"She'd be cross with you." Vhalla began kneading the dough she'd been working on before setting it in a bowl to rest, a cloth draped over top. "How's the well now? The creeks?"

"It has been a more arid year than normal, but they are fine enough for planting," he responded. "Don't worry on that."

"I *do* worry." She sighed. "The fields need ploughing—"

"It's not time just yet."

"—the barn door is broken—"

"As it has been for years."

"You're not taking care of things," Vhalla finished pointedly.

"I am." Rex Yarl laughed. "The farm's fine; I'm fine. I don't have some herbs. I always enjoyed bland foods."

"You do not." Vhalla crossed her arms on her chest stubbornly. "You loved mama's cooking, and she used them every day."

"I did because your mother could've made anything and I would've loved it."

Dinner passed quietly and peacefully. Fritz's soup was ready before Vhalla's bread, but there weren't enough bowls to go around. So they waited and talked until the small loaves had time to bake.

She'd forgotten where the sweet spot in their oven was and some of the loaves were a little too brown. Thankfully, Jax diligently adjusted the fire as she'd demanded, as best he could after the hearth had heated, so they were all edible.

Vhalla thought herself clever for gouging out the top of the bread and filling it with soup, even though she'd burned her fingers for handling them too quickly after cooking. They'd not eaten a real, hot meal since Fritz's home, and it was better than just about anything Vhalla could've imagined. Perhaps some of it was the semi-starvation they had been enduring, but everyone had seconds gladly, eating until their bellies were rounded.

It wasn't long after that they all collapsed on the floor. Fritz and Elecia were asleep in moments, Jax not long after. Their cloaks served as blankets; Rex's clothing was rolled to create makeshift pillows. After spending so many nights in the open, having two nights in a row under a roof was pure bliss.

Rex insisted that Aldrik take his small rope bed, but Aldrik refused, opting for the small palette that would've been Vhalla's. When he realized they couldn't both fit, he offered it to her, but it was Vhalla's turn to refuse. Her Emperor had a hard enough time sleeping, and if the thin layer of straw helped, she wasn't about to take it from him.

Everyone fell asleep quickly. Everyone but Vhalla. She was exhausted, but sleep wouldn't come.

She watched the red glow of the hearth fade into the darkness. The moon played hide and seek with the clouds, which she viewed through the window by their table. She listened to Fritz's soft snoring, the shifts as Elecia rolled around, Jax's boot scrape against the ground as he twitched in his sleep.

Vhalla pulled herself to her feet, glancing to her father's bed. He was curled in the opposite direction, the rise and fall of his chest slow and even. Like a child, she crept out the door.

The ladder was where it had always been, propped near the chimney. It was worn and old but could bear her weight without trouble. She situated herself near the stones and used the radiant heat they still held from the baking earlier to fend off the night's chill.

All her worries and assessments were correct. The roof needed to be re-built. But for now, the beams below the thatching were protected enough that they hadn't rotted and gone soft. Vhalla reclined back on the slope of the roof, looking up at the endless sky.

The ladder creaked and shifted, and then her father's head popped over the roof.

"I thought I'd find you up here," he said softly, climbing up the rest of the way. Vhalla shifted closer to the warmth of the hearth and pulled her knees to her chest to make room for him to sit. "You're still seeking places like this to roost?"

"I suppose so." Vhalla thought back to her window seat in the library, how it offered her a view of the entire capital. She thought of her Tower room and the small balcony she so loved. She thought to her fearlessness the night Aldrik had brought her to the top of a spire. She'd never connected her love of high vantages before. "You knew what I was, didn't you?"

"What you were?"

She finally had her father all to herself. She had the opportunity to ask the questions that had been burning for weeks. And now Vhalla was terrified of the answers.

"You and Mama, you knew I was a Windwalker," Vhalla asked in spite of her fear.

Her father was silent for a long moment, speaking volumes. "We had suspicions."

"And you never told me?" Vhalla twisted in shock. "You *hid* it from me?"

"Little bird, what were we to say? That we thought you may wield magic? Neither of us possessed such powers, and we barely knew what they meant. All we knew was what your grandmother had taught your mother."

Even her father's pet name for her suddenly had new meaning, even as he revealed new facets to her past. "What grandmother taught?" Vhalla knew her grandparents had worked in the post office of Hastan, but she'd always been told they had fallen out with their daughter when she'd married Vhalla's father.

"She also possessed the gift of winds." Her father sighed heavily, visibly pained by Vhalla's hurt. "When your mother expressed concerns, you were just a toddler. Your grandmother demanded we send you to her so she could teach you how to live hidden.

"But your mother wouldn't give you up. She read and heard as many tales from old Cyven as she could, learning what she could about the Windwalkers. She loved you, Vhalla, and she wanted to raise you."

Vhalla rested her chin on her knees. She debated internally if it would've been better to have been sent off. To know what she was. If she had been, if she had never been removed from the East, perhaps none of the current events would've happened.

But Vhalla didn't know what it felt like to have a child and be faced with the choice of giving up that child. She tightened her arms around her knees. She never would. Because if and when she did give birth to her first child, he or she would be taken to the North—*it was already decided. There would be no opportunity for conflict.*

"Don't harbor any anger toward your mother," her father sighed.

"I don't," Vhalla replied back before he could misinterpret her contemplations. "I just, wish I'd known sooner. I wish *someone* had told me." *So she wouldn't have had to be pushed off a roof.*

"If I'd known what would've happened, I would've done things differently," he confessed.

"What's done is done." Vhalla shrugged it away. "I know why you and Mama tried to hide me. I know what the East teaches about Windwalkers and magic." Vhalla considered it for a long moment. "But in the end, while I wish I had done a few things differently . . . I wouldn't change all of it."

"And why is that?"

"Because I stopped reading and started doing." Vhalla smiled faintly at the memory of Aldrik's words at their first meeting. "I messed up so badly. I didn't love some friends enough. Sometimes I focused on myself more than others. But if I hadn't made those mistakes, I wouldn't be strong enough to look to the future now and not be afraid."

"A future that involves you being Empress," her father probed.

Vhalla relented easily. "I should've written you more. I should've found a way to tell you sooner. I should've come home."

"You were off ending wars." He laughed his hearty laugh. "Don't be so hard on yourself, little bird."

She sighed. "Papa, do you think I will make a good Empress? I've done so many horrible things." Vhalla wanted to confess her sin of unleashing Victor upon the world. But some guilt was too heavy to share with her father.

"The best," her father said without hesitation. "I have no doubt in you; I know the sort of Empress you will be. But about our young crown prince, I know little more than the rumors from the soldiers during the War of the Crystal Caverns. Tell me the sort of Emperor we will have."

Vhalla obliged her father. Words spilled from her mouth as though she were the font from which they were created. In telling her father about Aldrik, she had to tell him how she came to meet Aldrik, how she came to know the man that had the reputation for being one of the most shut-off, cold people on the continent.

She didn't make him out to be perfect. Vhalla knew Aldrik was horribly flawed. But so was she. He was prone to anger and she prone to selfishness. But they strove together to be better, for themselves and for each other.

In it all, she told her father of everything that happened since she had last seen him. Years were summed up in minutes and hours. He frowned at her pain, and praised her for overcoming her trials.

Vhalla and Rex Yarl sat in the breeze until the dawn.

CHAPTER 8

HER CHEST ACHED at the smell of the air, at the way the dust settled in the early light, at the sweet scent of wet earth from the morning's dew. It all pained her. Each sensory input filled her with the heaviness of longing for a world that was long gone.

She'd only crawled back to her place near Aldrik an hour or so ago, but she couldn't fall asleep. She listened to her Emperor's slow and steady breathing and let it lull her into a heavy-lidded doze. But she didn't sleep. She wanted to savor every last moment in her home.

The dawn was insistent, and Vhalla eventually sat up. She glanced at her father, who was thankfully sleeping. He wasn't a young man any longer, and she'd kept him up until the first light.

On light feet, she tip-toed over to the pile of wood that was kept indoors. Her mother had always performed the ritual of lighting the hearth first thing in the winter months. *Now it would fall to her*, Vhalla's heart told her.

"Let me help you with that," Aldrik whispered in her ear.

Vhalla nearly jumped out of her skin, dropping the small log of wood she held in the process. His hand reached around her and caught it deftly.

"Thank you, my phantom," she teased coyly, having not heard him so much as stir.

"What's the cause for the old pet name?" Aldrik hummed, nuzzling the hair by her ear.

"I didn't realize it had become a pet name," she breathed in hushed amusement.

"Perhaps it was just my wishful thinking early on." The corner of Aldrik's mouth tugged up into a grin. Fire lit in the hearth next to them, summoned by his passing thought.

"Was it?" Vhalla hummed, resting her palms on his chest. "A prince thinking wishful thoughts about a library girl?"

"What magic you've woven over me." Aldrik leaned forward.

Vhalla's hands twisted in his clothes and pulled him to her. His palm smoothed out her shirt over her hip while the other left a trail of gooseflesh along her neck. The faintest of groans rose to meet his mouth. *She had not kissed him enough.*

The turmoil, the endless days on the road, the persistent company. It all pushed affections away as trivial. But Vhalla had never felt anything more essential to her wellbeing than his mouth on hers.

"When are you going to wake me up like that, my liege?" Jax quipped, not specifying to whom he spoke, so Vhalla and Aldrik both jumped away from each other.

"By the Mother, Jax, it's too early," Aldrik bemoaned.

"It's too early for all of you," Elecia echoed venomously.

"We finally agree on something." Fritz was awake as well.

"We agree on lots of things," Elecia insisted.

Fritz grinned. "No, we don't."

"You're just doing that on purpose."

"And you take all the covers."

And with that, everyone had risen for the day.

Vhalla began preparing an Eastern breakfast—sliced salted pork stuffed into bread left over from the night prior. She may have never cooked much, but she did know how to make *some* things.

"Rex," Aldrik began in a tone Vhalla instantly didn't like. She just knew. "I was thinking that it's not safe for you to stay here."

She stilled, leaning against the counter under the window by the hearth.

"The knowledge that Vhalla and I live will spread rapidly. As it does, we will become even more hunted." He paused to wash down some bread with water. "We will go West, after Hastan. My yet-living family through my mother is in Norin, and my uncle is the Lord of the West. That is where I want you to go also."

"I see." Her father rubbed the knuckle of his index finger over his lips in thought.

"You want my father to come with us?"

"Not quite." Aldrik's apologetic eyes told her everything before his lips spoke the words.

"Alone?" Vhalla shouldn't have let the panic slip into her voice. "You've seen what's out there, Aldrik."

"You know it's the right decision," the Emperor insisted.

Vhalla looked away with a sigh. She did, even if she didn't want to admit it. She knew her father was no one by himself. With her, with Aldrik, he became a target.

"Papa?" She returned from her thoughts, seeking out her father's opinion on the matter.

"I will be fine, little bird." Her father crossed over and pulled her in for a tight hug. "Remember, you're not the only one in this house who's ridden to war. I'm not that old and rusty."

Vhalla sighed softly, closing her eyes and resting her face on her father's shoulder. Having her father home was right. He smelled of the earth under his nails and the soot in the hearth. As long as he remained, there would always be somewhere she could run back to.

If he left, it meant the world had truly changed.

"Take my sword, then. You'll need a weapon." Vhalla insisted; there was no point in further argument. Everything had been changing for years, and would continue to change. That was life.

The preparations didn't take long. Bladders were filled from the well. The remaining bread was split among them with Vhalla insisting her father take the larger of the pieces.

Rex Yarl left first, heading straight for the Western border. He promised her he would only make one stop at a trusted friend's house before continuing onward. He didn't bring anything with him that could confirm his identity, in case he was stopped by Inquisitors. That had brought on a debate as to how he would prove his association upon arriving at Norin.

"Aldrik," Vhalla summoned his attention once they were on the road. "You must think of a new code."

"What code do you speak of?" he asked, reminding her that he couldn't read her mind.

"What is most beautiful just before it dies? A rose," Vhalla repeated what he had told her father to recite for Aldrik's uncle in Norin. "You told it to me after Baldair's death."

"I did." Aldrik's voice tightened some at the memory.

"Victor knew it; it's why I went with him."

"He would." Aldrik muttered a curse under his breath. "I've only ever used it with people I trust implicitly."

"Wait, so that means you trust me, right?" Fritz was over eager about the fact.

Vhalla was pleased to have a convenient change in topic. She'd said her peace, and she knew her Emperor's mind. It would stew in his brain until Aldrik had worked through a new solution and alternate code phrase. She smiled at Fritz. "I think that's exactly what it means."

"Technically, Elecia was the one to pass along the knowledge," Aldrik remarked dryly.

"And I wouldn't have done so if I wasn't confident I was passing it along to someone whom you trusted implicitly." Elecia's tone was part defensive, part jest. "Fritz, you are quite welcome in the Ci'Dan fold."

Fritz laughed nervously. "Not sure if I want that."

That set Elecia off on a long history of the noble Ci'Dan family. Vhalla knew she should listen—it was Aldrik's lineage and therefore important to her. But all she found herself focused on was the approaching end of her family's farmland. Her father not bringing identification meant that everything that declared her family remained here.

Vhalla turned in her saddle, looking at the farmhouse fading in the distance. It was empty and unassuming, waiting for renegades to come ransack it, to steal their few meager things of worth. Or it could be waiting for Victor's men to come and level it, purely out of spite for her.

She stopped her horse.

"Vhalla?" Aldrik slowed his to a stop a short distance away the moment he noticed she'd fallen from the group.

Vhalla gripped the reins tightly. She wanted to run back and take whatever she could that would remind her of home.

"Is everything all right?" Fritz called.

"Everything's fine," Vhalla forced herself to say. *Memories were not tied up in things.* She turned back to the group. "Let's go; Hastan is waiting."

The following days to Hastan passed blissfully uneventful. So much so that it was almost possible to imagine that they were merely five travelers on a trip because they wanted to be. They stayed at inns along the way, keeping their identities a secret. Every night, Vhalla pretended that she was just a woman and Aldrik was just a man, a couple engaged to be wed. She staved off worry with his kisses and quieted the noise in her mind with his blissfully breathy sighs.

The deeper they pushed into the heart of the East, the less they saw of Victor's hold. People knew what was going on; a few may have even seen one of the abominations Victor had crafted. But for the majority, life still continued with almost relative normalcy.

That normalcy ended the moment they reached the capital of the East. Hastan was the opposite of the towering Southern capital. It was not perched upon a mountaintop, but grew slowly from out of the surrounding plains. All farmland ended and the houses stopped for a long barren stretch before the city began. A no-man's land that set Hastan apart from the rest of Cyven. Very few people actually lived in Hastan proper; it serving more as an apex for government, commerce, and culture for the people of Cyven.

It was the first time Vhalla had laid eyes on the city.

"Why is the West laying siege to Hastan?" Vhalla scanned the army encampment set up around the whole of Hastan. Crimson pennons bearing the Western phoenix fluttered in the wind.

"I don't know." Aldrik frowned.

"I'd venture a guess they might." Jax pointed at the line of soldiers blocking the road into the city.

"Halt," one of the soldiers called out to them as they approached. "From where do you hail?"

"Now that's the question, isn't it?" Jax sniggered under his breath, glancing at their odd mix.

"We have come to speak with the Senators of Hastan." Aldrik had put back on his Emperor voice.

"Senator, you mean," one of the men clarified in a heavy Western accent.

"Senator?" Vhalla looked between them. "There should be four senators from the East."

"There were, until the Supreme King got his hands on the three that were still in the capital when he usurped the throne."

"By whose order are you here?" Elecia asked.

"By the order of the only ruler who still holds claim to the throne." Vhalla glanced at Aldrik from the corners of her eyes as the soldier spoke. "The Lord Ophain Ci'Dan."

Relief pulled at the corners of the Emperor's mouth, folding it neatly into a small smile. It exuded confidence and betrayed his ease at the soldier's omission. Elecia caught Vhalla's eyes for a conspiratorial look as she pulled them away from Aldrik's profile. She'd seen Aldrik's expression as well and seemed to get equal amusement from it.

Aldrik shook his head. "Well, my uncle's claim is something I cannot argue. Were I not alive."

The soldier opened his mouth to speak and paused, looking at Aldrik, and then looking at his comrade. They both struggled to put together what Aldrik had said.

"Usually you kneel before your sovereign lord," Elecia helped them along.

"No, no . . . The nephew of Lord Ophain, of our late princess . . . Prince Aldrik is dead."

"But there were rumors—"

"You know how people will talk," one soldier interrupted the other.

"Oh, we're wasting time." Elecia sat straighter in her saddle. "Bring us to whomever is running this operation."

"We will not trouble Lord Sevin for you imposters."

"Excuse me?" Elecia had gone deathly still. Vhalla expected some form of verbal lashing after being called an imposter. "Who did you say was leading this?"

"The honorable Lord Sevin Ci'Dan."

Elecia dismounted. She balled one of her hands into a fist, clasping the other hand over it—a motion Vhalla learned long ago was her physical act of opening her Channel. The curly-haired woman stalked over to the unsuspecting guards. The rest of them didn't move as their Emperor remained still, content to forfeit the soldiers to Elecia like mice to a cat.

"Don't come any closer or we'll be forced to engage." The man drew his sword. "Go on your own way and there needn't be bloodshed."

Elecia pressed forward, the man swung for her shoulder and the blade split open Elecia's shirt, but it stopped hard with a ring against her stone skin. Elecia looked at the offending sword for a long moment, before turning her eyes back to her attacker. The man was startled into silence.

"I'll tell the Lord Sevin to overlook that, if you do as we ask." Elecia raised her head with a triumphant grin. "Now, take me to my father."

Elecia was recognized not more than a few steps off the road. That was all it took. The soldiers leading them were suddenly wanting to make sure they accommodated every little thing the travelers asked for—*now that they realized they were in the presence of the Emperor.*

A messenger reached the Lord Sevin before they did. He was already running as they approached the heart of the camp, the tent flaps fluttering behind him. Elecia dismounted, crossing to where her father was skidding to a stop.

"My girl," he uttered in awe.

Vhalla immediately noticed two things about Sevin Ci'Dan. The first was that he didn't seem much older than Aldrik. The second was that the two could almost be brothers by appearances alone. Aldrik's mother, Fiera Ci'Dan, Western Princess, was the sister of Lord Ophain Ci'Dan, Sevin's father. That would make Aldrik and him cousins, so the family resemblance made sense, Vhalla reasoned.

"*Fiarum evantes,*" Elecia spoke the Western greeting strong and proud.

"*Kotun un knox,*" her father replied.

They clasped forearms, and the man lowered his forehead to his daughter's briefly. It was a restrained greeting and, compared to the Eastern embraces Vhalla was used to, she would expect it to seem cold. But there was true admiration in their movements, still waters ran deep here. It was different than what she knew, but the love remained.

"My Emperor." The lord dropped to a knee.

"Sevin," Aldrik spoke, dismounting. "No need for that. It is good to see you well."

"I cannot say enough of the same." The two men clasped forearms as well, an easy reunion between family members. "We heard you were dead."

"My lady has a habit of cheating death." Aldrik motioned to Vhalla. "She shared a bit of her luck this time."

"Your . . . lady?" The man followed Aldrik's hand to Vhalla.

"Vhalla Yarl," she announced and dismounted.

"There is much to tell." Sevin's eyes looked across their group before turning to his men. "Take their horses, see them rubbed down and the dust off their coats. Bring dried dates, cohi, bread, and whatever perishables are freshest."

They were ushered into the lord's tent. It was large enough for a table, cot, and a number of personal affects. However, it was unlike Aldrik's tent on the march. This had been set up with the intention of not being moved for some time.

"Are you in contact with your father?" Aldrik asked, sitting on one of the large pillows atop the hide that surrounded the low table.

"Regularly." Sevin sat next to his daughter. "I will send word to him immediately."

"I would like to include a personal letter." Aldrik motioned for Vhalla to sit at his right hand, and she did so without hesitation. Fritz and Jax filled in the rest of their small circle. "He may think you've gone mad if it's not in my hand."

"Of course." The lord paused as soldiers brought the requested foods. "Going mad is something that he may have suspected already, given the East's nature."

Vhalla cleared her throat, unappreciative of the tone of the last statement. "Why *are* you here?"

Sevin looked to Aldrik, confirming that she did, indeed, have the authority to ask outright. Aldrik stared expectantly.

"When the first messengers were received in Norin, they spoke of the fall of Solaris and demanded Father bend his knee and the West recognize King Victor's rule." He snorted, amused at the notion even recounting it. "Naturally, we killed the abominations and have begun to aggressively oppose the madman.

"But the East was unresponsive to our letters. We feared that they had already fallen or aligned with King Victor."

"So he prepared to subdue the Eastern front as well," Aldrik concluded.

Sevin nodded. "But we came to discover that the delay was only a result of one senator waiting to see if the other three had made it from the South alive." He mumbled under his breath, "The fool."

"What is the hesitation now, then?" Aldrik asked.

"You know the East; they don't want to fight even if war is at their doorstep. They're stalling to see if they can side with the winner and then belly up like they did with the Empire."

"Doing so saved countless lives." Vhalla frowned slightly. "The East knew they were beat, rather than fighting a ten-year war."

The lord didn't seem to appreciate her mention of Mhashan's longer, but inevitable, fall to the Empire.

Vhalla sighed softly; divisions would get them nowhere. "But this is different," she conceded. "This is not a force that can be reasoned with. This is a man beyond sense and logic. He will kill us all just because it would suit him to do so."

"You have seen him." The lord heard something in her tone that made his words a statement, rather than a question.

"I was the one to give him this corrupt strength." Vhalla met his eyes, and the lord leaned backward involuntarily. "And I will be the one to take it away. I will be the one to kill him and end the blight of crystals once and for all."

"What have you seen?"

Vhalla was the one to summarize their tale. She had earned the floor, and she kept it. Even Elecia kept her interjections minimal to only when Vhalla omitted an important detail.

"Terrible," the lord breathed in horror when they had finished listing the events that led them to his tent. "We knew it was something wretched, but—this?"

"It will only worsen." Vhalla balled her hands into fists. The phantom sensation of magic washed over her, her body creating the illusion of a Channel to meet her need for strength. "We must unite, and we must fight. Shaldan will fight on our side."

"Shaldan?" He turned to Aldrik with his confusion. "How? I assumed that if—" Sevin's eyes darted to Vhalla, struggling to make sense of what was before him, "—if your lady sat before me, then the Northern Princess had perished."

"She did not." Aldrik's jaw was tight. "We made a deal for the sake of the continent."

"I see." He clearly did not, and he was deeply curious about the details, that much was apparent. But the lord's upbringing won out, and he did not press. "Well, I am certain the West will praise your union with our Duchess with much fervor. And, for the time being, having an Eastern Empress will help us all."

Vhalla swallowed hard and tried to make sense of the emotions that rushed through her at the thought. She'd barely become accustomed to Aldrik outright calling her his lady, and now she was to be called Empress. She was not groomed for the title, but Vhalla would do whatever she must to fit it.

"Not quite Empress, cousin," Aldrik corrected, sensing Vhalla's struggle.

"Oh?"

"We have yet to speak our devotion before the Mother Sun."

"You wait for your throne to be restored?"

Vhalla stared on in confusion as Aldrik shook his head. His words echoed in her ears. "We will wed in Norin."

In Norin? He planned for them to wed not in months or years, or when his rule was restored, but mere weeks away? She'd been his lady openly for days, and now she was to be Empress by Gods and law in mere *weeks*?

"There will be a later time to speak nuptial details." Aldrik stood, keenly aware of her turmoil and acting before it could burst from her. "For now, we will go speak with this Eastern senator."

Fritz, Elecia, and Jax all opted to relax in the lord's tent during Aldrik's and Vhalla's mission. Elecia reluctantly picked up on the notion that it was a matter better served by allowing the rulers to rule, but Fritz and Jax seemed all too eager to finally be out of the saddle and stuffing their faces with as much food as they could.

It suited Vhalla because it meant that the Lord Ci'Dan walked a few paces behind with his men, leaving Vhalla and Aldrik alone. She had to physically bite her tongue to keep the questions from spilling out. They didn't get more than a few paces into camp toward Hastan when they came rushing forth.

"Norin? We will wed in Norin?"

"I'm sorry I didn't have a chance to run it by you." He at least *sounded* honestly apologetic.

"You didn't think running it by your bride would be important?" Vhalla gave her Emperor a small glare.

"Vhalla, now is not the time."

"When will the time be? The next time we are speaking to a member of your family?" she muttered.

"Tonight." He leaned forward, making it impossible for her not to meet his eyes. "Tonight, my Vhalla—"

"Your honeyed words have no effect on me, Emperor Solaris," Vhalla lied.

The arrogant royal knew it, too, judging by the small smile he gave her. "I promise we will speak on it tonight."

"If you promise," she sighed, letting the topic go for the time being.

Hastan was quiet. Despite having more people, more shops, more buildings, more everything than all the small farm towns they'd travelled through, it was so quiet that the wind sounded loud. Vhalla stared back at the men and women who looked upon them, curious but reserved. She tried to smile reassuringly, but it didn't seem to help. *At least it didn't hurt.*

The main government building of Hastan was a large, circular structure at the end of the East-West Way. The builders had chosen a circle to signify that all was made equal in that there were no sides. It had only one floor for much the same reason. The fact had never stuck out to her in all her reading, but after seeing so much of the world, she had never appreciated her own history or culture more.

"Back again?" A farmer who had been dressed up to look like a guard—and was failing—yawned from the doorway. "She's not going to see you twice in one day."

"Inform the senator that the Emperor wishes to meet with her." Vhalla made mental notes about how Aldrik put strength behind his words. How he could make a statement, said calmly, seem like both an order from a friend and a threat from a ruler.

"The Emperor is dead."

"The father, but not the son," Vhalla clarified.

The man looked at her, as if for the first time. "You're not one of them."

"I am. As are you. We are all the Solaris Empire. An Empire of the Sun for its people, for peace."

"Who are you?"

"Vhalla Yarl."

By the way he reacted, she would've thought she had told the man that she was the chaos dragon, burst free from the Father's prison in the night sky. The man stumbled back, holding his shirt over his chest in surprise. He stared at her for a long moment, ignoring the presence of the man who had proclaimed himself the true Emperor.

"You . . . You come with me." The man started for the door. "The rest of you stay."

"Excuse me?" the Lord Ci'Dan balked.

"The senator said no more Westerners, but I will take the Windwalker to her." The farmer-guard paused at the door.

"The Emperor will come with me," Vhalla insisted.

"Unnecessary." Aldrik rested his hand lightly on her arm, summoning her attention. "Once the senator meets with you, I'm confident she will be willing to hold an audience with the rest of us."

Vhalla paused, stuck in limbo. Aldrik had such confidence in her. It thrilled her. It terrified her. But she was becoming the woman she had hoped—because it was more elating than frightening.

"Very well." Vhalla nodded. She caught his hand, briefly lacing her fingers against his. "I'll go, and come back once I've gained an audience for you all."

She followed the guard into an entry room, it arched slightly with the curve of the building. They crossed through it, passing a long hall.

"You believe me?" she asked.

"I do," the man affirmed with minimal hesitation. "No one in their right mind would admit to being Vhalla Yarl if they weren't actually Vhalla Yarl."

Vhalla laughed, unable to argue. Claiming she was Vhalla Yarl was a virtual death sentence in the world they lived. He led her through another doorway into the center of the building. A circular auditorium descended three levels into the earth. Sun shades were pulled back from an open roof, letting in the sunlight. A woman, with brown hair that grayed at the ears, looked up from where she was toiling over some letters spread out at a circular table.

"Who is this?" The question was pointed, but not sharp nor unkind.

"Vhalla Yarl."

The senator looked Vhalla up and down for a long moment, squinting. "You're supposed to be dead."

"I've been told death doesn't suit me."

"It didn't suit the Vhalla Yarl I knew, either." The lines by her eyes deepened as she smiled. "If you are really Vhalla Yarl, tell me what you did to throw the court into disarray during your trial."

"I stopped Master Mohned from falling," Vhalla answered easily. "Senator, your Emperor seeks an audience, but he is being refused because you have already had your audience with the West today."

The woman considered this for a long moment. "Speak honestly; is he truly the Emperor?"

"You will know it to be fact when you see him."

The senator proved Vhalla correct. The moment she laid eyes on Aldrik, her hesitation vanished. Within minutes, they were sipping cool wheat tea and heatedly discussing plans to implement with the West. By the time they were finished, the sun was low in the sky.

It was easier than Vhalla had expected. The East and West seemed to just fall into place. Without the complication over whose claim to the throne was the strongest and who would likely garner more support across the continent, the East had little hesitation in supporting Aldrik's assertion.

"This feels too easy," she remarked to Aldrik as they walked through the curving hallway on their way to where the messenger birds of Hastan were kept.

"Let it be so," he chuckled. "We have had enough hardship."

"So it's what I expect." Vhalla linked her arm with his, enjoying the quiet. It felt like forever since they had last been alone. Elecia had chosen to sleep in the camp with her father. But Fritz and Jax were joining Vhalla and Aldrik in the government building, so Vhalla expected such times to be limited.

"My father," Aldrik said thoughtfully. "For all his flaws, he had a vision that takes roots in the hearts of men. A vision of a single banner, uniting us all. Of struggling for a better future rather than against each other."

Vhalla gripped his arm for a moment, debating if she should bring up the Crescent Continent. She put a quick end to her debate. *He didn't need to be reminded of his father's ruthlessness.* She would allow him a memory colored with fondness.

Aldrik continued, "It's an ideal people are still willing to fight for. Because we were so close we could taste it."

"You will end this war and be an Emperor for peace." Vhalla permitted herself a tiny smile at the notion.

"We will end it. And *we* will be the rulers for peace."

CHAPTER 9

THE NIGHT'S DARKNESS enveloped the last messenger bird. Vhalla's hands were ink stained and tired. She'd written triple the number of letters Aldrik had, but only a third had been sent. She had never written letters as an Empress before, and it proved more difficult than expected to capture and hold the right tone.

Vhalla had scrapped the first batch on her own and then the second after Aldrik's critique. Eventually she developed a formula for informing the Western lords and ladies that their Emperor was alive. But by the time she'd mastered it, Aldrik had already finished the majority on his own.

"Come." He took her hand in his, drawing her attention away from the window. "We should rest."

Vhalla appreciated the simple elegance of the Eastern government building. It was the original senate hall, and it was as opulent as could be expected of the East without being needlessly lavish. The floors were multi-colored wood, inlaid in a zig-zag pattern of light and dark. A handful of portraits in tasteful frames lined the hall at wide intervals. Candlelight gleamed off the floor polish.

But the beauty had a certain darkness tainting it at the

shadows. This place stood for a government created by the people, to serve the people—the East's great experiment. As long as Victor was alive, it would only be a shade of its former glory, its growth stinted by the shade of a madman.

She rubbed her shoulder absent-mindedly. The scar no longer ached to the touch. It had healed over to an ugly, but otherwise harmless, mark.

They passed Jax and Fritz's temporary chambers on the way to their rooms. Vhalla would have stopped in to spend time with her friend, but no light peeked out from under his door. Vhalla hoped that he was getting some much needed sleep in a real bed.

She and Aldrik had separate rooms, as was deemed chaste and appropriate for their standing. It made Vhalla roll her eyes at the notion. Apparently the senator thought similarly, as the rooms had a connecting door. It fit the East's lax mentality when it came to physical affection. The notion of sacred chastity was a loose construct placed upon them by the West rather than an important tenant of their culture.

Vhalla naturally found her way into his bed most nights. Their proximity was impossible to fight and, in some ways, she needed him now more than ever. His arms reassured her that she had a place in his world, that she wasn't a girl pretending to be noble.

Vhalla listened to his slow and steady breathing, debating the words that were burning her tongue. They both needed rest, and he was nearly asleep. Vhalla nuzzled her Emperor's jaw gently.

"What is it?" Aldrik uttered into the darkness.

"Norin?" she replied.

He sighed softly, pressing his cheek into her forehead. "I did promise we would speak on it."

"And I will hold you to that promise."

"We absolutely must have the full support of the Empire," he began. "Standing against Victor will otherwise be impossible."

She didn't disagree.

"Our Empire is in disarray, threatened by being torn apart and scattered. My life is enough to rally the West. Your becoming Empress helps cement the East's support. But the North depends on the deal we have struck with them."

Vhalla held her tongue as, technically, the deal Sehra had made was for *Aldrik's* heir, irrelevant of which woman produced said heir. Vhalla had no guarantee she would make it to the end of the war.

"Beyond that, the people need a display of strength. That their leadership is whole, united, concrete. A wedding will do just that."

"Are you certain?" She was unconvinced. "Wouldn't a wedding look as though we are focused on ourselves when we should be focused on our people?" It was odd how phrases like "our people" were becoming easier to say.

He chuckled and pressed his lips firmly to her forehead. "I adore your compassion for our Empire. But I beseech you— have faith in me on this. I understand the workings of the court and the displays the people expect."

"I do have faith in you, but that doesn't exempt me from feeling uncertain."

"My Vhalla." His arms tightened around her. "Grant it to me. If something should happen to me—"

"Don't say it." She twisted to find his face in the darkness, stealing the words from his lips with a firm kiss. "Don't you dare say those words, Aldrik Solaris. We've been through too much to entertain morbid possibilities."

Vhalla knew where his heart lay. It was in the same place that had told her to go West if he fell in the final battle of the North. It was the truth, but Vhalla did not want to give it the credence of words. She knew the title of Empress would ensure her protection. She knew Aldrik desired nothing more; he didn't need to say it.

"Very well," Aldrik sighed, gently kissing her back for a long moment. "If it is truly something you do not wish, then we won't speak on it. But consider the notion, come to terms with it, before you outright reject it."

"That I can do." Her words were a hushed whisper, but a cacophony of noise filled her brain as her mind tried to think too many thoughts over top each other.

A few hours later, she had almost quieted the noise in her mind when her restless sleep was interrupted by a screech ripping through the sky. It sounded as though the heavens were being torn asunder, and it awoke both of them with a start. Another cry echoed the first. It was pure agony given form, as though a thousand men and women cried all at once.

She was out of bed and to their window in an instant, throwing open the shutter and looking skyward.

"What do you see?" Aldrik asked, trying to look as well.

"Nothing from here." Vhalla squinted into the darkness of the night.

Another screech came. Creatures zipped through the night air and gusted wind against her cheeks. Vhalla's eyes caught a glint of something unnatural descending upon Hastan. The brief outlines of hulking abominations were visible, glowing faintly in a familiar turquoise shade.

"Monsters," she breathed. "Victor's attacking."

"Did you see him?" Aldrik took one more look out the window before starting for the door.

"Not him, but one of his crystal experiments." Vhalla wasn't actually sure what banked through the sky, but it was unlike anything she'd ever seen before. The creature they had encountered on the road with Daniel seemed child's play compared to this. Even just as a shadow in the night, it was a nightmare given form—a monster that one wished to remain in the void from where it came.

Aldrik cursed loudly, slamming the door behind them. "He knows we're here."

Vhalla was about to ask how, but the words stopped short. She remembered the Inquisitors in Paca and her foolishly proclaiming about where they were going. She'd wanted to spark inspiration in the people, she'd wanted to sway the men from Victor. *But what if they hadn't been swayed?* The heat of betrayal flushed her cheeks.

"What's going on?" Jax met them in the hall.

"Victor's attacking," Aldrik spoke without stopping.

"Vhal?" Fritz yawned, rubbing his eyes. He'd barely been roused by all the noise. The man might be able to sleep through the end of the world.

"We're under attack," Vhalla pulled her friend along.

The main entryway was already buzzing when the four of them entered. The senator was trying to pull threads of organization through the chaos, but it was proving a futile attempt. Aldrik cleared his throat.

"I need the fastest horse," he announced, projecting the demand throughout the room. "And whatever armor is closest to my size."

The room stilled.

"Any who are skilled in combat are to come with me. We will join with the Western forces outside the city to thwart this attempt from the false king." Aldrik glanced at her and guilt clouded his eyes. Vhalla knew why instantly, and she wanted to hate him for it. "My lady will remain here. Her will is to be considered an extension of my own."

He was leaving her behind. "Aldrik," Vhalla whispered hastily. "I can carry a sword; I can fight."

His eyes flicked to the rest of the room, the people watching their discourse. "You're more valuable to me here. Keep things in order. Help me lead from within."

"I'll stay with the Lady Yarl," Jax announced from her side.

"No, you will go with the Lord Solaris," Vhalla demanded. "Fritz, you will go as well. Both of your skills will be of use on the field."

Another screech interrupted any of Jax's potential objections. The smell of smoke wafted in through the open doors of the government building, cries and shouts riding the wind along with it. The three men exchanged a look as Vhalla stood resolute.

"Go, the field needs leaders."

They listened to her, and Vhalla swallowed her frantically beating heart as she watched the three leave with a handful of others. The room remained still as the world beyond devolved into chaos before their eyes. Vhalla clenched her fists.

Maybe there was more to Aldrik's leaving her than Vhalla understood. Panic was a wildfire that was quickly growing out of control in the people around her. Vhalla realized that Aldrik's words of her value may have been more than appeasement. They needed leadership here and now.

"Senator, how many civilians are currently within Hastan?"

"A couple hundred," the woman replied.

"What stone buildings are there? Any basement cellars or storehouses for the city?"

A few others listed varying responses. Three or four seemed promising.

"We will move civilians into these locations," Vhalla decreed. "As we do so, seek out any who have experience with healing or clerical skills. We will set up a triage here, central to all points. I need at least four runners to function as messengers."

Men and women volunteered instantly. The room was quickly divided into those who would remain and those who would help move civilians. She trusted those who lived in Hastan to know their city and to be motivated to protect their kin without her help.

"Triage will be here," she explained quickly to those who had remained. Her clerics ranged from old women who had seen every type of injury, to experienced veterans, to mothers, and a handful of those with formal training. She left the elderly in charge of the initial assessments.

"Those with the worst wounds send back into the hall, the least to the right. Take whatever you require and use whatever rooms you need."

"These rooms are to be used for nobility, the Emperor's guests," someone spoke up.

"Pardon?" Vhalla stilled her instruction.

"We cannot take from the Emperor . . ." another added uncertainly.

"I am your future Empress," she pointed out. "They're just blankets and sheets and beds. The Emperor and I want to see them used as bandages, tourniquets, or comfort for the ailing."

They were finally spurred to life. The most experienced clerics and veterans had the easiest time coming to terms with the fact that all bets were off when it came to warfare. Led by their example, everyone hastily began the process of setting up their clerical stations.

It couldn't have come a moment too soon. Wounded were carried in with returning messengers. It only took an hour for the floor of the main entry to the Eastern government hall to be slick with blood.

"Report," she demanded of the next messenger she saw.

"My lady," the young woman began, "seven winged beasts brought nearly one hundred soldiers to our city." Her voice wavered slightly with fear, but she persevered. "They landed to the north and quickly tore through the Western militia."

"Is the army trying to flank them to recover the ground?"

"They're trying," she affirmed.

"Go out and make sure all the civilians on the northern side of the city have been moved to safe houses elsewhere, should any remain," Vhalla ordered. "Then head south. Implore those who are in command there to split their forces and push through the city to defend and help those to the north."

"Understood," the messenger agreed and raced back out into the night.

Vhalla massaged her shoulder, looking out into the darkness past the main entry of the government building. She wondered at the extent of the carnage. She wondered if her friends were all right.

A soldier stumbled in, hunched over.

"If you can walk, head to the right," Vhalla instructed absent-mindedly.

"Good to see you, too." Jax raised his head with a tired grin, his presence pulling Vhalla from her thoughts.

"Jax!" Vhalla sprinted over to the man. "Are you all right?"

"I've had better. I've had worse." He slumped against her.

Vhalla caught sight of his back. It was in tatters. A deep gash ran from shoulder to waist, two others framing it on either side.

"I need a cleric!" Vhalla called, helping Jax into a chair in a nearby room.

Her order was heeded; a man quickly rushed in, assessing the state of Jax's back. Vhalla quickly helped by cutting Jax's shirt off his shoulders.

"Lady Yarl, I had no idea you held such affections." Jax waggled his eyebrows suggestively. "Cutting off another man's clothes isn't becoming of the future Empress."

Vhalla rolled her eyes. "Oh, hush." She gave a small glance to the cleric that she hoped conveyed the silent request that any of Jax's jests were not to be repeated elsewhere. The man seemed too focused on assessing the wounded Westerner to give much heed to what they were saying.

"How did this happen? What's it like out there?" Vhalla wasn't sure if she wanted the answers to her questions.

"A mess." Jax grimaced as the man packed some salve into the wounds. "We may have had some of Mhashan's might, but the soldiers were far from ready for an attack.

"We've taken down three beasts so far, but the bastards are nearly impervious to magic. The crystals give them some resistance and heal them at the same time. Takes three powerful sorcerers to bring them down."

"Sorcerers are one thing we should have," Vhalla hopefully thought aloud.

"We do, but not many at the level we need, and it has been slow communicating that the other soldiers need to protect our sorcerers exclusively."

She knew what Jax was saying. Aldrik was one of those sorcerers, one of those skilled enough to take on the beasts. Vhalla didn't know if she wanted to ask her next questions or not.

"Aldrik? Fritz? Elecia?"

He didn't torture her. "All fine."

"Were they injured as well?" Vhalla asked as the cleric worked on the last of his stitches.

"Not as of when I left." Jax grinned. "I was the only one foolish enough to be willing to throw his life away to save a lovely lady in distress."

"Well, I'm glad you were unsuccessful in throwing it away." Vhalla patted his shoulder, standing. "Go to your room and rest when the cleric is finished."

Jax looked utterly exhausted. Vhalla rubbed her own eyes tiredly. However worn she was, it was nothing to what the soldiers were facing at the front.

As the battle outside slowly began to quiet, the noise within the government building grew. The cries and groans of men and women, engaged in a different sort of fight for their lives, filled her ears and punctuated Vhalla's every order. These people were in her care, and she would do everything she could to protect and save them.

Fritz was the next to return. Vhalla caught sight of him instantly as she had kept one eye on the door. She crossed over to him quickly, weaving through the men and women arranged on the floor of what was once her orderly medical station.

"Fritz," she breathed in relief.

"Vhal." He tiredly returned her embrace.

"Thank the Mother you're all right."

"You too, Vhal." Her friend released her. "I was nervous something broke through."

She shook her head. "The army held the line." She'd been asking messengers all night for reports on the state of the city. They hadn't even lost one building. "What's the status?"

"The abominations are all dead. Aldrik is passing judgment on the remaining sorcerers now."

Vhalla glanced at the room. If the battle was winding down, there wasn't likely to be another influx of people to attend to. The clerics had developed their own systems based on her original suggestions as the night had waned, and Vhalla felt confident leaving them to it.

"Do you have a horse?" she asked her friend.

Fritz nodded.

"Stay here, get cleaned up."

He stopped her. "Where are you going?"

"I should be there." Vhalla shifted her arm to take his hand rather than gripping his wrist. "I need to be with him for this."

"Vhalla, do you understand—"

"Of course I do." She squeezed his fingers. "That's why I must be there."

Her Southern friend smiled tiredly. "Go on then, Miss Empress."

Fritz let her go, and she was off. Vhalla appreciated that he hadn't insisted upon going with her for her protection. She borrowed a sword from a soldier who would no longer need it, strapping it to her back. Even if the fight was over, she knew better than to charge unarmed into a battlefield. She had too much training now to even think otherwise.

With just the one weapon and a leather jerkin, she struck a course northward. Given all the reports she'd been receiving, it seemed like the most logical location for her Emperor. A red sunrise streaked across the sky, mirroring the crimson land before her.

The casualties had been heavy, heavier than she expected given the number of soldiers who had been in the Western force surrounding the city. But the hulking corpses of giant winged beasts offered a chilling explanation. Teeth longer than her body jutted out from their massive jowls. They had almost canine-like heads but with thick leathery skin pulled taut against oddly shaped muscles. Some had two arms, some had four, one even had six. They had the wings of a wyvern and scorpion-like tails. It was a creature that the Gods had never intended to exist, and the now-dormant crystals embedded in their bodies glinted like dull obsidian in the sunlight, slowly cracking into dust.

A handful of men and women were surrounded, forced to their knees. Soldiers waited around them, sorcerers and Commons alike, ready to execute the traitors who had ridden in to kill them all on the backs of monsters. The lean figure of a man was mounted before the lot—an Emperor casting judgment on those who fought against his throne.

". . . forsake the false king." Vhalla could hear Aldrik's

words as she approached. "Those who give information will be rewarded with their lives."

No one spoke.

"You protect a coward," Vhalla called out, announcing her presence. Aldrik turned in surprise as she rode up next to him. "You stand with a man whose power comes not through his own merit—as he would have you believe—but through theft."

"What would you know?" one of the kneeling sorcerers demanded, curiosity drawing the words from him.

"I know all too well," Vhalla replied quietly, "because I was the one whose powers he stole."

Now she had their attention.

"Victor could not open the caverns on his own; he wasn't strong enough to manage the crystals. I know because he needed me to help him do it. When he had what he wanted, he stole my magic to make him immune from the taint."

"Lies!" one sneered. "The taint only affects those of weak will, Commons, and lesser sorcerers."

Desperation carved the way for stupidity in the hearts of men.

"You can't possibly believe that. Is that what Victor has told you? That you are the strong ones and immune?" She shook her head with a bitter sorrowful laugh. "He has written you off as expendable with his lies."

"Are you really the Windwalker?" a timid voice asked from among them.

"I was." Vhalla spoke only to the man who had asked. "I was the Windwalker until he stole my powers. Now I am a Commons. It was my magic that unleashed this monster upon the world—"

"Vhalla . . ." Aldrik had a cautionary note.

"—but because of that, no one will fight harder than me to do what is necessary to right that wrong." The words hurt. They hurt like the wind still hurt on her cheeks, plain and un-magical. But it was finally the right kind of hurt. The hurt of a confession that needed to be said. "This is but a night. The sun will rise again, and I stand with the dawn."

She looked to the Emperor. His eyes were a chameleon over the past few weeks, constantly changing to match the woman she was becoming.

"Who will stand with the sun?" He tore his eyes away from her to make his final demand.

The man who had asked his timid question stood slowly. "A false king sits on a false throne."

"You disgrace sorcerers," another loyalist spat. "You'll follow a liar and a Commons."

"Strength channels its own magic," the man said in reply, looking directly at Vhalla.

"Who else will stand with us?" Vhalla demanded.

Two more stood.

"Why take pity on them?" a Western soldier finally spoke. "They fight against your Empire. Put them to death."

"Because a wise woman taught me that no soul is beyond saving," Aldrik replied easily.

Vhalla's chest tightened, instantly thinking of Larel.

"Those who stand with us, live; those who do not, die. Make your choice. Dawn comes and it will wait for no man." Aldrik turned back to Victor's sorcerers.

Two more stood, five in total. That was all who were spared. Vhalla bore a silent witness to the other sorcerers who died for Victor's ideal. Men and women who had become so tainted with his lies that they valued his dogma more than their lives.

Vhalla counted every man and woman put to death. *Twenty-three in total.* She shifted in her saddle and felt the sword pulling heavy on her shoulder. The next time she saw Victor she would stab him herself, Vhalla resolved, twenty-three times.

CHAPTER 10

VHALLA RODE BACK to the government building in silence. She visually checked Aldrik over several times. He had countless bruises and a gash by his shoulder, and she was prepared to scold him for not seeking treatment sooner, but he was okay, overall. A sickly feeling had bubbled in her stomach, but it was quelled at the sight.

How many more times would she have to watch the people she loved ride off to war?

She stayed a quiet shadow at Aldrik's side until a cleric demanded his attention, and then she slipped away. Vhalla drifted through the halls, suddenly exhausted. She'd put everything she could think to the test, to be the Empress the people needed, and she wasn't sure if she had even come close.

Her feet moved with the intention of seeking out Fritz, but she paused just before a different friend's door, the sliver of light stretching across the floor from Jax's current accommodations.

". . . worried about me?" She could barely hear Jax's quiet words.

"I had other things to focus on." *Elecia*, Vhalla realized. She took a step toward the open door, relieved to hear the woman was well enough to have the usual sarcastic bite to her voice.

"Aww, you were," Jax teased.

"Are you all right or not?" Elecia sighed heavily.

"I am." There was a long pause. " 'Cia, truly, I'm fine."

"You better not be playing hero again," the woman murmured.

"If I hadn't, you wouldn't be here now."

Vhalla stilled. Jax had said he sustained his wound while saving a damsel in distress. *Elecia wasn't much of a damsel.*

"Thank you." Elecia's gratitude was forced and awkward, but it was as sincere as anything else Vhalla had ever heard the woman say. Elecia was often times abrasive, certainly sarcastic, but she was usually sincere in what she said—good and bad.

"Think nothing of it, Lady Ci'Dan."

"That's not going to be possible. You know this changes things—"

"I said, think nothing of it." A nerve was struck.

"Fine, Jax, I won't." Elecia's footsteps neared their door, and Vhalla knocked softly on Fritz's, not wanting to be caught eavesdropping.

"You know, you're one of the few," Jax's words stopped both women, "who doesn't still call me lord."

"Your title was stripped."

And Vhalla still didn't know why.

"And it doesn't stop the Western Court from reminding me of such by using it ironically." Jax's voice had changed.

"You know how court is." Elecia's voice indicated indifference, but there was a sorrowful and sincere echo that followed her words. "Some of them still take your side."

"Who knows why," Jax murmured.

"I still do."

Fritz opened the door, distracting Vhalla from whatever was said next. She quickly pushed her way into the Southern man's room before he said anything that Elecia would hear. The Western woman would never let Vhalla listen in on a private conversation. *Rightfully so*, Vhalla admitted to herself. But she wanted to know about Jax; she needed to know why he was attached to the crown. Why he was practically enslaved and yet so revered by his masters.

"Everything all right?"

These thoughts were shelved for another time the second Fritz asked his question. Vhalla wrapped her arms around his waist, holding her Southerner tightly. He still smelled of battle—sweat and the metallic tang of blood. But his arms wrapped around her without hesitation, without question. He held her silently as Vhalla took a breath and just let the world move without her for a brief moment.

"I'm glad you're all right, Fritz."

"Me too," he laughed lightly.

"Why are you here?" The question escaped her as suddenly as she thought of it.

"I told you when we left my home: Larel would haunt me if I let you go alone."

"That's not good enough." Vhalla shook her head.

"It's not?"

"No, you're still fighting. You're at war on my behalf. Why are you doing it?"

"Silly Vhal." Fritz sighed gently, and the sound transformed into a smile. "You were at my house, you met my sisters."

Escaping the chaos of the Charem family home didn't seem like a good enough reason either.

"They all have their place in the world. They each know who they will be. Cass is going to inherit the home. Reona will be an amazing wife and mother. Nia will be a chef or baker or something. They all have something. I never did."

"You had your sorcery," Vhalla pointed out.

"And it took me away from them." Fritz had never seemed sorrowful about his magic before. His family was so accepting of it. "I went to the Tower and expected to find my place. And

I'm still figuring that out. Grahm, Larel, you, you all know what you want. I want to know that, too. I want purpose."

Vhalla clutched her friend's hands tightly. "I don't really know what I want."

"Yes, you do." Fritz actually laughed out loud at the notion. "There was a time when you didn't, but you found it. Now I'm trying to find it, too."

"Well . . ." Vhalla sat with Fritz on his bed. "What do you want to be? What do you *want* to do?"

Talking things through with Fritz was therapeutic. She gave him advice she needed to heed herself. It wasn't any wonder why her messy-haired friend had stayed around for so long. They were so similar in all the ways they needed.

When Vhalla finally returned to her room, she saw the low glow of a fire coming from the door to Aldrik's quarters. Her feet dragged forward, compelled by her heart. Aldrik worked dutifully at a small table by the fire, scribbling across parchment.

"Letters?" she asked.

"For my uncle and other Western lords," Aldrik responded without turning.

Vhalla pulled off her boots, leaving them at the door. On light feet, she padded over to the hunched Emperor. Aldrik didn't move as she slipped her arms around his shoulders.

"Ask for reinforcements, my love," she requested.

"An order from the Empress?" His quill paused, but when it picked up writing once more, Vhalla saw he worked in her request.

"If the Emperor permits it."

"Judging from how you handled affairs during that attack, I have little to worry about permitting," Aldrik hummed, a relaxed and pleased sound, like the purr of a cat.

"I'm still scared," she confessed. "Of being Empress."

"Really?" He sounded genuinely surprised. "It doesn't show."

"I've just been pretending when I could think of nothing else to do."

"Then you are more ready than you thought."

"I'm afraid of losing my friends, of making the wrong decision," Vhalla admitted. The load was easier to bear when she lightened it with words. "I crave peace, and I fear that I am a creature whose fate is written in bloodshed."

"More untrue words have never been spoken." Aldrik rested his quill on the table to look at her. "You spent eighteen years in peace. If anything, it is I who have placed this mantle of death upon you."

Vhalla shook her head, but he continued before she could object verbally.

"I know what I have asked of you. I was born into it, I was raised for it. Now I expect you to accomplish acts and diplomacy, tasks that were groomed into me for years." Aldrik pulled her down into his lap, running his hand over her cheek. "But hear me, I say born into, not born for. I may have the advantage of education, but you are as naturally fit to rule as I am, perhaps more so."

She held her forehead against his, rubbing the tips of their noses together lightly. "Teach me?"

"Always."

He taught her quite a few new things that night, ones that normally weren't offered in Empress training. And, afterward, with heaving chests and sweat-dotted bodies, he spent well over an hour telling her the long histories he knew of the kings in the South and West. Aldrik made it a point to detail every failure and what led them to recovery or demise. He highlighted the stories he'd always admired and why, which were usually the tales that encompassed salvation through the admission of one's shortcomings.

He teased her the first time her eyes fluttered closed. But

the Emperor didn't keep his lady awake. He spoke softly until exhaustion finally claimed her, holding her to him.

The next day, he took charge again. Before they even emerged from their respective rooms, he detailed every plan he had for the day, what he hoped to accomplish, and how he planned to go about doing it. He asked her to watch and learn.

As they met with the senator to discuss additional fortification of the East, it was finally like seeing the man emerge from behind the curtain. Aldrik deftly navigated his goals, accomplishing new plans and securing intangible reassurances of loyalty to Solaris. Knowing his approaches, the silver-tongued ruler was reduced to a parlor magician, and Vhalla knew his every sleight of hand.

He punctuated every decision with a long-term solution that would ensure the East remained bound to his leadership. When Aldrik brought up replacement senators, he did so in such a way that demanded the senator to naturally ask who he thought they should be. Vhalla had no doubt that the names he spouted weren't off the top of his head, but a planned list of people who had some debt owed or had already passed some prior test of loyalty.

After the meeting, they set out to take lunch with the merchants of Hastan. On the way, he quizzed her on his wording and methodology. He asked her for her thoughts on why he chose one thing over another, how he had turned the situation. He demanded she find imperfections and make suggestions for improvements. Looking for his shortcomings only made Vhalla study the whole affair more closely.

Just before they arrived at the host's modest manor, he shifted the conversation.

"I want you to lead this."

"Lead how?" Vhalla was uncertain in what capacity he meant.

"These are your people." He paused to lovingly brush some hair away from either side of her face. "I have an Eastern betrothed. Why would I not use it to my advantage?"

"I see." She gave him a conspiratorial grin.

"Will you be my clever Eastern bride?"

"I suppose, if my Emperor demands it," Vhalla sighed dramatically.

The levity calmed her nerves as they entered. By the time Vhalla sat at the dining table, she was relaxed. These were her people. And while Vhalla had little experience negotiating with merchants beyond the grocers and bakers in Leoul, she understood their wants and needs just as well as any Easterner could.

She indulged their questions of her childhood. Vhalla answered questions about her father's field rotation and method for using the least amount of water possible. Tales of the Windwalker had spread throughout the East, and they were hungry for knowledge of the woman behind the stories.

The Emperor and Vhalla engaged in a verbal waltz, spinning in and out. Aldrik would steer the conversation to official business, and Vhalla would take the lead. When a lord bristled at Aldrik's suggestion, Vhalla would act as a balm and drum up fond memories of Eastern festivals. If one of the ladies was put off by Aldrik's determination, Vhalla took her hand with a smile and shared some of her bread in a gesture of good faith.

Following lunch, they proceeded out to the Western camp. It was still in disarray from the battle, and Vhalla wondered what she could do to help both them and the citizens of Hastan. *There weren't enough resources to go around.*

The senator was waiting with Lord Sevin in his tent.

"Apologies for the delay," Aldrik said with minimal sincerity. *The Emperor could keep people waiting*, he had told her. The world waited on them.

"No need to apologize, my lord." The senator gave a small bow of her head in respect to each of them. "And lady."

"Sevin, do you have final counts on men and supplies?"

"I do." The Western Lord produced some papers.

"Excellent." Aldrik began to read with Vhalla reading over his shoulder.

"Most of the supplies made it through the battle, but we sustained heavier casualties than expected," the lord summarized.

"We have already requested further support from the West." Aldrik turned his attention away from the parchment.

"Reinforcements may be slow," Vhalla mused aloud. "And the East should learn how to defend itself."

"What are you thinking, Lady Vhalla?" the senator asked.

"We should set up a system to spread the word that we need recruits. Five riders carry a message to the five nearest towns. There, they command five more riders to carry the word outward to five more towns."

"And create a web across Cyven," the senator finished Vhalla's logic. "It's not a bad suggestion."

"It would depend on Lord Sevin's men being capable of training them." Vhalla looked to the Western lord. "They will be farmers and stable boys, as green as they come."

"We can train them," Sevin affirmed with a nod. "So long as they're willing to be trained."

"Once trained, they can help defend Hastan and build the army here for mobilization against the South when we are ready to attack." Vhalla finally turned to Aldrik.

"I would like to see my betrothed's suggestion made reality," the Emperor ordered.

Vhalla remained quiet for the second half of the meeting, once more watching Aldrik work and learning everything she could. She fully expected to be questioned on his methods afterward, and she was proved correct.

On the way back to the government building, Aldrik inquired on his approach and offered her both criticism and praise. There were ample areas for improvement that quickly became apparent, but Aldrik was good to sandwich praise around them. Some were as simple as pointing out that she needed to improve her posture. Others had layers of nuances that Vhalla still didn't completely understand as they entered the main building.

"And, above all other things," Aldrik continued, "you must remember that you are their Empress."

"But how can I relate to them if I am distanced?"

"Practice, to a certain extent. But it's difficult," he confessed. "It is more important for them to see you as their sovereign rather than their friend. That they know you are above them."

Vhalla nodded, deep in thought.

"You are unpleased." He smiled tiredly.

"You could tell?"

"I don't need the Bond to see it. I know you well enough."

Vhalla shook her head. There was a time where she worried that their affections were entirely a product of the Bond. *How foolish that seemed now.*

"Can I be both? Their leader and their friend?"

"To some, yes." Aldrik nodded. "But not to the masses."

"I suppose it's a good thing I like books more than most people," Vhalla muttered.

"A superb ruler in the making, indeed." Aldrik gave her a knowing smile, and Vhalla relaxed further.

CHAPTER 11

VHALLA WOKE TWO mornings later with a sickness in her stomach.

Aldrik briefly insisted upon fetching Elecia, but Vhalla refused. There wasn't a clerical solution to nervousness, and she knew of no salves that cured stress. The medicine she needed was bound between leather and delivered with silence. She'd been avoiding asking because their days were so filled with preparations to leave for Norin in another two mornings' time. When she finally broached the subject with her husband-to-be, he made her feel silly for even being concerned about leaving him to deal with the responsibilities alone.

The city's records room was dusty and stagnant. It hadn't been aired out in quite some time, and she went into a coughing fit with the first heavy scroll she pulled from the shelf. It wasn't her first choice, but Hastan didn't boast an impressive library, and she knew she'd be alone here. All she wanted was a quiet space and something to read.

Hastan's governmental logs weren't exactly thrilling material, but Vhalla had a new appreciation for the eloquence of politics and the importance of maturity in governance that made the reading more engaging than previous experiences.

Two scrolls in, Jax poked his head in and quipped, "Oh, Empress."

"I'm not the Empress yet." She adjusted the parchment before her.

"Close enough." He grinned and let himself in the rest of the way. Jax leaned against the door as he shut it. "Our Emperor has asked me to check on you and see if you need anything."

"I'm surprised he didn't send Elecia," Vhalla mumbled.

"He tried to." Jax laughed at her correct assumption. "Elecia said if you were not well you were 'quite capable' of seeking her out on your own."

"The woman has sense." Vhalla gained yet another reason to appreciate Aldrik's cousin.

"That I cannot argue."

Jax's unfiltered praise reminded Vhalla of the conversation she previously overheard. While she wouldn't dare bring up the details, there was one thing that still nagged at her. Vhalla turned away from the scroll, studying Jax's dark Western eyes. She tried to forage through their blackness, hoping they would somehow reveal the secret everyone had been so content to allude to but never speak of.

"Why are you owned by the crown?"

Panic flashed across his face. She'd caught him off-guard, and the defensive walls quickly rose in response. Vhalla pressed her lips together and fought a sad smile. She'd been with Aldrik now for so long that she knew what it looked like when a man was trying to smother the truth behind a mental defense.

"That's not a story you want to hear." He laughed suddenly. "Trust me."

"That's not for you to decide." Vhalla leaned back in her chair and motioned to the only other seat in the room across from her. "Sit and tell me."

"I do not think—"

"It's an order, Jax." She tried to make the words as gentle as possible, but no amount of tenderness could remove the hurt in his eyes. She'd crossed a line commanding him, a line she might not be able to erase.

He fell heavily into the chair, starting his tale with hasty resentment. "I was born into a noble family in the West. We weren't important, not like the Le'Dans or Ci'Dans, but my family had pride and a few generations of nobility. I was the eldest and the only son, my sisters just a few years younger."

"So you were set to inherit the estate." Vhalla shifted in her chair and leaned forward, placing her elbows on the table. For the first time, she was getting a glimpse of the man underneath the madness.

"I would have," Jax affirmed. "It was all set, and I was quite the little lord. The only thing that remained was finding a suitable match with another noble."

"An arranged marriage," she pieced together. It brought back memories of the last arranged marriage she had experienced: Aldrik's. It tugged at the corners of her lips, pulling them into a frown at the thought.

"I loved her." Jax wiped the expression from her face with three words, and Vhalla listened in surprise. "I loved her like the Father loves the Mother. I loved her more than the sun, more than life itself. I would have waited a thousand years had she needed it to be ready to accept my hand."

"Did she need it?" Vhalla tried to weed out the imperfection in his currently glowing tale.

"No, the feelings were mutual." Jax looked at nothing for a long moment. Then a shift. Vhalla wasn't sure if she imagined it. But his expression clicked into something different. "Or rather, I thought they were . . .

"We would spend days on end together. Every chance we had we would see each other, be with each other. We wanted nothing more than to be around each other just breathing each other's air. Everything was going to be so perfect, a love arranged but that was also meant to be."

There was an uneasy shroud hovering over his words. He rattled them off his tongue with nearly rehearsed precision. As though it was no longer Jax speaking, and he was possessed by the shroud of someone else, someone who had not actually endured what he was about to tell her.

"Until, one day, I decided I would surprise her. I was studying at the Academia of Arcane Arts. Or maybe I was instructing a class. I don't remember why . . . maybe they needed my assistance." He shook his head. "Either way, I was early home. Earlier than anyone expected.

"It had been a few days since I had seen her. Days that may as well have been eternity. I surprised her at her family's home . . . It was quiet, so quiet."

Vhalla's heart slowed with unease at the mad glint overcoming Jax's eyes.

"So quiet that I could hear them. I followed the sounds, the cries, to her room. I found her there. I found her completely bare and beneath another man." Jax began to chuckle. It was dark and as ominous as low thunder across a stormy sky. "I'd never even had a woman. I thought it romantic that I'd save my flesh for her hands alone. But she had known this man. Time and time again from what I discovered in that dim room.

"Coupling has no romance to it."

Vhalla bit her tongue at an immediate objection. The man before her was a world away from reason.

"Trust me, Vhalla. It is the most animalistic need that craves satiation. I've scoured the world for something more, but I've never found it. We're all just carnal beings, hunting, clawing, seeking to consume each other to fill the holes we've carved into our hearts from trying to scrape out our own inadequacies."

"What happened next?" Vhalla spoke after a long moment. She wasn't sure if she wanted to know the answer. But she knew she *needed* to know it.

"I killed them all." He leaned back, slouching in his chair until his head rested on the back. His limbs were like long, willowy branches all stretched out. "First him. He had to die. He had to burn. He had touched her and oh, oh I killed him for it. I made her watch and she—" Jax choked on his tale a moment, but quickly regained his composure, "—she *begged* me to save him. She screamed for his life, as though she somehow loved him.

"Her family tried to stop me. They returned at her screams, and they tried to stop me. But they knew. They knew what had been happening. They needed to die as well. They burned, and she . . ."

Jax began laughing. It was a growl that rose from the depths of his throat and had him howling in morbid amusement in a moment. Vhalla failed to see the humor, but it was clearly the truth to his insanity. He stopped suddenly, looking back at her.

"Then, there was only me. I honestly don't even remember half the magic that leapt from my fingers as arcs of fire across their flesh. But I do remember the satisfaction when they burned. Their blood was the first on my virgin hands."

Vhalla was mortal. She'd had her streaks of jealousy, and she'd overcome them. She understood the nasty feelings that could rise in people; she'd lived enough now to have seen it from all sides. But this, *this* was more than she could comprehend. No matter what situation, she could never imagine herself harming Aldrik. *What kind of love was a love that led a man to kill that which he coveted?* Was such a love stronger than the one she held?

"I didn't resist capture. By the Mother, I even pled guilty! There was nothing more for me. My future died with her, the woman I loved, the woman I killed. Lord Ophain stripped me of my title and rank." Jax stood, wrapping up his tale with a nonchalant motion. "I should've been killed; that is the punishment for murder, after all."

"Why weren't you?" She tried to make sense of it all. Jax had survived for years. He had served under and even been respected by Baldair. Vhalla knew well what opinions the younger prince had held toward men who harmed women.

"You want me dead that badly?" Jax laughed.

"Answer the question." Vhalla was no longer in the mood for his games.

Jax rolled his eyes and obliged. "I had a friend, someone better than I deserved. His brother and I had studied at the academy together, which was how we met. He came to my defense, pleading madness. He argued that the woman was the one who erred in breaking our contract. He came from an old family, and his name was both a help and a hindrance in court."

"Erion." Vhalla pieced it together. If Lord Ophain Ci'Dan had been overseeing Jax's trial, the only name that could be a hindrance was the Le'Dan name. It also explained Jax's connection to the guard.

"Bing-bong," Jax chimed. He was morbidly chipper for being knee-deep in rehashing his dark history. "He managed to stall everything long enough for him to explain things to his friend, who was even higher."

"Baldair . . ." Just the name evoked sorrow.

"The two of them constructed a new punishment for me. One that even Lord Ophain decided was fitting." The Westerner paused at the door. "I would serve in the Golden Guard to pay my debt back to the people. If I did anything questionable, I would be killed."

The terms were all too familiar to Vhalla. "For how long?"

"Until the end of my days."

"Forever?" Even though she was once owned by the crown, Vhalla couldn't imagine the notion of never-ending servitude. "You're a slave."

"I still prefer the title soldier." He shrugged. "Though some still prefer to call me lord, as though it never happened, as though I could have been justified in what I did, as though I still have a family. Others at least add 'fallen' first."

"Have you ever sought freedom?"

"No." Jax looked through her. "That would be something I'd need to earn, not ask for. And my sins would never merit a pardon."

"But your family—"

"I can't look at myself in the mirror. Do you think I could ever face them again? I died to them the day I killed the woman I loved."

Silence settled between them, still and heavy. Vhalla knew that, as the Empress, she'd have to face ugliness, horrors. But she wasn't ready for those horrors to come from those she considered her friends. Then again, what were she and Jax now? It seemed she'd never really known the man.

Vhalla looked at him with fresh eyes, and it seemed he did the same. Things had changed between them, and Vhalla knew it was on her to decide how that change would manifest. Luckily, Jax didn't seem eager to force her into a choice.

"If you require anything, future Empress, call for me and I will fetch it." Jax gave a small bow. "Don't forget, our Emperor decreed that my life is yours."

"As if I needed a reminder . . ." Vhalla muttered at the door as it clicked closed behind Jax.

She leaned back, gripping her shirt over her stomach. She had been feeling better, but that unsettled sick feeling had returned in all its fury. Vhalla barely had enough time to escape the records room, bolting for her own chambers, before the sickness bubbled up.

"Vhalla?" Aldrik emerged from the door connecting their rooms.

Vhalla peeled herself away from the basin. Her knees felt a little shaky, and she leaned against the wall for support. She hadn't expected Jax's story to affect her so strongly.

"I thought you'd be out with the Western lords."

"I came back to change before lunch." He cast aside the muddy trousers he'd been carrying, crossing over to her. "Are you still unwell? Have you seen Elecia?"

Vhalla shook her head. She didn't need a cleric. She needed the truth. She needed to know if everything Jax had just filled her head with was real.

"You and Jax." Vhalla focused on the corner of the room instead of the bare-chested man before her. "Are you truly close?"

"He told you," Aldrik breathed.

"How can you let him stay as he is?" Vhalla couldn't fathom why Aldrik tolerated Jax's presence, how Aldrik seemed to consider the other Western lord his friend. It seemed against everything she thought she knew of her lover.

"He wants it this way," Aldrik said gently. "I never had the ability to free him until recently."

"You would free him?" she balked. "He-he did something wretched."

"Men who have done worse walk free." Guilt crossed Aldrik's features.

"What he did is nothing like what happened with you and the caverns." Vhalla gripped her Emperor's hands tightly. Aldrik looked surprised a moment, confirming that she'd guessed correctly. She'd come to know the demons he carried as well as the man himself.

"Very well," Aldrik thought aloud. "You were able to forgive me and my crimes, perhaps you will be able to forgive his. I attached his life to yours, so it's only fitting."

"What is?" She frowned.

"You control his freedom, his fate."

"Aldrik, I—"

"Vhalla, you will be Empress someday. If you cannot decide the fate of one man, how will you ever be able to pass judgment on the masses?" *The infuriating royal was using this as a learning experience.* "I wish I could spare you from it, but—"

"But you cannot," she finished for him. The words were as heavy as lead. This was the price of her love. The cost of being with the man she had chosen. "What if I never decide that he has atoned?"

"Then that is your decision to live with."

"You can be heartless," Vhalla weakly replied with a small smile.

"You wound me." His palms rested on her hips. "If I am heartless, it is because a library girl stole my heart."

"You think you can distract me with your honeyed words?" She played coy, resting the back of her head against the doorframe.

"I think I can," he proclaimed, and kissed her lightly.

Vhalla didn't want to agree with him, but the Emperor could be persuasive when he wanted.

CHAPTER 12

"**N**OW, VHALLA, I know I am one gorgeous specimen of a man, but I fear you will make your intended jealous if you continue to stare like that." Jax grinned at her.

"I was not staring," she mumbled, looking at the road ahead. They'd been riding for three days straight and were nearing the border between the East and the West. And the only easiness she clung to was that her stomach had thankfull quieted down.

"My lord," Jax called across her to Aldrik. "I do not think it safe to have your lady around me."

"I do not think I have much cause for concern from the likes of you," Aldrik remarked dryly.

"Vhal's only ever had eyes for one man," Fritz added helpfully.

Elecia hummed and glanced at Vhalla from the corners of her eyes. The woman kept her mouth shut, but the look put the thought of Daniel into Vhalla's mind. Vhalla met the other woman's gaze and held it until Elecia looked away. Elecia didn't know what she and Daniel had been or, rather, hadn't been. She would not be made guilty for it.

The moment Elecia's attention was no longer on her, Vhalla shifted in her saddle, hiding another look in Jax's direction.

She still felt uneasy around the long-haired Westerner whose

life she now owned. She knew this was a test of Aldrik's to keep
her calm and to learn how to manage herself around someone
who made her feel conflicted emotions. If she couldn't figure
out how she felt about Jax, she was going to be hopeless when it
came to managing the snakes at the Southern court. *Assuming
the Southern court was ever in session again.*

Word of the attack on Hastan had rippled throughout the
East on the backs of the messengers Vhalla had sent to call for
soldiers. The towns they had stopped in and the inns they stayed
at held a quiet that hadn't been present before. War was coming,
and it didn't care if the people were ready or not.

The fields around them changed, crops differing with the
shifting landscape. The soil was lighter, sandier, and the small
rivers and streams that wove through the East were less full as
they approached the West.

At the end of the third day, they ran into another Inquisitor
group. Aldrik offered them the same deal he'd offered the prior
Inquisitors, and the Southerners were all too happy to forsake
the false king. *At least, that's what it seemed like.* Vhalla held her
tongue and let her expression betray nothing throughout the
encounter. She wasn't going to give away their intentions like
before and endanger more people.

Through the former-Inquisitors, they learned of Victor's
latest decrees. The madman was finally acknowledging Aldrik
and Vhalla were alive, though they were being painted as
demons who rose from the dead, twisted and corrupt. It wasn't
the first time Vhalla had been called a demon, and she'd happily
wear the mantle again if it cracked the resolve of Victor's
followers.

The Inquisitors told them that dissenters in the South were
becoming commonplace and more citizens were using the
opportunity to be an Inquisitor to escape the perpetually red
streets. Victor's personal army—the Black Brigade, as they were

called—weeded out anyone who was potentially loyal to the old crown.

But one force gave birth to another counterforce. Before the Inquisitors departed, they gave one more interesting piece of information—the Silver Wings. The name was not lost on Vhalla, and it filled her with memories of the Tower sorcerers, proudly wearing their silver wing pins when she returned from the war. The description of the secretive group and the fierce loyalty among its members confirmed her suspicions. The Inquisitors said that those in the capital saw the Silver Wings as the only possible way to fight the false king's tyranny.

This information improved their spirits on the following day's ride. Knowing that Victor's strength was wavering and the people were beginning to create organized forces against him put them all in a good mood. It was the most hope they'd dared to feel since leaving the South, and it was needed more than ever the next day.

An innkeeper had warned the group of what was waiting for them at the Western border, but nothing could prepare the group for what they actually encountered.

The border had been completely closed. A massive crystal gate stood over the road with walls stretching endless in either direction. Perched atop it were two winged beasts, the kind that had attacked Hastan. Vhalla stared at the shimmering, unnatural structure. All she could think about was Aldrik's and her request for more soldiers from the West.

It didn't matter if they'd sent all of the Western soldiers if those men and women couldn't reach their destination.

"This looks a lot like Victor is compensating for something," Jax appraised the size of the gate with a snigger.

"Now isn't the time," Elecia muttered from the other side of the Westerner. Her eyes were fixed forward.

"How are we going to get through?" Fritz asked outright.

Their horses had slowed to a walk as they stared at the ominous and impenetrable barrier.

"I doubt they'll just let us pass," Elecia stated as she eyed Victor's guards. She pointed to the small collection of structures built by and out of the crystal. "I also doubt that Victor would put just anyone here. They're likely half-mad with taint, and even if they're not, they're certain to be the most loyal."

"It doesn't look like the walls stop, either." Vhalla raised a hand to her brow, squinting in both directions. Even if they could go around, it would take them days in either direction. Time they didn't really have.

"So what do we do, Emperor?" Jax asked.

"We watch," Aldrik decided, pulling his horse to a stop.

They followed their sovereign's orders, setting up on the edge of the road. They squinted in the distance, staying among the tall grasses of an unkempt field. Vhalla absentmindedly brushed out Lightning's mane with her fingers.

"Why did Victor even make a gate?" she said suddenly. Her comrades jumped at the sudden break in the silence. "He wants to keep the East and West from helping each other. I think we can be certain about that. Split up the continent, break it down one piece at a time until everyone kneels." No one argued with her. "So why make a gate at all? Why not just a wall?"

"That's a good point," Fritz agreed.

"He needs to move his men as well," Vhalla continued her logic. "If he crushes the East by pouring all his forces here, then he'll need to get them to the West, which explains why it's on the main road."

"Why wouldn't he just destroy it when he needs to?" Fritz mused.

"Management of troops, being able to control entry points; maybe it exhausted him too much to build the wall that he didn't want to take it down." *Now that was an interesting thought,* one she shelved to muse over later. "So if he wasn't planning on returning, his forces would need to be able to move themselves."

Vhalla squinted at the gate, putting her thumb on the uneasy feeling that had surrounded her from the moment she saw it. It reminded her of the Crystal Caverns, the one Victor had forced her to open using Aldrik's magic. Vhalla couldn't keep herself from seeking out her Emperor, her heart aching dully at the thought of their lost Bond.

Then another thought came to her. "Aldrik." She waved him and Elecia over from where they had been talking. "I know how to get in."

"You do?" Elecia sounded surprised and impressed, but not skeptical.

"He's tuned the gate to his magic, to open and close it, like—" Vhalla swallowed hard. "Like the Crystal Caverns."

"It's possible." Aldrik's jaw was taut at the mention of the caverns.

"It's the only way to open them; he's the only one with enough power, immunity, and crystal knowledge to do it." Vhalla couldn't stop herself from wondering if she would've been able to help open the gate if she still had her magic. But she didn't dwell. Her magic was gone, and there was no possibility of getting it back now.

"So are you saying there's no hope of opening them unless Victor decides to stroll by?" Jax asked.

Vhalla shook her head. "That wouldn't make sense. Because if he was going to come back and open them himself, why make a gate at all? Fritz is right, he could've just destroyed it then. He must've left a key, a crystal vessel with the essence of his magic in it that the gate will respond to, allowing the troops to move back and forth as needed."

"So what would this crystal look like?" Elecia asked.

"It could be in any shape, but you wouldn't find it with regular sight. If I—If I still had my magic sight, I'd look at the magic on the gate and then find a spare crystal that matches it. These men and women must be half mad with taint; Victor couldn't have made it too hard for them, so I imagine it's somewhere fairly obvious."

They were all silent for a long moment.

"Fritter," Elecia said suddenly.

"Fritter?" That name was new.

"I'm going to need illusions. And yours are just wonderful." She flashed Fritz a brilliant, toothy smile.

"Mine are all right," Fritz replied with modesty.

"Elecia?" A marked concern had set up shop in Aldrik's voice.

"What?" she sighed in exasperation, giving her cousin a hard look. "It's not as though you can go. You're our Emperor *and* you don't have magic sight. You wouldn't let her go—" Elecia motioned to Vhalla, "—even if she still had her magic sight."

"I have magic sight and am not the Emperor or Empress," Jax said suddenly. "Let me go."

"No, the fewer people the better," Elecia insisted. "Plus, you have your own obligations: you need to protect our Empress. Isn't that your responsibility now?"

Jax didn't argue. He sidestepped closer to Vhalla.

"Fritz will make an illusion just after nightfall to send them on a wild goose chase. I'll use the confusion to sneak in and find this key. How do I make the gate open once I have it?"

"You should just need to make contact with the gate." Vhalla rubbed her shoulder absentmindedly.

"Easy enough."

"I don't like it," Aldrik announced. "It's too risky."

"Ah yes, and shall we sit here and wait for it to become less risky as the world is spiraling into chaos around us?" Elecia shot back in all her snarky glory. "Aldrik, I am going home. I want to see my mother and grandfather. I want letters on my father's status." In Aldrik's silence, Elecia turned to Fritz. "Are you in?"

"I, um . . ." His blue eyes darted between the two nobles.

"You are," Vhalla encouraged her friend, placing a palm on his shoulder. She addressed Aldrik, "It's the best chance we have."

"Is this what you choose?" the Emperor asked her.

Vhalla smiled tiredly at his sad eyes. He knew what he was doing. More training, more grooming, more assurances that she would be ready for the crown that he would place upon her brow in Norin. If she said no, her friends would remain safe for a while longer. Perhaps, with enough time, they could conceive a new plan.

"It is." There wasn't a trace of doubt in her voice. No matter what turmoil brewed within her, she didn't let it show. Aldrik never betrayed his uncertainty; she wouldn't either. "We will move tonight."

Elecia gave her an approving nod before immediately launching into a conversation with Fritz about the type of illusions she needed. Vhalla tuned them out for a moment. She watched the sun set over the gate and knew it would set on their fates all too soon.

Come nightfall, Elecia had almost completely changed and reequipped herself. Her father had not let her leave Hastan without a good set of leathers and an even better set of steel. She had two blades strapped inside her boots, a small dagger on her hip. The woman checked the weapons ten times over, militant that they were just so.

The rest of them followed suit. The Western army had been honored to spare weaponry for the Imperial company. While they didn't wear heavy plate for ease of mobility and wanting to remain inconspicuous, they all had some leather and steel.

The five of them left their threadbare travelling cloaks at the roadside; once they passed into the West, it mattered less to keep a low profile.

Vhalla, Jax, Fritz, and Aldrik mounted as the stars winked into existence. Elecia remained on foot, hidden by the tall grasses.

"Start the fog," Elecia commanded Fritz. "Slowly at first, let it thicken when I'm halfway."

"You got it, boss." Fritz failed in his attempt at levity.

"The rest of you, don't forget my horse." She tilted her head toward the rider-less steed. "I'm running through the gate, but I want to ride to Norin."

"Be careful," Aldrik ordered.

"Don't be foolish enough to start doubting me now." Elecia grinned and took a couple steps away. "You, both of you," she pointed to Vhalla and Aldrik. "Just focus on getting through. Especially you, Aldrik; our world needs you to rally behind. No one else can fill that role."

Vhalla knew what Elecia was really urging Aldrik to do. So did Jax, judging from the way he inched closer to her. Their Emperor couldn't be reckless on her behalf. Vhalla patted the dagger on her thigh thoughtfully. One way or another, she wouldn't let that happen.

"Stay close to me," Aldrik whispered softly to her.

"I will," she promised.

The dim light of the half moon was fading. Elecia crouched low, almost on her hands and knees, and began her slow trek through the fields leading up to the gate. It was a longer distance than Vhalla had originally thought, since they had stopped far enough out that they wouldn't raise suspicion.

Elecia slowly blended in with the earth as she inched forward; eventually she became completely invisible in the darkness. Fritz squinted, watching a distant point, where they assumed Elecia would be. As he focused, a fog began to rise from the fields. Fritz slowly lifted an open palm and the clouds intensified.

"Won't they realize it's magical?" Vhalla breathed, not wanting to risk breaking her friend's concentration.

"If they look carefully, they can." Aldrik gripped his reins. "We'll have to hope they don't have a reason to look carefully."

The gate was growing hazy. The torchlight of the encampment surrounding it faded to floating orbs in the mist.

"We should move." Some mental timer of Fritz's had clicked into its next cycle.

Slowly, they inched their horses through the fog-filled expanse. For the time being, they remained on the fields, the soft earth masking the horses' hooves. Vhalla struggled to remain as still and taut as possible so her saddle didn't rattle and ruin everything.

Crossing half the distance, they stopped again. Sweat rolled off Fritz's brow. His hand was balled into a white-knuckled fist and the world held its breath between each of his soft pants.

Suddenly he sprang to life. Fritz drew his hand fast across his body, as though he was throwing something off into the distance. Upon the road, hazy figures appeared. Up close, they looked like nothing more than dense fog, but from the gate they would certainly be seen as riders.

"Emperor," Fritz spoke between gasping breaths. He was using an unfathomable amount of magic. Vhalla wondered how long he could hold such a complex illusion for. "Throw flame from there to the gate, on my mark."

Aldrik followed Fritz's nonverbal gestures and gave a sharp nod. There was a whole shift in the Emperor's form. Vhalla watched him transition from the man she adored into the Fire Lord the world feared.

Without further warning, Fritz cast his arm forward, nearly

falling out of his saddle in the process. He grunted at the unseen magical exertion. The shadows began their phantom attack.

Aldrik flicked his wrist, sending a tongue of flame from the illusion soldiers to the camp. It was more effective than expected as one of their non-crystal shelters burst into flame. Cries and shouts filled the night air, followed by a screech that rattled the heavens. One of the beasts had left its perch in response. Large, leathery wings flapped, and the gleam of talons was barely visible through the haze.

"Come on," Fritz pleaded.

"Come out and play," taunted Jax with a bloodthirsty gleam in his eyes.

The beast swooped down off its perch, gunning for the illusions. Fritz swept his palms to the side and the fog riders dodged effortlessly. He pushed the magical burden to the right side of the camp and a good many of Victor's loyalists poured out.

The beast cried, ascending once more to circle the sky. Vhalla wondered if it had somehow seen what was happening. Or if *Victor* had seen what was happening through his magical connection with the crystals. Its screeches could be a language in their own right, and it was trying to convey to the soldiers below the truth. If it was, she hoped no one could understand it.

Aldrik snapped his reins without word, trusting the three of them to follow his lead. They charged together, a second blurred streak through the fog. Fritz struggled to remain upright in his saddle, but he hung on.

The distorted and formless blur of Victor's camp gained shape. Things had been set up to stay. Buildings were erected rather than tents, and latrines had been dug. Vhalla scowled at the crystal jutting up from the earth. Such a thing should've never existed.

The moment their horses crossed over onto the pristine

stone of the East-West Way the soldiers who had remained in the encampment were alerted to their presence. Shouts rose only to be echoed by those who had chased the shadow riders. Vhalla's head whipped back to Fritz. The Southerner was blinking, bleary eyed, his body halfway limp. *The thinning of the fog wasn't just her imagination.*

Her heart raced. It pounded in her ears louder than Lightning's hooves, and, for a brief moment, it gave her the illusion of the Bond. Vhalla gained strength from the beautiful lie.

The other beast launched off the gate, and fire arced through the sky. Aldrik and Jax moved in unison, creating a protective canopy of flame above them, thwarting the monster's attack and setting buildings to flame at the same time.

With a flash of light, the gates sprang to life. Vhalla let out a holler of laughter in relief. There was no sign of Elecia, but if the woman had made it this far, she'd see it through the rest of the way. The massive doors sighed as they pushed against the ground, easing open.

A burst of desert air hit Vhalla's cheeks, and she'd never felt anything sweeter. It was as though, despite everything, the wind still reached out to her. That it knew her Channel still lived deep within her, seeking it out. It called, promising that her future was there in its dusty breeze.

"Single file!" Aldrik bellowed. The heavy doors were moving slower than a glacier.

"Close the gate!" a man shouted from a high crystal ledge.

"Not on your life!" Elecia proclaimed, triumphantly. A dagger protruded from the man's eye, and the Western woman threw the corpse aside, adjusting her bandana proudly.

"If you have time to pose, you have time to get down here!" Jax called up to her, throwing out another arc of fire.

Elecia ran down the pitch of the short roof below her, falling to the ground with a roll. She recovered, scrambling to her feet and launching into an all-out run. Two screeches filled the air, and Aldrik focused on maintaining a shield of fire large enough to cover the three of them.

Vhalla did as she was supposed to do. She focused on getting herself through the gate. Everyone had a job, and hers was to follow orders and keep herself alive.

"It's the Fire Lord!" a woman growled.

These were Tower sorcerers; of course someone would recognize Aldrik's magic. But when Vhalla cursed, Aldrik laughed.

"If you know who I am, why do you even try to fight?" He opened both arms wide. Two walls of fire ignited the camp, and most of the soldiers who were trying to rain their own magic upon them.

A scream wiped the expression from Aldrik's face.

Elecia rolled on the ground, tackled by an icicle-wielding Waterrunner.

"Elecia!" Vhalla cried.

" 'Cia!" Aldrik used the childhood nickname in anguish.

Elecia threw the man off, pouncing on his chest and slitting his throat viciously. "Go!" she screamed.

Vhalla began to turn Lightning.

"By the Mother, woman, *go*."

Vhalla's heart beat in her throat. She had fallen to the last in their line, and if she didn't go, Elecia likely wouldn't make it. Another tongue of flame licked at a sorcerer behind Elecia, the woman running in a desperate attempt to catch up.

She turned forward and braced her heart at the feeling of leaving her friend behind.

They crossed through the doors, barely enough clearance for them to race through single-file. A whole encampment greeted them on the other side. But the crimson, phoenix-bearing pennons that fluttered were a welcome sight.

Western soldiers, likely those who had been sent to help the East, had been roused by the commotion. A line stood across the road, swords at the ready.

"Let us pass!" Aldrik ordered at the top of his lungs. "By the order of your true Emperor, let us pass!" He shot a ball of flame high into the sky for emphasis, and it lit up the ground below like a small sun.

The soldiers parted, and the Emperor's company continued to race down the East-West way. Fire and ice erupted above them as the Western army joined the fray, fighting off the beasts and pushing through the gates. Vhalla swept her eyes quickly over her group. Aldrik in front, Fritz at her side, Jax pulling up the rear.

Vhalla whirled her horse in place, Lightning whinnying in protest at the sudden demand.

"We must go back."

Her heart was about to break a rib, her breath frozen in her chest. Vhalla tried to make sense of the commotion at the gate. Western soldiers swarmed the opening. Groundbreakers attempted to raise stones to prevent the gate from closing. Firebearers kept the abominations at bay. They had kicked an ants' nest, and Vhalla only cared about finding one in the swarm.

"Vhalla—"

She knew Aldrik would tell her to keep going. She knew she had made her choice. She was the one who had agreed to Elecia's plan, knowing the risks. Now she had to live with the knowledge that she had gotten her friend killed.

"No, no, it's my fault. I must go back for her." Vhalla's voice cracked for the first time in a long time.

"Vhalla—"

"I shouldn't have left her behind. I was closest." Vhalla remained focused on the gate, not allowing Aldrik to interrupt her. "She was my friend, she was to be my kin, and I just left her! Why did I let her do it?"

"Because you knew I could." A female voice stopped her. Vhalla slowly drew her gaze to Jax's horse. Wrapped tight and pressed to the back of the Western man was a set of emerald eyes Vhalla knew well. She'd been hidden by Jax's cloak, but now she grinned in all her triumphant glory. "I didn't know you cared so much. I want to make sure you're at my real Rite of Sunset when the time comes. I think you'll bring a tear to every—"

Elecia's word was reduced to a grunt as Vhalla threw her arms around the other woman. It was awkward from their saddles and Jax seated next to her, but Vhalla didn't care. She squeezed Elecia tightly, reassuring herself that the woman was alive and well.

"I thought you were dead."

"Is this whole embracing nonsense going to be common when you become my cousin?" Elecia drawled. "Because it's really not a *thing* here in the West."

"I thought I killed you." Vhalla smiled at Elecia's abrasiveness and pulled away some.

"If I got killed, it would've been my fault because I wasn't where I was supposed to be—not because you had given the order for us to move as we did." The woman's voice had softened significantly. "It may be hard for you to believe, Vhalla Yarl, but the world isn't always about you."

Vhalla laughed in relief. Elecia freed herself from the Easterner's clutches and dismounted to return to her own mount. The woman gave Vhalla one more small smile, and a nod to Aldrik.

"Let's keep moving while the beasts are distracted." Aldrik appraised the gate once more. "We'll rest at the first noble estate we come to."

They rode into the dawn. Vhalla watched the sun rise over

the dunes, and relief swept through her. They'd made it from the East. There were a million things that remained for her to worry over: her father, Hastan, Victor's advances, and the creation of abominations. But, for a brief moment, she let herself appreciate the wind in her hair. She relished her friends surrounding her. And she believed that something great awaited them.

CHAPTER 13

WHEN THEY FINALLY rode up to a manor, the lord was all too honored to put up the Emperor, future Empress, and their company. He welcomed them with open arms the moment they made their identities known. Over breakfast, he prattled off a long-winded explanation of how he was some distant relative of Aldrik's. Thankfully, he finished just in time for them to be shown their rooms. Aldrik had his own, Elecia paired with Vhalla, and Fritz with Jax.

It was the first time Vhalla had really found herself alone with Elecia, Vhalla realized as she dabbed her face dry with a washcloth. She'd known the woman for over a year, and she had never spent much time one on one with her.

"So, is he really related to your family?" Vhalla struck up conversation, using the lord's story as an easy starting point.

"Who knows?" Elecia yawned, collapsing into the bed. "The West is old, and the branches of the family trees are wide-reaching."

Vhalla thought about this for a long moment. She vividly recalled her prior experiences with Western nobility. Vhalla sat heavily on her edge of the low bed.

"What is it?" the curly haired woman asked tentatively, clearly unsure of offering her ear.

"I won't trouble you with it."

Elecia rolled her eyes dramatically. "Poor Vhalla, shouldering her burdens all alone when she has so many people wanting to help."

"You can be rather sharp, you know that?" Vhalla grinned faintly.

Elecia shrugged. "I'm honest. I can't help it if you take that harshly."

"I like it about you."

"You *like* something about *me*?" Elecia gasped dramatically. "And here I had been thinking we were enemies."

"I didn't know what to think of you for a while." Vhalla reclined, settling the covers over herself.

"Well that much was mutual. I had no idea what Aldrik saw in you."

"Had, past tense," Vhalla pointed out.

"Past tense." Elecia didn't try to scramble away from her word choice. "I still think you've a long way to go, but you're making strides."

"Thank you, truly." It meant a lot coming from the Western woman.

"Yes, well . . ." Elecia was clearly uncomfortable. "That wasn't what had you sighing earlier."

"Are you sure we can trust this lord?"

"Has he given you indication otherwise?" The question was serious when it could've been skeptical.

"He hasn't, but . . . how do we know he's not a Knight of Jadar?" Vhalla knew better than to think the Knights of Jadar were gone just because she'd thwarted Major Schnurr. He had certainly been one of their leaders, but the organization had survived over a hundred years, and she suspected it would survive a lot longer.

Elecia considered this for a long moment. "Even if he

was, the Knights would be unlikely to make a move right now."

"Because of Aldrik?"

"In part," Elecia agreed with a nod. "If it's between having one of Western blood or a Southerner sit on the Empire's throne, I have no doubt which they'd choose. Even given their loathing of our family." There was bite to the last remark. "Beyond that, their goal has always been the crystals. With the caverns opened, they sort of lost that race. I'm certain they're in the middle of a crisis of purpose and, since my grandfather is smart, he'll use it to his advantage to regain that loyalty."

"I don't know if I'd want their loyalty."

"Bitterness is unbecoming, Lady Empress," Elecia teased.

Vhalla snorted.

"So is that," Elecia laughed. "You'd think you've never been to a finishing class in your life." Vhalla rolled her eyes at the face Elecia made. "Now, I am tired; snuff the light and let me sleep."

"But of course, Lady Ci'Dan," Vhalla proclaimed with dramatic flair, obliging the request.

"Lady Ci'Dan, don't you forget it," Elecia murmured. "For I expect to be appointed the next Lady of the West for my service when this is all over."

"Deal," Vhalla replied easily and honestly.

For the next two nights, Vhalla and Elecia shared a bed. On the third, they were able to find an inn, and Vhalla relished being in Aldrik's arms once more. Elecia wasn't a bad bedmate; in fact, Vhalla was beginning to enjoy the woman's company more with each passing day.

But nothing was better than the feeling of Aldrik's breath on her skin, the way he moved, the way he whispered in the dark. Vhalla relished it all. It was one of the many things that reaffirmed she had made the right decision—to stay with the man she loved—in spite of the chaos in the world around her.

It was easier with each passing day to stand gracefully at his side as he introduced them as a couple. Grabbing her stomach to try to quell the butterflies was still a regular occurrence, but it happened less and less. *It was all practice for a new life*, she reminded herself, one that would begin in Norin.

"It's been a pleasure to have you this evening," a lord praised them after dinner one night over drinks. Aldrik had reluctantly accepted a glass out of pure etiquette. Though he hadn't touched it after the obligatory sip with the lord's toast to them, his eyes did dart to the glass from time to time in silent debate.

"I knew the day you came out to the Southern Court that you were destined for greatness. I think we all did."

She smiled as he lied through his teeth. "Is that so?"

"You had such natural grace and elegance, born of the Empire. Only fitting for you to be with our Emperor over that Northern girl."

"I stand by what I said then. This Empire would have been lucky to have someone like Princess Sehra as its Empress." Vhalla was not going to tolerate any animosity between the regions. *An Empire of peace*; she wouldn't lose sight of that dream as long as she drew breath.

"Of course." The lord clearly was not equipped with the eloquence to reply to Vhalla's praise of Aldrik's former betrothed.

Aldrik brought his lips together in a small smile, enjoying the lord's struggle at Vhalla's words. As Vhalla became more adept at navigating nobility, she began to play small games alongside Aldrik. She didn't think she'd quite reached puppet master status, but she certainly was improving.

"I hear you have plans to wed in Norin. Quite exciting."

"I am looking forward to making our love official." Aldrik squeezed Vhalla's hand lightly.

Vhalla gave him a small smile. He'd invited her to speak any objections she had to wedding in Norin, but Vhalla had never said a word. Everything had been in such turmoil before their escape from the East that she hadn't had much time to think on it. By the time she could, it had already cemented in her mind as fact.

"The other lords and ladies I keep in correspondence with are also surprised that you will marry before reclaiming your throne."

Aldrik obliged the lord, answering his unspoken question. "When I return South, it is to reclaim the home of my forefathers and present my bride with her future home. The Empire Solaris is strong still. Why wait to lay the foundation of the future?"

"I couldn't have said it better myself." The lord seemed satisfied with the answer, and Vhalla wondered how much of the ways of nobility, ways that had led Aldrik to deciding to wed in Norin, she didn't understand. "While I realize that the Imperial chapel in the capital may be the preferred place for the ceremony, I am looking forward to a Western wedding. Perhaps a new tradition?" he mused aloud. "Our late princess had her wedding to the Emperor in Norin as well."

Vhalla stole a look at Aldrik. His face betrayed no change in emotion, but she could almost physically feel him withdraw at the mention of his late mother. Vhalla put her glass down on the table, hardly touched out of solidarity for her betrothed.

"Please excuse me." She stood. "I am weary from the day's ride."

"My lady, allow me to escort you." Aldrik was on his feet as well, along with the Western lord.

"I'm fine, Aldrik, just tired. Please enjoy the company," she encouraged.

Vhalla knew he needed to mingle with all the lords. Their Empire depended, in no small part, on their unquestioning loyalty and resources. She also knew, justly or not, that some things were more easily shared between men, and she trusted Aldrik to take advantage of the opportunity.

Despite what she said, Vhalla didn't retire to her room. She hadn't had much time alone with Fritz since the East. She found her Southerner curled up in a plush chair by the fireplace in his room.

"You look cozy." Vhalla shut the door softly behind her.

"Quite cozy. Come join me, Vhal." Fritz lifted up the edge of his blanket.

She was happy to accept his invitation and wedged herself next to him on the oversized chair. "Cozy indeed. What book did you find?"

"Something awfully boring. A collection of family autobiographies. They're all talking about how amazing they are."

Vhalla laughed, flipping through a few pages. She shook her head. "Nobility."

"Hey now, *you're* a noble. Soon to be the noblest of them all."

Rather than laughing it off as she would any other time, Vhalla paused, studying the fire. "Do you think I will do a good job?"

"Nope."

She blinked at him in shock.

"I *know* it." Her friend nudged her playfully. "Don't doubt yourself."

"If I do, will you be there to reassure me?"

"Always."

Vhalla closed the book in her hands, leaning on Fritz's shoulder. "You're right, this book is boring. You should tell me a story about you instead."

"Well, I suppose if the Empress demands a story, she will get one."

"I'm not the Empress yet."

"*Yet*," he agreed only on that one word. "All right, let's see . . ." He shifted before settling into a more comfortable position. "When I joined the Tower, I was mostly alone. I didn't really know how to make friends. I'd always had my sisters, and they *had* to tolerate me. But, well, you know, our home was far from the village, and my family was nervous about my magic freezing another child or something horrible. So I didn't have much interaction with other kids."

Even in the best of cases, like Fritz, magic was still a separating force.

"I was finally around people like me, and I had no idea how to bridge the moat that I had unknowingly dug around myself. Larel took pity on me, after one instruction, and went out of her way to sit with me in the library. For three months we met there at the same time, same table, every day. It was never formally said, but we both knew where we would wait for the other."

"Was that the table where I found you?" Vhalla thought back to the first time she had laid eyes on the messy haired Southerner. It felt like a lifetime ago.

"It was." He rested his cheek against her forehead. "I met Grahm there as well . . . One day, I walked in, and my table was taken. Now, the old me would've just sat somewhere else. But that was *my* table, and my friendship with Larel had made me bold. Plus, he was really, *really* cute."

Vhalla laughed softly and closed her eyes. She wondered how often Fritz thought of Grahm. Right before she dozed off, she wondered if the Eastern man she had befriended was even still alive.

CHAPTER 14

J UST A HANDFUL of weeks after leaving her home, Vhalla
found herself once more in the Crossroads. It couldn't have
been a happier sight. The hustle and bustle of the market,
the shades of every type of person strolling about. Victor's
tyranny and Vhalla's last, less than favorable, experience at the
Crossroads couldn't diminish her fond memories or the good
energy that was palpable in the air.

It was the center of the world. It was where she had confessed
her love for the man she would marry. It was where she had
made and lost friends. It was where she had found strength. She
had dreamed, cried, laughed, and—it dawned on her in short
order after arriving—gained a glimpse of the future.

Her gaze was locked on the main market as they passed,
headed toward the standard Imperial hotel. Vhalla was suddenly
very curious.

That night, Aldrik's breathing was slow and consistent in her
ear. He curled around her back, as had become their habit. It
had been an hour since he'd last moved and, for once, Vhalla
had outlasted him when it came to the race of who would be
the first to slumber. The prince who was once unable to sleep
was now an Emperor who slumbered mostly through the night
and fell asleep relatively quickly after his head hit the pillow—so

long as he wasn't kept awake engaging in any *activities* with his future Empress.

With small wiggles over a painfully long period of time, Vhalla freed herself from his grasp. He stirred, a soft murmur in disapproval, but she had waited long enough that he was well and truly asleep. He was barely visible in the darkness, but with the slit of moonlight streaming between the curtains, Vhalla could make out his face.

His brow was relaxed, and he looked almost peaceful. Tonight, she had gone to bed with a very different man than the last time they had curled together in the Crossroads. His skin had a healthier glow, and the circles underneath his eyes had lightened. The journey in the West had been easy so far, and it felt like they were thawing out after an impossibly long winter.

Vhalla stood slowly, easing her weight off the bed. His fist curled around the blankets where she had just been, but Aldrik showed no other signs of waking. She retreated into the bathroom, easing the door silently closed behind her. The tile was cold on her toes as Vhalla began to rummage through the wardrobe. Word of the Emperor's eminent arrival had spread, and the hotel had stocked the closet with clothing in advance, welcoming them with much pomp and circumstance.

She massaged her scarred shoulder after slipping a tunic over her head, thinking of their praises. The Western lords and ladies applauded what a smart match the *Windwalker* was for their Emperor. They never seemed to hear her when she corrected them, that she was just a Commons. It was no easier to bear the misplaced mantle now than it was when they first set out in the West.

Dressed, Vhalla poked her nose out into the dark room. Aldrik hadn't moved and remained still as she crept past the sliding door. Vhalla ran a hand through her hair, teasing out the knots Aldrik's eager hands always left in her tresses. She knew she should feel guilty, sneaking away from him as she was, but some things demanded answers.

She avoided the main lobby, staffed all hours of the day, slipping out a back door. No one paid her any mind, her hood drawn and her head down. She wanted to remain as inconspicuous as possible. She willed herself to fade into the shadows.

The late hours of the Crossroads were a very different place. Most stores were shuttered for the day, save for the more creative establishments that were just opening for halfway drunken and seedy-looking patrons. Men and women leaned against the corners of alleys with come-hither stares, beckoning those who came and went with promises of dreams and pleasure.

Vhalla drew her hood tighter; now was not the time to be the future Empress Solaris.

As one particularly shady-looking character beckoned to her, forcing Vhalla more into the middle of the road and out of the shadows, she wondered again why she had left the hotel. There was a touch of shame about what she was about to do, shame for the doubt that still lived in her heart despite all her friends' assurances. Aldrik swore that their future was one of love, prosperity, and happiness. But he did not know what the next day held, let alone what would come in the years before them.

A familiar storefront seemed to materialize out of nowhere, interrupting her thoughts. It was completely dark, save for the light of a single candle on a table. Vhalla's hand slipped from her shoulder to her neck, and she silently begged Aldrik to forgive her for her doubts.

The drapery in the doorway was drawn to the side, as if inviting her, and Vhalla entered boldly. Some unseen force pulled the curtain shut behind her, and Vhalla turned in surprise, her eyes trying to adjust to the sudden darkness. When her gaze swept back within once more, a face—illuminated by the candle—peered back.

"I knew you would come." The woman's voice was as smooth as silk and more melodic than any instrument Vhalla had ever heard. It beckoned. It beseeched. It hinted at promises that people wanted to give but were too afraid to make.

"You did?" Vhalla realized the low display case the woman stood behind was empty. Shelves that were once cluttered with all manner of items were now barren, occupied only by shadow.

"That was not the first time you have heard such, Vhalla Yarl." The woman stepped into the circle of light created by the candle, and Vhalla could see her more clearly. She was once more draped in robes, but this time they were of a pristine white, trimmed in gold. Her long black hair cut a sharp contrast against the garment. Vhalla blinked in surprise at someone so boldly wearing the Imperial colors. "Wasn't it true then, as well?"

"What are you talking about?" Aldrik's face from the first night they had met in the library was clear across her memory.

"You know of what I speak." The woman placed her fingertips on the table, dragging them as she slowly walked around. "The man whose crown you have worn spoke those words to you."

"How do you know that?" Vhalla raised a hand to her forehead, remembering when Aldrik had placed his crown upon her brow in his chambers at the palace. There was no one else there then, and neither she nor Aldrik had told anyone.

"I know it the same way I knew your name the first time we met. This knowing is why you have sought me out."

"If you know so much, then you know why I am here." Vhalla reminded herself to be brave. She would not show fear, no matter what powers this woman possessed. Her bravery came easy, a soft whisper in the back of Vhalla's mind reassuring her that she would not be harmed here.

"I do." The woman folded her hands before her, leaning against the case. With the candle at her back, the woman's features were shrouded in shadow. *But her eyes.* Vhalla was surely imagining their unnatural glow, a trick of the light, perhaps . . .

"Then let's begin. Do you still have the supplies?" Vhalla looked around the empty room.

"Let us," the woman agreed. "But I do not need supplies this night."

"Isn't that how curiosity shops work?"

"You have already cast your future to the flames and marked the three intersections of fate, Vhalla Yarl." The woman held up a fist, uncurling fingers as she spoke. "At one such intersection I tried to guide you. At the other, I made an effort of saving you. You only have one meeting left now with me."

"What?" Vhalla struggled to comprehend the woman's meaning. She had only met Vi once before, and that was in this shop. Or so she thought. The night she stole Achel, the image of magic, glittering through the air like *feathers*, came to mind. "In the North? Was it you?"

"It was."

"And the Knights of Jadar, the windmill." *Wheat.*

"It was," she repeated.

"What are you?" Chill horror poured ice into Vhalla's veins. The Crossroads suddenly felt a world away, and Vhalla felt very alone with the woman before her. "Why are you doing this?"

"Tonight is not a night for your questions," Vi declared. "I possess great strength, but coming to you when you are not at an intersection of fate is exhausting for even me."

"If you will not answer my questions, then we have no further business." Vhalla stepped backward, reaching for the curtain of the door and unable to find it.

"Tell me, do you love this world?"

The question caught Vhalla off-guard. "Of course I do."

"*Of course*," the woman repeated. "You don't realize how much you say that. Of course you will do this, of course you will go there, of course you will oblige the demands made upon you."

The many times Vhalla had said those words rushed through her mind. She didn't say it *that* often, did she? Surely no more often than anyone else.

"Do you know why?" Strands of hair slipped over the woman's shoulder as she tilted her head to the side quizzically. The question was clearly rhetorical as she continued, "Because it is what you were made for. Those things were what you were meant to do. Long before you ever met your prince or arrived at his castle, red strands of fate pulled you from the East, setting it all into motion."

"You speak of the Mother."

"If that is the name you choose." The woman smiled. "You are trapped in a vortex. Time and again, you will repeat your fate dutifully. If we cannot change fate itself and save our world."

The woman stepped away from the case. Barefoot, she didn't make a sound as she floated over to Vhalla. Closer now, Vhalla could no longer deny the red glint to Vi's eyes.

"Let me see you," she whispered.

Vhalla was transfixed, helpless to do anything more than let the woman lower her hood. The woman's face held an odd sort of longing tinted with sorrow.

"You are younger than I expected, and so much weight on your shoulders, future Empress."

"I will be the Empress?" Vhalla jumped at the first definitive thing she'd heard in the Firebearer's words.

"You will be." The woman stepped away. "I told you then, you would find what you sought."

"But I never sought—"

"You sought him," the woman interrupted with a sudden

intensity. "You knew who he was and what his title meant. You knew, even if you didn't admit it to yourself; you knew what being with him would lead to. And now you have him."

"I know all this already." Vhalla was desperate for her to return to whatever comments she had on the future.

"Tell me, was the sacrifice worth it?" The woman once more folded her hands and leaned against the counter.

"Sacrifice?" Vhalla could think of a good many sacrifices, but she wasn't about to let them roll off her tongue freely.

"The sacrifice of this world."

"No, I didn't—"

"For him, you hesitated in eradicating your magic when it was first born. For his defense, for his Empire, you took the axe, the last of the crystal weapons, and returned it to its birthplace. When you could have remained hidden, you sought answers to his truths. You cast aside the night's shroud and dreams of home to stand on a sunlit stage."

"No . . ." Vhalla's heart was beginning to race. "No, I-I thought I was doing the right thing. Not just for him, but for everyone. I didn't know. You should have told me all this before."

"I did." The ghost of a smile haunted the woman's cheeks.

"No, yes, no!" Vhalla shook her head in frustration.

"Not in so many words," Vi relented. "But the language of the Gods is hard to translate into mortal tongue. I did my best for you."

"If I had known—"

"You wouldn't have done anything differently." Now there was a heavy sorrow in the woman's voice. "I know that now. I have seen the vortex of fate clearly."

"That's not true," Vhalla insisted.

The woman paused and passed judgment on Vhalla for a handful of minutes. "You were drawn by a man who ran the Black Tower, just as Aldrik was. You were taken to the caverns, just as he was. You were used to open a gate, just as he was. You were raised without a mother, just as he was. Pushed to battle, just as he was.

"In many ways, just as his father was before him."

"You lie."

"Your mother was forced to watch her mother live in hiding, be persecuted and face the threat of judgment, or worse." Vhalla's fairly recent discoveries about her childhood added extra gravity to the woman's words. "Your mother saw the same future in you."

"You don't know any of this," Vhalla said stiffly.

"Just as I did not know the first words he ever spoke to you?" The woman arched a dark eyebrow.

"Who are you?" Vhalla's voice was beginning to rise.

"I am the one who is about to offer you a choice. A choice that will change everything and set into motion that which can break the vortex." Vi had finally reached her point. "Tell me, Vhalla, with what you can see in your limited view, how will a child of the Emperor grow?"

"What?" She didn't even realize the palm that had instinctually covered her lower abdomen.

"*Think.*"

Vhalla's eyes widened as the woman's words finally hit home. She had lived without her mother. Aldrik had lived without his. If the woman's implications were to be believed, then his father had lived without at least one of his parents. In light of recent information, Vhalla was forced to wonder about the exact details of why her mother had lived without her grandmother.

"No." Vhalla had seen the briefest glimpse of the vortex the woman spoke of. The spinning fate that had trapped her and everyone she loved within it. She stumbled over to Vi, grabbing the woman's warm hand. "Tell me this is not the truth you see in the flames!" Vhalla didn't plead for her own mortality, but at the thought of leaving Aldrik and a child she had never met.

"Do you want me to lie?" the woman's voice was a cool contrast to her skin. "I will not lie to you, but I will offer you a choice."

"A choice?" she repeated numbly, a strange tingling surrounding Vhalla's body, starting from the woman's fingertips.

"If you leave now, you will remain trapped. You and all you know and love will continue onward, time and time again, forever. Fate has grown too hungry, and it will never have its fill."

"Or . . .?" Vhalla braced herself.

"Or you build a new fate." The woman reached into the wide sash wrapped around her waist. She pulled on a silver chain, producing a familiar plain pocket watch. "Regain your powers as a Windwalker and be the crux by which balance can be restored to this world."

"Is that . . ." *Had she made an unintentional vessel all those months ago?* "Of cour—" Vhalla stopped herself, changing her words. "Yes, I want to build a new fate."

The woman pulled the watch away, snapping it into her palm when Vhalla reached for it. "I told you, fate is hungry, and it must have its due. You cannot gain a future without sacrificing the one that lies before you."

"What must I do?"

"You choose if you will be the Empress this world needs. If you will sacrifice your future upon the altar of fate, before the eyes of Gods and men. If you will become an Empress that can save this world. If you will enter into a pact with me to ensure that the vortex is finally quieted." Vi watched Vhalla's reaction carefully with her glittering, dangerous eyes. "Buy time, with time."

A hand clasped around Aldrik's watch, knowing instantly what the woman wanted.

"Do you think if you give it to regain your magic, he will vanish from your side?" She gave a thin smile.

"Will he?" Vhalla pressured.

"No more insights; I cannot afford it. You have your choices: leave as you are and be trapped in the vortex that threatens to consume this world. Or give that which is most precious to you, the future you carry, for something far greater than you or I."

Vhalla's whole body trembled. She wanted to leave. Every inch of her screamed for her to run back to the bed she should have never left. She wanted to pretend she had never heard Vi's words. Vhalla urged her mind to pretend that the woman was no more than a hoax.

But her heart knew. Even if her mind could not comprehend everything that was happening, Vhalla knew somewhere deep within her soul that what Vi said was true. She ached at the sight of the watch, at the thought of her magic once more.

"Let me come back," Vhalla attempted. She wanted Aldrik; she wanted to at least discuss it all with him.

"No. The next time you come you will not find me. There is only one more time I can come to you."

"So I'll make my decision the next time we meet." It was foolish, but Vhalla would be the hopeful fool.

"Choose now. It must be your choice alone."

Vhalla couldn't handle the woman's eyes as her hands began to move. She couldn't bear a witness on what she was about to do. Vhalla's fingers closed around the clasp of the watch that she had hardly removed since Aldrik had promised his future with it.

"Tell me one thing." Vhalla paused, just shy of handing over Aldrik's token. Vhalla remembered the princess's words, that it was a vessel holding his magic. "This will not be used to hurt Aldrik, will it?"

"I did not use this to hurt you." Vi twisted her hand and dangled the watch with two fingers. "I could have sold this at a great price to the man who sits on the Southern throne."

Vhalla looked down at the watch Aldrik had given her, unable to argue. Its once polished surface was scratched and beginning to tarnish from never-ending wear, but she loved it more now than the first day he had given it to her. Aldrik had said he had made the watch at the Crossroads. There was a dark poetry to losing it here as well.

With a trembling hand, Vhalla held out her most precious possession.

Just like that, it was gone. Vhalla looked on as the Firebearer curled her fingers around Aldrik's gift. The thing he had put so much love into was gone. *She had given it up.*

Vhalla looked at the blank watch in her hand. It was a clean slate, perfect and unblemished. She had traded Aldrik's gift for power. Was she any better than Victor?

The flame extinguished, and Vhalla's head snapped back up, startled. The darkness pressed upon her, pushing at her chest.

"V-Vi?" Vhalla took a step backward to where she knew the door to be. "I-I changed my mind. I can't give it up."

Silence was her only reply.

"Please, I didn't." Vhalla's neck already felt barren. "I don't want to lose that. I've lost so much, not that. Our Bond is gone; the watch is the only part of him that I can carry with me."

The darkness was oppressive, setting her ears to ringing. Vhalla clutched the blank watch tightly in her palm. A chill swept through the room, and Vhalla no longer felt that she was alone. The hair-raising feeling of being watched set her on edge.

Vhalla turned and fled as fast as her feet would carry her.

Stumbling into the street, Vhalla looked back frantically, with the feeling that something terrible was about to pursue her. The moon stared down at her, time continuing as normal. Vhalla felt dizzy and sick, looking back into the perfect blackness of the shop.

Her feet felt like lead. Her brain swam in her skull, and the world swayed. Vhalla struggled back to the hotel as fast as she could go. She was certain she was going to be sick. Just when another step was going to be too much, Vhalla was plunged into the bright light of the lobby.

"My lady!" The woman behind the desk blinked in confusion, startled to her feet. "What are you doing out? Are you all right?"

"I-I, yes." Vhalla raised the back of her fist to her head, the watch still clasped within. She was clammy and cold. "I just need to lie down . . ."

The woman nodded but was clearly biting her tongue at the state of the Empress. Vhalla gripped at her shirt above her stomach. She hurt all through her middle, a strange and growing agony. Vhalla looked upward. She would feel better once she was with Aldrik once more. Once she could pretend everything that had just happened wasn't real for a few hours longer.

Vhalla's foot slipped on a step, and she fell with a cry. Something shattered within her as she hit the stairs. Vhalla hardly registered the woman rushing to her side.

"I will go fetch the Emperor."

Vhalla forced her eyes open through the pain, staring at the watch in her hand. A wave of nausea hit, and Vhalla swallowed hard. "No. G-get Lady Ci'Dan. I need Elecia."

The woman was off and running, leaving Vhalla to struggle to catch her breath alone. Wrapping her arms around her middle, Vhalla curled into a ball. Something was very, *very* wrong.

"Vhalla?" Elecia's voice quickly cast aside the groggy tones of sleep as she knelt down before her. "What are you doing at this hour?"

"Help me," Vhalla beseeched the Groundbreaker, one of the best clerics in the world.

"Come." Elecia took one look at Vhalla's sweat-dotted brow and began helping her up the stairs.

"Should I fetch a cleric?" the desk woman called.

"I am a cleric," Elecia snapped back. "Not a word of this to anyone."

The curly-haired woman practically carried Vhalla up two flights of stairs to her own room on the third floor. She gingerly helped Vhalla over to one of her chaises, easing her down before shutting the door. Another round of pain jolted through her, and Vhalla was once more doubled over.

"I don't know." Vhalla grimaced. "I don't know, but it hurts."

"Let me look at you." The woman pulled Vhalla's arms away from her abdomen, taking both her hands in hers. Elecia blinked her eyes and began looking from top to bottom with magic sight. "Why are you even awake at this hour? I thought you—"

Elecia's eyes stopped on her abdomen.

The woman was a flurry of movement and offered no explanation as she dragged Vhalla into the bathroom. She tore at the ties of Vhalla's cloak, pulling it off. Looking at her reflection, Vhalla could see what Elecia had seen moments early with her magic. Blood glistened darkly on the fabric covering the insides of her legs.

One fate sacrificed for another.

Vhalla gave an uncontrolled cry and collapsed in on herself.

CHAPTER 15

"VHALLA, COME, WE need to get you cleaned up." Elecia's hands were on her trembling arms, hoisting Vhalla back to her feet. There was a clinical force to the other woman's voice as she shut out every other emotion but the drive to act as a healer.

One of Vhalla's hands clutched the watch so tightly her whole hand was white, blood pooling by her nails. The other hand covered her mouth, muffling the sobs that racked her body at the realization of what she'd unknowingly done. Another lightning pain jolted through her abdomen, and she was leaning against the counter as Elecia began to draw a bath.

"I can't believe you both were so stupid. I trusted that you were being careful. That one of you would come to me if you needed Elixir of the Moon. I assumed Jax was getting it for you," Elecia rambled. She began rummaging through various supplies before returning to Vhalla. The other woman's hands registered on Vhalla's bare skin as Vhalla was helped out of her clothes.

"Listen," Elecia's voice dramatically softened. "It's all right. It will be all right. I can help lessen the pain, make it pass faster. This happens to more women than you know. I've seen it a lot, and, really, try thinking of this as a kindness from the Mother.

The Goddess is looking out for you. The child would have grown up like Aldrik if you'd carried it to term, under speculations of being a bastard."

Tears streamed off Vhalla's cheeks, pooling on the floor. *The child would've grown up like Aldrik, a kindness from the Mother;* the words whirled in Vhalla's head faster than a twister. As impossible as it was, there was a greater force within the world that Vhalla had seen a glimpse of in that curiosity shop. It was beyond comprehension, and it had traded her fate. No, *it* hadn't traded her fate. This had been Vhalla's choice. She wanted to scream or vomit, and the combination gave birth to nothing but silence and clotted blood.

"In the water with you now."

"I-I can wash myself," Vhalla fumbled over her words. She didn't want any more of a witness to her shame. She wanted to be alone, to dunk her head beneath the water and muffle the world.

"No." The edge had returned to Elecia's tone. "I am not leaving you alone right now."

Vhalla tried to help Elecia, but her hands shook too hard to do much of anything. She felt raw. Like she had just been reshaped by the maker Herself.

"What's this?" Elecia asked, bringing Vhalla back to the present by tapping on her fist.

"It's . . ." Vhalla didn't have an explanation other than the impossible truth. "It's a vessel of my magic."

"What?" The other woman looked at her as though Vhalla had gone insane. "No, that's—" The words froze in Elecia's mouth as she blinked at the token in Vhalla's palm. "By the Mother, where did you get this?"

By the Mother, indeed . . . Could there be another explanation for what had transpired? "I traded for it."

"That doesn't make sense." Elecia sighed. "Later."

The other woman allowed Vhalla to keep the token while she

finished bathing and drying her. Vhalla tried to help, to a point. But she felt too tired and numb to care.

Pulling her back into the attached bedroom, Elecia put two layers of cloth atop the bedsheets. Vhalla lay down as instructed. Her abdomen and back ached in a manner she had never quite felt before.

"I'm going to get Aldrik." Elecia started for the door.

"No!" Vhalla sat up instantly, hissing in pain at the sudden movement. She had no explanation for Aldrik yet; she needed more time. She needed some kind of glue to piece together the shattered reality first. "Don't tell him yet."

"What?" Elecia stalked over back to the bed. "You mean to tell me he didn't know?"

Vhalla could only shake her head.

"What did you both think when you stopped having your monthly bleed?"

"It had gone away on the march North," Vhalla tried to explain. "I thought it the same. We hadn't been eating well, and all the travel, strain . . ."

Elecia pinched the bridge of her nose with a heavy sigh. It wasn't an illogical leap, and the woman couldn't immediately refute it. When she opened her mouth to speak, she was cut off by a banging at the door.

"Elecia!" Aldrik was barely keeping his volume under a shout. "By the Mother, open the door."

" 'Cia, are you there?" Fritz called also. "Is Vhalla?"

Elecia looked between the outer door and the bed.

"Don't—" Vhalla pleaded.

"I'm sorry." Elecia actually looked it. "But you will appreciate this later."

"No!" Vhalla tried to swing her feet over the edge of the bed, stopped short by the pain the movement caused.

"Lie down!" Elecia barked.

Vhalla resituated herself and pulled the covers over her head. She didn't care if she was being childish. She had been strong for so long that all she wanted to do was spend a moment hurting. She wanted to hide from the shame that was about to be heaped upon her the moment she saw Aldrik's eyes.

"Don't shout," Elecia snapped from the outer room, presumably opening the door in the process.

"Is she here?" Aldrik was relentless.

"She is."

"Where?" Aldrik's footsteps fell across the floor.

"Aldrik, you need to calm down first." There was a tone in Elecia's voice that Vhalla had never heard the woman take with her cousin before. "And Fritz, you should go now."

"Is she in here?" Aldrik's voice grew louder, and Vhalla shrunk further into herself.

"Listen to me—" Elecia's attempt was too late.

A large beam of light stretched across the bed like an accusatory arrow the moment Aldrik opened the wood and paper door between the bedroom and the main room. Vhalla didn't move, her shoulders trembled, and she hardly breathed. *What could she possibly say to him?*

"Vhalla," he breathed, relief saturating her name. It put an aching in her heart that competed with the pain of her middle. "You worried me so much. I woke, and you weren't there." She felt his weight as he sat on the edge of the bed. "I couldn't find you, and when you weren't in Fritz's room, I—"

He reached out his hand, barely brushing the blanket that covered her shoulder.

"Don't touch me!" She cringed from his reach.

His hand hovered, obliging her wish but clearly uncomfortable with it. "My love . . . What could make you want to shy from my touch?"

"Aldrik . . ." She choked out his name.

"Let me reassure you," he begged. "Was it a dream? A nightmare? There is nothing to fear."

Delicately, tentatively, his palm lowered once more. Vhalla whimpered her consent, and it curled around her upper arm. It was equal parts reassurance and turmoil.

"Aldrik," Elecia started.

"Don't!" Vhalla sat, clutching the blankets around her.

"Where are your clothes?" Aldrik blinked, staring at her bare back.

"He deserves to know." Elecia crossed her arms over her chest. "If you don't tell him, then I will."

"It is not your place to tell!"

"Then talk to the man who will be your husband!" Elecia slid the door closed so hard Vhalla and Aldrik jumped.

"Tell me what?" He rested his palm on her back, lightly kissing her temple. "Fear not, for whatever it is, we can tackle it together."

"I-I lost our son," Vhalla confessed, wide eyed. She remembered the note Aldrik had written, the one she had clutched to her breast. Her, him, their son.

"What are you saying?" Aldrik's voice had gone monotone.

"We were careless." She couldn't bring herself to say the words.

"How were we careless?" He was too smart not to know the answers.

"You know how!" She turned to him, and a particularly sharp pain pulsed from deep within her abdomen. Vhalla collapsed back onto the bed with a choked sob.

Aldrik could only stare at her as it sunk in, and Vhalla avoided his gaze.

"Elecia." He was on his feet, storming for the doors. "Elecia, tell me—"

"Stop being stupid," Elecia said curtly, snapping open the doors and allowing herself back into the room. A hand, cooler than Aldrik's, smoothed over Vhalla's forehead. "Vhalla, here, drink this. It'll help things move along."

"I don't want it." She deserved every wave of pain she was to endure.

"Don't start this. You promised me that your life would—"

"You don't even know what my life means!" Vhalla twisted, ignoring the pain to stare down the Westerner. "You don't know the sacrifices I've made. You think this—"

A small bottle was unceremoniously shoved into Vhalla's mouth between words. It clanked against her teeth and her lips wrapped around it as Elecia forced it into her face. Vhalla swallowed the liquid within, resigned.

"Stop. Stop trying to make the illusion of strength. You don't need it. Not here. Not now. Let yourself be sad until the real strength returns." The empty bottle was gently pulled from her lips, and Elecia smoothed some of the hair away from Vhalla's sweat-dotted forehead. It was a tender gesture that had no precedence between them.

"Cousin," Elecia walked away as she spoke, "however completely idiotic I think you both have clearly been . . . However much I believe this could be interpreted as a blessing in disguise . . ." There was a long pause. "I am sorry."

The other woman left, closing the doors once more behind her and resigning her room to the Emperor and his lady. The couch beyond sighed softly as Elecia settled upon it, and Vhalla couldn't help but remember she had slept on couches in this hotel the last time they were in the Crossroads, spending her night hours healing.

Aldrik hovered for several long breaths before finally returning to the bed. Her love settled on the bed next to her but did not touch her, the small distance between them feeling like the world.

The silence crossed the threshold into agonizing when he finally spoke. "Look at me."

"No."

"Do not fight me, not now." His hand pulled on her shoulder. "Please."

It was the please that called through to her. Vhalla rolled and looked up at her Emperor with red and burning eyes. Her face was twisted in grief and glistening with snot and tears. Aldrik caressed the expression, replying with tenderness.

"I am . . ." He took a deep breath, "Relieved you are all right."

Vhalla squeezed her eyes shut. He didn't even understand a fraction of how she'd wronged them.

"I was so worried." His lips ghosted against her forehead. "I woke, and you weren't there. I went to Fritz, and when you weren't with him . . . If I'd not found you, I was ready to burn down the Crossroads in a rage to find you."

"Don't say that," Vhalla hissed in agony.

"It's the truth."

"You said it before." She remembered him bidding her farewell at a secret door the first time they were at the Crossroads. "Do not say it again. We have to be different than before."

"Different?"

"I traded fates. We must break the vortex. We must do better." Vhalla felt sick at herself all over again for what she'd done. The night was becoming a messy blob of memories that were distorting with time. Did she really have any idea what the truth was? *Or was she just slowly losing her mind?*

"What are you talking about?"

"There was a Firebearer." Vhalla struggled to collect herself to say what needed to be said. "I met her the last time I came. She . . . then she told me . . . She told me I would lose you. She told me of Victor. I didn't understand. I was worried, so I went—"

"You went out? Tonight?" The tender tones were fading from his words.

"I wanted to go alone . . ."

"To some curiosity shop? To a Firebearer with some smoke and mirror tricks? Why didn't you tell me?" Justified agitation furrowed his brow.

"I didn't want you to tell me not to go."

"So you knew I would disapprove?" His touch vanished, and Aldrik withdrew. "You couldn't respect my wishes. No, not even enough to try to talk it over with me?"

"I should've explained."

"You should have. You don't keep secrets from me, not you." There was genuine pain now in his voice. His old insecurities flared brightly, and the wounds that had scarred his heart saw light once more.

"You know I don't." Vhalla looked at him for a long moment, challenging him to object.

He cursed softly and looked away.

"I'm sorry, I handled this poorly. I just wanted to know if . . . if we would really make it."

"You shouldn't have to ask a Firebearer to know that," he mumbled.

"It isn't as though we haven't been on the run for weeks! I was scared, Aldrik. I thought that I could find something, some small reassurance to sooth the worry in my heart but . . ." She'd talked herself to the threshold she'd feared all along. How could she summarize what had transpired in a way that he would take seriously?

"But?" Aldrik pressed. "This Firebearer, did she touch you?" he growled. There was a protective dangerous gleam in his eyes. "Is it because of her that we lost . . ." Aldrik couldn't bring himself to say it.

"No." This was her responsibility, and Vhalla would accept it. "That was my fault alone."

"It's not your fault," he mumbled.

She had to take a second and brace herself for what had to come next. Vhalla wanted to put the night behind her so badly, but she couldn't do that if there were truths left unsaid. Through the slowly thickening haze in her head, she forced herself to carry on.

"I gave away the watch you made."

He was so silent she wondered if he somehow hadn't heard her. "You . . . *what*?"

"I had a reason!" Vhalla freed her hand from the blanket, thrusting her silver trophy before him. "This, Aldrik, with this—"

"Another pocket watch? Did you tire of mine so you wanted something more—"

"It's a vessel!" Their pattern of interruption ended with that. His mouth hung open on the unformed word she had stolen from him with the truth. "It's a vessel."

"What?"

"It's an unintentional vessel I made back when the Firebearer last looked into the flames to answer my question," Vhalla explained quickly. "With this . . . With this I should be able to . . ."

Her words failed. Despite what she had just told him, the hurt had yet to vanish from his expression. Vhalla suspected she could've said she traded his watch for the entire Crescent Continent, and Aldrik would've still been pained. Tonight, she hadn't paid the price for her choices. Aldrik had.

"It's my fault . . . I wanted you, so I stayed. And because I stayed, I was where Victor could get me. All the people who have died, Erion, Craig, Raylynn, your father—it's all because of me. All the pain is my responsibility. With this, with my magic,

I can right what I wronged. I can beat Victor at his own game. He thinks he can kill or force all Windwalkers into hiding. But I will stand against him. I will do what I must for our people before I do what I want for myself."

He was as still as a statue. Vhalla took the weight of his gaze upon her shoulders as well. She was carrying the world, and he was but one point upon it. Everything was lost if she did not make her vow a reality.

"I wanted to make things right. I hurt you while doing so, and I'm sorry. I never wanted to. But I . . ."

The heat of his palm on her lower abdomen silenced her. Vhalla stared at the man who was to be her husband. A storm raged just behind the darkness of his eyes.

He sighed. "What have I done to you?"

"Nothing I didn't ask for." She'd asked to be Empress. She'd chosen it the moment she'd chosen him. She'd been so busy surviving that she hadn't accepted what that really meant. Now it wasn't just about her survival, but her people's.

"You should sleep. Your body needs to heal."

Vhalla leaned forward, pressing her forehead into his sternum. Aldrik shifted to snake his arms around her. "I lost him," she breathed.

"No."

"The son of your dreams—" she tried to continue.

"Was not this child."

Vhalla wished she could make him understand. His dreams had been scattered to the wind. Their future, the red lines of fate he had looked forward to, had been interrupted. But Vhalla didn't try to make Aldrik comprehend the truth that was filling the hollow within her. Only one of them would have to bear this truth, and that would be her.

"We will try again." He kissed the top of her head. "When we are wed, when I have my throne. That is when our child will be born. And when that day comes, this night will be nothing more than a forgotten nightmare."

She needed his optimism. Her head was thick and heavy. Vhalla suspected the potion Elecia forced down her throat had been laced with Deep Sleep, but the cleric knew best. She closed her eyes, and Vhalla gave herself to that welcoming blackness.

The bed was cold, and dawn hovered in the morning air when Vhalla finally stirred. She heard Aldrik's voice from the adjacent room, the sound pulling her the rest of the way from sleep.

"How did you find her?"

"She just appeared in the night," Elecia responded.

Vhalla blinked groggily, the Deep Sleep slow to release her mind.

"She said she went to a curiosity shop. Jax, I want every last one in this Gods forsaken city turned up-side-down with the most discretion you can manage. If even one confesses any knowledge, I want to know everything. And—" Aldrik's voice dripped acidic malice off his tongue. "—should you find one that laid a finger upon her . . ."

"No one will ever find the body," Jax filled in the blank with methodological viciousness.

Vhalla shook her head, pulling herself into a seated position. Vi was long gone. Whatever that woman was, it was nothing like any of them had ever seen, and there was no way she had remained. Still, there was little point in trying to call Aldrik off on his demands. Vhalla was happy to concede to them if it pleased him and eased his pain.

"Now, Fritz, she claims this is a vessel."

"It-it does feel like her magic," Fritz confirmed with evident surprise.

"I already told you that." Elecia's eye roll was heard by Vhalla from the other room.

"You will help withdraw the magic so her Channel can be restored."

"I've never—"

"I am not asking you, Fritznangle, I am telling you as your Emperor."

Vhalla rubbed her abdomen. She needed to get up and call off her protective love before he made an ass of himself to their friends.

"But not yet," Elecia said firmly. "I see what you are doing."

"Elecia—" Aldrik warned.

"No. You are trying to fix it all and force it back to where it is comfortable for you. But you cannot force her. Her body is healing. This isn't a battle scar, and it's not going to be fixed when we don't see blood anymore. You are healing, too."

"Aldrik," Vhalla called.

"Vhalla, what is it?" The doors were thrown open, and he rushed to her side. "What hurts?"

"I woke, and you weren't here." She tried to force a small smile.

"I was only taking care of a few things, my love. I'm here. I'm with you."

"Stay," Vhalla demanded.

Aldrik's hair was a mess, and his eyes looked sunken. Somehow, his face had become gaunter in one night. Elecia's advice to Aldrik hit Vhalla's heart. They were both hurting, and that hurt would only be soothed by being together and letting themselves be sad.

Elecia came in as Aldrik situated himself next to her. She had clearly spent some of the night acquiring and preparing a new flight of potions for Vhalla to ingest. As the healer was leaving, Aldrik requested that she find a book for them to read.

Vhalla wondered if he had known what she needed to feel better. Or if, somehow in his own turmoil, he needed the same things as she. They spent the day tucked together, ignoring the world.

Aldrik didn't even part from her when it came time to bathe again. He sent Elecia away, announcing that he would do it himself. Vhalla tried to avoid either of them helping her, but her attempts were futile.

"I can do it myself," she insisted. "I don't need you."

"You're right, you don't *need* me. But I *want* to help you." He guided her to the steaming bathwater.

"Aldrik, you don't want to do this, it's . . . very messy." She had more eloquent words to describe the situation, but she didn't use them. Clarity and eloquence bred heartbreak for her as they laid out neatly the situation she was in.

"Blood does not scare me." Aldrik begun undressing her.

Vhalla grabbed his wrist. Tears of frustration and anger welled up in the corners of her eyes. Every word was trapped in her throat with no hope of freedom.

"If you want me to go," he whispered. "Tell me plainly. Tell me to leave your side, and I will."

She shook her head. She didn't want him gone. She needed his presence and his love just as he seemed to need hers. The emotion persisted even when his hands washed away the blood that slicked her thighs.

The distance in his eyes eased as the days passed. The only time pain showed was when he focused on the sight of her barren neck. But Aldrik didn't speak of it, and Vhalla didn't force the issue. She could apologize and make excuses until the world ended. But it wouldn't change anything.

The only thing that mildly helped was the day that Elecia deemed her healed enough to attempt recovering her magic from the vessel. It reminded them both that, despite what Vhalla had given up, hopefully something was gained.

"All right, Vhal," Fritz began. "There isn't much here. It should—*should*—be enough to have a Vessel to start calling to magic through your Channel. But you'll need to withdraw every last bit of magic, to be certain."

"Might it not work?" Vhalla asked nervously.

"If there's not enough to unblock your Channel, the magic will just fizzle the first time you try to use it."

"How do I withdraw it?" She didn't allow herself to be scared. There wasn't any other option but success.

"I'll help you," Fritz encouraged. "You hold it and imagine the watch is your Channel. Feel it, know it, and welcome it into you." He curled her fingers around the watch and grasped her hand. "I'll help push the magic out, help it move towards you."

Vhalla nodded, nerves stilling her tongue.

"Are you ready?" He continued at her small nod, "Here it goes . . ."

He closed his eyes, and Vhalla did the same. Just like the very first time she had ever tried to use her magic, Vhalla imagined something just beyond herself, and tried to touch it. The world didn't rebuild magic on a whim, nor did she feel a whisper of sorcery on the wind. There was only a subtle tingling in her fingertips.

Vhalla guarded her every hope. She felt as though she was on the edge and only needed one more good push to hold everything in her grasp. Her breathing echoed in her ears as she mentally reached for the truth the watch held.

She was the Windwalker. She would fill up the hollow that had been carved from her, fill it up with a new future.

"Vhalla, enough." Fritz released her fist. "Don't push too hard now."

"But you said get it all." Her eyes fluttered open.

"I think you did." He inspected the watch. "You don't want to expend magic, looking for magic."

"So did it work?" Vhalla stared at her hands.

"We'll know soon." Fritz blinked his eyes a few times, shifting his vision to study her. "Your Channel will need more time to restore, if it's going to. By the Mother, Vhal, if you think you even feel the hint of magic, do not be too eager to use it, or you'll drain it all and be back in the same position as before."

For the rest of the day, Vhalla remained on bedrest. She was getting bored of it, especially now that the bleeding had slowed to occasional spotting. But between Aldrik, Elecia, Fritz, and Jax, she had no option but to take it easy.

"How do you feel?" Aldrik asked as they settled for sleep.

"Tired." Despite resting all day, it was true.

"I've always loved watching you sleep. Seeing you at peace." He brushed hair lovingly away from her face. "I plan to do it forever."

"Even now?" she whispered, wanting to hear the words between his words.

"Even now," he affirmed.

There was pain still, but it was beginning to fade even for Aldrik. No matter how much they lost, they still had each other. And, so long as that was true, they could continue to meet the dawn.

Dawn, however, came too early for either of their tastes. Vhalla rolled over tiredly, a light sneaking through a crack in the curtains to hit her face. She felt so exhausted. Aldrik's arms tightened around her, and he nuzzled the back of her neck.

"It's bright," Vhalla complained. "Make it go away." She motioned to the curtains. The room darkened, and they both woke with a start.

Vhalla stared at the now drawn window dressings, as they swayed in the remnants of an unseen breeze.

CHAPTER 16

VHALLA STARED AT her fingertips in dumb shock, her eyes darting between the unassuming digits and the settling curtain. Raising her hand, she took a shaky breath, determined to re-witness the truth that had just revealed itself to her.

Long, warm fingers curled gently around her wrist. "Don't." Aldrik shook his head at her. "Don't push yourself."

"But what if . . ." Vhalla stared at the window.

"The curtain closed by a draft?" His smile was small, but there was genuine joy in his eyes. Cupping her face in both palms, Aldrik graced her lips with a brief kiss. It felt like the first kiss in forever, and a butterfly emerged from its cocoon in her stomach. "Do not be silly, my sorcerer."

"Am I?"

Aldrik held out his hand, palm up, and a tiny flame appeared in its center. "Blow it out. But only this small test, and then more rest."

Slowly, hesitantly, Vhalla raised her hand. Aldrik shifted closer, the orange glow of the tiny mote illuminating his bare chest. Her fingers tensed, straightening and relaxing in an instant. The fire was snuffed, the light extinguished to nothing more than the ghost of a blue glow when Vhalla blinked.

"My magic," she breathed.

The covers flew through the air as Vhalla tossed them aside. Swinging her feet off the side of the bed, she was stopped, mid-lunge, by an arm snatching her around the waist. Aldrik pulled her back to him, racing heart and all.

"I want to see."

"You just saw." He held her to him.

"No, no, it's not enough."

Aldrik nuzzled her neck, the tenderness stilling her. "You still must rest. You have been through a lot."

"I know." Ice surged through her veins at the memories. "I gave up everything for this, so let me go."

"You did not." Aldrik's hair tickled her shoulder as he shook his head. "You gave up a child that you should have never even carried. And one of my many pathetic attempts at silver working."

Her insides clenched, but not like it had over the past few days. She had witnessed a memory in which he'd presented a gift to the woman who should've loved him as her own child, and it was rejected. Vhalla twisted, seeing beyond him back to that young, nervous child.

"It was not pathetic." She spoke firmly enough that it commanded his attention. "It was the best gift anyone had ever given me, and I would have loved it had it been misshapen and half-finished—because you were the one to give it to me. That's what was truly important, that's why I could give it up. Because our love is more than something I can wear. Our time is far greater than what can be counted by two hands and some numbers. Because, even without it, I still have you."

The edge of a question slipped into her last statement, and Aldrik sighed, an exhausted smile curling his lips.

"You shall always have me." He pulled her back onto the bed with him holding her as close as possible. "Our love is more than physical trappings. Be it tokens of affections or the bodies our eternal souls inhabit while we are chained to this mortal coil. I would have made a hundred watches if it would have returned your magic to you."

There was pain in his words, even still. But there was also truth. He shared in the joy of her magic returning. Vhalla sighed softly and pressed closer against him. If she was going to continue to be restricted to bed, then she would make the most of it by filling her hours with him.

When Elecia and Fritz finally deemed Vhalla strong enough, physically and magically, to leave the bedroom, she paid the price of vanishing from the world for a short week. Letters had piled up from both Norin and Hastan. A new timeline also needed to be addressed for the rest of their journey to Norin.

Their break in the crystal gate at the border of East and West had held long enough for Western reinforcements to get through and march to Hastan. Elecia's father reported that they couldn't have come a moment too soon, as Hastan had sustained another attack by Victor shortly thereafter. This time, Victor had sent a larger force on foot, marching from the South and laying waste to cities and towns along the way, Leoul included.

That was when Vhalla realized that she was never going home. She had to continue to believe that her father had, indeed, moved ahead of the gate's construction and she would meet him in Norin. In truth, home had always been where the people she loved were. For years, that had been the farm in Leoul. But now it was where her father, Aldrik, and friends were.

The news cast a somber cloud over her for a different reason as well. Leoul was farther north than Paca, which meant Daniel's town had been right in the line of Victor's marching forces. His fragile state lingered in the back of her mind; the sight of Victor's sorcerers would have caused agony in the man who cast a shadow across her heart. Vhalla wondered if her friend had escaped safely, or if he had met the fate of nearly a third of the East.

If Vhalla had lacked any purpose before hearing this news, she certainly didn't after. Rather than hardening, her heart became hotter. It burned and pushed hot blood through her veins faster than sandstorm winds. Vhalla racked her brain, considering all the information that had come through the reports sent from Hastan. She stayed up until her eyes crossed and blurred, trying to find the best way to distribute the East's limited fighting forces.

The largest sites of food production had to be protected first, alongside Hastan as the head of the East. But there was no choice when it came to sacrificing some smaller towns as a result. It was among the hardest decisions Vhalla had ever made, and she allowed herself to feel pain at it. If she became numb, it would be a disservice to the people whose lives she was deciding.

To save the most lives, more messengers and more reminders were sent to those interested in joining the fight, reminders that they could retreat to Hastan. Vhalla made her will known through letters, sharing with the men and women of the East exactly how and why she was moving them. That it was, indeed, a choice made by the person claiming to be their leader. Vhalla knew she could never accept their loyalty if such facts were ever hidden.

Aldrik fussed over her incessantly. He worried constantly. Vhalla tolerated it, the guilt of Vi's trade making her oblige Aldrik as recompense for her transgressions against him. But Elecia finally snapped.

The woman began dictating how Aldrik could—and could not—take care of his wife-to-be. She was having none of his doubts over her methods of healing. He finally relented and began running the Empire at Vhalla's side in earnest.

Jax remained ever present as well, especially when Aldrik disappeared to grant some face time with a prominent lord or lady who ventured to the Crossroads to meet them. Jax's revelations about his past lingered with Vhalla, but she didn't give it much thought. There were far bigger concerns facing her than the crimes Jax had committed years ago. She'd sort through it eventually.

Only once had Aldrik pressed for Vhalla to show him where Vi's curiosity shop had been located. They circled the market several times, but Vhalla couldn't find the small curtained entrance or anything even remotely resembling it. Her Emperor did his best to hide his frustration, but Vhalla was unbothered. She hadn't expected to ever encounter Vi again. The woman would only reveal herself on her own terms, not Vhalla's. And as badly as Vhalla wanted to understand Vi's actions, she'd felt Vi's unnatural darkness and the weight of the woman's eyes seeing more than Vhalla's physical form too many times to question too deeply. *Some things may not be meant to be understood.*

The more time that passed, the fuzzier that night became. Vhalla finally stopped fighting it and let the memory hide away into the hazy shadows of the back of her mind. It happened more slowly for Aldrik, but they soon stopped talking about it. By the time a letter from Sehra arrived with the status of the North's preparations, it had faded away into little more than a dark spot on their journey to Norin.

What had not faded, however, was Vhalla's elation at regaining her magic. At every opportunity, Vhalla called upon her winds. Things were lifted and pushed, opened and shut. She demanded to sleep with the windows open just to feel the night breathe across her skin.

There was so much to do that the days slipped away from them, and they were late to leave the Crossroads. The last letter they received from Ophain began to question if they had any intention of coming to Norin or if they intended to make the Crossroads their headquarters. Vhalla broached the idea with the Emperor that night.

"Wouldn't it make more sense to stay?" She pointed to Ophain's letter.

"Why?" Aldrik glanced up from the other end of the table where he had been working on finalizing troop numbers.

"Because Sehra will bring her army here, to the Crossroads." Vhalla rummaged, looking over one of the maps that had been marked and crossed one too many times. "If she's going to start her journey shortly, then we could tell your uncle and the troops from Norin to do the same. They should arrive within days of each other. It would save at least . . . at least two weeks of travel compared to us going to Norin and back."

"We must wed." Aldrik paused his quill, giving her his undivided attention.

Vhalla stared at the map for another long moment. She knew he saw it as such, that it was something they must do as a symbol. Even if she was growing more concerned about the timing by the day, Vhalla continued to concede.

"Then we will do it here," she suggested.

"Impossible."

"Are there no Crones who could perform the ceremony in the Crossroads?" She laughed at the ridiculousness of the notion.

"It must be done in the Western Sun Temple in Norin," Aldrik insisted. "That is where my father wed."

"Now hardly seems like the time for sentimentality," she gently pointed out.

"Far from it," he agreed. "But now is the time for putting on the right display for the lords and ladies, for the world. We are strong, and we do not allow a false king to force us to wed in hiding. Or hint that there is something illegitimate about our union that we should do it in a small chapel on the run."

"I'm sure we could explain . . . It's just so much time to lose."

Aldrik considered it for several slow breaths. Making up his mind on something, he reached forward and grabbed a slip of parchment, beginning to scribble as he spoke, "We shall write to my uncle and tell him a date. We'll invite the lords and ladies in advance so that the amount of time we must spend before the ceremony is limited to necessary preparations and appearances."

Vhalla glanced back at the map, thinking of the waste it seemed. "Thank you," she said finally. *It was something.*

They replied to Lord Ophain that night with the request of the date along with their promises to depart the Crossroads before he received their reply.

Shortly after, Aldrik started the task of making them new armor. It was a good distraction from the worry that blossomed in her chest by the fact that Lord Ophain had yet to make any mention of her father. Vhalla kept her fears in check and her hands busy with helping Aldrik in the smithy. Just like she couldn't allow Jax's presence to distract her, she couldn't allow fears over her kin to distort her priorities. *Her father would be all right*, she assured herself. He'd been a soldier once and knew how to handle himself. There was nothing else for her to believe.

Vhalla's first experience with the craftsman habits of her Emperor was enlightening. Aldrik tested and felt each piece of steel before he began working with it—he was nothing if not particular. Not one smelter denied him, naturally, and he was finally satisfied with his base materials.

They worked together to make flames hotter than he could alone. Aldrik worked in simple clothes, and Vhalla appreciated the look of the man with his hair pulled back from his face and soot rubbed into his nose. It was an elegant orchestration of their magic, but it was one that held melancholy notes. Had they still been Bonded, his flames wouldn't hurt her and they could've been far less careful. His magic was no longer in her, but there was still something different about it. Vhalla knew it like an old friend. She recognized every spike, every subtle flux in his power and could account for it.

They were not Bound, but they were not separate either. They had become something new yet again.

Aldrik finished the armor the day before they were set to leave. He put on the final touches alone while Vhalla spent the day bidding farewell and reaffirming the loyalty of the lords and ladies in and around the Crossroads. When she returned to the room that night, the matching sets waited on stands. Aldrik smoothed over portions with his thumbs, unable to stop working the metal.

"Well, what do you think?" he asked, finally.

Vhalla tilted her head. Sitting cross-legged on one of the chaises, she studied the pieces on the stands. Something was off, and it took her too long to put her finger on what it was. "The color."

"You don't like it?" Aldrik sat down at her side.

"It's not that I don't like it." Vhalla struggled with how to encapsulate her feelings.

The armor was indeed lovely, very identical in craftsmanship and style to her prior suit with some additional embellishments. Smaller shoulder pauldrons matched his, gold detailing lining their edges. The scales were more angled, giving it a sharper and stronger look. The outer steel had been layered with an alloy that shone white, setting off the gold detailing—like the pair of wings that sat with a sun in their center at the armor's collar.

"It's white."

He laughed, but it sounded forced. "White is the Imperial color." The man was nervous by her reaction.

Vhalla knew he understood her statement, but she played along. "You've never worn white, on anything."

"That's not true," he objected.

"I'm not counting in private," she hastily clarified. "Why not black?"

"Because—" He paused, abandoning the quick remark he'd been readying. Aldrik turned back to the two suits of armor and took a deep and slow breath. "Because that time is over.

"I need to lead my people—our people. I must be someone they look to, and I must *look* like that person." Aldrik waged an internal battle with the armor. "I have no more family, so I am no longer a black sheep. I no longer have my life overshadowed by my father's missions and visions for his Empire. I cannot afford to let a personal tantrum, or bitterness, distance me from the subjects whose trust I so need. I need their loyalty, and I would rather earn that through admiration than fear."

He peeled his eyes away from the simple thing that had caused him so much introspection. He looked to her, and the man still managed to look uncertain at the exact moment that Vhalla thought he had attained clarity. He was no longer a wildfire burning with rage. He was now the fires of the forges he'd stoked. He burned for a purpose and remained focused on that singular goal.

Vhalla rested her hand on his, initiating touch for the first time since the night she had traded with Vi. Aldrik's eyes darted over her face. It had been so long since she was nervous around him that the butterflies in her stomach were awkward, though not unwelcome. She reached up to touch the face of the man she adored, to pull it toward her. To hook his chin and guide his lips to where they belonged—against hers.

Delicate exploration paid quick dividends as a breathless chorus filled the room when they pulled apart. Neither of them were ready yet, Vhalla realized, to be as intimate as they had once been. But the fact that something was still there, given all that had happened, the fact that he was still capable of wanting her and that her body had not forgotten how to want, returned to them a level of closeness that had been woefully missing.

For the first time in nearly two weeks, the Emperor and Empress slept peacefully through the night—completely folded in the other's arms.

CHAPTER 17

DESPITE KNOWING THE armor's color and the reasoning behind it, nothing could have prepared Vhalla for the next morning when Aldrik strapped himself into it for the first time. His hair was combed back and his helm had been attached to a saddlebag so that the people could see him on their ride out. Vhalla did the same, following his lead in their departure from the Crossroads.

He was radiant, every bit of the leader Vhalla had always known he could be. He was a seedling that had been transplanted from the dirt in his father's shade and placed in the sun for the first time. He greeted the assembled masses and waved to merchants and lords alike as the Emperor's company wound its way out the main road. Vhalla witnessed their people finally seeing what she had known all along: he was born for this.

On their way out of the Crossroads, Fritz had his first opportunity to comment on her armor. "Your symbol changed." Fritz fingered a corner of the cloth that went down to her waist, somewhere between a cape and a cloak with a slit in the front for mobility. It was fixed by the sun and wings at her collarbone. Vhalla touched the new symbol, the same one that was emblazoned in gold on her back.

"I suppose it did." Vhalla glanced over to Aldrik. He wore a similar garment, though his only had the sun of the Empire on its back.

"Why?" Fritz mused aloud to no one in particular.

"A second wing, because the Windwalker has been born again," Aldrik answered. "The whole Imperial sun because she will wear this armor after she has formally become my Empress."

"No longer cutting it in half and pretending it's not obvious?" Jax grinned.

Aldrik rolled his eyes.

"He has a point," Elecia teased her cousin. "It's unlike you, Aldrik, to have given her something so overtly Imperial."

Vhalla remained silent through the teasing. It hurt. Her friends didn't mean for it to. But they didn't know that her watch, the one Aldrik had given her, was gone forever. Judging from the long look Aldrik gave her, he was thinking much the same.

Then the wind shifted and, with it, her Emperor's expression.

"This is what is obviously Imperial. It's a new dawn for us both, and she wears my craftsmanship upon her once more," Aldrik spoke only for her.

"As I should," Vhalla replied gently.

They set a good pace through the desert. The East-West Way made an easy path from the Crossroads to Norin, and they once more found themselves spending time in the company of lords and ladies along the way. The further West they went, the stronger the culture of old Mhashan became.

Vhalla was on-edge the first time she saw the Western phoenix with a sword in its talons. No one questioned her decision to ride hard into the next day for the next opportunity for shelter. Like the scar on her shoulder, there were some wounds that could be mostly forgotten day to day, with enough time and healing, but would always be tender when probed.

As summer came early to the desert, Vhalla and Fritz used

their magic in tandem to keep them from cooking alive in their armor. Fritz applied thin layers of ice atop the metal, which Vhalla's winds quickly evaporated. At first, they were wet and windswept. But Vhalla and Fritz managed to get the hang of it enough that soon the five of them were not only kept cool, but they were comfortable as well.

The ride progressed without problem, and they woke before the sun on their final day of their ride into Norin. They'd stayed with one of Aldrik's distant cousins, sending word ahead to Ophain that they were only a few hours from the city proper. Vhalla had wanted to keep pushing, but Aldrik was insistent that certain conventions must be observed, and their arrival would be one of them.

Normal butterflies were replaced by a whole flock of birds in her stomach as the city began to grow around them. Sunlight sparkled over their recently polished armor, and they had all washed properly at the lord's home before the final leg of the journey. Elecia was all smiles at the idea of returning home, but Jax had grown quieter and quieter as the days progressed.

The man had reduced himself to nothing more than a silent shadow. The lords and ladies along the route had maintained only the bare minimum of etiquette toward the man. A select few treated him with as much respect as the rest of his noble company. However, there was a moment when the lords and ladies first saw his face, a moment where they had to check their reactions at the sight of him.

All thoughts of Jax's odd mood vanished like pennons flapping in the wind. Sand changed to a more soil-like consistency, and large palms appeared in the growing density of the city. Norin waited before her.

It was a city unlike any she had ever witnessed before, and it had surely been built by giants. The outer wall of Norin was so tall that Vhalla wondered how they had engineered mechanisms to carry stones that high. The houses within the outer wall were constructed of clay and wood, simple structures packed one atop the other in a mission to rival the wall with their height. Vhalla remembered Master Mohned's history, and she wondered if this was the place that he had grown up. The thought was quickly accompanied by a pang of sorrow at the fact that her master likely met an untimely demise at the hand of Victor.

The inner wall of Norin separated the squalor of the slums from the working and middle classes. At present, men and women lined the streets in the first section of the city; common folk, lords, ladies, merchants, dignities, and all shades between them encroached on Vhalla and Aldrik's forward progression. Vhalla would have felt uneasy by the mass had they not been happily crying her name alongside Aldrik's.

They threw rose pedals from rooftops and sent tongues of flame into the sky. They waved small pennons, all crying for her attention. Men, women, children, all reached for those who had returned from the dead to lead them. Vhalla was thankful for the strong legs of the horse beneath her.

The castle of Norin appeared before them, stretching up in defiance against the sky. In the sunlight, the clay and stone used in the construction seemed to glow scarlet. A red castle that skewered the sky with its flat-topped spires and arched walls. It was set apart from the most affluent section of the city by a wide, dry moat, a single drawbridge spanning the distance.

Vhalla understood how the West had nearly taken a decade to fall.

"My lady." Aldrik pulled her from her thoughts by offering her his palm.

Vhalla shifted Lightning's reins into one hand in order to take his hand. In the light of the sun, before all their subjects, the Emperor and future Empress rode together. Vhalla wondered if the people had ever seen the man with a wider smile across his lips.

She doubted it.

A man waited for them at the end of the drawbridge, a man who was the spitting image of Aldrik, plus a few years, gray hairs, and darker skin. The courtyard surrounding the drawbridge entrance was filled to the brim with people, so much so that the newcomers could barely cross. Lord Ophain met them halfway atop his massive War-strider.

"The Emperor Solaris has returned home to the West!" Lord Ophain announced proudly.

"It is my honor to be among so many of my kind once more," Aldrik replied. Despite being close to each other, they shouted in an attempt for all to hear.

"But you have not come alone." The lord's verbal dance for the people's sake was obvious.

"No." Aldrik raised their joined hands slightly, putting them on display. Vhalla swallowed any discomfort, reminding herself that this was now her world and her duty. "I have come with the first Windwalker in nearly a century and a half. She is the hero of the North, a lady of two courts, a woman who has not only saved my life countless times but is one whom I have found to be peerless."

For being a man who had a reputation for not being well loved, Aldrik had a natural talent for working the people into a frenzy. The cries of the masses nearly deafened her as he rose her hand to his mouth, kissing its back.

"I present to you all the woman I have chosen to be your Empress, the Lady Vhalla Yarl!"

After that, all hope for further announcement was lost as the raves for an Imperial wedding drowned out everything. Lord Ophain said a few more things to Aldrik as they began moving once more, but Vhalla couldn't hear the words. Her free hand had been lost to the outstretched palms of the people surrounding them. They reached for her as though she was the hope by which their lives depended.

Vhalla would do all she could to not let that hope be in vain.

The cries echoed with them as they started down the drawbridge, finally free to move once more. They steered their mounts toward waiting stable hands, who stood immediately within the castle. Aldrik relinquished her hand for his reins once out of sight of the people, and Vhalla breathed a small sigh of relief at no longer being on display. As proud as she was to be his, there were some feelings that Vhalla knew would take time for her to become accustomed to.

"It is truly good to see you, Uncle," Aldrik said as he dismounted.

"I prayed to the Mother every day for your safe arrival." The two men briefly embraced as the horses were led away.

"I did not think I would ever have the opportunity to see you again," Vhalla said as she dismounted and adjusted the cape about her shoulders.

"I confess, there was a time where I, too, was uncertain." The lord rested both hands on her shoulders in a familial motion. "But I should have known the Mother would not intertwine two people so carefully, only to deny them." Ophain released her and moved toward the castle. "Now, there is much to be done."

"We will need to organize a careful timeline," Aldrik agreed.

"Indeed, but first," the lord of the West paused and gave a conspiratorial smile to Vhalla, "there is someone who I think very much wishes to see you."

Vhalla stared at the lord while she mentally reminded her heart to beat. "Where is he?"

"Just up the stairs to the right when you first enter. We'll all go together."

She couldn't wait. Vhalla bounded away as fast as her feet could carry her. Her heart pounded, and she felt dizzy. Every feeling that she had suppressed about her father traveling alone to Norin came rushing to her all at once. She prayed she hadn't misunderstood the lord's unspoken meaning about who waited to see her.

Vhalla skidded to a stop at the wide open doors to a parlor. They framed a man who stood looking out over the window at the city below. The trellised glass perfectly framed the street she had just rode upon.

Her father's Eastern hair and complexion looked odd in the bright colors of Western fashions. She'd never seen him in a vest before, and it fit him so well that it nearly took years off his appearance. The man turned at the sound of the panting woman.

"Papa!" Vhalla cried.

"Little bird." He didn't quite share the same shock at her existence as she did for his.

Rex Yarl opened his arms and accepted his daughter—windswept, sun-kissed, sandy, armored—into his embrace. Vhalla held him fiercely, her face pressed into his shoulder. She hugged him as though he would disappear the moment she let go, like nothing more than a wishful illusion.

But he was still there as her arms finally slackened and Vhalla took a step away. Vhalla studied him carefully, looking for the smallest thing amiss. But her father was as he'd always been. Sun-leathered, burnished skin folded around his gentle smile.

"You made it." She beamed from ear to ear. "You made it before the gate. You're here, in Norin!"

"Did you ever doubt me?" Rex said with mock offense.

"Of course not." Vhalla shook her head and allowed herself to fully believe her own half-truth. "How long ago did you arrive?"

"Not too long before you." He motioned to a large recessed area before the hearth. "I hoped to be a pleasant surprise."

Vhalla took in the room for the first time. The hearths were decorated in mosaic tile and precious gems that went from floor to ceiling and lined the bottoms of the wooden beams that broke up the clay ceiling. The floors were wooden and stained a deep red. Their polish picked up the silver accents throughout the space.

"Papa, you're limping!" Her attention was quickly restored to her father the moment they started for the sitting area.

"It's nothing."

"What happened?" Vhalla asked, concern lacing every word as she unnecessarily helped her father sit.

"Oh, I was clumsy." He laughed the laugh she so loved. "I made it all the way to Norin without problem only to slip on some stairs and bend my ankle oddly."

Vhalla rolled her eyes and collapsed down next to him. She avoided the lush fabrics of the pillows and blankets in the sitting space and instead chose the hard wood around it. Her armor was likely to snag on fine fabric and her boots would grind in dust so fine it would be impossible to get out.

"You should be more careful," she scolded, starting on the clips of her cape. "What if you really hurt yourself? You would've had me worrying the whole time while I was here."

"And the last thing I want you doing is worrying during your wedding," her father interjected.

Vhalla paused and time stopped. Her father had known about her and Aldrik in the East. But something had changed; the way he looked at her now was completely different from any gaze her father had given her before.

Rex picked up her discarded cape thoughtfully. His fingers ran over the emblem of the sun reverently even as he folded it. Her father, the soldier, he'd been the one to instill in her the deep concern and reverence for their Empire and those who stood as its figureheads. Now she had become a person her father would always look to.

It was an odd reversal from the man whom Vhalla had always admired.

"You looked like an Empress out there, little bird." There was a note in her father's voice that made Vhalla's heart want to break.

"It was what she was born to do," a voice as dark as midnight slid across the room in agreement.

Vhalla turned. Aldrik and Ophain had finally caught up. Elecia was in their company as well and stood beside a woman Vhalla assumed easily was Elecia's mother. The woman had the exact same rich shade of darkened skin and beautifully curled hair that seemed to defy gravity in its brilliance.

Bringing up the last of the nobility were two more women. They both had straight dark hair and piercing black eyes. One was shorter and carried a little more weight on her form. She wore her hair cut at the shoulders with a side-swept fringe. The other was tall, but sturdy—much like Aldrik's build—and had a long thick braid running down her back. Vhalla knew who they were without the need for introduction. Their high cheekbones and thin lips marked them of the Ci'Dan stock. Aldrik's aunts.

"Let me help you." Aldrik sat next to Vhalla as the rest of the company assumed places around the perimeter of the sitting area before the hearth. His fingers deftly reached for the clips that were in hard to reach places, allowing Vhalla to shed her metal skin.

"It is a pleasure to finally meet you, Lady Yarl," Elecia's mother said, breaking the short silence on behalf of the group.

"Likewise, Lady . . ."

"Ioine," the woman finished for her with a bright smile. "Though no title is necessary."

"Then I must ask the same, just Vhalla."

"Are you certain?" The woman had an easy elegance about her. It was quickly apparent who Elecia modeled herself after.

"Of course. We are to be family." Vhalla put the matter to rest with that simple truth.

"Family, indeed," added the woman with the braid, as she crossed her arms over her chest.

Vhalla struggled to assess if the motion was hostile, skeptical, or merely curious. "I apologize; I've not yet caught your names."

"Tina."

"I am Lilo." The younger woman smiled wide enough to make up for her sister's blank expression.

"An honor to meet you both." Vhalla gave a small nod of her head in respect. It didn't matter that she would be the Empress in a short turn of the moon. These women were Western princesses. They had been commanding respect for decades before Vhalla was even alive.

"We have heard much about you." Tina was as expressionless as Aldrik was when Vhalla had first met him.

"I can only imagine." Vhalla didn't let her voice waver. The woman was trying to intimidate her, and Vhalla was determined to disappoint her in that endeavor.

"There is good reason why the West has not had much surprise regarding your betrothal," Tina spoke as castle help entered the room to serve dark Western tea and rice pressed into shapes. "The Western court has been rampant with talk over the woman who not only earned the first crimson proclamation in years but also earned the prince's heart.

"And then," she continued. "It was rampant with the Knights of Jadar howling foul against that same woman. Crying wrongs against them. You can see how it could be difficult to know what to think."

"Actually, I cannot." The woman arched a dark eyebrow at Vhalla's remark. "I would think that you should know exactly what to think of anyone who displeased the Knights of Jadar. Those who have so wrongfully cast aside your noble lineage in exchange for madness and fools' missions."

The corners of Tina's mouth tensed briefly. Vhalla would have missed it had she not just spent years of her life breaking down the subtle mannerisms of the most private man in the Empire. Acceptance flashed across her face as she reveled in the momentary amusement Vhalla had provided her.

"Speaking of families and upsetting the Knights of Jadar," Lord Ophain interrupted as he set his glass aside with a chuckle, "we have a wedding to plan. The false king's seat has been successfully thrown into question with our current successes against his forces and the truth that both of you live. To meet your aggressive date, there are quite a few details to be formalized."

"I think a wedding will be just what the people need," Lilo chimed in brightly. "Take their minds off decay and death, and give them a reason to be happy. Your wedding will be such a joyous reminder that the sun still burns brightly."

"Speaking of, let us show you our home, Lady Yarl." Tina stood. "This is not where the ceremony would be, but the audiences leading up to the wedding and the revelries following would occur within these halls. You should know the place that is to become your home as well."

"A wonderful idea, sister!" Lilo was on her feet as well. "Then we can show you your chambers, as I'm sure you're tired from the day's ride."

"Very well." Vhalla would agree to anything if she felt it would make things go faster. Her wedding was evolving into more of a chore than she'd ever expected. Every mention of it brought back memories of the decisions she had to make about the East's defense. *Her people were dying and she was planning a party.* "Father, would you like to come?"

"Leave the men to chat," Tina spoke before her father had a chance.

Elecia and Ioine stood as well at the subtle command.

Vhalla raised her chin and looked the Western woman in the eye for a long, hard moment. She had just reunited with her father after fearing for his life. Being told to dismiss him didn't sit well with Vhalla, and the words slipped her lips before she could stop them. "Father, would you like to join me as they show me the castle?" Vhalla asked again slowly, ignoring Tina's order.

Aldrik tore his eyes away from the exchange, hiding his face in the process. Vhalla could've sworn she saw a satisfied smile escaping across his mouth.

"My ankle still pains me," her father refused gently. "Plus, I have had a few days to explore. You enjoy it now."

"Take dinner with me later." Vhalla knelt to kiss both her father's cheeks. "I want to catch up with you."

"I won't refuse that, little bird."

"Good, I didn't want to have to beg you," she teased lightly.

"Enjoy the home of my forefathers." Aldrik caught her hand, holding it for a long moment before relinquishing her once more. His eyes shifted to his eldest aunt. "Do not show her the library."

"There's a library?" Vhalla gasped.

"Call me selfish." His mouth curled into an irresistible and utterly unapologetic smirk. "Take care of her, Aunt Tina."

"Yes, my Emperor." Tina revealed the most expression Vhalla had seen from her when the woman referred to Aldrik as such.

Vhalla was led out of the room, with Elecia and her mother following. She barely contained a belated eye roll at the thought of Tina's previous suggestion. Perhaps outlawing the notion of "words amongst men" would be her first decree as Empress.

As far as Vhalla had ever experienced, men and women spoke the same words and there was no reason why men couldn't say certain things in her presence.

Her ire quickly faded to awe as she marveled at every wonder the castle held. In the richness of its history, the home of Mhashan's ruling family rivaled the palace in the Southern capital. In architecture and art, they could not be more different. There were countless rooms to sit and lounge within. Steel rang out on steel from well-fitted training grounds. Hundreds of years of history were packed into every hall.

"How did you and Aldrik meet?" Tina asked as they strolled through a large room of statues and paintings.

"Through notes in a book," Vhalla answered vaguely. She tried to make a show of studying the sculpture before her to avoid further questioning. It didn't work.

The woman arched a dark eyebrow. "Notes in a book?"

Vhalla briefly wondered if the ability to do so was passed down in the family or if they were tutored in it. She'd seen Aldrik give her the same inquisitive look countless times. Her palm rested on her lower stomach without thought. *Would their children make such a look?*

"They were notes that were ultimately of help to him." Vhalla didn't want to give up much more than that, as the thought of their lost Bond hurt. "He reached out to me after that."

"That was forward and most unlike our nephew." Tina may as well have screamed that she suspected there was more to Vhalla's story than she was being told.

"Well, I didn't know it was him for the longest time." Vhalla smiled faintly at the memory of their first notes exchanged. "I called him a phantom then."

"He did have a liking for all things dark," Lilo agreed. "Though he seems to have finally taken to the color of his station."

"The color doesn't matter." Vhalla strolled onward as she

mused. "Underneath it all, he will always be Aldrik, the man who was born to lead us."

"And . . ." Tina stepped into Vhalla's personal space. Her voice dropped to a hush, glancing pointedly at the guards positioned at the far ends of the room. "Do you know clearly what that is? What lies underneath the clothes he wears?"

"What?" Vhalla spun, frowning up at the much taller woman. Elecia sniggered, and Vhalla felt a flush on her cheeks. All hope of denial was gone, and Vhalla shot her friend a frustrated glare.

"My dear." Tina wrapped an arm around her shoulders, pushing Vhalla along to the next painting. "Do not be shy. We have our suspicions already. Your secrets are safe with us."

"We would never hurt our little Aldrik." Lilo linked her arm with Vhalla's open one, effectively pinning her between the two sisters. "Remember, he's all we have left of our sister."

They stopped at a large portrait, and Vhalla's breath caught in her throat. The woman sat, swathed in an Imperial white robe with a golden trim. A crimson shawl about her shoulders pooled on the floor. One hand held a mote of flame, the other a golden scepter with a sun at the top. The fire that lived in her eyes existed beyond death and time. It was complemented by a familiar curl at the corners of her mouth, betraying an air of confidence that could easily border on arrogance. Angular eyes and high cheekbones were framed by long black hair that fell under her shoulders unbound.

The woman looked like authority incarnate. She looked as though she could kill the person who stood before her—or save them for a heaven that man had never known. She was everything Vhalla would have expected Aldrik's mother to be, and more.

"Would she have liked me?" Vhalla murmured, the thought escaping her mind as a quiet musing.

"For what you have done for her son, she would have loved you," Lilo answered before Tina could.

"She looks just like him." Vhalla realized that Aldrik was already older than the woman in the painting. That idea carried a new weight to his mother's death. Vhalla was nearly the age at which his mother had died.

"The Ci'Dan blood is strong," Tina said proudly. "I am sure your children will look much like him also."

Vhalla couldn't speak. She grabbed her shirt above her stomach where a phantom pain rippled through her at the thought. Elecia looked on with silent concern as Vhalla struggled to find the right words. She'd already failed once; she had traded the future where an heir was assured. Now she carved her own path, and no one knew what that may hold.

"Do not be nervous, dear!" Lilo sensed the right emotion but for the wrong reasons.

"Listen to my sister," Tina agreed. "After all, your greatest duty will be producing an heir."

"What?" Vhalla freed herself of the women's grips so she could read their facial expressions. She'd always known such to be a fact of their union. But, her *greatest duty*?

"Surely, Aldrik has spoken on it . . . As soon as you are wed, you will need to bear him an heir."

"After the war," Vhalla whispered.

"That won't do." Tina shook her head and spoke as though she was leading a child into the world for the first time. "We live in uncertain times. You will need to leave the fighting in the South to him and the armies."

"But—" Vhalla wasn't even allowed protest.

"If he dies, the Solaris name will then live on. You can rule in his stead until the heir is of age," Tina continued. No matter how much love she spoke of her nephew, the words rang heartless.

"This will ensure the future stability of the Empire. We can keep you safe here as you bring the child to term."

"No." Vhalla repeated herself before the softness in her objection could be mistaken for weakness, "No."

"Vhalla, this is—"

"This is for the best? Is that what you will tell me?" Vhalla stared intently at Aldrik's aunt and, for once, the woman held her tongue. "Forgive me, but you know nothing about our history— not really. So I am uninclined to entertain your opinions. Separating me from Aldrik has only ever led to heartbreak and misfortune."

Vhalla paused, choosing to speak another truth, a deeper truth. "I may be a woman and I may be his lady, but I am capable of doing something that even he cannot. It is something beyond crowns and titles, and it cannot be given or passed along." Vhalla stood tall with the portrait of Aldrik's mother at her back.

"Aldrik can produce an heir with any woman who is healthy and of age. He can share the seed of the Empire so long as that one functional requirement is met. He cannot bring down the tyrant which spills the blood of our people. He cannot touch crystals as I can. He does not know them as I do. He has not been taken to the Father's halls and brought back for the purpose of saving this world, of breaking the vortex that spins outward from the Crystal Caverns. He cannot destroy the monster that has been wrought from greed and put an end to it once and for all.

"But I can." Wind swirled around her fingertips. "I can do those things. So if you are truly so worried for the stability of the Empire, then keep Aldrik here. Let me fight alone, and should I die, then let him bear the heir you so desire."

The three women she'd just met stared at her in dumb shock.

"However . . ." Vhalla couldn't help a knowing smirk from playing on her lips. "Do tell me if you plan on suggesting such a course to him. For, from what I know of my Aldrik, he will not handle the notion of sitting by while I fight as gracefully as I have endured the reverse suggestion. His reaction to such a thought is a sight I would much enjoy being privy to."

Vhalla looked between the four women, as if daring one of them to speak an objection. The wind slowly fell from her hands, and Vhalla questioned herself briefly. But only as briefly as a breath. She was the Empress-to-be, and Empresses did not doubt. They were confident and graceful creatures full of knowing smiles and organized secrets. Vhalla would soon be of the same rank as the portrait of the woman at her back.

"But please." She forced her face to relax and was proud when it fell into a sincere smile. "Do not think I will avoid future counsel."

"Right," Tina remarked cautiously as Vhalla proceeded to the next statue.

There were no future suggestions or recommendations on how Vhalla should act as Empress. They were quieter when she spoke and more attentive to her words from then on. Vhalla watched, without fully realizing, as the women from one of the oldest and noble families in the West submitted before her. They never did so physically, but they bent knee long before the others who would come to her throne in the days to follow.

CHAPTER 18

VHALLA SHIFTED IN her seat. It was the first time she had sat on a throne—though that was a loose term for where she was now located—and all she could think was how uncomfortable it was. She was positioned at Aldrik's right hand on a raised platform at the end of a long audience chamber. They sat upon legless chairs with their seats flat on the ground, simple compared to the thrones of the South. But what the furniture lacked in its simplicity, the room made up for in its opulence.

The wall behind them was decorated almost entirely in silver and ruby. It had script covering it that told the story of the very first King of Mhashan, written in the native tongue. The silver crept into the wall to their right, running the length of the room and glinting on the highly polished floors. Columns framed wide openings to their left, overlooking all of Norin—the world that they ruled on display before them.

It was certainly a space that had been designed to evoke humility at the might of the two who sat in the most revered spot. Rather than clashing with it, Vhalla blended in. They had dressed her in the traditional clothing of the West. Shining silks and intricate embroidery turned reds and golds into textile artworks.

On her bottom half was a large and flowing split skirt with a band of red trim. A crimson vest was worn atop a flowing shirt of golden silk, fitted that morning to her measurements. Pearl buttons made a line up the middle of her breastbone to the high collar that extended up towards her ears. Her hair had been coiffed and held in place by a delicate golden band, although it was determined to escape.

Aldrik was dressed in the same fashion, and Vhalla kept glancing at him from the corners of her eyes. He wore loose white trousers and a long-sleeved shirt beneath his own fitted tunic that was decorated in crimson suns. A large red scarf had been wrapped many times over his shoulders and it bore a long tail that he folded and carried expertly over his arm.

He'd easily transitioned from the fitted, modern, military fashions to Mhashan's traditional garb. Aldrik was poised and relaxed, the small golden crown across his brow making no difference in his dealings with the lords and ladies who came before them. Vhalla had not yet been bestowed a crown of her own.

Vhalla struggled to pay attention as the endless rotation of lords and ladies were ushered in and out of the large silver doors at the far end of the hall. Had the discussion strayed to anything that seemed remotely important, she would've been eager to lend her insights and opinions. But, for the most part, Aldrik seemed to be on repeat, and the nobility only varied their script slightly.

The Emperor began by giving a court member his thanks for their unwavering loyalty. The lords and ladies would then humble themselves and offer up some empty compliment or blessing on their union. Aldrik would promise that their loyalty would not be forgotten after the war, and Vhalla would chime in with hopes that their families would maintain positive relationships for years to come.

Repeat, again, and again.

It was a tiresome dance for her. Vhalla understood the necessity on paper, but she had a harder time coming to terms with it in practice. Aldrik had insisted on it late the night before and reiterated it that morning. He explained that there was more than met the eye to what was being done, that it served as a visual display of their power as a unified force. That the process inspired loyalty by discouraging others from being the "odd one out", which could lead to dissention.

Vhalla hoped that the Knights of Jadar would show their faces. They wouldn't dare bring Jadar's armed phoenix into the hall, but Vhalla hoped they felt forced to come and kneel before her. The idea of that satisfaction helped sustain her through the first half of the day and into lunch.

"We should resume soon." Aldrik had hardly touched his food. He'd been focused on the letters his uncle had given him. Vhalla's plate looked much the same as she'd been engaged in discussing news from the East and North.

"How many more are there?" she attempted to ask casually.

"Not too many," Aldrik encouraged.

"You're certain this is more important than reviewing troops?" Vhalla motioned to the letters.

"I am." The Emperor stood. "My uncle can review the letters and help the East, but he cannot sit for us in the audience hall."

"It is my honor to see the East protected," Ophain encouraged.

"Thank you." Vhalla relented with a tired smile.

"Endure this a little longer." Aldrik stopped her before they crossed the threshold back into the public chambers. "I have something special for you when we finish."

"Something special?"

"Yes, assuming my aunt granted my wishes of not taking you to the castle library." Aldrik removed his crown and adjusted his hair, soothing any fly-aways from its slicked-back perfection.

"I wondered how long you could keep it from me," Vhalla teased.

"Not very long, clearly." He cupped her cheek, caressing it with his thumb. "Would it please you?"

"How is that even a question?"

They shared a knowing grin and were off again. Vhalla continued to dutifully play her part as both future leader and respecting wife. Some of the friendlier noblemen specifically asked her questions, and Aldrik remained silent so that Vhalla could establish herself as their Empress. Unsurprisingly, he later had critiques on her approach.

She listened as dutifully as possible, but the second dust and parchment hit her nose, all hope was lost. The library was at the top of the castle, not far from the hall that held their quarters. Vhalla clutched Aldrik's arm in heart-pounding anticipation. But nothing could have prepared her for one of the most beautiful sights she'd ever seen.

The hexagon extended upward five floors, managing to be both intimate and expansive. Blood red carpet covered the usual hardwoods of the West, muffling her footfalls. The furniture was a mix of lower Western styles for lounging and higher Southern styles for studying. Two fireplaces crackled opposite each other, filling the bottom level with warmth and an inviting glow. Flame bulbs carried the glow upward, positioned on the six red beams that stretched up through the rows of bookcases at each of the hexagon's points. A massive iron chandelier lit the upper two floors and washed the room in a pleasant ambient light.

Despite the library's size, each shelf was crammed full. Narrow walkways outlined each level, giving access to the plethora of knowledge. Vhalla tried to assess how many books this library contained in comparison to the library in the Southern capital, and added the two together to gage the size of the entire Imperial collection.

"Do you like it?"

Vhalla didn't know if her head spun from the wondrousness of it all or his voice rumbling at her back. "It is amazing."

"And it is all yours." His hands smoothed over the silk covering her shoulders.

Vhalla felt like a princess. It hit her all at once. Like a fairytale come true. She was garbed in foreign finery, revered as nobility, preparing to marry the Emperor. It was more than she could've ever dreamed—and it had come at a cost that was far greater than she could've ever imagined.

"Mine," she repeated softly.

"Every book in our Empire will belong to you. It will be your choice if you share them or keep them." He intertwined his fingers with hers, beginning to lead her up a side stair.

"Knowledge should always be shared," Vhalla decreed thoughtfully.

"I don't know if I agree." He surprised her as they rounded the second stair. Aldrik continued, "If we could have kept the knowledge of the caverns from Egmun, Victor would have never known to pursue them."

"But," Vhalla followed his logic, "if I had known the full truth about the caverns from the start, I may have done some things differently."

"A fair point," he conceded.

All talk on the failures of the past and what knowledge—or the lack of—had wrought ceased as Aldrik led her through a small door wedged between bookcases. Vhalla blinked against the bright unfiltered sunlight in contrast to the dim light of the library. A wave of heat hit her cheeks, followed by the quiet whispers of wind through leaves. A familiar scent greeted her nose.

Her senses adjusted, and Vhalla took in the garden before her. It was familiar, yet different, from the smaller glass greenhouse in the Southern palace where she had read with Aldrik. This was its own room, tucked into the walls of the castle tower. Glass replaced stone on two of the walls and above. Roses, giant and beautiful, wound up trellises that arched over the pathway cutting through the modestly sized space.

"This way." Aldrik hooked her arm, offering no further explanation.

Vhalla was well aware of where they were. It was as though the wind itself here had been trapped by time, weighted in the scent of roses. There was the hum of magic around them, different and yet so very similar to the man who was leading her toward a marble obelisk. The figure of a woman sat atop it, a ruby sun at her back. She recognized it from a dream of Aldrik's she'd viewed so long ago.

"This was her garden," Vhalla stated.

"It was." Aldrik looked only momentarily surprised at Vhalla's ability to piece together where he had taken her. "My father proposed to her here, asking the youngest of three princesses to take a throne that she was never meant to have."

Vhalla attempted to push her resentment for the former Emperor aside. In some ways, he was like her original perceptions of the North. Vhalla had a very limited scope as to who the late Emperor Solaris really was. She'd known him during the final years of his life, the point in time where all he'd seemed to covet was his Empire and his legacy.

But perhaps—behind the weathered, bearded, and scarred face of the Emperor she knew—there had been a young man. A man who had been as attractive as Aldrik. Vhalla saw a woman who was tall, given Aldrik's family's propensity to height, looming over a kneeling Emperor. She would make him wait, in Vhalla's vision. The late Princess Fiera would be one to smile coyly and keep her true wants hidden just long enough to make the man tremble, to remind him that she was in control.

"They must have loved each other very much."

"So my family tells me." Aldrik didn't look anywhere but his mother's face. "My father took rose clippings and had them transported South for her so that she would feel at home."

"A garden she never saw," Vhalla thought sadly.

"My father told me once that he was still glad for building it. That it helped my mother live on. Though, eventually, I think it caused him more hurt than anything."

"So you took up the mantle of tending to it." Vhalla reflected on Aldrik's story, on the history that she had, for so long, barely understood surrounding his family. His mother had given up ever seeing that garden, ever spending time in it, for the sake of saving her son from madmen.

Vhalla's eyes met the statue's once more, and she wished she could speak with the woman whose visage she now looked upon. Vhalla understood what had compelled Aldrik's mother to run to the caverns that night, and it was something they now shared across time and life and death. She had known a truth about the world. Be it of her own insight or of some unknown guidance—like a Firebearer named Vi—Aldrik's mother had known what the caverns could reap.

It would stop with her, Vhalla vowed. She would end the cycle that they were trapped within, enslaved to the Caverns across time and generations. It would all end with her.

Over the next week, Vhalla tolerated the audiences with the lords and ladies with poise. She smiled and said the expected words, doing what was now the dance of her station. It began to pay off in the war councils that were held in the evening.

She was discovering how strong the West really was and how deep old Mhashan's pockets ran. Vhalla began to ransack the library for records of famous noble families and began keeping a list of their names, which she reviewed at night. By day, she would smile wide and loudly praise lords and ladies from these houses. Unsurprisingly, it became just that much easier to secure promises for supplies for the war and checks to be cashed when it came time to rebuild the Empire.

Aldrik must have pieced together what she was doing, but he made no comment against it. In the language of the Emperor, his silence was as good as resounding approval. So when the Le'Dan family appeared on their docket for the morning, Vhalla knew she was about to deal with the second oldest family in the West, the only name to rival power against the Ci'Dans.

"I am sure Richard will have much to say regarding your union." Ophain passed the list of appearances for the day back to Aldrik.

"I'm familiar with how that family operates. You forget that my brother kept a Le'Dan on his guard," Aldrik replied.

She'd overlooked it. Vhalla had known Erion's last name, but she'd been so wrapped up in everything else. Her spoon paused on the plate, shuffling her food like the thoughts in her head.

"My Emperor." A thought had occurred to her. "Let me lead the meeting with the Le'Dans."

Ophain and Aldrik both gave her shifting stares. Their expressions went from startled, to surprised, to intrigued.

"I've been listening," she explained. "I know what to say and what to do. And I think it would be wise."

"Why so?" Aldrik didn't seem to be objecting.

"Because your family holds bad blood with them. Whereas I doubt the Le'Dan name has any distaste for clan Yarl." Vhalla grinned slyly and was given a similar expression in return from Aldrik. "Beyond that, in the North, Erion said his family stood with the Windwalker. Given light of recent events, I want to be the one to talk to them."

Comprehension raised Aldrik's brows a fraction. The Golden Guard had been entrusted to protect her alongside the crown.

She wanted to be the one to apologize for the death of their son. *She needed to be.*

"Very well. You shall lead."

The contents of Vhalla's stomach mirrored a spinner's wheel all morning. Every lord and lady that was marched in was one closer to the Le'Dans. She was just thankful they were the last before lunch, otherwise Vhalla was certain that she wouldn't have been able to eat a thing.

"The Lords Richard and Erion, accompanied by Lady Cara Le'Dan," the doorman at the end of the hall announced.

Vhalla was on her feet.

"Vhalla—" Aldrik hissed.

She didn't hear. All she saw was the doors swing open. A man she didn't recognize stood alongside a pretty Southern woman. Vhalla's eyes widened at the cane-wielding soldier standing to the man's right.

"Erion!" Her slippers made no sound as Vhalla sprinted across the length of the hall. She threw her arms around his waist and pulled him in for a tight embrace, her momentum nearly toppling the unsuspecting and unsteady lord.

"Son, you didn't tell us you were so close to the future Empress," the man to her right remarked with a chuckle.

"Easterners." Erion clearly didn't know how to handle her unexpected affection.

"You're all right." Vhalla looked up at Erion's face. He had dark circles under his eyes, and there were gray strands of hair that Vhalla hadn't seen before. *But he was alive.* "I was given no indication, I thought, Daniel said—"

"Daniel?" Erion's face became serious. "You spoke to Daniel?"

"We found him on the way to the East," Vhalla tried to explain hastily. "He was feeling, he said that Craig had—"

"My lady," Aldrik interrupted her sharply.

Vhalla turned back toward the Emperor, who still held

his place on the raised section of the room. Vhalla knew she had completely botched the test she had earned from him in this respect. She straightened, taking a deep breath. If she had already broken all decorum, she may as well do whatever she wanted at this point.

"My Emperor, I did not realize that I would have an old friend among our company. As I have already disturbed this audience, I seek your permission to escort my friend through the galleries."

Aldrik was visibly conflicted. It wasn't an elegant situation no matter what they did. The worst thing he could do would be to refuse her now and make the interaction awkward.

"Very well." Aldrik forced a horribly fake smile. "If the Lord and Lady Le'Dan give their permission as well for you to not be in attendance for their audience."

"Of course, my lord," Richard Le'Dan said hastily. "We would never wish to go against your lady's desires."

Vhalla heard Aldrik begin speaking a somewhat different script than usual as the doors closed behind her and Erion. It took a lot to throw Aldrik off balance, and Vhalla wasn't sure if she should be proud or concerned at the fact that she had accomplished it without even trying.

"My lady." Erion offered her his elbow.

"You don't mind, do you?" Vhalla asked as she hastily took his arm. She tried to subtly offer him support on his wobbling legs, remembering what Daniel had said about Victor's abuse.

"Not even in the slightest." He shook his head. "You said you had news of Daniel?"

Vhalla's chest tightened. She recounted the story of how she had found Daniel, glossing over some of the darker aspects of his mental state. The distance in Erion's eyes told her that he already had a reason to suspect how bad it had actually been. It was out of respect for the horrors that the man had so clearly known that Vhalla left out the fact that Daniel's hometown, the place that *she* had left him, had fallen to Victor's troops.

"You inherit an Empire full of broken and half-people, Vhalla." Erion motioned to his now lame legs with his cane.

His trousers hid what she suspected to be scarred and ravaged flesh. In truth, she was surprised he was walking at all after Daniel's testament regarding the injury. The young lord watched her face tensely.

"I will kill him." She didn't apologize. Apologies wouldn't return Erion the life he had earned as a warrior, that he had fashioned for himself since he was a boy. They were men and women of action. She'd offer him solutions. "I can find you work here, in the palace."

"I decline your offer." Erion's cane clicked along softly. "But I will thank you for it."

"Are you certain? I know you cannot fight, but you have a wealth of experience with tactics and—"

"And most of my brainpower has been spent healing and relearning how to walk. Most of my willpower goes to getting out of bed." The words were heavy. "My days for battle are over, and I am sick of its taste. I may never expunge the blood from my dreams, but I am done washing it off my hands for this lifetime. I've decided to manage my family's shop here in Norin, and learn the trade of my forefathers." They began walking again. "When you win the war, the Empire will need to be rebuilt. That will take gold, and gold comes from commerce. I hope to serve our Empire in that way. I'm commissioning some ships to be made for longer trips to the Crescent Continent, even."

"Have you ever been?" Vhalla remembered what the Emperor had said about the magic of the Crescent Continent.

"The journey across the barrier islands is perilous and one not many dare make." Erion shook his head. "I am merely orchestrating the voyages."

"Right," Vhalla mused, mostly to herself. *Perhaps the difficulty was a good thing.*

"Have you been to the harbor in Norin yet?" Erion asked.

"I haven't even left the castle since we arrived," Vhalla confessed.

"I imagine a soon-to-be Empress would be busy. But if you find the time, it's a wonderful place and unlike anything you'll see anywhere else. I'd offer to escort you there myself but—" he looked down at his legs. "I think you would prefer a guard who could actually protect you should something go awry."

"Oh, I'm sure if I left the castle that Aldrik or—" Vhalla stopped herself for a second, quickly collecting her thoughts. "Have you seen Jax yet?"

"No, I was going to head to him after our audience. I was quite elated to see him well and riding at your side."

Vhalla studied the brotherly smile on Erion's cheeks. This man had been Baldair's right hand, and they'd both held Jax in high esteem. Two men, who Vhalla had nothing but respect for, deemed Jax acceptable. Combined with Elecia and Aldrik's general acceptance . . .

"How can you call yourself his friend?" Vhalla blurted.

"Pardon?" Confusion stilled him.

"You defended him in his trial, even after what he did." She wanted so badly to understand what everyone else seemed to know. Vhalla was giving Jax the benefit of the doubt based on those around her, but she was tired of being expected to have blind faith.

"He told you, then?"

"He did." She frowned. "I have barely been able to look him in the eye for weeks. I don't understand."

"*What* did he tell you?" Erion asked slowly.

"The truth of how he came to be in Baldair's service."

"*The* truth? Or *Jax's* truth?"

His words stopped her heart. Vhalla hadn't even thought to question that the man would be lying to her. It had been so horrible. *Who lied to make something worse than what it was?*

"A murder in cold blood for a lover's revenge?"

"Something like that," she admitted, wondering the source of the shift in Erion's eyes.

"Even after all this time," Erion muttered then cursed under his breath.

"No. What?" she demanded, refusing to let Erion pull away.

"It's not my place."

"He said you spoke for him in court." Vhalla thought quickly, not wanting to let the conversation die. "You can tell me why. That *is* your place to say."

Erion considered her for a long, hard moment. "He told you I spoke for him?"

"He did."

"And you still believed him?"

"Well . . ."

"I'm hurt, Vhalla." Erion's expression echoed the truth of his words. "You think I am the type to rise to defend a man who slays innocent women in their beds?" She had no real answer. "Do you think Baldair would permit a man with a history of violence toward the innocent into his guard?"

That was exactly what she'd been struggling to reconcile. "So, he lied about it? Why would he lie?"

"You know his full name. I'm certain, as Empress, you have access to those records." Erion stepped away. "If you want to know so badly, go and find out."

"Should I walk you back?" She glanced at the hall from where they'd come.

"I know the way."

"Erion, I'm glad you're all right." Vhalla gave him one more quick embrace. This time the Westerner was ready, and his arms tentatively wrapped around her shoulders.

"I am glad you are as well, and that one of my brothers still defends you as Baldair would have wanted." There was a waver in Erion's voice when he said the late prince's name. "Fight for us all, Vhalla."

"Always," she vowed.

He let her go, and Vhalla was off. She tore a path through the castle unapologetically, a woman on a mission. The library wasn't prepared for her whirlwind as Vhalla scanned the shelves with purpose. The old records were kept on the highest floor, and Vhalla searched for manuscripts and scrolls similar to what was kept in Hastan.

If the truth was on the shelf, she would find it. Manuscripts littered the floor around her, and the scrolls were mostly unrolled. It was in the fifth book that she had finally found what she suspected was the right year. On the first page, Jax's name stared back at her in the list of trials and decrees the book contained.

Vhalla flipped eagerly, opening to the page.

A frayed edge of parchment stared back at her. The pages, five or six by the looks of it, had all been ripped from the book. Only the first page, introducing the crimes, and the last page dictating the sentence, remained. Vhalla snapped the book shut and took a deep breath. *Were some truths better not to find?*

She stood, resolute. She'd long since banned lies in her world. It was time to make sure Jax Wendyl understood that fact.

CHAPTER 19

THE DAY WAS hot. It already felt like the late days of summer in the South, but spring was barely upon them. Vhalla's cheeks were flushed by frustration as much as from the weather.

The guards and soldiers parted before her as she stormed through the grounds. The bottoms of her split skirt brushed upon the hard-packed, sandy dirt, wind flying under her toes. Vhalla clenched and unclenched her fingers.

"Major Jax," she called the moment she spotted his high bun among a group of soldiers performing drills.

Jax paused. Aldrik had trained her well because Vhalla didn't miss the flash of panic in his eyes. Her expression had instilled the appropriate amount of concern in him. *Maybe this time it'd be enough for him to tell her the truth.*

"Why, Lady Yarl, been some time. And here I thought you'd forgotten about little ol' me," he chuckled.

"Not quite." She folded her hands at the small of her back. "I require you."

"That's what they all say." Jax gave a lecherous wink to a nearby soldier, who laughed uncomfortably.

"In there." Vhalla pointed to a castle entry, a gust of wind unlatching and opening a door.

Jax followed her orders, and she followed him into the privacy of the small storeroom. Her hands were nearly shaking as she eased the door shut, trying not to slam it.

"As much as I appreciate your Western-clad beauty, I feel obligated to tell you that the men will talk." Jax leaned against a table, adjusting his high bun.

"Why are the records missing?"

Jax froze. His hands slowly fell from his hair. Vhalla watched as the madman began to take over.

"What records are you asking about?"

"Don't play coy, and don't lie to me. Your records," she snapped.

"I never lied to you."

"How dare you." The hurt was real. It was just as bad, perhaps even worse, as Jax's original tale. "You told me I could trust you with my life, and you didn't trust me with your truth."

"I did not lie." The man gripped the table, digging his nails into the wood. "Don't chase this."

"You did. I know you did," she insisted.

"You drew your own conclusions, and I didn't correct them." Jax slapped the table and stood upright. "Now leave this be."

"No." Vhalla moved in front of the door. "If you are my friend, you will tell me."

"Who said I wanted to be your friend?" Jax snapped back. "Let me leave, Lady Yarl. And don't go chasing ghosts again."

"I will not!" She had such precious few people in the world. The idea of losing Jax to old crimes immolated her senses. Their friendship would only be salvaged if he could trust her.

"Why don't you just ask Aldrik?" Jax was suddenly unable to look at her.

"I want to hear it from you." Vhalla lifted her hands, trying to calm them both. "I need to hear it from you."

"You already heard what I had to say. I owe you nothing more."

"You didn't kill her, did you?" Vhalla rested her hands gently on his upper arms.

He flinched at the touch. "I did," Jax insisted, but his resolve had fractured just enough that he continued. "But I never meant to."

"What happened?" Vhalla prodded gently.

"Nothing that should have."

"Was it an accident?" She tried to tilt her head to meet his eyes.

"Partly."

"Tell me please," Vhalla whispered. "I want to help you."

His shoulders began to tremble. Vhalla thought he was crying, but mad laughter echoed hauntingly into her ears. Jax wrenched himself away, throwing out his arms. "Oh, oh you siren. You wretched wench. I see now, I see now how you ensnared Aldrik." Jax pointed his finger in her face, and Vhalla was too startled to react. "You think you can save everyone. You think you're a damned Goddess, glowing high above the masses who cower at your feet. You think you can fix the broken and heal the wounded because you *want to.*"

Fire sparked around his finger, close enough that Vhalla's nose was nearly burned.

"You want to know something? You-you misbegotten noble, you are as bad as every other who has stepped before you. You are pathetic, useless, inept. You can barely defend yourself, and you think you can defend those you love."

Vhalla leaned against the door. She endured his insults, his raving. She held her head high and waited out the madness.

"I can help you." Vhalla had never believed anything more than those four words in that moment.

"You can't help! I couldn't help!" Spit flew from his mouth, landing on her cheek. He raged on, "She could not help herself as she ran into the flames to save her father. To save that worthless sack of putrid flesh that didn't deserve to die a clean death of fire."

"Her father?"

"Yes, her *father*, you simpleton!" Jax lunged for her, and Vhalla's head cracked against the door hard as he shook her by the collar. "What would you have done? Tell me. *Tell me!* They knew, they all knew, and they didn't stop him!" he howled. "A father is meant to protect his young, to love them. But not like that. Never like *that*."

She blinked away the stars from where Jax had knocked her head. He was right, he hadn't lied to her. He'd said he'd discovered a man with his bride-to-be, a man who had taken her multiple times. But it hadn't been just any man. Vhalla felt sick.

"You were trying to save her."

Jax growled and threw her to the side. He leaned against the door, his head hanging between his arms. His back heaved with his rasping breaths. "Go . . . go and never speak about this ever again."

"Jax, it wasn't—"

"Go!" Fire flared over his shoulders as he spun, its heat making her blink water from her eyes. "If you ever speak of this to me again, I do not care who you are, Vhalla Yarl, I do not care what clothes you wear, or what title you bear. *I will kill you.*"

The man had been pushed far enough. Vhalla took a deep breath and waited for the fire to disappear. It left a dark burnt spot on the ceiling.

"I'm sorry for hurting you and making you recall this." She rested a hand on his shoulder and looked him in the eye when she said it. The contact stilled him and panicked him once more. But it was a different kind of panic, something more akin to a lost child than a lunatic.

"I said go," Jax demanded.

Vhalla obliged him and stepped back into the sunlight of the dusty training ground.

She ignored every look from the soldiers, unashamed of her

activities with Jax. There were some things that, as Empress, she didn't have to explain. Vhalla didn't want to exercise her authority often or without good reason. But this qualified as a good reason.

Vhalla escaped their eyes and started up a small stair that wound straight up to the king's and queen's—or now the Emperor's and Empress's—chambers. She made it several steps before she stopped to catch her breath, leaning against the wall for support. Her knees trembled, and her arm couldn't seem to support her. She slid down the wall and sat on the steps, her chest heaving for air.

She'd gone hunting for the truth, and she had finally found it. *But what did she do with it?* Aldrik had said that he'd put Jax's life into her hands. That it would fall to her to pardon the man or let him continue on with his service.

After meeting all the lords and ladies, Vhalla knew that the West valued tradition above all other things. They saw Jax as a fallen lord; pardoning him would likely earn their ire. But Vhalla didn't want to keep him under her command by holding a leash that she didn't think was necessary.

Though, did Jax even *want* to be pardoned? Was justice still just if it went against the person's fundamental wishes? She had so many questions but not a single answer.

Vhalla pulled herself off the floor. There was someone else she hadn't fielded thoughts from. Someone who had just as much noble training as Aldrik. Someone else who'd been born to lead.

She knocked on Elecia's door and waited.

"Enter," the woman called.

Vhalla obliged and was surprised to find she had company. "Fritz? What're you doing here?"

" 'Cia is teaching me how to play carcivi." He pointed to the board that sat on the low table between them.

" 'Cia? Does everyone get to call you 'Cia but me?" Vhalla joined them in front of the open window.

"We'll see if I ever deem you worthy," Elecia joked back. She studied Vhalla for a long moment from the corners of her eyes. "So, future Empress, why are you here when I'm fairly certain you have other far more important people to be meeting?"

"I wanted to talk to you."

"Me?" She seemed surprised that Vhalla would seek her out.

"Yes. I want your advice," Vhalla affirmed.

"What about mine?" Fritz squinted at Vhalla, making a show of pouting.

"Yours is always welcome, Fritz." The Southerner would add a completely different perspective from someone who wasn't of the West and wasn't nobility either.

"Don't you have an Emperor you could ask?" Elecia ignored the carcivi board entirely now, giving Vhalla her full attention.

"I do, but I know what he'll say. I want to know what you'll say." Vhalla gave the skeptical woman a small smile. "What kind of Empress will I be if I ignore some of the best counsel available to me?"

Elecia seemed surprised. She tapped on one of the carcivi tokens for a moment in thought. "Very well, what is it you seek?"

"I spoke with Jax." Vhalla let the weight of the interaction with Jax pull down her voice, taking the smile off her cheeks with it.

"I see." Elecia heard everything Vhalla had hoped for.

"I know the truth now."

"He told you?" Elecia seemed surprised. "The truth? Not one of his colorful lies that he uses to scare people away?"

"He told me one of those first." Vhalla wanted to put to rest any confusion over what she really did or did not know.

"And you got the truth out of him . . ." There was a concerned glint to Elecia's voice that Vhalla affirmed with a small nod. *Got the truth out of him*, that was a good way to put it, because it certainly hadn't been graceful. "So, if you know, what do you need from me?"

"What are you two talking about?" Fritz reminded them both that he was still there.

Vhalla and Elecia shared an uncertain look. "Fritz—" they started at the same time.

"Fritz," Vhalla took the lead. This was her responsibility now. She was the one who had dredged it up, she would be the one who would handle it. "Jax is owned by the crown as a punishment for a crime."

Fritz didn't seem shocked, but his expression told her clearly that this was the first time he was hearing it put so simply.

"But the crime, however heinous it seems on the surface, isn't what it appears. He's innocent."

"Not quite," Elecia interjected with a heavy sigh. "He did kill the lord—"

"But, given the circumstances—"

"I understand that." Elecia held up a hand, indicating that she now had the floor, and Vhalla would wait to speak. "But that fact remains. And while that murder may have been in the defense of another, he killed the lord's wife and other child in cold blood."

Vhalla wouldn't quite have described Jax's blood as *cold*. "But only because they knew what was happening."

"Even still," Elecia shook her head. "It's all a gray area mess. When his betrothed ran into the fire, his emotions were too far gone to stop the flames. He's not as guilty as he makes himself sound, I'll grant you that, but he's not innocent either."

"Did he—does he—feel sorry for it?" Fritz asked.

"Somewhat," Elecia conceded.

"Why does he lie about it?" Vhalla quickly corrected herself, "Or tell half-truths."

"To save her memory." Elecia looked out the window, avoiding eye-contact for what may have been the first time in her life. The woman's voice was soft, almost gentle, contemplative. "He loved her deeply, and he would rather endure people scorning him than try to clear his name at the cost of letting the world know how she had been violated. And the only one who knows the real truth of what happened that night is Jax; he's the only one alive to tell the tale. The rest of us who know certainly won't violate his trust by doing so."

"Do you believe him?" Fritz stole the words out of Vhalla's mouth.

"I do." Elecia returned physically and mentally to the group. "When I first found out, I went to Aldrik, who pointed me to Erion. He told me how Jax had hand-picked through the char for her bones, carrying them in a box along with his confession, begging for a proper Rite of Sunset."

"What would you do if you were me?" Vhalla outright asked Elecia. She didn't bother explaining herself further because she knew she didn't really need to; Elecia's expression told her as much. The woman was smart; she knew full well the power and nobility that Vhalla was marrying into.

"I am not you, Vhalla Yarl," Elecia said after a long second of contemplation. "I have grown up in a world of rules and regulations. I have been taught what can and cannot be done from the moment I could speak my first word.

"You, you are not so chained. And so you see the world with eyes that I could never have. You have hopes that no one else would allow themselves to even dream of." Elecia gave the tiniest of smirks. "Forgive me, but I wish not to sway your actions in this matter. I want to see what you will do. I want to know what kind of Empress you will be."

CHAPTER 20

I WANT TO *know* *what kind of Empress you will be.*
The words repeated, again and again, in Vhalla's mind the closer the wedding neared. She would be Empress. There was no more denying, dodging, or burying the fact under obligation. Her calendar soon became filled with as many wedding planning details as it was with audiences and war councils, and it drove her mad.

At least with the audiences, Vhalla could smile through the necessities knowing that she was working toward strengthening their army. When it came to picking one fabric or another for a dress, Vhalla couldn't care less. She felt as though it did nothing but take her away from actually being useful.

It put Vhalla on edge, and her annoyed, frayed nerves didn't do anyone any favors.

"What do you mean, we can't do anything?" She couldn't stop the words, just like she couldn't keep herself from glaring at the map before her.

The continent was covered in multi-colored figures, each representing civilians, military, Victor's forces, and just about every other factor that could be an influence in the happenings of the world. It reminded her of all the times she had mentally thought of nobility as a game. Well, now the pieces were spread out before her.

"It simply doesn't make sense," a lord answered. Vhalla had forgotten his name already, and she could imagine quite a few colorful titles to fill in the blank.

"We are to just ignore them? To forfeit? That is no small portion of the East. Victor's hold will go from a quarter to nearly half."

"But they are just farmers; they don't offer anything with regards to military strength or stalling the false king's army. They are already lost," a different major remarked, almost casually. It wasn't until her sharp inhale and cold stare that he realized where he had just placed his foot.

"Forgive me, major." Vhalla tried to keep her voice even. She did not want to sound like a petulant child, but a noble lady. "They are certainly *not* just farmers."

"Lady Yarl, I did not mean to offend you or any of your noble kin." He gave a small bow of his head.

Vhalla wanted none of it. His fake sincerity was as valuable to her as coal in the face of diamonds.

"Very well. Lord Ophain," Vhalla began boldly, pointing to the West's border with the South. "If I understand your major's logic correctly, then these towns should be considered lost."

"M-my lady!" the major balked.

"They are just some mining towns, no?" Vhalla knew the West's terrain by now like the back of her hand. She could possibly list more cities and towns than even some of the nobles in the room. So she continued, not letting her rhetorical question hang too long. "Do they offer anything to our military strength?" The twenty or so nobles around the table were silent. "Then let us pull back any defense that is currently there."

"That is the West!" Another joined the conversation with his impassioned declaration. "The West protects its own. I will not stand for this."

"And neither will I." Vhalla silenced the murmurings of the

table, her words quick as a whip. "It's easier if it is not your own kin; I understand that truth." Vhalla paused, staring at the map for a long hard moment. "But the real truth is this."

She plucked a quill from an inkwell and began to cross out and scribble over the lines on the map between the East, West, South, and North. Vhalla triumphantly returned the writing instrument to its place. She smiled briefly at the map that the majority of the room now considered ruined.

"These are your kin." She motioned to the whole continent. Vhalla looked at the assembled lords and ladies, most of which were twice her age and possibly had three times her experience on the field. Almost all had olive-hued skin and darker Northern tones. She had to speak to her audience and make them understand. "Each of you are part of this Empire. I witnessed every person in this room kneel before our Emperor and swear your lives and your futures to his hand. He is not *your* Western King, but *our* Emperor. Your brothers and sisters are here in the West as much as they are in the South, East, and North. If you truly believe that the West looks after its own, then that should extend to all those under the light of Solaris."

Vhalla glanced at Aldrik from the corners of her eyes. He'd let her lead through the majority of the exchange, as he had done when it came to anything involving the East. But his expression was difficult to read.

"I want to assure you that I understand the sacrifices war can, and will, demand of those engaged in the bloody business. I know that not everyone can be saved." Vhalla tapped on the map. "But I will not stand by and allow lives to be written off carelessly—no matter where those lives are—because it is more convenient when it is not a place that you were born into."

"Bleeding heart Easterner," someone mumbled.

"Out," Aldrik snapped suddenly. Given the fiery stare he

was giving one particular major, Vhalla suspected he knew the source of the insult.

"My Emperor, I—"

"Out." Aldrik's voice took on a dangerous quiet that Vhalla knew well. "I will not have you speaking to my intended that way."

"Aldrik," Vhalla interjected. "It's all right."

"Vhalla, he should not be permitted to say such to you." His eyes darted between her and the major.

"If he is to say such things, then let him say it where my ears can hear, rather than as a coward behind my back." Vhalla spoke loudly enough for the table to hear, only pretending to be speaking to Aldrik. "But I want him to stay so that he knows I ask nothing of him that I am not prepared to give myself. I will protect the East, South, West, and North as though they are all my family. I only ask the same of those I fight with."

Vhalla appreciated the few nods of approval she received. The man in question had the sense to look at least moderately ashamed by his outburst. Under the table, Vhalla felt long fingers curl around hers in support.

"Shall we continue?" she prompted the group.

"The question remains, how to manage our troops?" Another major pointed back to the map.

"We can send some additional aid to the East; granted, it will weaken our own borders."

"If we spread these out here," Aldrik moved some red soldiers along the West's southern line, "it should give enough to spare."

Vhalla stared at the black figures indicating Victor's forces. They were fewer, but they were spread wide, and growing. Every time a soldier fell, Victor leveraged the corpse by turning it into a crystal-walking abomination. Vhalla tried to put herself in the mind of the madman: *what would he do next?*

"If we move those troops, we can expect at least these two towns to fall." Another set of hands moved the pieces.

"We could send some from Norin," another suggested.

"No, he will likely make an attempt on the Imperial wedding." The idea was shot down. "What's the word on the North?"

"The North is just now marching. Princess Sehra has moved ahead to show her support for our union, but the main forces will not reach the Crossroads until just before we are set to arrive," Aldrik answered.

"We're keeping troops here for the wedding?" Vhalla thought aloud, her introspective considerations slowing her response.

"Certainly," Aldrik responded. "It is a public affair. There should be little doubt that Victor knows of our pending nuptials, and he will use it as an opportunity to strike us down or remove all joy from the people's symbol of the continuing Empire."

You are a symbol. Baldair's words from long ago returned to her, and Vhalla loathed them. She was tired of being a symbol. Symbols were stagnant, frozen, representative, and spurring of action but never the action itself.

Vhalla looked at the map with new eyes. They were playing the part that was expected of them by nobility, and while they did, they were a predictable target for their enemy. The wedding kept troops from moving.

"This could be the chance for us to strike first," she said suddenly.

"What?" Aldrik spoke the surprise of the table.

"Victor expects us to be rendered immobile for the ceremony. It makes more sense for him to use the wedding as an opportunity to pick off half our forces spread across the Empire than strike us directly." Vhalla moved some of the dark wooden sculptures and tokens along the East and pushed them into the West.

"However, if we attack in force now, when he least expects

it . . ." She quickly shifted their tokens of war, pushing them down through the Southern border and into the weak point of Victor's army at the bottom of the West. "We can move before he has time to react. We can punch a hole straight for the capital."

"We cannot change the date of the wedding now." Aldrik turned to her. "There are still arrangements to finalize, lords and ladies who have yet to arrive."

"We can do something small, say our vows and be done." The war was more important than a grand ceremony. "Or, we could even keep up the wedding for appearances, making our attack even more of a surprise."

"Vhalla, there are certain expectations," he replied with a careful glance at those assembled. "The ceremony is not an option."

"I am sorry, but I did not realize my wedding was dictated by the nobility of the realm," Vhalla snapped. Aldrik's eyes widened slightly, and her face instantly relaxed, apologetic. She hadn't meant to be so sharp, not to him.

"My lords and ladies, please excuse us a moment." Aldrik's eyes didn't leave hers as the entire room shuffled out, leaving the Emperor and Empress alone. "Vhalla, what are you doing?"

"Aldrik, it makes perfect sense." She motioned to her play with the tokens on the map. "This is an advantage; it's a chance at deception. If we wait, Victor will only become stronger, and we'll be playing into his expectations."

"In theory." Aldrik spoke before she had finished exhaling the last word. "But I can tell you what is not theory—the fact that those lords and ladies, whom you seem so ready to insult, give us their gold and supplies to pay for our army's needs. We cannot shun them."

"They should look at what we are doing and understand that we are trying to put their gold and loyalty to good use, rather than losing what could be a key advantage to formality," she countered.

"We have already announced one thing; nobility and people will lose faith in our word if we do anything different." Aldrik frowned.

"Not if we win." Vhalla shook her head. "All will be forgiven when Victor is dead."

"So you hope." Aldrik leaned on the table with a sigh. "Vhalla, you don't understand. Noble families hold grudges like no other. Nothing, no slight, no matter how small, is ever forgotten."

"If we go on as planned, we may not even have subjects to be angry at us."

"You do not know war," Aldrik muttered.

"I know war better than most, Aldrik Solaris." She rounded in front of him. The insult had lit a tiny flame in her that Vhalla struggled to keep under control. "I have spent the past three years of my life at war. I have been utilized as a weapon and coveted as a tool. I have killed countless men and women. And while I may not have made as many hard choices as you for as many years, *do not tell me I do not know war.*"

Aldrik stared at her in surprise before pulling his eyes away with a touch of shame. Vhalla hadn't intended to make him feel guilty for his role in the events that had put her in a position to experience war. Reaching out, she took his hand gently in hers, trying to soothe the tension.

"I know you," she whispered. "I know you well enough to know you think I'm right."

"Were things not as they are, yes, yes, your theory holds merit." Aldrik sighed heavily. His hands held her face, underscoring the tenderness. "But there are so many forces at play here. And, sometimes, the safer course is the best one. Let us do this one thing right."

"One thing?" She didn't understand.

"I-I took you to bed for the first time on sweat-stained sheets in a war camp. I took you because I promised myself that I would make you mine properly one day."

"I had not thought poorly of our first time together." Vhalla stepped away, pulling her face from his palms.

"Then I shamed my love for you by allowing myself to be engaged to another. By allowing that engagement to push you away."

"You saved my life with that engagement." Vhalla wondered if he had somehow forgotten the sword at her throat when his hand was forced to sign that fateful paper. "And I acted harshly towards you that night as well. It's forgiven and forgotten."

"I let my family and those beneath me witness my stealing you away when Bal—" his voice cracked. He cleared his throat to continue, "—when Baldair died. I let you become the other woman, the prince's whore."

"There was hardly enough time for anyone to know with all that happened after," Vhalla contested. "Any who would remember are friends or will long forget when your throne is restored."

"I asked you to remain mine when I had no future for you, and I vowed to do things right." He reached for her hands, holding them tightly. "I have yet to live up to that vow."

"Aldrik, you have not wronged me." She tried to smile encouragingly.

"Then, the baby."

She bristled at the words. A chill ran up Vhalla's spine, triggering uneasiness in her mind. It was like magic across her flesh, reminding her of what happened, of the murky night that was being lost to time—that she *wanted* to lose to time.

"I know it was the Mother giving us a chance to do things right. To not harbor a child in secret or rush a marriage to make it a legitimate heir."

"Our marriage was already rushed." Ice water ran through her veins. "It was not the Mother who lost our child, it was—"

"Hush. Please, Vhalla, just listen to me." He squeezed her fingers encouragingly. "I want to see you as my bride and do this one thing right. I want this wedding."

"Aldrik, this wedding is nothing more than a formality of something that already lives between us." Vhalla sighed in frustration. "It doesn't matter when and how we marry; we know our bond."

"It matters to everyone else."

"I am not marrying everyone else!" Her patience cracked. "I am marrying you, and your thoughts and my thoughts are the only thoughts that matter on the subject. I am not going to put my own wedding before the lives of our people. How can I look at them when there are innocent people dying, and I am keeping soldiers from saving them so that I may say some vows?"

"I will not have them whisper rumors of you as they did of my mother." Aldrik pulled away and pinched the bridge of his nose in frustration. "I will not have them speak more poorly of this than they already do."

"Speak poorly of this?" she repeated.

"Enough."

"No." Vhalla rounded him as he tried to avoid her stare. "What do you mean, 'Speak poorly of this'?"

"It does not matter."

"It does," her voice rose a small fraction with her insistence.

"Fine." Aldrik scowled. "Fine, you infuriating woman. You want to know of every uncertainty presented by the Western lords and ladies to me or my uncle? How you are too thin, too wild, too risky, to be trusted with carrying an heir? How you have won yourself above your station by giving the lonely prince what is between your legs? How you are too young, too soft, too inexperienced to lead? How I should have taken a Western bride, or even kept the Northern one, to strengthen ties and support my armies? How I am a fool's Emperor for taking a no-named commoner as my bride? How you are only with me for power and gold?"

Vhalla stared at him in shock. *She'd been kept completely unaware.* That burned more within her than the shame and embarrassment of the accusations.

"Were you going to tell me?" she whispered.

"Vhalla—"

"Were you going to tell me?" The dam broke within her. "Or were you just planning on keeping me in the dark? Were you going to prove them right, that I am too soft for the truth, that I am ignorant and unfit to be your Empress? Because not even you trust me with what is said!"

"Vhalla, you prove them wrong just by being you. I did not want you to worry and change." Aldrik's voice already sought her forgiveness. Forgiveness she didn't want to give.

"Were you going to tell me?"

"I don't know." He withdrew.

"Fine." Vhalla glared. "Since you clearly have such a handle on managing what I can and cannot hear or think, see or do, then you can just manage your wedding and your war as you want."

"Vhalla! Vhalla!" he called when she was halfway for the door.

"But if we wait on this wedding, you can make my dress crimson. I will not wear gold if my Imperial nobility is bought with the blood of innocent civilians who died while I had a party." Vhalla glared back at him once more. She never heard if he said anything else because she slammed the door on his attempt at further words.

Vhalla stormed up the castle alone.

CHAPTER 21

HER CHAMBERS IN the Western castle were opulent. Low platform beds covered with expertly woven silks complemented endless polished floors that picked up the shine of gemstones and silver embedded into the ceiling. Warm, summer-like breezes flooded the room through open windows, blocked only by chiffon curtains and tall pillars.

It was an exercise in excess by the original architect and decorator. A decadence that Vhalla should have every right to appreciate, an experience that she could never otherwise have.

But now it felt cold.

She hadn't been spending her days in these chambers; hiding there now only served as a reminder of the harsh words she'd spoken to Aldrik. She'd actually retreated here because she knew it was the one place that he would not come. The lord's and lady's quarters were across the hall from each other, and while Vhalla heard his door open and close, he made no effort to seek her out.

Not that she blamed him. Or perhaps she did. The man did an excellent job at making her feel so justified one minute, only to have her feel wildly conflicted the next.

After pacing ruts into the floor, Vhalla decided that lingering wasn't going to solve anything. She undressed quickly, rummaging through the virtual mountains of clothes to find something simple. Riding leggings that were no doubt intended to be worn underneath a skirt were paired with an oversized shirt that Vhalla fashioned as a tunic. It was certain to horrify the staff and Western nobility. But apparently her existence was already offensive, so she might as well be comfortably offensive.

On the way down to the training grounds, Vhalla walked on air, fluttered pennons, and played with the wind. She delighted in everything that she had taken for granted in the years prior to losing her magic. Things that she would never let be taken from her again.

Fussing with the tail of her braid, Vhalla entered the training ground. Here was another relationship she had ruined with harsh words and pushiness. She wasn't sure if she was ready to see Jax again—or if he was ready to see her.

"Where is Major Jax?" Vhalla asked the first woman to cross her path on the dusty field.

"Major Jax?" the woman repeated. "I think he's training with sorcerers in the pit."

"Can you show me?" Vhalla folded her hands at the small of her back, quickly releasing them when she remembered how imposing Aldrik looked while doing so.

The young woman bowed deeply and stiffly guided her future Empress. More than one soldier gave pause and looked at her. Vhalla wondered if it was because she was the future Empress, or as a result of her prior run-in with Jax. *She knew how soldiers talked.*

The pit was exactly as the name suggested. Recessed into the ground and hexagonal in shape, the large fighting arena had all kinds of people at its edge cheering or shouting suggestions to two Firebearers sparring within. Jax was situated on one side, shouting with the rest of them. But he was one of the last to quiet and turn as her presence was noted.

"Major Jax." Vhalla swallowed the silence between them before it became far too obvious. "Could I perhaps join in a spar or two?"

He stared at her a long moment, looking her up and down. Where Vhalla expected the average Westerner to look disapproving at her relaxed and more masculine clothing, she found Jax's stare appreciative.

"If the lady wants a spar, than a spar she will get!" Jax's voice had not changed at all. It was back to how she'd always heard it: jovial, jesting, and entertained with the nature of existence. "Which one of you wants the honor of going against the first Windwalker in nearly a century and a half?"

No one moved. No one seemed able to look at her. And, most certainly, no one volunteered.

"Come now," Jax encouraged. "Ren, you're up!"

The man who Jax tasked with this duty appeared to be of Northern descent. Vhalla assessed him as she was helped into a leather jerkin, coated in something sweet smelling. She recognized the greenish sheen as something the Northerners used to protect against Firebearers.

"Ready?" Jax called. Vhalla gave a definitive nod, but Ren gave a hesitant glance. "Go!"

Vhalla wasted no time, and the man was on his back in an instant. Vhalla stared dumbly as Ren stood, gave a bow, and quickly retreated from the ring.

There hadn't been a single spark of fire, chill of ice, or rumble of earth. Vhalla frowned. He'd not tried to attack her in any way.

The next soldier Jax threw at her acted much the same. A quick start and quick finish left her uncomfortable. As the dust settled atop the third, Vhalla couldn't contain herself any longer.

"Why won't you spar with me?" she demanded of the woman who pulled herself off the ground.

"What?"

"What was that?" Vhalla persisted. "You didn't even fight back."

"I-I-I . . . your prowess is such that none of us could hope to match." The woman retreated awkwardly, eager to escape the ring.

Vhalla's arms dropped limply to her sides. *They were letting her win.* Vhalla had been through war and had trained under a multitude of soldiers, but she no longer had the Bond to draw from, and these people had been soldiers the majority of their adult lives. Vhalla should at least have to struggle against them.

"Oh, this just won't do," Jax admonished. "You sorry lot have done the worst thing someone can manage: disappoint a pretty lady." He pointed across the pit toward something Vhalla couldn't see. "Fritz! You're needed."

Vhalla's heart soared from just hearing her friend's name. The second he actually stepped into the ring, Vhalla was nearly tackling him in an overpowering embrace. She wondered if Jax had figured out her mental state upon entering the training grounds.

"Vhal, it's only been two days since I last saw you," Fritz laughed.

"It feels like forever," Vhalla insisted.

"Well, now I'm going to beat you up!" Her friend grinned.

"You can try!" she retorted playfully. "Jax, thank you; this is exactly what I needed."

"Oh, Lady Yarl, I always give the beautiful ones what they want." Jax winked.

Vhalla rolled her eyes playfully and returned her attention to Fritz. "I don't want you to go easy on me."

"I've seen you fight," Fritz snorted with amusement. "The last thing I'm going to do is go easy on you."

She was unsurprised when Fritz bested her right away. Vhalla was rusty, and she'd forgotten all the tricks this Waterrunner kept up his sleeve, from ice daggers to illusions. They went two out of three, and Vhalla could only get the upper hand once. It was satisfying. She was certain her losses weren't just a result of her own lack of training but because Fritz had improved.

Jax scolded everyone watching by pointing out how Fritz hadn't held back, despite going against their Emperor's betrothed. Vhalla gave a supportive nod when Jax explained that the best soldiers fought with everything they had, every time. He shot her one wary look from the corners of his eyes. Things had not quite gone back to normal between them, despite how experienced he was at faking it.

Vhalla pulled her friend from the training grounds. They wove up through the palace and made their roost around a table in the library. Along the way, a servant noticed them, and Vhalla sent for tea and candied lemon peels.

"Aren't you supposed to be doing audiences or some such?" Fritz finally asked.

Vhalla sighed heavily.

"So the afternoon war meeting gossip was true?"

"News travels that fast?" Vhalla gave in without struggle.

"Some majors came to the grounds while you and Aldrik were talking," Fritz explained.

"I made a real mess of things, I think." Vhalla collapsed back onto the pillows and stared up at the library that stretched above her. She longed for the days where her biggest decision was what book to read first.

"Even if you did, Aldrik is still over the sun for you and you know it," Fritz spoke while chewing through a lemon peel. He was on his fourth one. "That means everyone has to love you."

"I don't want forced love." She couldn't help but think of Jax, still strapped to his obligations with the crown. What if his display on the grounds was because he had to tolerate her?

What if he hated her but was still obligated to protect her? The notion made Vhalla sick.

"You're going to have it—and don't give me that look." Fritz flopped next to her. "You won't ever have everyone love you, just as you won't have everyone hate you. Find the right people to love you and return the hatred of others with ambivalence or hatred of your own."

"Since when did you become so philosophical?" Vhalla twisted to consider her friend.

"I've always been brilliant, and you know it." Fritz kissed her nose lightly.

"You have been." Vhalla's eyes fluttered closed, and she enjoyed Fritz' simple closeness. "Thank you for staying with me."

"If you ever had doubts, I'll scold you." She could feel him considering her thoughtfully without needing to see his eyes running over her face. "What is bothering you, really?"

"I'm going to be married so soon," she whispered. "What if I am not meant to be Empress?"

"Who is meant to be anything?" Fritz sat. "Are you worried because of the mutterings of a few crusty nobles?"

"You sound like Jax." She opened one eye to grin up at her friend.

"There are worse things. Jax is cute." Fritz gave a little smile at the idea.

Vhalla kept her mouth shut, wondering where his heart would lead him after Grahm. Surely, the man he had known and loved had died with the fall of the Tower. There wasn't any other likely scenario. Vhalla couldn't imagine Grahm kneeling to Victor.

Fritz didn't say anything about his love either, and they let the memory of their friend rest like so many others who were at the capital during Victor's takeover.

"I think," Fritz hummed, "that you should leave the castle."

"What?" Vhalla sat as well, stuffing two lemon peels into her mouth at once.

"You and me, let's go out." Her friend was on his feet. "No one has to know; that way they won't make a fuss."

"Fritznangle . . ." Vhalla cautioned. It wasn't as though she was trapped, but she was already publically shirking her duties for the day.

"I think it'll do you good," he encouraged. "When was the last time you were around *real* people? Not soldiers or nobles? Those are the people whose opinions really matter, Vhal. Sure, nobles are important and support the crown. But you know who supports the nobles? The common man. So stop hiding in your literary roost and come out onto the street."

Vhalla allowed him to pull her to her feet.

"Plus, I really want to see the Port of Norin, and Elecia still hasn't shown me." He gave her a conspiratorial grin that was too infectious not to return, and they were off.

The main street stretched out from the castle, the street that they used to enter the city and reach the castle. It looked far different without the masses crowding it. With the normal ebb and flow of people, it reminded her of the Crossroads as merchants and patrons alike lingered under large sun shades.

They'd barely made it off the main street when she was finally noticed. Every peddler and shop owner wanted her to try something, wear something, or simply "bless their shop" with a breeze. Vhalla obliged with smiles and did her best to accommodate everyone. If Fritz was frustrated by the slow going, he didn't let it show. He seemed equally enamored by the dried dates, strawberries, mangos, and all manner of exotic fruits. By the end of just one street, they both had new necklaces of braided leather and bellies full of sweets.

The castle loomed over them, barely visible between houses

and towering high above the canopy of fabric that lined every stall. The farther she stepped from the place, the better she began to feel. Fritz had been right; this was what she'd needed. She needed to feel welcomed by the people, to see the blazing sun framed by two wings, and to forget about obligations and duties for just a little while.

The houses of Norin began to grow as they neared the harbor. Stores became richer and more elaborate, each competing for the attention of shoppers milling through the honeycombed streets and lavish squares. Live models posed in store windows, slowly changing pose to show off the fabric or cut in a new way. There were jewels as big as her fist, and Vhalla eyed the skilled craftsmanship of one shop, stopping long enough to be recognized by its owner—Erion Le'Dan.

With that, they gained a local guide for the rest of the day. Erion told them interesting notes of history and facts about the wealthiest nobles who lived around the harbor. He even gave his own take on the largest port in the world. But no amount of explanation or reading could have prepared Vhalla for what awaited at the Great Port of Norin.

Ships upon ships were docked as far as the eye could see. Some Vhalla recognized from reading, large hulls and wide sails with endless lengths of rope hanging and coiled about their decks. Others were strange and foreign. Some were long with flat oars sticking from the sides. Farther down the docks sat boats with sails that looked like the fins of a fish, pointed and folding like a fan.

Some vessels were in dry dock, supported and suspended mid-air. Workers scrubbed the hulls, repainting and repairing as necessary.

Others ships were leaving to make space.

Somehow, in the bustle of Norin's mecca of trade and commerce, even the future Empress could go unnoticed. Burly men carried chests up and down gangplanks. Nets full of fish were hoisted from cargo holds and dragged to shops, where the fish were then butchered and sold. People of every shape and color went about their business as if the world was as it had always been.

War did not affect these people, Vhalla realized. Famine, religion, nobility, or turmoil, it did not change their lives. One thing reigned supreme, and everything else fell around it: gold.

She expressed such thoughts to Erion over an icy cocktail, a red dragon, while they rested their legs.

"That's astute of you," Erion praised her without any apparent ulterior motive. "Because these men and women have little care for who is in power. They'll work for the highest bidder."

"Is that how your family is?" Vhalla asked. The question struck a surprising cord, one she hadn't expected.

"Do you think so?"

"I can't say I know your lineage well enough to have an opinion."

"Don't dodge the question," Erion scolded lightly.

"There must be a nugget of truth." Vhalla could blame the alcohol for her loose tongue. It'd been months since Vhalla had really drank, mainly out of respect for Aldrik's continuing struggle to avoid alcohol in times of stress. And while she wasn't about to lose her head, the liquor had a welcome burn. But she didn't use the likely excuse.

No, her loose tongue was entirely the fault of the sun, the warm sea breeze on her cheeks, and the freeing sensation of not feeling like the world was on her shoulders. "You seemed very quick to support me in the North."

"Fair enough." He raised his glass in acknowledgement of her point. "Any family who has thrived for as long as we have didn't do it by strapping themselves to dogma. Even if you were chosen by a Ci'Dan, that Ci'Dan happened to be the Emperor's

Elise Kova

crowned son, and supporting you could support us in the long run."

She laughed at his candor and let the fact lie, picking something else that had been nagging at her to focus on. "Then why does dogma seem so important to the Western Court?"

"This has been bothering her," Fritz outed.

Vhalla shot him a look that he just grinned away.

"They want to see what you do when rules are imposed upon you. They want to push you and see if you break," Erion answered easily. "They're testing you, Vhalla."

"But how do I pass? Do I do as they ask? Do I thwart them at every turn?" She honestly was at a loss.

"You're thinking too small." Erion hummed, looking out over the port. "You see all these ships?"

She nodded.

"When do you think they come and go?"

"When they have somewhere to be?" She assumed the merchants had deadlines and the rest were chartered.

Erion shook his head. "When the wind is good," he answered his own question. "All that rigging and lumber and men, it's all at the whim of the wind. Now they try to tame it, they try to control it. They have created hulking sails and innovative drafts to cut through the water as quickly as possible. But they remain at the whim of the wind. A force that cannot be understood, nor explained, for it just happens."

The lord looked back at her, but Vhalla had already processed his point.

"They are the ships, and you are the wind. You do not lower yourself to their rules or expectations. You blow in whatever direction you feel is needed and leave them with no choice but to oblige."

Vhalla thought about Erion's words as they finished slowly strolling through the port. The only thing that distracted her was when he pointed out a particularly colorful vessel. She noted that it was a trade ship from the Crescent Continent, an uncommon sight even for the grandest port in the world. Vhalla wanted to investigate further, but that was the one thing Erion advised against. He cautioned that the people of the Crescent Continent could be quite backwards and barbaric, and it was best to leave any dealings to their approved liaisons.

Vhalla held her tongue that "backwards and barbaric" were often times only used when one culture didn't properly understand another. She had heard people describe the North that way before she'd come to properly understand a region of the Empire that she now held in deep respect.

By the time Fritz and Vhalla returned to the castle, the sun hung low in the sky. The stable hand who had helped them tack the horses earlier in the day reported that the Lord Ophain and the Emperor had inquired about where they had gone. Whatever the lad had said must have been sufficient because neither had launched any kind of search.

Vhalla bid farewell to Fritz and ended her walk in silence. She eased the door open to Aldrik's room, uncaring if there was a servant walking by who saw her entering the Emperor's chambers. She was done with their propriety. She wanted to see the man she loved.

Taking her shoes off at the door, Vhalla walked on small pockets of wind, avoiding making a sound. She stopped the second Aldrik came into view. His hair was still styled for the obligations of the day, and he sat facing the hearth. He had an empty cup by him, but no sign of a bottle anywhere that could betray what its contents may have been.

Gathering her resolve, she walked as silently as possible around the couch upon which he sat. He had one leg bent, his lower calf resting on the thigh of his left leg. A book was open, but Vhalla could see no sign of ink or quill. He was researching lightly or reading purely for pleasure, judging from his lack of note-taking supplies.

Dark eyes rose slowly and froze upon seeing her. Those eyes that glittered and were wonderfully illuminated by the fire. Across the world and all the time that had passed between them, those eyes could still hold her in place.

"Aldrik—"

"Vhalla—"

"Go ahead," she encouraged softly.

"Did you have fun in the city?" he finally asked.

"I did." Vhalla nodded and watched the flames flicker and dance upon the marble hearth. No fuel for their blaze crackled, and the fire felt warmer knowing it was his.

"I'm glad." Aldrik returned to his book.

Was that all there was? No, she took a step forward. That could not be it. They could not pretend away this impasse. She could not let the day fade away in a manner that widened the gap forming between them since their arrival in Norin.

Vhalla crossed the distance between them and knelt at his feet.

"Vhalla—" he sighed tiredly.

"Listen." He leaned back in the chair, clearly unamused at being interrupted by her yet again. "Listen, please. If you listen, I will listen to what you need to say, I promise."

Aldrik motioned for her to continue.

"I need you to know that I trust you." Vhalla looked at the book in his lap as she spoke, as though the mere sight of it could bring her support. "I know I am not well versed in interacting with the society that our marriage will require I interact with. And I know full well how that can make a mess. The truth is, Aldrik, I don't care about the ways of nobility."

He was about to interject but she continued too quickly.

"But I care about you." For once, Vhalla pierced him with a

stare. She felt that exhilarating sensation of looking right into him and seeing his inner mechanisms. "I am the wind, Aldrik, but you are the compass point to which my passions gust. And I will learn to be perfect for you."

Vhalla shifted, her legs falling asleep beneath her. Aldrik placed both feet on the floor, moving the book. The unspoken invitation was accepted, and Vhalla rested her cheek on his thigh. His long fingers wove through her hair, and Vhalla could not stop the contented sigh that escaped her lips.

"I don't want perfect," Aldrik uttered. "I will never be perfect, and I will never deserve perfect."

"But I can try."

"Why?" He chuckled deeply. "Vhalla, we will always have our tiffs; even the best couples do. What matters to me is that you come to me and I go to you. That we embrace love more than hate."

"Everyone around me is so philosophical today." She shook her head in amusement.

"My Vhalla." The long pause drew her eyes open. Aldrik waged a mental war with the fire, the flames flashing and dimming a few times. "I moved some troops. The borders will receive further support."

"How?" Vhalla straightened.

"I forfeited the defense that was remaining here in Norin for our wedding."

"But—"

"The city will remain defended," he inserted the answer before the question could be asked. "But there will be no extra. The more I thought it through, the more I felt you were right. Victor will attack from the south and continue to push his line of influence before trying to jump straight to Norin. He'll chip away at our strength while we wed. So perhaps we can give him a small surprise with the new placement of force."

"Aldrik . . ." She struggled to find words.

"We will march shortly after the wedding." A glint of desperation appeared in his eyes, one she had never noticed before. "I have already sent word to the princess's mother, beseeching her to have their warriors waiting for us in the Crossroads. We will end this war soon enough."

"But first." He took his hands in hers, leaning forward. "My Vhalla, my lady, my love, please marry me properly. Not for the appearance for the nobles or the war. Marry me because—" Aldrik looked away, and Vhalla swore it was only the red of the fire on his cheeks. "Because I want a proper wedding for us."

It was then she realized what a fool she'd been. Certainly politics was a factor, but Aldrik truly wanted it. More than anything, he wanted a ceremony, and he was clearly doing all he could to appease her enough to earn her consent.

"I'm sorry, Aldrik."

"Tell me, what else can be done to reassure you? If you want a red dress, then it shall be so, but can we not make it for a better reason than—"

"This isn't about colors of dresses." She laughed weakly. "I'm sorry I never realized how much it meant to you."

Aldrik's lips parted in surprise, and his brow relaxed. Aldrik looked away, suddenly bashful. With just her fingertips, she guided his attention back to her.

But Vhalla was hungry for more than just his attention. Her lips met his before any more words could be exchanged. A low growl rumbled up his throat, a sound she harmonized with, full of yearning. Vhalla stood slowly, prolonging the kiss as much as possible.

"Come," she whispered over his lips.

"Vhalla . . ." his voice was low and dangerous in a way that made her knees weak.

"Come," she repeated, guiding him with a tug on his hands.

The book fell from the Emperor's lap as he rose to meet her. It may have been the first time in her life that Vhalla let a book fall without frantically checking to see if any pages were bent. Aldrik's arms pressed her against him. One kiss, one step, and they made their way toward the bedroom.

They were perfectly imperfect. Vhalla knew they would fight again. She knew fire and air had a tendency to burn hot. But she wouldn't have it any other way. For tonight, she would beg for their flames.

Chapter 22

VHALLA ROLLED OVER, groping at the bedside table. Her fingers searched for something wooden, round, and heavier than the rest. It rolled away, and she stretched with a groan.

"Trouble?" Aldrik shifted, loosening his hold on her waist.

Picking up one of the vials, Vhalla inspected its lack of stopper and cast it aside with a hollow thud. "I wouldn't have trouble if half of them weren't empty," she muttered. "Why are they all still here?"

"We can't really discard so many without raising suspicion."

"You're a Firebearer." Vhalla rolled her eyes, even though she couldn't see her face in the dim light of the room. "*Burn* them."

"You and your logic." Aldrik finally gave up on the unspoken idea of going back to sleep and sat up, burning every empty vial she tossed into the air. Vhalla scattered the ashes with a gust of wind.

Elixir of the Moon had been something that Elecia was all too prepared to provide since the events of the night at the Crossroads. In the eyes of the court, they were still playing the role of proper man- and wife-to-be, keeping their separate sleeping quarters until their wedding. But more often than not, Jax slotted himself for the night shift, a shift he made sure was scheduled until late mornings. Even more mysterious was the fact that he didn't show up half the time, which was noted without comment.

Downing the foul liquid in one quick gulp, Vhalla tossed the vial with a grimace. It exploded in a final burst of flame before hitting the floor. She barely had time to scatter its remnants when an arm pulled her against a very naked man.

"Are you pleased?" he hummed. His voice was deep and throaty with sleep.

"With what?"

"With everything."

Vhalla thought for a long moment before replying, as was their morning ritual. "As pleased as I can be until we finish with our wedding and can march once more."

"Soon." He nuzzled the base of her neck, his lips brushing over what must be the makings of a bruise. "Tell me what it looks like."

"My answer was no last night, and it is still no this morning." Vhalla laughed breathily at the way his morning stubble rubbed against her chin.

"I will see it tomorrow." He was making every attempt to convince her to spill the details of her wedding gown. And if the revelries of the night before couldn't, then his kisses in the morning certainly wouldn't.

"Yes, you will." Vhalla wiggled beneath him and freed herself.

"Stubborn." He rolled onto his back with a small grin.

"You love me that way."

Vhalla was the first to escape the bed, which ended their escape from the world.

Following their small tiff about their wedding, they had discovered that no matter how bleak the world was, if they wanted to survive, then they had to savor the things that gave them joy. So each morning they woke and pretended they were nothing more than two lovers enjoying the dawn. Vhalla had felt guilty about it at first. But it made them stronger as a unit and put them in a better place to lead their people.

The second part of their new morning ritual was to go through the letters and notes that multiplied in the night while they slept. They would alternate reading them aloud over breakfast, once more just the two of them, and would decide together where they stood on matters. At the same time, Vhalla would go over her notes from the previous day's council. They were regularly corresponding with Sehra now, which gave Vhalla hope that their support from the North would arrive in time.

Her efforts to utilize more silent smiles amid the nobles was paying off. She wore out her quill with notes about what to discuss with Aldrik in private. This habit didn't stop her from interjecting her thoughts into those public discussions, but it was improving her diplomatic relationships. She also found it helped her organize her thoughts better, so that when she did speak she did so with more tact.

Aldrik had taken to doing the same, which surprised her, and it helped them present a unified front on all matters. The first comment of praise had come through Elecia, saying Vhalla seemed more reflective in meetings.

But the time Vhalla could spend in meetings had been shortening as Lilo and Tina began to buzz more with wedding preparations. They were frustrated on more than one occasion by her lack of opinion, but Vhalla told them that she was content doing things in the traditional Western fashion. The things that mattered most to Vhalla was that she and Aldrik wed, that Aldrik was content, and that they could move onto fighting their war.

However little it had mattered to her, Vhalla still woke on her wedding day with a small family of butterflies in her stomach. Music wafted up from the streets, and the revels began long before the ceremony. Vhalla woke alone so that there was no risk of the wedding preparation crew discovering her in Aldrik's bed—she was really growing tired of *that* façade.

Fritz kept her company throughout the day, and Elecia played messenger between Vhalla's and Aldrik's rooms. Vhalla inquired as to what Aldrik was doing as she prepared; she was certain he was not having his face powered ten times over. Elecia informed her with a dramatic eye roll that Aldrik was on a mission to pace the room until his shoes had to be replaced.

The wedding was set for midday, when the sun would be at its apex, which left little time for anything else. As Vhalla's gown was undergoing the final pinning around the hem, and the last embellishments were being stitched on, her aunts-to-be graced her with their presence. Tina eyed Vhalla up and down, passing silent approval.

"You look like a Solaris Empress," she finally spoke.

"That's what I'm supposed to look like, isn't it?" Vhalla smoothed her hands over the skirt. Golden silks draped in the Southern fashion underneath a more Western-styled jacket that went from her hips all the way to her neck, capping her shoulders.

"It is."

"We have something for you." There was an odd mix of excitement and sorrow in Lilo's voice. "However, it is silver, over the Imperial gold."

The older woman motioned for a servant to bring forward a medium-sized box. Vhalla watched in curiosity that quickly turned to awe as it opened to reveal one of the most beautiful crowns she'd ever seen. Diamond-shaped rubies hung from delicate pointed archways that rose from the base of the crown. The silverwork around the brow looked more like lace than metal. It was delicate, feminine, beautiful, and strong in equal measure.

"She would have wanted you to have it." Tina's usually steely tones had gone soft as well. "Fiera was not one to change who she was. Even when she married an Emperor of the South, she wanted a crown of silver."

"So, this crown truly is . . ." Vhalla looked between the women in shock.

"Our sister's, Aldrik's mother's." Vhalla had never seen a more joyfully heartbreaking smile than what Lilo wore on her lips. "She was the Empress this realm needed, if only she'd lived to fulfill that role."

"But she gave us Aldrik. And hopefully he has brought us an Empress who will be worthy of picking up my sister's crown." Tina's words left little doubt on what she truly thought of Vhalla.

"I will be," Vhalla swore.

"Good. I would expect no less." The older woman gave a firm nod.

Eventually, Vhalla and the crown were left alone. Aldrik's aunts talked with her for a little bit longer, but they left shortly before the last servant. Vhalla sent away all remaining help, preferring the company of her thoughts in her final moments as an unmarried woman. It wasn't that she was nervous about her and Aldrik. The time for such things was long gone. Their perfect imperfection, constantly striving and pushing each other to do better, it would be her life's mission and joy—with or without crowns and vows.

The sound of the door opening again brought Vhalla back to reality. Her eyes met a pair nearly identical to her own, and Vhalla gave her father a small smile. Rex Yarl had been dressed up in Western fashions, but styled in Eastern purples. She had to stifle a laugh fueled by nerves at the sight of her father so polished.

"Little bird." He opened his arms, and Vhalla went to him without hesitation so that he could wrap her in a tight embrace. "You're beautiful."

"Thank you." Her mouth had filled with cotton, and she was suddenly terrified she'd forget her vows. "You clean up well yourself, for a low-born, Eastern farmer."

They shared a knowing laugh at what had been used against both of them.

"Well, this farmer's daughter is about to marry a man befitting her status."

Vhalla's heart threatened to explode. In her father's words, Aldrik was vying to be worthy of her, not the other way around. She leaned up and kissed him on a clean-shaven cheek.

"Was Mother nervous?" Vhalla whispered. Her parents had nothing but love for each other; in Vhalla's mind, they'd had nothing to fear going into their union.

"She told me so the second we had said our vows before the Mother." Rex offered his arm to his daughter. "Every chance worth taking will make you a little scared. That means you're taking a risk. And where there is risk, there is reward."

Her father rode with her in a closed carriage to the Cathedral of the Mother. Vhalla remained out of sight from the prying eyes of the public. Her hand never left her father's as her heart threatened to choke her—it felt like it was beating in her throat instead of her chest.

Vhalla waited in a small antechamber with her father. She could hear the talking of people through the gilded doors before her muffled like it was a world away. She was about to cross the threshold to a place she thought she would never see, to be with a man she should've never met, to become someone she was never meant to be. The room fell to a hush, and Lord Ophain's voice boomed through the following silence.

She took a deep breath as the doors swung open before her, and Vhalla didn't look anywhere but forward. Her hand gripped her father's elbow so hard that she'd have to apologize for bruises later. But, for now, she would just focus on being the Empress the people needed. Love, war, life was a series of battlefields strung together with the courage to march forward.

A sculpture of the Mother reaching out her arms, holding a giant fire that lit the entire room, dominated the center of the dome above. Men and women packed the large hall, blocking out the imagery of the Father depicted in the lower part of the room, that showed how he yearned for the Mother above. Vhalla walked toward a circular marble space where Lord Ophain waited next to a cowled Crone.

Aldrik entered from the far side of the room, descending a grand stair from the domed ceiling. The fire flared brighter as he made his entrance, arcing around him as though he was hand chosen by the Gods to be their leader.

The men and women who sat on the wooden risers along the outside of the room whispered. Their whispers traveled unhindered on the wind to her ears. *How dare this Eastern commoner marry their Emperor?* A smile carved into Vhalla's lips. She'd let them have their words. No matter what she did, they would talk. Today was hers and Aldrik's, and she wasn't even going to let thoughts of others trouble her.

The Emperor paused for half a breath as their eyes met. It was silent acknowledgement of the precipice upon which they stood. They were the most unlikely of pairs who had travelled an extraordinarily unconventional path.

Vhalla wanted to run to him.

They met before Lord Ophain and the Crone, mirror images of each other. Vhalla's dress was gold, trimmed and embroidered with suns in white. Aldrik's clothes were white, lined with gold up along his trousers and at the top of his large cuffed sleeves.

There wasn't a scrap of black on him, other than his raven hair. For the first time, Vhalla realized that by wearing white, he didn't look like a sign of defeat. It didn't look like a color he'd worn to appease his father. It didn't look like something he was forcing himself to do for his people. It was as natural to him as the replica of the sun crown that was settled upon his brow.

Her father extended her hand, and Vhalla's palm practically leapt to meet Aldrik's. Her fingers hooked around his, and he half pulled her a step. In a complete lack of form, Aldrik drew her knuckles to his lips, giving her a satisfied grin as he shocked the court. The rest of the world vanished for one blissful moment, and Vhalla savored the fact that she was *indeed* going to marry the man who had so claimed her heart.

Lord Ophain cleared his throat softly, pulling them both back to reality. The crowd wore looks of surprise, accompanied by whispers. Vhalla gave the tiniest of smiles when her eyes fell on Fritz, and he risked breaking his wrist with his frantic, not so subtle waving.

"It was here, upon this spot, where our last Emperor married our princess, my sister," Lord Ophain began his opening remarks, addressing the crowd. "The West lives in the blood of the Empire, and our Emperor is one of our own. And, while unjoyful events have led him to being our Emperor so young, the circumstances of this world have seen him to our most sacred of halls for yet another Imperial union.

"I have long since born witness to the lines that connect our Emperor, Aldrik Ci'Dan Solaris, with the Lady Vhalla Yarl." Lord Ophain's focus rested upon them, and only them. He produced a scroll from his jacket pocket for emphasis. "It is with the blessing of the West, East, and North that this union will be the foundation upon which a harmonious Solaris Empire may be rebuilt."

Vhalla followed the direction of Lord Ophain's nod. Za and Sehra returned the motion. *They had made it.* The acknowledgement wasn't lost on the other nobles in the room, and Vhalla contained a sigh of relief.

"Eons ago," the head Crone began to speak, "the Father lived in a land of eternal night. It was in that darkness that he met the

Mother. She was a brilliant star, a point of light that cut through the night like a sword of law and order. It was with her dazzling radiance that she brought the day."

The Crone raised her wrinkled hands, and the fires that hovered above burned even brighter.

"The Mother could not live with the Father in that world of night, and he could not live in her world of day." The Crone dropped her hands and motioned to the stone floor beneath them. "So they began to spin in an eternal dance, one where they could look upon each other from the beginning and until the end of days. In this dance, their children were born, and the first men walked upon the new earth.

"The Mother watches over our lives, bringing us life and joy. The Father watches over our timelessness, seeing us safely into the lands beyond." The Crone produced a long red ribbon from within her sleeve. "From our births to our deaths, we are bound to the plans which they have laid. We walk the red lines they have given us."

Vhalla resisted the urge to shift uncomfortably. She wondered what the Crone would say to someone who had changed their fate. Or if the very notion that fates could even be changed would be blasphemous. Vhalla wondered if, perhaps, just perhaps, Vi had been wrong from the start. If every last thing had been as Ophain said, the red lines of fate that the Mother had laid. *After all, who could change things, like time and fate and futures, other than the Mother herself?*

"By this, it is not for us to question those who are called to each other, just as it is no more our place to question those called to greatness. To do so would be an affront to the divine." The Crone's voice was powerful in its frailty. "From the highest nobility to the lowest of common, we are no different from each other in the Mother's eyes. We are all threads in the same great weave."

The Crone stepped forward. With gnarled fingers, purple

veins spider webbing under the thin skin of their backs, she wrapped the red ribbon around Vhalla and Aldrik's outstretched hands.

"Vhalla Yarl." The faceless Crone turned to her. "May the Mother bless you with the greatness of her warmth." She wrapped the ribbon again and turned to Aldrik. "Aldrik Ci'Dan Solaris, may the Father bless you with his resolution."

The Crone carried on in this manner, binding their hands after every blessing. The Mother was to give Vhalla beauty, kindness, and many heirs. The Father was to give Aldrik strength, determination, and foresight. Vhalla had the distinct feeling that he was getting the better end of the bargain, but she held her tongue. They'd practiced the ceremony enough times that she knew every stage of what was coming.

"Vhalla Yarl, what do you pledge to your Emperor?"

"I will be yours," she spoke with raw and delicate earnest. "I will be faithful to you. I will be yours from this day, and every day, into eternity."

"Aldrik Ci'Dan Solaris?"

"I will be yours," Aldrik replied. Vhalla's eyes widened a fraction. He'd gone off-script. It was slight, and he quickly returned to the expected words, but it had been there. He had offered himself as much to her as she had to him. It was a subtle statement, but a statement nonetheless. "I will shelter you. I will protect you. I will keep you as my own, as my Empress."

"These vows have been said before Gods and men," the Crone continued, as though Aldrik's modification hadn't even happened. "May they never be broken, and may these two never prove unfaithful to the words that have been spoken.

"Should the Mother above bless this union, may she touch this couple with her flame. Should the Father above bless this union, may the Mother's flames leave their skin unmarred." The Crone raised her hands.

A golden flame sparked at the short bottoms of the ribbon wrapped around their hands. Vhalla held Aldrik's hand tightly. Her fingers already bore burn scars, and she could endure the pain for formality's sake.

But the fire did not burn her. It consumed the ribbon, but only licked lightly on their skin. It was true magic, a type she had never seen before.

"With this sign from the Gods themselves, you are now united as one, husband and wife. May your life, and reign, be one of light," the Crone announced.

Just like that, it was done. The crowd burst into fierce applause, and Vhalla blinked as if returning from a trance. Even if it was just for appearances, the masses seemed happy. They celebrated. And, for that moment, Vhalla, too, allowed herself to pretend that the world wasn't at war. That they wouldn't march out at dawn.

"Vhalla, kneel," Aldrik whispered.

She swallowed hard and adjusted her skirts. Falling as gracefully as possible to one knee, she suddenly felt more nervous than she had all day. Aldrik released her hand slowly, making sure she was stable, before turning to his uncle.

The box Lord Ophain held was of no surprise to Vhalla. But, judging from the look on Aldrik's face, it was a surprise to him. His hands paused, hovering mid-air just before opening the box.

"Uncle . . ." he breathed.

"She would've wanted it," the lord insisted.

Aldrik's long fingers ran over the top of the box before settling on the latch and opening it. Reaching in, he produced the same glittering crown Vhalla had seen earlier. Clearly, some of the nobles recognized it and were all too eager to tell their friends in the near vicinity all about the important history of the relic.

"Lady Vhalla Ya—" he caught himself. "Lady Vhalla *Solaris*."

Hearing her new name was quite a strange, yet wonderful, sensation.

"Wife of the Emperor, common born and nobly appointed." Aldrik lowered the crown upon her waiting brow. The moment his fingers vanished she felt the weight of it upon her head. "Rise and stand with me—as Empress Solaris."

Just like that, the world changed. Aldrik held out both hands before her and helped her to her feet. Vhalla stood, not as a common-born library girl, a soldier, a sorcerer, or a lady, but as an Empress.

If the cheers for their wedding had been loud, the cheers for her coronation were near deafening. It was as though the people truly believed that, by having a whole royal family again, they stood a better chance against the madman in the south.

"My Empress." Aldrik gripped her hands tightly, a beaming smile threatening to break through his trained decorum. "Ascend with me."

Vhalla walked at his side up the stairs that he had descended earlier. She held her skirts with one hand, his hand in the other. She was terrified but hopeful. And all she wanted was him.

The door at the top of the balcony closed behind them, and the sound broke her trance. Vhalla found herself in a dimly lit hall, alone with the man who was now her husband. There were no words for the joy, the triumph. Vhalla threw out all necessary decorum and forced the Emperor against the door.

Her mouth crashed against his, and Aldrik's arms closed around her waist. They had done it. In spite of it all, they had found each other. He tasted of pure elation and of something much sweeter, something she hadn't dared even breathe in for some time: *hope.*

CHAPTER 23

"Sooo," Jax drawled from the end of the hall. "You two skipping the party?"

Vhalla pulled away, grinning wildly. She still had his jacket balled in her fists. His hands were halfway under the upper layer she wore overtop her skirts.

"What do you think, Empress?" Aldrik cocked his head to the side with a small grin.

"I think we are our own party."

Aldrik laughed and pressed his lips against hers. Vhalla returned his kiss in earnest. Though she couldn't commit to it fully due to the sensation of someone else's eyes.

"Jax, are you . . . just going to stand there?" She fell back down onto her heels.

"It's not every day you get to watch your sovereigns put on a show like two raging teens." Jax leaned against the wall, his arms folded across his chest. "Since it's in a public place, I figured that meant you didn't mind spectators. Or maybe you'd finally take me up on my offer of a third."

"Oh, by the Mother." Vhalla rolled her eyes and finally stepped away from her husband. "I suppose we should go."

"If we must." Aldrik's cheeks held a faint rosy flush.

The rest of the royals and highest nobility were waiting

for them in a small antechamber. Tina and Lilo both pressed their cheeks to hers in modest signs of affection. For the West, however, they were overt displays. Ophain welcomed her to the family as well.

Vhalla was momentarily distracted by Aldrik and her father sharing a brief familial embrace. He had lost his family in the South, but, in their own way, they were rebuilding anew. She hoped that her father could be someone Aldrik felt comfortable with.

Her eyes shifted towards foreign whispers. Za and Sehra stood a few paces away from everyone else, talking between themselves.

Vhalla crossed over. "I'm glad you could make it."

"Are you?" the princess asked thoughtfully.

"I am," she affirmed. "It was an important display for the Empire." Vhalla didn't mince words. She knew the princess wouldn't want it, and there was no longer time for it.

"You seem to be settling into your crown already, Lady Empress," Sehra praised.

"The crown has little to do with it. I am no longer interested in fronts. I want action."

Aldrik walked over, placing his palm on the small of her back.

"Emperor Solaris." Sehra gave a small nod of her head, the most subservience the girl had ever demonstrated.

"Princess Sehra." Aldrik mirrored the motion. "How did you find the ceremony?"

"Long and needlessly cumbersome, as I find most things in the South to be." She gave the tiniest of smiles. "And one that I am very glad I was not forced to be at the center of."

Vhalla should be offended, but she found herself amused. "Join us in the carriage?" she asked as they started for the large doors out of the cathedral.

"I would think those just married would seek some time alone," the other royal hummed.

"We have had ample time to be alone. I am much more interested in speaking to you regarding the status of the North's armies and any strategies you may have for reclaiming the South." Vhalla readjusted her crown as the doors to the cathedral opened.

They lost the ability to converse due to the deafening cheers. Aldrik's fingers remained entwined with hers as the Imperial couple waved at the gathered masses. Firebearers sent tongues of flame toward the heavens, and Commons waved pennons. With the world at its most beautiful and his hand in hers, for a second, it was a perfect dream. But Vhalla had yet to earn her happily ever after, if there was one to be had after the long march South.

Sehra and Za entered the carriage first and settled as Vhalla and Aldrik continued to smile and wave. Za was awkward with her bow and quiver, tools that never left the warrior's side. Vhalla and Aldrik navigated around them while they took their seats.

"We have amassed an army of three thousand strong from Norin and the surrounding coastal cities," Aldrik said, wasting no time in bringing Sehra up to speed on the most recent numbers. "That will join with another fifteen hundred from around the Crossroads and the East."

"So then we will have nearly five thousand in total," Sehra summed up gravely. It was a number that most strategists would be pleased with. But the princess's emerald eyes still carried weight.

"What do you fear?" Vhalla asked.

"These men, they're green. We have spent much time using our best to kill each other that we are now lame before a real force," Sehra replied. "The earth quivers before this man's magic.

Even in Yargen, the trees shudder and cry out. He is tapping into something great."

"That is why we will move as fast as we can." Vhalla glanced at Aldrik, who gave an affirmative nod. They'd fulfilled their obligations to the nobles and secured their crowns and their armies. "Our army is set to march in three days' time."

"My warriors will arrive at the Crossroads in five."

"Then forgive me, princess, because I know you have just arrived, but I will ask you and Za to ride ahead and meet them. The Western nobility will feel more at ease if they know the Northern army's leader is present to keep them under control."

"You think Shaldan people need keep under control?" Za frowned.

"No, I—"

"Peace, Za." Sehra rested a hand on her guard's knee. "She is worried for perception, not reality. The Southern peoples yet fear our might."

Vhalla didn't correct Sehra. She was truthfully afraid of the Western lords looking for any reason to pick a fight with the people who had been their enemies only months ago. Vhalla knew men and women whose sons and daughters had died in the Northern campaigns. If Vhalla and Aldrik could send letters in advance informing them that the North had an appointed and native commander who was holding them accountable, it would help keep the chain of command streamlined and respected.

"We will rest for two days at the Crossroads to replenish stock and rest the horses," Aldrik said to no one in particular.

"Then I will tell my people that they will expect to move in about two weeks' time," Sehra reasoned. "Have you plans to get through his walls?"

"Was there a crystal one to the north?" Vhalla frowned. Sehra nodded. "How did you get through it?"

"I used the power of Yargen," Sehra replied, as though that fact would be obvious.

Vhalla accepted it at face value. When the war was over, she was going to ensure she sat down and learned exactly what the power of Yargen was and how it worked.

"But that will not work in the Waste. It is too far from the old trees."

"I see." Vhalla adjusted her crown, the jostling of the carriage threatening to throw it off her brow. "Aldrik, has anyone scouted south?"

"We can send someone. It should take—" he was cut short as the carriage came to a sudden stop with a loud whinny.

"Tainted!" Vhalla heard someone scream. "She's tainted!"

A commotion rose outside the carriage. The four inside shared a brief look before bursting out the doors. Vhalla clenched her fists, prepared for whatever she was about to face.

A group of people blocked the path to the drawbridge of the castle. They surrounded a single horse and rider. Guards lined the drawbridge, swords drawn.

The rider looked as though she had come a long way. Her body was frail and her clothes threadbare. Her shoulders heaved, and her hands shook. Vhalla's eyes lingered on the woman's hands. Black veins bulged under the skin, as though trying to break through. Old cuts lingered open, having turned raw and leathery rather than healing. The woman raised her face. What was once Southern eyes had been turned nearly entirely red.

"Take," she rasped. "Take me—to Vhalla Yarl."

There was something about the voice that cut deep into Vhalla's consciousness. Something that was familiar in the most terrible of ways. To everyone else, the woman looked like a tainted monster. Blackened gums receding away from lengthening teeth, blood red eyes and gnarled hands—it all made for a terrifying picture.

But Vhalla mentally smeared away the blood and decay. She imagined the woman's eyes to be blue and her frame thicker. She imagined her hair was not matted and, after a wash, would be blonde. But not the fair shades of blonde. A darker shade, one that could almost pass for Eastern.

"By the might of the Mother, we will smite you down," a guard boldly proclaimed.

"Wait!" Vhalla stepped forward, and the crowd melted away from her.

Heat registered next to her as fire crackled around Aldrik's closed fists.

"What do you want with Vhalla Yarl?" she asked the familiar creature.

There was a delay, and the tainted woman swayed. She looked as though she was about to make an effort to dismount, but gave up halfway through. Her body fell to the road below with a sickening thud.

"Vhalla, stop." Aldrik caught her wrist, stopping her from running to the prone creature. "Don't go near it."

"It's Tim." *At least, she hoped it was.*

Shock relaxed his jaw, and Aldrik looked between the woman he held and the one unmoving on the ground. He squinted, trying to see what she had seen. Vhalla didn't have time for it.

Wrenching her arm from Aldrik's, she sprinted over to the prone woman, stopping a step out of her reach. The taint was even worse close-up. It looked as though the very thing that was holding Tim together had somehow turned sour, and now her body was falling apart from the inside.

"Timanthia?" Vhalla breathed.

No one made a sound.

The woman struggled, gasping for air through bleeding gums and black saliva. She half snarled, half cried, as she tried to will her body to move. Vhalla knelt down, hearing Aldrik's footsteps behind her.

"T-take it. Take it. From him. I came. For you," Tim's voice crackled and rasped. She raised an arm weakly.

Vhalla's hands closed around silver. She felt the etchings along the outside of the bangle, familiar and almost warm to the touch. It was scratched and scuffed. But it was undeniably the token Larel had given to Vhalla years ago.

"Listen to. Listen, and help them," Tim pleaded. She gripped Vhalla's skirts, blinking away bloody tears that poured over her cheeks. "Take it and kill me."

"Can nothing be done for her?" Vhalla whispered to no one. She was unable to tear her eyes away from the other woman's face. At the grotesque shade that had been cast upon what was once beauty.

"She's too far gone," Sehra responded.

Vhalla wanted to scream. She had a thousand questions. How had Tim made it to Norin? Why had she come? How had she survived, and what had she endured? Vhalla needed hours to dissect all the information locked within Tim's story. And all she was giving Vhalla was a bracelet. Vhalla carefully twisted the bangle and slipped it off while holding Tim's wrist steady.

"Lady Empress, I don't think it wise—" the highest ranking guard began cautioning.

"I did not ask what you thought." She put the jewelry on her own wrist and slowly returned Tim's arm to the woman's side. Vhalla stared down at the face of suffering. *This was what their time had cost.*

They were partying, while their people were dying.

Vhalla caressed Tim's cheek gently, unafraid of crystal taint. Sorrow was being smothered by anger, by pain. She didn't want to cry. She wanted to end it all, once and for all. She wanted to see that there never was another day, ever, where crystal taint would be feared.

"K-k-kill..." Tim's lower lip quivered overtop her unnaturally shaped teeth.

"Tim, thank you." Vhalla's hand shifted to cover the woman's mouth. "Thank you."

Just enough magic, just enough to turn her insides to liquid. To shred her lungs and tear through her heart. Wind roared under Vhalla's skin and poured into Tim. The woman shuddered and the second her neck burst Vhalla withdrew her palm.

Everyone looked on as the Empress slowly stood. Vhalla balled her hand into a fist, blood dripping between her clenched fingers. Vhalla raised her voice for all to hear.

"We march at dawn!"

CHAPTER 24

"**M**Y LADY, THE army can't possibly march at dawn." One of the majors tried to catch up with her as she strode through the castle. "That's not enough time."

"Find time," Vhalla demanded unapologetically.

"We need more supplies, carts are still being packed, and—"

"Essentials first, everything else second. The climate will be temperate in the West; we can forego some of the bedding now and pick it up at the Crossroads for the South. We'll send word ahead on what we need." Vhalla glanced at the party that developed around her. "Tina, please write to every Western lord and lady between here and the East demanding that supplies be sent to the Crossroads."

"Major . . ." Vhalla didn't know what the man's name was and didn't care enough to wait for him to say it. "Go with Lady Tina and help give instructions on everything we may need."

They crossed through a series of inner gardens and back through another slew of halls before Vhalla broke out to the training grounds. She held up her hand, imagining she was winding a ball of wind in its center. The sky screeched briefly with the noise of the unseen twister she created, summoning every soldier's focus.

"Men and women of the Solaris Army." The woman in the golden dress, silver crown, and blood-stained hand captured their attention. "For too long we have sat quietly. For too long we have talked about preparing. For too long we have practiced. And I am no exception."

Vhalla held out her dress, uncaring for the blood she smeared on the gold fabric. She hadn't expected to be so right when she'd told Aldrik that she'd wear the blood of their subjects. "I have fulfilled my duties as a noblewoman at the cost of my duties as a soldier."

She never thought she'd identify as a soldier.

"No more." Vhalla had no idea who was behind her, listening to her words. She only remained focused ahead. "Tomorrow, I ride with the dawn. I make for the Crossroads and for the South. I march to put an end to the false king.

"The lords tell me that there is not enough time, that you are not ready." Vhalla held out her arms, beseeching. "Is this true? Are you not ready to reclaim your Empire?"

They objected with a swift and powerful, "Nay!"

"Good. Go now, and do what you must to ready yourselves. I only want the best at my side!"

It was like she'd kicked an ants' nest. The soldiers began running, quickly organizing themselves under their own ranks. Majors stepped forward to bark quick orders.

Vhalla turned. Aldrik stood at her side, his mouth made a firm line.

"Let us get into more fitting clothes for war," he suggested.

Their momentary escape from the growing madness was unquestioned, and they quickly ascended away from the chaos to what was now *their* chambers. The morning of preparations and nerves was gone. In its wake came renewed purpose.

"Aldrik," she started as soon as the door closed. "I know you likely do not approve."

"Vhalla—"

"But we have lingered long enough." She held out her hands. Vhalla wanted him to understand. "We are ready for this. Sehra is ready. Every moment we wait is another death."

"Vhalla—"

"I know you can't speak against me publically, but give me counsel here. I will not back down on this, but I want to know how you think we should go about it."

"Vhalla." He took both her hands firmly and silenced her. "I support you."

She blinked. "You do?"

"I wouldn't have proclaimed it in the street. I may have pushed in private." Aldrik shook his head. "But we have done things as I wanted. You are Empress now, and your word holds just as much weight as mine, publically. I will let you lead this war."

"We will," Vhalla amended. "It is not *I* or *you*, it is now *we*. We will, for our people."

"Don your armor," he suggested as they broke apart to dress. "At least the chainmail. It will set the right mindset."

"Help me from this?" Vhalla asked as she was half sewn into her dress.

Aldrik obliged, chuckling softly. "This was not why I imagined I'd get you out of your dress on our wedding day."

"My Emperor, there will be ample time for such things at a later date." Vhalla rolled her eyes, hunting down clothes substantial enough to go under her chainmail. Vhalla paused, staring at the bangle Tim had given her.

Take it. From him. Listen.

Vhalla stilled, trying to logic through what Tim's presence had really meant. Her emotions cooled, and her mind spun. She had clearly been trying to deliver the bracelet to Vhalla. Listen; that could mean that Tim wanted Vhalla to pay attention to her. *Unless, it didn't.*

She was a blur from the room, not even bothering to put on her shoes.

"Vhalla!" Aldrik called after her, confused.

Fritz had been at the wedding with Elecia, but the castle was now in utter chaos. Still, she had to start somewhere, and it seemed just as likely if she could find one of them she'd find the other.

"Where's Elecia Ci'Dan?" Vhalla demanded of a guard between panting breaths. "Have you seen her?"

"My lady?"

"Elecia Ci'Dan?" she repeated.

"I've not seen her . . ."

Vhalla muttered a curse under her breath and started for the Westerner's room. They weren't there, and they weren't in Fritz's either. Vhalla finally found them on the training grounds helping organize and prepare.

"Fritz!" Vhalla practically tackled the man as she tried to pluck him out of a stream of people walking in the opposite direction.

"Vhal? Vhal, what?" Fritz teetered and regained his feet. "Are you all right? I heard what happened and—"

"We need to listen to it." Vhalla held up the bracelet.

"Is that?" Fritz recognized it instantly, but he didn't believe it.

"It is," she insisted.

"How can you be sure?" He looked skeptical still.

"I know one way we can find out." Vhalla pressed the bracelet into Fritz's hands. "We need to listen to it again."

"Nothing will have changed."

"Fritz, please," Vhalla pleaded.

He finally obliged, and they went to the nearest vacant guest room, stealing the washbasin from within. Aldrik caught up with them along the way, and Vhalla offered a short explanation as to the importance of the token.

"This may not be the best of ideas." The Emperor was suddenly uneasy as Fritz placed the bangle into the water. "It may be from Victor. There could be magic within it that will activate when it is tampered with."

"No," Vhalla insisted. "If Victor was going to attack me with it, he would have done so when my hand first came into contact with it. I know what crystals feel like, and that does not feel like crystal magic."

Though, if one of Vhalla's two theories were correct, they might hear Victor's voice.

"It will be fine." Fritz's words were braver and more certain than he sounded. "Larel would never hurt me."

Before any further objection could be made, his fingers dipped into the bowl. The water rippled, and they all held their breath as Fritz drew the words out from the vessel. *Listen*—that had been Tim's dying wish. Vhalla braced herself for what she was about to hear.

First, a familiar voice filled the room. It was the same as Vhalla and Fritz had heard an eternity ago. Larel's words of encouragement and hope, echoed through the room, and Aldrik's fingers slipped between hers. He had never heard the message, and Vhalla watched from the corners of her eyes as Aldrik listened to the farewells of his first true friend.

The last words faded and silence followed. Just as Fritz was about to pull his hands from the water, a new voice began to speak. Vhalla had braced herself for the mad voice of a man drunk on crystal magic. But what she heard instead was harder to handle.

"Vhalla, if you are listening to this, then Tim made it." Grahm's voice echoed across the water. It was weak and thin, whispered as though his lips were brushing right across the bracelet itself when he recorded his hasty message. "Tim, she—they-they did things to her. Anyone with a wing meets such a fate, or worse. We tried to get her out, but she was lost, she volunteered. She wanted to get our message to you before you left Norin.

"We've heard word that you will be our Empress. You and our Emperor rose from the dead; you're the only one who can stop him now. You have defied him once; you can teach us all how to do it."

Guilt burdened her heart. Her perceived resurrection was giving the people in the South a false hope. She was not their savior. She had been the one who dammed them to begin with.

"We've grown a Silver Wing network, there are many of us now. We will help, when the time comes. We could smuggle people out, but our routes have slowly been closed off. The best we can offer you would be a way in." Grahm's speech began to pick up pace. The man poured words frantically into the vessel. "When you come, carve a wing into the sky. We will know. We will lower the guard at any cost so you can enter. If—"

Grahm's voice broke, and he rasped heavily.

"If there are any of us left." He drew a long and quivering breath. "This place, is not what you remember. It is a city of taint, and death, and crystal. Be careful and-and . . ."

There was one final pause. So long Vhalla worried that he had somehow been caught and was never able to finish his impassioned plea.

"And if-if Fritz is still with you . . . If he's there. Fritz, by the Mother. I am doing all I can. Tell me he is well. Tell me my dreams are not lies. Because I still, I can still dream."

The water stilled and mirrored the motionless trio standing around the dish. Fritz made a strangled noise and dropped his face into his wet palms. Vhalla was at his side in a rush, clutching him, supporting him as his knees went weak. His sobs burned her eyes and ripped through the remaining shreds of her heart.

"Vh-Vhal, we must go to him."

"We are," she soothed, rubbing her friend's back.

"He-he sounds so scared!" Fritz buried his face where her neck met her shoulder.

"I know." Vhalla took a deep breath. "But he is also strong. Just as you are. We will stand with him on the other side of this."

Her words may have been lies. Vhalla knew she would live with that forever if they were. But as the truth had yet to unfurl its grand design upon the tapestry of time, Vhalla was content to make such a vow.

She helped Fritz back to his room. Aldrik excused himself to handle other business, giving the two friends time with just each other. The sun was already setting, and, in a complete reversal of what he had once done before, Vhalla saw him bathed and tucked into bed before leaving. Reminding him that the sooner he slept, the sooner the dawn would come.

The day had been one somber reminder after the next that death was at their doorstep. Their time of preparation and—for lack of more eloquent, *nicer* words—hiding was over. They were about to stand upon the precipice and greet true evil. And Vhalla only wanted people to join of their own free will.

She found Jax and Elecia talking near a back storeroom in the training grounds. They were arguing over how many potions of this or that to bring when Vhalla interrupted them.

"Jax, a moment."

"Ah, how I have longed for the moment you seek me out by your lonesome when the moon is in the heavens above," he held out his arms dramatically, as though Vhalla would believe a word of what he said as sincerity.

"It's important." Her words shifted Jax's expression from the light-hearted and fun-loving major to the darker soldier that Vhalla had become more familiar with during her time in Norin. Elecia was keen enough to excuse herself.

"What is it, Lady Solaris?" he asked as Vhalla shut the door behind him in a small side hall. "I don't think either of us need to be reminded of, or want to repeat, the last time you pulled me off the training grounds for a private little chat."

"Why do you think I picked a hallway this time?" Vhalla motioned to the left and right. "Look, we can both pick a different escape route."

The Jax she plucked from the grounds would've laughed. This Jax remained solemn at her remark, assessing her warily. Vhalla clenched her fists, opening her Channel for good measure.

"We march with the dawn."

"You didn't pull me here to tell me that."

"Do you want to go?" Vhalla cut straight to the point.

"I don't know where else I would be. I have not been told to vacate my post as your guard. I realize it's not been necessary here, but when we march again—"

"Is that what you want to do?" she interrupted him. "Do you *want* that post?"

"It is an order." The panic she'd been expecting all along finally began to sneak up on him.

"No, that's what I'm telling you; it's not."

He shook his head in horror. Vhalla could feel him willing her not to say the words, but she would say them anyway, for them both.

"I pardon you." Vhalla stood as tall as she could, trying to evoke the Empress that people expected to see. An Empress that Vhalla didn't even know if she'd ever be. "Jax Wendyl, for your crimes—"

"Don't," he breathed.

"I hereby grant you an Imperial pardon. You are a free man and you can now go where you will."

"Your first Imperial pardon, on *me*?" His words were cut with laughter. "They will make a fool of you."

"Let them." Vhalla shrugged. "You know how I care so

deeply for the opinions of others. I will write my name and your pardon in the Western record. A record no one will ever see. It's up to you from here."

"So I am your shameful act in a dark hall?" he sneered.

"No." Vhalla remained resolute. "If you want to tell the world, then tell them. I merely am respecting your choice as a free man." Vhalla braved a step forward. "Jax, if you stand with me as my guard, I want you to stand with me of your own will. Not because you are ordered. Not as my slave. But as my friend and comrade—or I don't want you there at all."

"You don't understand . . . I'm the mad dog. I'm the fallen lord. I'm the one who the lords hide their daughters from and only feel safe around when I am on an imperial leash!" he snapped. "Do you think you can make me worth her? That you can absolve me and make me someone that she could look upon with fondness from the Father's realms?"

"No." Vhalla kept her voice calm and level, realizing he was very close to lashing out as he had last time. "That's something that is well beyond my power to give. Such a thing must come from you."

"What do you want from me?" he cried.

"To be your friend."

"I don't have friends, I have masters!"

"What was Baldair, then?" Emotion betrayed her the second the younger prince's name was mentioned. "Was he just a master? Is that all his memory is to you?"

Jax stared at her, in a complete loss for words. Vhalla took a step away and started down the hall to leave him to his thoughts. She went straight up to the library, hunted down a familiar tome, and found the page listing Jax's sentence. Alone in the library, Vhalla penned her name as the Empress for the first time, and she freed a man.

CHAPTER 25

C OME THE DAWN, Jax rode at her side. He remained at her left hand for the entire march to the Crossroads. It was as though their conversation had never happened. He didn't bring it up again, and Vhalla honored his silent wish by doing the same. The only person she even told about the small confrontation was Aldrik.

The Emperor supported her decree with Jax like he did with most of her other decisions. Vhalla demanded a hard pace through the West and regular training for all groups. Sehra had been right; many soldiers were green, and she was determined that, by the time they arrived at the Southern border, all soldiers would have a shot at surviving the upcoming battles.

She intentionally kept her meetings short and restricted only to the mornings. Vhalla and Aldrik settled into a rotation where he focused on the appeasement of the lords and majors, and Vhalla spent her time among the soldiers. As much as possible, she wanted to lead by example. If she wanted them to perform three rounds of drills each day, she would perform them herself.

Vhalla also made sure the men and women saw her learning. She split her time between training with sorcerers and training with the sword. One where she could be a teacher, the other where she was still much the student.

Before leaving Norin, she'd commissioned a new blade. It was short and light, well balanced but sturdy. The pommel was wheat, in the shape of wings.

Every time she felt the weight of the blade in her hand or on her hip, every time the wind soared through the skies at her command, she thought of Victor. Vhalla tried to envision what his face would look like when she killed him. There was no other alternative in Vhalla's mind. She would be the one to do it. She had created him—she would be the one to destroy him.

On the ride into the Crossroads, Vhalla tried—once again—to find the small curiosity shop where she'd met Vi. But between the crowds, the sun shades, and the tongues of fire celebrating their arrival, she couldn't find it. It lingered on her mind for the rest of the day as Vhalla tried to recall exactly where it had been or what it had looked like. She began to wonder if the whole encounter was nothing more than a walking dream. Exhausted, Vhalla pushed it from her mind and fell into the arms of her lover in the first bed they'd had in weeks. If she was to meet Vi again, Vhalla was fairly confident that the woman would be the one to find her.

The next morning Vhalla met with the high-ranking warriors in Sehra's forces. She took careful note of the princess's advice on what was likely to offend those from the North and learned a few phrases of greeting in their native tongue. Despite her mouth struggling to form the words, the Northerners seemed to appreciate that an effort was made. It was one of the only things they appreciated about being faced with the Solaris family, who they still very obviously considered to be their Southern oppressors.

Elecia was at her side, in place of Aldrik, for the greetings. The woman couldn't speak the Northern tongue either, but she already knew a few key words and phrases and could make the sounds with ease. Vhalla made her now-cousin promise to teach her a few phrases when the war was over so she could be a better delegate to the Empire's newest addition.

Decisions became no easier to make with time. The day before they were intended to leave, they received a message that Hastan's scouts had confirmed movement of Victor's army further north. An attack on the Eastern capital was likely. Vhalla knew that if they pushed the army East, they may be able to make it to the capital in time to crush Victor's offense. If they didn't, Hastan had a fifty-fifty chance of enduring or falling.

Vhalla's hand shook as she quilled the response back to the Eastern senator. Aldrik had offered to do it, but Vhalla was insistent. These were her people, and she had always made sure they knew orders that put them in danger—the decision that they could sacrifice the East—came from her and why.

Her world kept producing rainbows of conflict cast in deepening shades of gray. The only black and white was her ink on parchment informing Hastan that help would not be coming. That they would use Victor's attack to strike when the Southern border was likely to be weaker.

Rested and restocked, the army proceeded south from the Crossroads. Vhalla resumed her previous regimen of training among the soldiers. As much as possible, she made herself available to them. Fritz had been right: the day that they had escaped from Norin's castle, these were her people.

Her favorite Southerner was at her side one night when she took dinner with the swords she had trained with that day.

"My lady," one remarked during a lull in the prior conversation. "I was there when you stopped the sandstorm."

"Were you?" Vhalla smiled politely. She'd heard this story at least one hundred times on the march.

"We all thought she was suicidal." He began speaking more to the rest of the group than to her. "I was in the late prince's legion, but in the back. So not really that far from where our Empress rode."

Everyone seemed more interested in the man's story than the woman who was the living topic of the tale, but Vhalla was content to let them tell it as they saw fit. Fritz still got great amusement at all the embellishments the men would include, and Vhalla elbowed him in the side more than once to curb his snickering.

"I knew then," the man wrapped up his tale. "I said to my mates, 'This woman is special.' I knew she was far better than I saw others giving her credit for. But the prince, now the crown prince is a man with a good head on his shoulders. Well learned. He sees it."

Vhalla tore off a strip of dried meat and chewed it to tenderness. *That was another recent hobby*, soldiers and nobility claiming that they knew her and Aldrik would be together. Certainly the support pleased her, but it rested uneasily in Vhalla's heart. She had no doubt some of them had seen it, but she also had no doubt that many of them had spoken ill of their former dark prince.

She kept her feelings to herself, except for Aldrik. He agreed with her that it was a relief to have the soldiers supporting them. It helped keep a balance. Whatever issues the nobility still harbored toward her, the common man's love kept their lips still.

Golden wings and suns were emblazoned upon nearly every breast. They looked to her for strength; they believed her wings would never be still, that she really had risen from the dead. It was a mantle she never wanted but had no choice in wearing. There was precious little hope, and, as the giant crystal wall closing the border of South and West came into view, Vhalla knew they needed all the hope they could get.

The weather had begun to chill, the heat of the Western

Waste giving way to firmer ground and the cool winds of the South. The army halted for the majors to convene, to discuss the best plan of attack. Scouts with telescopic lenses peered at the wall, reporting what they could discern.

Five hideous crystal beasts prowled the wall's top. Vhalla knew that if they could see the creatures, the creatures and their all-seeing eyes could see her. That was the most immediate threat. Then came opening the gate. This wasn't like the East where they only needed to slip a few horses through. The army needed the doors to be wide open and hold that way. Finally, logic dictated that Victor had more forces on the other side of the wall, bracing for such an occasion.

It would need to be a three phase attack. The first would focus on the monsters. If they were lucky, the forces on the other side of the wall would be slow or dumb, or both, and the army could pick off the abominations.

When the creatures were gone, they would need to open—or destroy—the gate. Vhalla volunteered herself to investigate it first. She could practically feel Aldrik bristling at the notion, but he held his tongue. They had gone through too many conversations over the weeks regarding her necessity to the war. She was the only one who could manage crystals and was brave, or stupid, enough to do so with reckless abandon.

Once the gates were opened, the army would tackle whatever else Victor had waiting for them and venture forward into the largely unknown southern territory. The meeting with the majors ran late in the day. They carefully watched and planned.

Whatever the beasts were, they didn't seem particularly intelligent. They remained stoic guardians as the army moved forward. Archers lined up on command, Vhalla at their center point. Jax, not Aldrik, was at her side. The Emperor was positioned not far off with the Black Legion—a term they were already discussing retiring in light of Victor's naming system.

"I will dislodge the beasts from the walls." Vhalla rode down the ranks, reminding the soldiers of the plans their leaders should've trickled down to them. "One or two, I will pin to the ground for the swordsmen and pole arms. While I do this, you will need to fend off the others in the sky."

The Black Legion was lined behind the archers, and they all gave her their full attention.

"Archers, sorcerers, even if your attacks do not hit their mark, so long as you keep them at bay, you have been successful."

Vhalla paused her mount, her eyes meeting Aldrik's. The Emperor gave her a small nod, and Vhalla adjusted her grip on the reins. Her heart willed him to be safe in the impending skirmish.

"He doesn't want you here," Jax spoke only for her ears.

"No, he would rather I was still in Norin," Vhalla agreed.

"Well, I want you to know that I told him he need not worry." Jax sat back in his saddle, adjusting the high bun on his head. "For I will protect our delicate and most innocent Empress."

Vhalla snorted in amusement. Laughter was a precious commodity these days. And if Jax was good for anything, it was creating that rare resource in droves.

Clenching her fists, she opened her Channels, directing her attention to the beasts. Raising her hands, she felt the world for miles around. The winds of the Western Waste had always been a monster of their own. Now it was time to pit monster against monster.

Dropping her hands suddenly, and with a grunt at the magical exertion, two of the crystal abominations were sent crashing from their perches by the sudden and unseen force of her wind. Vhalla pulled toward her, the wind literally tugging at her taut fingers. The beasts tumbled awkwardly in their struggle to become airborne.

Panting and determined, Vhalla pressed down harder. Their

leathery, crystal-tipped wings functioned like sails, catching her gusts. Palms flat and open, Vhalla held two creatures against the sand.

The roar of the soldiers could barely be heard over the cries of the other crystal monsters taking to the sky. Fire and arrows rang out. Every time one tried to swoop down, a giant inferno or swarm of arrows kept it at bay.

Beads of sweat ran down her forehead. She could feel them, as though her hands were physically upon them. Struggling, twisting, writhing, they fought against her physically and magically.

Vhalla was so focused on her magic that Jax's shout of warning went completely unheard. She had to keep the beasts down long enough for the soldiers to overwhelm them. She had to keep the wind focused only on them, but not on the swordsmen and women who had begun their bloody work of slaying the beasts.

A pair of arms closed around her, and Vhalla was pulled against Jax's chest. Sand filled her mouth as she was tackled to the ground, face first, off her horse. Flames burst around them, burning as hot as she'd ever seen. The heat was suffocating and Vhalla struggled to breathe, her body shielded by the one atop her.

A crack and sizzling noise threatened to split open the earth, and Vhalla cried out at the discomfort as electric magic pulsed through her mind. Sweat dripped from her face, and she stayed still, letting Jax's body shield her from the flames as much as possible. Magic, powerful and wild, surged about them, barely diffused by Jax's shield of flame.

"Jax! Too hot!" She was boiling alive.

"Well, I didn't know they could use lightning!"

"You can't sustain this for much longer." Vhalla twisted, ready to make a break for it.

"Someone will take it down," he insisted.

"After the next shot, Jax, send the fire straight up."

"I am keeping you alive!" Jax shouted.

There was another crack, and his shield wavered.

"Quit this noble nonsense and be the insane asshole I want!"

His shoulders shook, and the man sprung to his feet. The fire that had been blazing about them shot up as a pillar through the air. Vhalla swung her hands down with a cry, giving the beast no option but to be impaled upon his flames. The creature's cry was as loud as it was agonizing. And it only made Jax's flames burn all the hotter and her winds blow harder.

With a mad dash, they both narrowly avoided the charred remains of the creature as it crashed down to earth. The crystals that had shone so brilliantly on its wings went dull, like scratched obsidian, then cracked. Vhalla scrambled to her feet, feeling her Channel in preparation for her next attack.

The remaining two beasts were engaged with different groups of sorcerers and soldiers. Fire, ice, and arrows sought purchase against their nearly impenetrable bodies, trying to bring them out of the air. Vhalla picked one at random, sending it out of the sky. By the time she could turn to the other, the sorcerers had finished it.

It was a small victory, but a victory nevertheless. It would be the first of many, she vowed. One after another, the tainted wretches that stood against them would fall.

CHAPTER 26

THEY QUICKLY MOVED on the wall. There wasn't time to waste. Each moment that ticked threatened enemy reinforcements and monsters. Vhalla brought her fingers to her mouth and gave a sharp whistle. With a half jump and step on the air, she mounted Lightning in a single motion.

"Make a path!" she called at the top of her lungs. Soldiers were quick to oblige.

Like thunder, a War-strider appeared at her side. Aldrik's new mount was as large as Baston ever was. Vhalla gave the Emperor a quick glance-over, looking for wounds—and he did the same to her.

He looked uneasily at the gate. "Are you sure about this?"

"Do you have a better idea?" Vhalla glanced at the Northern forces slowly regrouping around their princess. "Sehra said she can't help here. What other choice do we have?"

They both pulled their mounts to a stop before the wall. Vhalla knew Victor would be aware when each of his beasts died. There was a connection between him and the crystals. She'd known it from the first abomination she'd encountered.

"Don't come any closer, Aldrik." Her words of caution were needless; the man knew as well as she the risks associated with crystals.

Vhalla dismounted, blinking her eyes. The magic was unlike anything she'd ever seen. It swirled in a tight jumble just above the crystal. But it was strangely familiar. She was reminded of the axe, the layers of magic that lingered upon it.

Holding out a hand, Vhalla made contact.

It was a mess of power, pulsing through her fingertips, testing her as much as she was testing it. It was like professional musicians sitting together, skilled but all strumming notes to a different song, creating nothing but a cacophony. Yet there was an underlying beat, one she knew. It resonated deep within her; it echoed across her being and accepted her.

Vhalla's magic called to itself.

She broke away, peeling her hand from the wall. The residual magic swirled between her fingers, slowly fading. Vhalla began to laugh, dazed and shocked.

"What is it?" Aldrik took a cautionary step forward.

"It's mine," she observed. Amazement and resentment fought for her heart. "All of this, he's doing by lacing my magic under it to hold the crystals together in the shapes he wants."

"The crown . . ."

Vhalla gave a solemn nod of affirmation. There was much to think on with this revelation. Victor couldn't tap into her Channel. Having her magic in the crown didn't make him a Windwalker. Which meant that *perhaps* he had a finite amount of magic he was working with and slowly exhausting. The idea upheld their earlier theories of why he built walls with gates rather than building or tearing them down as he needed.

With two hands, she made full contact with the wall. Vhalla closed her eyes, thinking of it as an odd sort of Joining. She only needed to gain control of that underlying current beneath all the nonsense that was structured atop it.

Reaching out to the magic, she tried to welcome it once more into herself. It was just slightly different, the crystal magic and

Victor's pulling it in odd directions. It squirmed and slithered, resistant to accepting her. Resistant to letting her regain control.

Embracing the connection completely, she allowed what she thought was her magical pulse from the caverns to merge with her current magic. It connected with her in one breath—and horror settled in. The magic was not purely hers any longer.

A heartbeat echoed through her ears.

Mentally retreating, Vhalla tried to pull away. She tried to force the unwelcome presence that had piggybacked its way into her through her own sorcery. But it was already pulsing through her, poisoning her. Like spindly vines, it dug into her with deadly thorns. It joined with her essence.

She stumbled backward, a clamor of armor. Vhalla stared at her hands in horror as a maniacal chuckle echoed on the edge of her mind before fading away. She held her head tightly, trying to purge the slimy feeling that coated the underside of her skin.

"No."

"What is it? What happened?" Aldrik rushed over.

"Don't touch me!" She stopped him at arm's length. Too much had happened in those few seconds, and she needed to come to terms with it all.

"Vhalla—"

"*Not now,*" she grit out.

His brow furrowed and he frowned in concern. *But they were here to do a job,* and they both knew it. Aldrik's expression shifted as he visually invoked his training as both a leader and a lord to the forefront. "Can you open it?"

"I can do one better." Vhalla pushed herself to her feet, clenching her fists. There was a deep pleasure coursing through her in the realization of new knowledge gained. She just wished she could say for certain it was her own.

"You're trembling," he whispered.

"I'll be fine." Vhalla hoped saying it would make it true.

The power within her rumbled as Vhalla stared at the wall. Vhalla turned and marched back to her steed, mounting Lightning with confidence. She gripped the reins, hatred bubbling deep within her.

"Men and women of the Empire Solaris!" she shouted. The soldiers snapped to attention, near and far, as the wind carried her voice across the field. Aldrik mounted next to her. "Behind this wall is our land. For some of you, it is home. For others, it is the home of your children or your forefathers. The wall is a scar upon our Empire—when I remove it, you will push forward and you will kill every man, woman, and monster who does not mark themselves loyal to the true Emperor of this land!"

With cheers of bloodlust at her back, Vhalla returned her attention to the wall, summoning every ounce of her strength and of the new found understanding she'd gained of the dark Channel that now lived within her. Victor had made this wall. And if he could make it, she could tear it down.

Vhalla raised her hands slowly, shifting her magic. She thought of the crystal forces she had felt, of the madman's magic lying underneath it. She loathed the moment foreign magic churned within her, responding, bubbling up through her hands. Vhalla grimaced.

Pure energy flew from her fingertips to the center of the gate. It was shapeless and colorless. The only time Vhalla had seen magic of its nature was in the North and in the Crystal Caverns.

Aldrik's lips parted, and he looked away from the cracking gate. He focused only on her as the earth cried out in a monumental groan. He'd recognized the sorcery. It had been used on him as well. The Emperor shook his head slowly, horror spinning panic within his eyes. *He knew, he had to know what now existed within her.*

"To kill a monster, you must become one yourself." It was

all she could confess to the man she loved. Deep within her, rage spiraled out of control. Victor knew what she had done and could feel what it meant.

"Vhalla—" Her name on Aldrik's lips was a pained and strangled whine.

"There's no time now." Vhalla turned back to the gate. Cracks raced to be the first to the top. Large stones began to loosen and fall as the magic of the crystals faded and fell dormant. The gate crumbled, and the whole wall began to topple like dominos following. "We have a war to fight."

"Later." He grabbed her forearm. Her resolve cracked at the wild concern in his eyes. "This will not just fade away unspoken."

"Later." Vhalla tried to coax her voice into being as gentle as possible, which was difficult when a foreign feeling of loathing began to mix with the cries of battle.

Aldrik pulled away, jaw clenched and brow furrowed. He turned sharply toward the startled encampment on the other side of the gate and rained fire down on the enemy. Vhalla's eyes were alight with the flames as she heard the symphony of dying screams.

Kicking Lightning's sides, Vhalla rushed to the head of the charge. For the first time in her life, it was she who raced forward with an army at her back. Vhalla held out her right hand and swept it to the side before quickly repeating the process with the left. The rubble cleared for those behind her, making a path along the Great Imperial Way.

Victor's monsters and men were fending off the inferno Aldrik reaped upon them. The fire vanished when she crossed the line where the wall had been moments before.

"Swear fealty to the Solaris Empire, and you will be spared!" she cried. "Strike an 'X' into the black of your armor or clothes so that we may know who stands with the sun!"

"Long live the Supreme King Victor!" one sorcerer spat.

He didn't have time to even raise his hand before an icicle impaled him. Vhalla glanced over her shoulder, looking for Fritz.

One or two of Victor's soldiers attempted to accept her offer, hastily scratching a large 'X' onto their makeshift armor. It was an army enslaved, and their loyalty only went so far. But these had mostly become Victor's men. Whatever the false king had promised must have been tempting, because more sorcerers quickly turned on their allies, killing any who would try to return their loyalty to Solaris.

Vhalla kept charging forward. At the least, they could use the momentary confusion to their advantage. But for every one conscious sorcerer, there were five more tainted, mad, and under Victor's control. Her attempt had been made, but it was a fairly futile one.

Fire combusted by her side, and Vhalla barely had enough time to ditch the horse and roll. The smell of singed fur assaulted her senses, but she had more pressing matters than checking if her trusty steed was well. A sorcerer was upon her. With a gleaming sharp ice dagger, he slashed into the ground by her face.

Vhalla threw up an arm, and he flew backward. Just as she stood, a heavy greave kneed her in the face, shattering her nose. She was an easy target in white and Vhalla was quickly learning why nobility didn't usually lead charges.

She coughed up blood, surprised she had not lost any teeth or bit her tongue off. Just a laceration inside her cheek. A heartbeat began to race at the edge of her consciousness. It was both familiar and terribly different at the same time, and she struggled to fight it. It was an unwanted and unwelcome sound, a rhythm that beat to the drums of war and bloodlust.

The man with the ice had recovered and was lunging again. With a cry that was part animal, Vhalla thrust a hand onto his face, dodging the other man's second punch. Blood splattered the ground as the Waterrunner's head exploded.

She spun, wind under her toes, making her nimble. *Making her powerful.*

Her sword rang out against its sheathe, reverberating up her arms and into her chest. The sound echoed in harmony with the pulse that propelled her. *She would write their requiem in blood.* There was minimal resistance as Vhalla put the wind at her elbows to shove her blade clear through the man's skull, starting with his eye.

Vhalla kicked him off her blade. Laughter rasped against the inside of her throat. They would all die. Any who opposed her were weak. This was the only truth of the world. The weak would die to form the foundation of the world, the world the strong would inherit. *A beautifully, wonderfully, chaotic world.* It was only nature.

She turned her head, and, at her behest, lightning crackled across a sorcerer's flesh. He shuddered, his eyes lolling in their sockets as his body became coated in burn marks that quickly turned black. He fell dead, and Vhalla turned for her next victim. It was as though the battle moved slowly for her. She saw every pulse of magic from the sorcerers and from the tainted. Each flash of weaponry was seen in perfect clarity.

She was death itself. No, she was stronger than death. She had beaten death twice! That made it hers to administer. Her body moved without thought, reckless and wild.

A pair of arms closed around her torso.

"Vhalla," Jax's voice hissed in her ear. "Vhalla, *enough.*"

She blinked the haze from her mind. The familiar call of her name pulled her back to the present, like waking from a dream. The battlefield had changed from her prior recollections. The last of the soldiers had fallen, their victory apparent. Vhalla panted heavily, trying to make sense of it.

Turning her, his palms on her shoulders as though he would need to physically hold her in place, Jax checked her up and down. A frown weighed on the corners of his lips.

"What did I do?" she breathed.

His scowl only deepened at her question. "We should get you to Elecia; she'll heal you up."

Vhalla followed dutifully, noticing her feet when she followed behind the Western man. It was as though she had bathed in blood. The white of her armor was coated and splatted in bits of gore. Soldiers stared. Some began to cheer, but others looked at her with a touch of fear.

Elecia made quick work of fixing Vhalla's nose. But there was a reserved nature to her ministrations. The woman studied Vhalla carefully for far too long.

"We should get you washed up," she said finally.

"I can do it." Vhalla stood.

"I want to come, continue inspecting you." Elecia half blocked Vhalla's path and put on her best imitation of Aldrik when he was uninterested in any arguments. "We'll be setting up camp here for the night anyway."

"Very well," Vhalla sighed.

They walked through the beginnings of a camp being erected just beyond the edge of the carnage. Elecia paused, resting her hand on a tree before heading away in a diagonal direction. Vhalla dragged her feet along.

"What are you doing?" Curiosity still got the better of her.

"Seeing where the trees roots get the most water in order to find us a stream or spring." Elecia glanced over her shoulder. "You're painted red."

Vhalla looked back down at her armor with a small frown. *If only she could remember killing the people whose blood she wore.*

Elecia's magic delivered. The spring they found was small

and shallow, barely up to Vhalla's short-statured waist. They were still in the transitional shrub land of West and South.

Her armor felt heavy and her fingers uncoordinated as she tried to unclasp it. Elecia sighed softly and helped Vhalla. The women found a spot at the water's rocky edge to sit.

"Elecia, look, I'm fine." Vhalla held out her arms putting herself on display. "You don't need to be here to check or heal me."

"It's not your physical body I'm worried about," the woman solemnly uttered. "Now, in the water."

Vhalla obliged, wading into the center of the pool. The spring was chilly on her skin. It sharpened her senses and grounded her in the present. Vhalla watched as the water clouded with blood.

"What happened today?" Elecia demanded.

Vhalla cringed inwardly. She wanted to scream; she wanted to sob. Vhalla tilted her head back and looked at the unbroken sky. She opened her mouth and took a deep breath.

"The wall had my magic in it."

"*Yours?*"

"Alongside Victor's and the crystal magic," Vhalla affirmed. "I don't think he can quite control or manipulate the crystals without it. My magic was like a support structure holding the rest together."

"He's not a Windwalker, but if he has Windwalker magic to work with . . . I suppose it makes as much sense as anything else involving crystals," Elecia worked out.

"I thought I could pull out the scaffolding, or that I could reclaim it and gain control of the crystals. I invited it into me. I invited *him* into me."

"Who?"

Vhalla's eyes drifted over to the other woman. She dropped her head to one side, debating between laughing and continuing to stare at her incredulously. "You're not one to ask dumb questions."

Elecia frowned.

"I didn't want it." Vhalla returned to staring at her fingers, as though they were disconnected from her body. "But I didn't think it could or would come in alongside my magic. Now he has some of my magic, I have some of his. I *feel* him. It's like we, we're . . ."

The word was thick and heavy on Vhalla's tongue. It tasted like death. She was tainted, but it wasn't the taint everyone knew.

"We're Bonded."

There was nothing but the sound of the winds and the rustling of small trees and grasses. Elecia stared at her a long moment, blinking her eyes. Vhalla wondered if the woman could see it, now that she knew what to look for.

"You're shivering." Elecia quickly splashed some water over her own bloodstains and stood. "Come, we'll get you back to Aldrik and get you warm."

"I don't think I should be around Aldrik," Vhalla confessed.

"Well, you can tell him that, because I most certainly won't be the one to do so." Elecia held out a hand. "You're stronger than this, Vhalla Yarl."

Vhalla searched Elecia's emerald eyes for the hint of deception. If the words were a lie, Elecia did a great job of delivering them with confidence. Vhalla stood on her own, ignoring the offered help up. She didn't want anyone touching her. She had used crystal magic. She could be walking taint.

Night fell quickly and, despite Vhalla deciding to risk some magic to dry their clothing, they were both cold by the time they arrived back at camp. Jax and Aldrik stood around a campfire, speaking with Fritz and a few other majors who quickly cleared out when the Lady Ci'Dan and the Empress sat.

"Vhal." Everyone looked at Fritz in surprise. Apparently,

none of them expected him to be the one to break the silence. "What happened today?"

"A battle."

"No, I've seen you fight before. That wasn't you," Fritz said softly, almost fearfully.

He had no idea what he needed to fear.

"I'm Bonded to Victor." It was going to come out sooner or later; Vhalla didn't see the point in delay.

"What?" Fritz leaned backward in surprise.

"Vhalla." Aldrik grabbed her hand from wringing her own fingers in her absentminded habit. "What are you talking about?"

"I'm sorry," she whispered and pulled her hand from his.

"No."

"His magic is in me, mine is in him. I feel *him* as I felt you." Vhalla didn't want to break her husband's heart just weeks into their marriage.

"How?" Aldrik breathed. The majority of his brainpower was clearly being used to process what she was saying, rather than mustering eloquent words.

Vhalla sighed and summarized it as she had for Elecia, about the wall and Victor's magic being atop hers and the crystal's magic.

"Vhalla, are you sure?" Fritz had the audacity to look hopeful, as if she were somehow mistaken.

"I know what this feels like!" Vhalla snapped. Fritz's eyes widened, and she immediately regained control of herself. "I'm sorry, I'm sorry. It's just—it's been a long day."

"Well, something *is* different." Elecia blinked her eyes a few times, and inspected her again. "I don't know enough to determine if it is a Bond or not. But there is some kind of strange synthesis."

"What do you think it is?" Aldrik asked.

"I just said I don't know." Elecia shook her head.

"Well, he doesn't have your magic in him," Aldrik pointed out with a finger. "It's just the crown."

"True." Elecia didn't put up much of a fight. "But who knows what he has accomplished with all his crystal work. Vhalla seems to already be able to use crystal magic like Victor. A feat she never really accomplished with your Bond, which was quite strong. Crystals break all the rules of magic we know, and those rules surrounding Bonding are fuzzy at best."

"But this could be good." Jax rubbed his chin, no longer the silent observer. "We saw it today; you can tear down what he makes like it's nothing. This could be a useful tool."

"I am not a tool." Vhalla looked at him darkly. "Would you want the madman in you? How would you like to feel his rage burning under your flesh? Then maybe you wouldn't think it's so damned convenient!"

They all stared at her in shock. Vhalla's mouth dropped open as well, struggling to find words—words that were truly hers. It was like a switch on her emotions that she no longer knew how to control. Jax, for once, had no dark or perverse retort. Vhalla buried her face into her palms.

"I'm tired," she mumbled, unable to face them a moment longer.

Hands, hot palms, slid over her, easing over the invisible wounds that bled under her skin. Aldrik engulfed her, smoke, sweat, fire, and scent all his own. Vhalla trembled, she wanted to push away the emotions that were threatening to break out. She tried to drown the unwelcome disgust that coated the back of her mouth with thoughts of Aldrik's love.

"Friends, leave us."

Vhalla heard shuffling and was almost content to let them leave without another word. But she had to clutch onto the things that made her Vhalla, and her friends were one of those things.

"Jax." She pulled her head away from Aldrik's chest. He

stopped, just within the light of the campfire. "I'm sorry. I didn't mean to."

"Don't let it trouble you, Empress." If Jax was putting on a front, he did quite a good job at feigning earnestness.

"Come, my Vhalla." Aldrik pulled her to her feet. "There is a warm bedroll waiting for us."

Vhalla stopped trying to fight him. She gave into the comfort of her husband's presence. One foot, then the next, it was the only thing that she filled her mind with, afraid if she went too far in any direction, Victor would take over.

Under the blankets, Aldrik coaxed out the stubborn stiffness anxiety had put in her shoulders and arms. His heated caress, his soothing whisper. It drew Vhalla against him, basking in his love as though it were the only thing that would keep her alive now.

"I don't want this . . ." she breathed in Aldrik's essence to fuel her frightful confession. "I can feel him. Even now, lurking back behind my thoughts. Waiting for the currents of magic and minds to let him have a hold again."

Aldrik held her hand bone-crushingly tight, bringing it to his lips to kiss her fingertips.

"I'm Bonded to that man. I lost our Bond, and now—"

"It is not a Bond," Aldrik spoke with conviction.

"I know this feeling, this—"

He silenced her with a firm kiss. One that was magical enough to muster hope. "We shared a Bond," he whispered across her lips. "A Bond is wonderous. A Bond is life. It is the most beautiful connection that can ever be shared. This—this is not a Bond."

Vhalla kept her mouth silent. A wolf was not a dog because you called it so. But she would give her husband hope, even if she couldn't share it. Vhalla closed her eyes and gave herself to his reassurances. She hoped that by morning she could actually believe them.

CHAPTER 27

"VICTOR." THE EMPEROR Tiberus Solaris was removing his plate with the assistance of various servants. He stood in an open space with polearms displayed on the walls, their points still sharpened and oiled. The tiling was vaguely familiar, white marble laid at a diamond pattern. "You know I am very busy right now with the festival starting soon."

"I know, my lord," the Minister of Sorcery acknowledged with a bow. "But you told me to come to you with the results of my research on your future campaigns."

"You have found something useful?" The Emperor looked at Victor through his reflection in a large mirror. His arms held straight out, the help had almost finished removing the many layers of complex plate that made up his ceremonial armor.

"Very useful." Victor struggled to keep the apparent glee from curling his mouth. "But tell me first, where is your eldest son now?"

The Emperor turned to the minister and arched a single brow. Victor smiled calmly. It was a smug little look that breathed of arrogance and assurance. It was a bold front to put before the late-Emperor Solaris, and one people only did when they were certain that the information they possessed outweighed any potential ire.

"Leave us," the Emperor ordered, his eyes focused on Victor.

The servants cleared the room on command. Dressed down to just pants and a thick cotton tunic, the Emperor took a step toward Victor, regarding him carefully. "Were it not for your manner, I would presume he would be making the necessary preparations for our court dinner for the start of the Festival of the Sun."

There was a long moment of silence while Victor clearly weighed his options for how to proceed. "What do you know of the common girl named Vhalla Yarl?"

"Vhalla Yarl?" The Emperor shook his head. "The name is not familiar. I usually make little effort to remember the names of the lowborn."

"He has not sent one report to you about her?" Victor stroked his goatee thoughtfully. He made a show of speaking to himself. "I'm sure it just slipped Aldrik's mind."

The Emperor's expression changed momentarily at Victor's words. The royal had taken the bait.

"I am sure her name will be well known by you soon enough," Victor assured.

"Why?" the Emperor asked cautiously.

"Your son is with her now," Victor reported triumphantly.

"Aldrik?" The Emperor seemed genuinely surprised, but quickly waved it off. "Aldrik is not one to fraternize with common folk. I try not to get in the way of his amusements when it comes to playing his mind games with them. Keeps a healthy amount of fear in those beneath our notice."

"If anything, she has played a mind game on him." Victor's tone turned serious, not wanted to heed the obvious dismissal of the topic. "Every time he comes to me, he inquires after her well-being. He trained her personally. He carried her to me following an incident, cradled in his arms and begged me to help her. He races to her side at every possible moment. We both know he has previously made some less than ideal choices off the lower rungs of society."

"*I am not worried about a child.*" The Emperor folded his hands behind his back and leisurely strolled over to a window, looking over his city. "*If she is a problem, I will remove her like . . . Oh, what was her name?*"

"*Inad?*" Victor finished easily.

Vhalla recognized the name of Aldrik's first love.

"*Yes, her.*" The Emperor nodded. "*I appreciate your diligence now, like then, Victor, but I am not worried. Now, I think this conversation—*"

"*This girl is able to give you the means to conquer the Crescent Continent,*" Victor interjected quickly.

"*What?*" The Emperor turned in place, too invested in Victor's words to be upset by the interruption.

"*That's why I thought Aldrik would tell you. I realize you've been keeping your overseas visions from him, but I thought he would tell you for the sake of taking the North.*" Victor sighed heavily and pressed his fingers against his temple. "*But he's so protective of the girl.*"

"*You have found me a Windwalker.*" The Emperor's words were nearly reverent, his excitement palpable. Then his expression darkened. "*Why would my son keep this from me?*"

"*Harnessing the true usefulness of her power, at the least, will require her enslavement. If not her death.*" Victor shrugged, as though the thought was nothing to him.

"*Aldrik, my idiot son with his mother's heart.*" The Emperor sighed heavily. "*Thank you for telling me this. I will have the girl conscripted into service.*"

"*If I may advise you . . .*" The Emperor motioned for Victor to continue. "*Be patient. The two are fire and air. Aldrik can be untamed, as you know, and she can barely control her magic at present. I think there will come an opportunity for you to use her to your advantage.*"

"*Or I will see one made,*" the Emperor remarked. "*Victor, I am thankful to have such loyal servants such as yourself. It is a refreshing change from my last Minister of Sorcery."*

"There is one more thing, my lord," Victor added, his eyes shining with manipulation. *"One more thing; to make her truly the key to your conquest across the sea, I will need something from the North to unlock the caverns."*

"A small price for what you promise. I will see that we acquire what you need."

"It is a treasure of Yargen, of the variety Egmun procured—an axe made of crystal. If I have it, I will see that you witness the true power of the caverns." Victor barely hid his giddiness, even as his words held more than one meaning.

"Consider it done. And report back to me with any further knowledge you gain on the girl . . . and my son."

"Of course, I am nothing if not your most obedient servant." A mad grin spread triumphantly across Victor's face the second he'd turned away from the Emperor.

That expression, the wicked glee, was what Vhalla woke to. She didn't wake screaming or thrashing, but her whole body ached, and her head hurt as though she'd run a marathon in her sleep. The sun had yet to rise, and the canvas above her was a hazy and dull blue. Aldrik's arm wrapped around her middle, and, judging from his deep and steady breathing, Vhalla knew he had yet to stir.

Vhalla didn't wake him. She stayed still and quiet, trying to dissect the dream. She turned it over in her mind and picked it apart. Victor had played them all. He played on their hatred of each other, their distance. He knew Aldrik well enough to know that the prince would never fully trust his father. He knew the Emperor didn't think Aldrik ready for his plans for the Crescent Continent.

Aldrik didn't want to use the word "Bond" to describe what

had happened between her and Victor, but Vhalla could offer no other alternative. She was Bonded to Victor. She had him within her. The madman, the monster who had stolen her magic. Vhalla was deeply connected with the one person in the world she truly wanted to kill.

Jax's suggestion echoed within her. Perhaps if she could manipulate the Bond, she could help them with the knowledge she could glean, with the powers she gained over the crystals.

With the sun, Vhalla began to feel a rise in other emotions, a dark sea that raged in the back of her mind stirring to life. She rolled away from Aldrik, unable to endure his tender touch a moment longer.

"Vhalla?" he mumbled, pawing at the empty space she left.

"Go back to sleep," she demanded quietly. "There's still time yet."

Aldrik opened a single dark eye, looking up at her skeptically.

Vhalla forced a smile onto her lips. When he still seemed insistent, she rested a palm on his shoulder. "Just the bathroom," she lied.

How far she had come. She, the library girl who was notorious for being a bad liar, was believed by the silver-tongued prince. Aldrik closed his eye and mumbled something about her coming back soon. Vhalla tugged on her chainmail and left him, hoping he could endure the disappointment of discovering her absence.

A barren land greeted her. The bloodshed from the previous day was still visible in the distance. Carrion birds picked at the remnants. Vhalla turned her eyes away from it and looked southward. That would only be a small portion of the destruction she'd reap. She'd turn Victor's power against him and take the world from under his feet.

She stood staring at the destruction before her until people began to stir.

Aldrik said nothing about her morning walk as they rode. He attempted to strike up various conversations with her, but none sparked, and he was left talking around her to Jax or Fritz. Elecia was equally quiet, her eyes heavy on Vhalla.

But Vhalla ignored them all. She kept her eyes trained on the great, distant horizon that she suspected would be her final battle field.

They marched through lunch into the afternoon, finally striking camp at dinnertime.

Vhalla sat at their shared campfire for a few moments as everyone eagerly dug into their portions. She passed her meat from hand to hand, and then passed it off to Jax. The man regarded her with concern but didn't say anything.

"You hardly ate," Aldrik said when she stood.

"Not hungry."

"Where are you going, Vhal?" Fritz asked from across the campfire.

"To spar." Someone would be willing to help her relieve the nervous energy that crawled under her skin.

"You should eat more." Aldrik caught her wrist.

"I told you, I am not hungry." There was an edge to his voice that only she seemed able to hear. It was an awful grating sound that didn't appear to bother anyone else.

"Vhalla, please," he encouraged.

"I will eat what I please!" She wrenched her hand from his grip. A frown crossed her husband's face, an expression that Vhalla couldn't endure. It swayed her mind into more familiar territory. "I just . . . want to work on my swordsmanship."

Vhalla vanished before any of them could say anything else—hunting down the first partner she could find.

One parry, two, repeat; the pattern rang through her head in time with the steel vibrating in her hand. *Turn, dodge, duck, lunge, kick*, she was getting better. The unsuspecting swordsman had claimed he would be all too honored to be the Empress's practice for the night, but he'd bitten off more than he could chew against the Windwalker.

Five exhausted partners later, Vhalla sheathed her sword. Sweat rolled off her face, and she panted heavily, but she was no closer to feeling satiated. Victor's energy still churned underneath her skin.

The next day, her head began to hurt on and off. She could feel Victor's presence, like a shadow clinging on her back, and it was becoming more and more difficult to sort her emotions from his. This Bond was unlike anything she had felt with Aldrik.

Damn crystals.

The forest grew denser with each passing day, and the ground began to turn into hills that would later become mountains and valleys. Vhalla kept her eyes down for most of the day, silent, focusing on keeping Victor's magic contained within her. *Closer,* she realized. Each sway of the horse was bringing her closer to her goal. *Shouldn't she feel happier?*

Happiness was illusive, and her dreams began to occur more regularly. No, they weren't dreams. They were memories. And their assaults were more aggressive than it had ever been with Aldrik.

"What're you gonna do about it, huh? Man witch?" a boy, barely old enough for a coming of age ceremony, taunted. *"Gonna use your magic on us?"*

Victor, no older than thirteen, stood with his back against a wall. Based on the construction of the buildings, he appeared to be somewhere in the capital.

"Yeah, magic boy, let's see it."

Victor scowled and ran his thumbs over the tips of his fingers. "You wouldn't want that, I'm warning you."

"*Warnings?*" *The first boy glanced between his two friends.* "*I think he's scared.*"

"*I'm not scared of a Commons,*" *Victor swore.* "*You should be scared of me.*"

"*We'll see.*" *The boy cracked his knuckles and swung.*

Victor dodged and put his hand on the boy's chest. Ice covered his torso, rendering his arms mostly immobile from the elbow up. The second boy stepped forward, and Victor repeated the process with confidence.

"*Don't want to fight me now?*" *he asked the remaining riff raff. The last boy shook his head.*

"*Hey, hey.*" *He held out his arms and placed his palms on the half frozen children. The ice vanished into the air.* "*Look, we can all still be friends.*"

Two just chattered, while the third looked too horrified to speak.

"*I need you to remember two things though . . . The first is to never think you're better than a sorcerer—ever again.*" *Victor patted what had been the leader on the shoulder, grinning brightly.*

"*The second is to remember that you belong to me now.*"

The boys, the alley, faded away like black smoke. There was only the young Victor before her, as arrogant and triumphant as his adult counterpart.

He looked up at her, and Vhalla was frozen, helpless to do anything.

"*Now, you've been very naughty, raiding my mind,*" *the boy spoke slowly.* "*Let's see what's in yours.*"

Vhalla felt him. She felt his magic like icy fingers peeling back and penetrating the depths of her mind without her consent. He probed her, taking what was most precious to her.

"*No . . .*" *Her protest was weak, his magic already within her.*

A young woman with a mess of hair sprinted through the darkness, a new world building under her footsteps. She put her shoulder to the Imperial library's door and pushed. Vhalla willed it to stop. She wished for nothing more than to stop the replay of her life before her eyes.

"There he is." Victor's voice echoed in her ears. "Let's see, did you find him attractive then?"

Vhalla remained silent, trying to hide her emotions. But she felt the echo of her dream self. The way Aldrik had first captivated her with his unconventional appeal. Victor felt it too; she knew he did by the satisfaction in his voice.

"I read all his little notes to you. The ones you hid away in your room. He never had time for apprentices, he always claimed, but I guess that didn't extend to girls whose legs he wanted to spread."

Rage betrayed her.

"There it is! There's the anger!" he egged on.

Vhalla focused on the young woman before her, watching Aldrik lead her past self through the bookshelves. They both looked so much younger. There wasn't a scar on her body. The dark circles under his eyes were only just forming.

"Yes, yes, you love him so much, you can't hide it from me. But, Vhalla, I-I can be kind. I will show you. Tell him to give up his claim to the throne, and I will let you both fade away. If his army bows to me, I will let you both flee across the sea."

"I will kill you." Her voice quivered with barely controllable rage.

"No, I think not." Victor chuckled, his voice growing distant. "The longer we are linked, the more our lives grow entwined. If I die, you will die."

"That's not true. Bonds don't work that way." She remembered Aldrik telling her so, and Vhalla needed it to be true now more than ever.

"But it is true. I will make sure it is. Because I don't think he will kill me if it means killing you."

"You lie," Vhalla screamed mentally. "You lie!"

Vhalla woke with a start. Her skin was flushed, and her blood boiled within her as if trying to purge Victor like an infection. She cradled her face in her hands and, for the first time, contemplated running.

No, Vhalla shook her head at herself. There was no one else. Even if she could find another Windwalker, they'd never withstand this burden. Even if they were willing, they would die before they ever had enough training to be a threat.

A movement from behind startled her. Vhalla turned, her hands flying from her face. Magic was ready upon her fingertips when Aldrik caught them effortlessly. She panted softly, withdrawing the power she'd been ready to unleash on him.

"Vhalla," Aldrik whispered softly. The blankets pooled around his waist as he sat. "What is it?"

"Don't touch me." She twisted, avoiding the hand that sought her cheek.

"Vhalla!" He heaped frustration upon her name. "You waste away before my eyes. I cannot convince you to eat. You thrash in your sleep. And now, now I may not touch you?"

Vhalla stared at her bare-chested husband. Their rations had yet to expire, and the training had been good on his body. In stark contrast, her arms looking more gangly, her waist thinner. She resisted a stirring of want, not the first she'd fought on the march since the gate. Monsters weren't allowed to want Emperors.

"No." She withdrew. "You may not."

Aldrik stared as though she had slapped him. He didn't utter another word as Vhalla dressed and clipped into her armor.

The Emperor let her go.

Jax waited outside the tent, scrambling to his feet as she stormed out.

"Go," Vhalla ordered. She was struggling to contain the rage within her.

"Someone woke up on the wrong side of the bed," Jax jested.

Vhalla spun on her heel, glaring up at the Westerner. Her hand had flattened and her fingertips stopped at his throat. The broken nail of her middle finger scratched lightly against the hard knot in his neck, right where she had been ready to gouge. Jax didn't even flinch. He either trusted her a great deal, or he truly didn't care about dying. Both seemed equally likely.

"Elecia's right, you are not well, are you?" he whispered.

Vhalla eased away. "I'm fine."

"Vhalla, you should—"

"I am your Empress!" Her voice raised half a fraction as she raised a finger, pointing it at the tall Westerner's face. "And you, you fallen disgraced lord, will not tell me what I should and should not do."

Jax blinked down at her. Vhalla's breathing was heavy. When he said nothing, she continued on her way alone. Being alone was fine, because if it came to it, Jax wouldn't be able to protect her. None of them could touch her any longer. The more she trained, the stronger she became. She was evolving into something better than them all.

CHAPTER 28

HER THEORIES WERE proven true when an enemy force greeted them halfway through the Great Southern Forest. Victor had planned this attack carefully, and it wasn't until giant flaming trees were falling upon the Imperial army that they even realized the enemy surrounded them. Vhalla watched as the first tree fell, soldiers scrambling out of its way ahead of her, and wondered if she should just let them die. Any who couldn't protect themselves didn't deserve life.

However, her hand moved and pushed tree after tree away with gust after gust, sparing her mostly Commons army.

The enemy charged from their hiding places on either side of the road. Vhalla was off Lightning within seconds, her sword drawn. She would tear them all apart herself, with steel or wind.

The first sound of her blade crunching through a skull was the sweetest sound she'd ever heard. Vhalla couldn't keep a gleeful smile off her face as she turned and depressed a hand into another's mouth. The woman's eyes widened and Vhalla savored the look. *There it was.* That moment right before someone's death. The split second when they realized their own mortality. That they were going to die by her fingers. She'd never allowed herself to enjoy it before and, *oh*, she'd been missing so much!

Licking her lips, tasting her kill, Vhalla was already onto the next one. The skies opened, and a late autumn rain drenched the field. Vhalla trusted wind more than ground to keep her feet from slipping.

The rain washed off her trophies, and Vhalla was forced to keep up with the downpour if she wanted any of the satisfying crimson.

Kill them.

Yes, she agreed.

Kill them all.

She vowed she would.

Enemy sorcerers were still in the treetops to rain arrows and fire down to the ground. Vhalla pushed them to their deaths one by one. She bobbled them like toys on the way down, deciding if she wanted to kill them from the fall or tear them apart with her hands.

The heartbeat in her ears would've driven her mad if she hadn't given herself to it. It was physically painful to resist. And it had always been her lifeline in battle.

Vhalla's hand clamped down on another mouth. *What number was this?* Too many to count. Too many to count! She stared at the wide eyes, a mad grin curling her cheeks.

A shoulder slammed into Vhalla's side, destroying her focus before the final blow could be delivered. Vhalla snarled, ready to assault the wretch who had dared interrupt her.

"Vhal, stop!" Fritz shouted over the rain. His hair stuck to his face like a wet mop.

"M-my lady," the soldier Vhalla had been about to kill stuttered. "The-the 'X' . . . I fight for you."

"Go." Vhalla didn't even offer an apology to the ally she had been about to slay. She just grabbed her head with her hands.

"Vhal . . ." Fritz walked forward slowly.

"Fritz, I don't want you," she remarked with blisteringly short temper. Even his face annoyed her.

He took another step toward her. "What's wrong with you?"

"If I told you, what do you think you could do?" she shouted. "You could not even complete your apprenticeship vessel creation!"

Fritz paled. He stared with eyes as hopelessly vast as the ocean. Vhalla panted, her nails digging into her scalp. Her head was beginning to hurt again, and, thanks to Fritz, she hadn't even been able to assess the field to see if they could afford to be talking.

"Vhal, I . . . I never told you that."

"Yes, you did," she muttered trying to recall exactly when.

"No, I didn't." He blinked rain from his eyes. "I was embarrassed. I didn't want you to think your friend was just a screw up."

"I already knew you were a screw up!"

The look of hurt that crossed her friend's face was so genuinely raw that it summoned something equally real from deep within her, a woman she once knew. A woman she'd been. Vhalla's hand rose to her mouth in shock.

"Fritz," she breathed at his back. "Fritz, wait—"

"Sorry, Lady Empress, I didn't mean to trouble you with the likes of a screw up like me." His voice was barely audible over the rain.

"I didn't mean that!" Her efforts were for nothing as he walked back toward the main host where it regrouped along the road.

Vhalla stared numbly at the battlefield. How many people had she killed? Had any begged for their lives? Had she killed another ally before the one Fritz had saved from her? Vhalla honestly couldn't say.

She dropped her head, her fingers digging into the blood and mud around her. This was not the Empire she had wanted to build. This was not the Empress she had wanted to be.

This is the Empress you were born to be.

"Lady Empress," Jax said stiffly, interrupting her from her thoughts. His voice echoed through her ears as though she was trapped underwater. She was drowning, and they all still thought she was breathing. "The majors are meeting to regroup."

He left her before she could say anything.

The meeting tent had clearly been treated by Waterrunners, as it was perfectly dry within. Flames hovered near every person, both drying and warming. Vhalla took her place at Aldrik's right hand at the front of the room.

"The swords sustained the majority of the casualties," a cleric reported.

"Though it is not so substantial that we would need to reform our ranks," another added.

"If the false king continues to attack by trees, we may want to consider spreading archers through the column for a faster response."

"It may be a safe thing to do," another agreed.

"My Emperor, what do you think?" the major deferred the responsibility.

"Let me consult with the Empress," Aldrik said suddenly.

Vhalla turned, realizing he'd been staring at her the whole time. The majors departed on command. Jax didn't so much as look at her, whispering hastily to Elecia.

"Vhalla . . ." Aldrik crossed the gap between them. "Are you hurt?"

"No." She avoided his gaze.

"You fought well."

She winced at the compliment.

"You are becoming a force to be reckoned with on the

battlefield." Aldrik tried leaning forward to catch her eyes. "So, what do you think we should do?"

"Whatever you and the majors think is best." She sighed heavily. "I am very tired. I trust you."

"I need your opinion." He was being relentless.

"Why?"

"Well, you said you could feel him . . ." Vhalla looked up sharply at the Emperor, a scowl growing on her face as he spoke. It only made him speak faster, and the more he opened his mouth the further his foot went into it. "I know, I understand, that you may not want to. But for us—no, for everyone—for all of our subjects, if you can find out what his next move is, then we can prepare."

The laughter escaped as a spasm of amusement. It quivered her breath, trembled her shoulders, until it erupted as a raspy noise between her lips. It silenced Aldrik and brought a paused, distant look she'd not seen in some time.

"I see." She stepped away from him. "I see. You are your father's son after all."

"*What?*"

"So willing to use *my* magic to get what you want. 'Hush, Vhalla. It's not a Bond Vhalla.' It's easy, not having him in *your* ear."

Aldrik stepped back as though she'd struck him.

"You don't know what it's like having him in your head!" she shouted and didn't care who may hear. "You want me to listen to him? To all the words he tries so hard to whisper into my subconscious? To all the visions he shows me if I dare shut my eyes and try to sleep."

"Vhalla—" Aldrik returned to life.

"How many times must I tell you not to touch me?!" She wrapped her arms around herself, her nails breaking as they dug into her armor. "Don't do it, Aldrik. Don't give him one more scrap of emotion to take from me and turn into something else. To use as fuel to break me down."

Her knees hit the ground, and Vhalla looked up at him, pleading. She looked at him as though he were the Father incarnate. Ready to beg him to take her to the realms beyond.

"By the Mother and Father, Gods, *make it stop!*" She could feel him in her. He wanted her to give him control. Victor wanted nothing more than to ransack her mind and claim her body. He would turn her into one of his crystal abominations if she let him. "Aldrik, I know you wanted it of me, but-but I can't."

Aldrik said nothing. Kneeling on the damp ground before her, Aldrik held out his arms. And the Emperor waited.

Vhalla's self-control finally cracked. He was a risk worth taking; he'd always been. Aldrik's arms enveloped her, and Vhalla pushed her face into his chest so hard it almost broke her nose again. She didn't even try to stop the tears, and he held her all the harder.

"I don't know—his magic is in me, Aldrik; it could hurt you." Sense wasn't winning as Vhalla sought out his comfort, her head finding its way to his neck and shoulder.

"You could never hurt me," Aldrik whispered.

Vhalla could not choke down a sob, praying that it was still true. His heartbeat pulsed within his neck, and Vhalla listened closely. She focused on it above all other noise in her head.

"I'm sorry," Aldrik continued, his breath ruffling her hair. "I shouldn't have let you endure this for so long. I didn't think it was this bad. I thought it was stress and war, and I was a fool. Forgive me." He pressed his lips to her temple. "I love you, Vhalla Yarl Solaris."

Vhalla closed her eyes and let her new, full name echo throughout her mind. It reverberated all the way down into the depths of emotions she had tried to hide. Her love for him would always be there, burning just under the surface. Vhalla opened her mouth to tell him the same, to make her own apologies, to commit to working together and building a new dawn.

But a scream was the only sound to escape as a stabbing pain knocked the wind from her chest.

"Vhalla!" Aldrik's voice was raised, frantic.

Vhalla, another voice seared at the edge of her consciousness. It sounded like a dagger being drawn across glass.

She gasped for air, a violent shudder coursing through her. It was as though someone had removed her lungs and replaced them with ice.

"Vhalla, what's wrong? What is it?" Aldrik was hopelessly frantic.

"Al—"

Don't say his name, Victor's voice purred. *Do it and you'll only make this worse.*

"Aldrik!" Vhalla choked out defiantly. "He-he—"

She couldn't utter another word. All the air was gone. Vhalla balled in on herself, trying to become so small the world would forget she existed. The agony was as great as some of the worst pains that had been inflicted upon her in the past two years.

"Major Jax!" Aldrik shouted.

Movement barely registered in her blurring vision. Her breath was quick and shallow, and she fought for every gasp. The firelight was reduced to glowing orbs in her quickly tunneling vision. More shouting, arguing, running footsteps, it was all happening to someone else very far away.

How badly does it hurt? Victor raked against her mind.

She couldn't even choke out a response.

All because you said his name. I did warn you. Do you know what this is, Vhalla? Do you know what's happening to you?

She was dying.

"Vhal, Vhalla!" a different voice cried for her.

Her eyes fluttered closed.

There is no pain here.

No pain, she agreed weakly. Darkness welcomed her.

If he truly loved you, he would take you away. But do you see what he does to you?

Victor smashed his way into her consciousness with the grace of a sledgehammer. He was pilfering from her awareness, encroaching upon all that she was. His essence was like a snare, the more she fought it, the tighter it wound.

"Vhalla! Don't - - - - -ave to fig- -t!" The voices were fading; she was reaching the bottom of that abyss she was sinking into.

The truth is, Victor continued. It was as though he stood right next to her. *He loves his crown, his Empire, his legacy. He fights for his own glory, just like his father.*

You're wrong.

Why do you still fight me, wretch? Do you not think the late Solaris started with pure intentions? You knew the man he was. Aldrik will be the same; he's tasting war, and he will hunger for it forever. The sensation of Victor pressed upon her, and Vhalla struggled to maintain her sense of self. *But what's Vhalla's role in his world? Why doesn't she fight for the winning side? Fight with me . . . What'll be your destiny?*

To kill you. Vhalla fought for—and meant—each of those words. He was like ice, invading her, freezing her in a prison of her mind where there was only him.

You know you can't. Look at you now, prone before my might. Your tenacity to resist is charming, but I am much stronger than you give me credit for. It will only result in the deaths of those you—

Vhalla didn't know if hers or Victor's scream was louder. A blinding white light penetrated through the darkness. It immolated the shade of Victor that had been moving into her mind. It scorched her and exposed her like a babe raw to the world.

She opened her eyes weakly, not expecting the face that stared back at her. Princess Sehra dominated Vhalla's field of vision. Her hands slowly pulled away from Vhalla's temples before she sagged into Za's waiting arms.

"Vhalla, my Vhalla," Aldrik coaxed from her side.

She shuddered violently, but squeezed his hand as tight as she could.

"She's too cold." Elecia pulled her hand away from Vhalla's face. "We must warm her up."

"What's happening?" Fritz asked the question on everyone's mind.

"He's using the crystals to entwine his magic with hers," Sehra answered, instantly gaining the floor. "I wondered, when she lowered the gate, but I did not expect this . . ."

"Y-you saved me." Vhalla couldn't believe it.

"I did," the princess didn't mince words. "But he will be back. He's stinging, but that was not a fatal blow."

"Thank you," Vhalla whispered.

Sehra regarded her for a long moment before giving a small nod.

"What did you do?" There was genuine gratitude in Aldrik's voice.

"I used the power of Yargen to put a stop to the crystals," Sehra spoke as though the fact should've been obvious.

"What *is* the power of Yargen?" Jax asked the question Vhalla had been meaning to.

Sehra and Za shared a look. After a quiet exchange in the Northern tongue, Sehra spoke again, although the rest of the room was keenly aware that they would be hearing an edited version.

"That which you call the Mother has a name, Yargen. She cultivated the earth and gave those tools to the initial peoples of this land."

Vhalla had heard this story before, she realized. Victor had mentioned it.

"One tool was an axe, Achel, capable of splitting the earth and creating life. It was given to the first Child of Yargen, and the place they did so was Soricium. When their job was done, they committed Achel to rest. I am a descendent of the first child, and Yargen has chosen me to hold her magic." Sehra went from addressing the group, to only addressing Jax. "So the magic of Yargen is her strength, the force of life and light and order."

"So, crystals are of the Gods?" Vhalla asked slowly as she warmed, thanks to Aldrik's fire burning near her.

"They are," Sehra affirmed. "It is their power in physical form. Something that we mortals can barely dip into without severe consequences."

"The taint," Fritz put "severe consequences" in more common words.

"And why I cannot do what I just did very often." Sehra looked over Vhalla solemnly. "I could not break the connection you have with him, only stall it for a time. He will come back for you. If you can harness his magic, the crystal magic, you are the thing which stands in his way."

"How often can you do it?" Aldrik asked.

"I'm far from Soricium." Sehra shook her head. "Even surrounded by life here, there is much wickedness and impure magic upon these lands. My link to Yargen is not strong enough to do it more than every few days."

"Every few days? She could die!" The Emperor wasn't pleased with the news.

"You kill Sehra if she does more." Za scowled. "Southern King be thankful."

Aldrik opened his mouth to speak, and Vhalla stopped him with a touch. "Za is right. And I wouldn't want Sehra to die for me." Vhalla turned to the princess. "How much longer until he can be back in my mind?"

"I cannot say." She shook her head solemnly. "It all depends on how badly he seeks it."

"How much longer until we reach the capital?"

"Fifteen days," Aldrik said finally.

He'd said a number. But all Vhalla heard was a death sentence.

CHAPTER 29

VHALLA HAD THE best sleep in what felt like years. There was no grating on the underside of her flesh, nor were there any nightmares. She could enjoy the loving support of her husband without fear, and Aldrik indulged her every want for comfort.

The next morning, Vhalla sought out Fritz first thing and apologized. Her friend was understanding, even apologetic himself for not being more understanding of the situation. They both said their peace and continued on as normal—as much as possible. She did the same with Jax, though the Westerner seemed to have already forgotten their tension.

Her heightened awareness did not serve her on the march, however. Vhalla forced herself to ignore the stares and whispers as the army mounted and began marching. She kept her head high and kept her face impassive. But her ears heard.

"Did you see how she fought?"

"The Empress of blood."

"Crimson twister."

"Death bringer."

Aldrik kept glaring from the corners of his eyes, a silent challenge for anyone to raise their voice to something more than a whisper. None rose to his challenge, and the gossip eventually faded. But it weighed heavy in her mind in the days that followed.

Vhalla woke from sleep with a searing pain through her mind.

All those things said of you.

She gripped her head, panting. Aldrik stirred.

They will never respect you. They will always fear you. You put your powers on display, your might, and that was their response? To call you a monster? Look at the ignorance of Commons. Victor's voice echoed through her mind right behind her temples.

"Go away," Vhalla hissed.

"Vhalla?" Aldrik sat, clearly hesitant to touch her. "Is he awake?"

Is that the man you claim to love? Tell Aldrik hello for me. I so look forward to killing him again. Do tell me, how did you survive the Crystal Caverns? The same way you forced me out of your mind yesterday? What power was that?

"I said go away." Vhalla closed her eyes and imagined her mind like the wide plains of the East. Vast and overwhelmed with wind. Someplace that she knew, but any other man could be lost within.

Why don't you come to me? Come to me, Vhalla. Victor's voice was already weaker. Sehra had been right, he was certainly recovering from whatever the princess had done.

"Go away!" she screamed.

Victor released his hold on her mind.

Their tent flap opened without permission, a pair of concerned Western eyes looking between them. Vhalla stared back at Jax and realized her responses to Victor had been said aloud. Aldrik shook his head, and the guard retreated.

Vhalla did not want to acknowledge the looks the next morning. She ignored the faces of the people who she was supposed to lead. She tried to hold herself together as the world felt like it was slowly falling apart beneath her. She didn't want to reveal the increasingly fragile sanity of their Empress.

No one would share her fire pit at night. No one would look at her for longer than a few seconds at a time. The majors spoke primarily to Aldrik. Everything she had worked for felt like it was falling between her fingertips.

The third night, the dreams returned.

Vhalla stood in a throne room, a place she once knew. On one end sat a large golden chair. On the other stood massive ceremonial doors, so large they required chains and two men each to open and close. Large vaulted ceilings displayed stonework reminiscent of the Imperial library. Where golden pennons once hung, black velvet strips featuring a silver dragon ran the lengths of the long columns.

A man sat in a chair, a crystal crown upon his brow. It glinted off the light from the windows overhead, but glowed mostly with its own unnatural aura. The glow was mirrored in the faintly shining crystals that were overtaking the room from the floor beneath the throne. Victor's hair had been cut, and he now wore it in a style similar to Aldrik—combed back. It was a slightly looser hairdo, but it was similar enough that Vhalla wondered if it had been a conscious change.

He looked every inch a king upon the throne, save for the stones marring his skin. The crystals were embedded into his flesh, jutting from his body, growing from his bones. His veins pulsated black around them, the taint struggling to take hold. On occasion he'd shift his attention from the scene before him to one of the stones. It'd flash faintly, as if whispering to him, communicating with some distant point.

She wanted to feel hatred at the sight of him, she wanted to be ready to launch herself—even in a dream state—into an attack.

But all Vhalla felt was empty. He didn't look like a man any longer, he looked like a God. A God who had worn her down past the point of exhaustion.

However, following his line of sight, the object that he looked at with such malicious delight, brought feeling back to her—and the feeling was horror. It compelled her to movement. She held out a translucent hand, as though she was more than just a spectator in the nightmarish memory to which she bore witness.

Laughter rang out from all sides of the hall. Men and women swathed in black robes sat on one side of long tables, feasting and enjoying in the night's revelries. In the center of the room were ten people, naked with sacks tied over their heads. They were of varying ages, from varying backgrounds, but the one commonality they shared was trembling fear.

"Who would like to go first?" Victor called from behind her.

"I found and put to death four Commons for besmirching your name!" a black robed man cried as he stood.

"I orchestrated the Eastern advance!" another shouted.

A third stood. "Two of the fare are women I supplied— Easterners!"

"To the man who is our benefactor goes the honor of the first spoils." Victor's voice grated through the cavernous space like rocks scratching over glass.

Stop, *Vhalla pleaded futilely with the memory. She knew the time she was witnessing had long passed, but the fragile sanity she'd managed to scrape back together was threatening to break if she was forced to endure another moment of what was coming.*

The man stood, walking around the table with a small applause from his peers. Arms folded over his chest, he strolled down the line of shivering people. Each one flinched as his boots clicked past them. Victor shifted in his seat, grabbing both arms of the throne in anticipation.

"They are Commons." The man walked back to one of the dinner tables, grabbing a long meat knife from a plate. "They are not worth our magic, not even to die."

With a swift kick to the shoulder, the Common man on the end of the line was sent onto his back. Arms and feet bound, he could do little more than whimper on the floor. Kneeling beside his victim, the hooded soldier gripped his blade firmly.

Placing the silver flat against the man's flesh at the elbow, he slowly worked the blade under the skin. With careful precision, he picked at the skin, pulling up a tiny flap. He pinched the stretching flesh, proceeding to flay the man's arm.

Vhalla wanted to scream. She wanted to shout. She wanted to be free of this nightmare. But she couldn't be. No matter how hard she struggled, she couldn't escape. So she gave in. She gave the people the only honor she could give them. She bore witness to the horrors Victor's men reaped upon the Commons. She saw with her own eyes the horrors that could thrive in men's hearts when their victims begged for freedom, mercy, and the end.

It was during their fifth torture when an arm shook her, freeing her and jolting Vhalla awake. Vhalla promptly retched, barely missing the edge of their sleeping mat.

Aldrik placed his hands on her shoulders, and she flinched. The memories seared behind her eyelids. Covering her mouth, Vhalla struggled to regain control of her body. Her head hurt, her eyes only saw the nightmares, and her shoulders wouldn't stop trembling.

That entire day, Vhalla felt that same horrible emptiness she'd endured in the dream. A feeling of hopelessness before the horrors. She didn't know anymore which feelings were her feelings and which feelings Victor was projecting into her. She was untouchable to her friends; no matter how much they yearned to help, it was useless. She had to endure the nightmares, the shakes, the horrors, his voice, one hour after the next.

Egmun had been right, Vhalla mused one night. He had warned them that this would happen if she lived. He had tried to kill her from the onset. He couldn't say why; his own history was a secret. But he had known. It was just another piece in a puzzle that came together too late. *What if they had all actually worked together from the start rather than casting doubt upon each other?*

Vhalla looked up at the sky tiredly, too exhausted to straighten her back. She couldn't remember the last time she'd slept. Her eyes drifted over to Aldrik; dark circles surrounded his eyes, his cheeks looked hollow, and his skin was translucent. Her condition was beginning to have a very real effect on their Emperor, the only one who could band the empire together and lead the army as they had.

If I die, you die. Vhalla hadn't believed Victor's words then. But if they were true, it could present an unexpected solution to their problem. Her mind circled around the notion for the rest of the day's ride.

That night, Aldrik presented her the last thing she'd expected.

"I thought we wanted to use this connection for me to find out information, to find something useful." She stared at the vial of Deep Sleep.

"You're not sleeping. You won't get to him at all if you keep this up."

"So you want to drug me?" The words could have been sharp, but they were only tired. She didn't see the point in fighting any more. "You'll knock me out because I'm too much of a hassle."

"That isn't what this is." His mouth said one thing, his eyes said another.

"I know what they're saying, Aldrik. I know this is easier for you." Vhalla reached for the vial. His hands clasped over hers, gripping her fingers fiercely. Vhalla hid her wince. Victor's magic and the crystals continued to increase their hold, and Aldrik's sorcery was becoming a searing pain every time they touched.

"I want you well," he insisted. "Please, Vhalla."

"If you insist," she reluctantly agreed.

When the host stopped for the night, a vial was forced into her hand. Food was shoved in her face, and she was watched carefully while she ate. Then she was told to drink.

Her friends had become her keepers. Her husband was now her overseer before being her lover. They were reduced to handlers, pushing her from one place to the next.

She felt stronger after getting rest each night. But darkness grew on the edge of her mind. It itched and beckoned to her. It told her that she was certainly still dreaming, the Deep Sleep just made her oblivious to it in the morning. She had a nagging sensation of forgetting something important, but she also bore the burden of that forgotten something.

Her improved strength proved to be more than useful at the next crystal barrier they met. Set up where the Great Southern Road forked with the path to the East, Vhalla barely exhausted a thought to dismantle the crystals that were attempting to inundate bolts of pure magic upon them. But once again, she couldn't recall the ensuing battle with Victor's forces. All she knew was that she had to swallow that sickening liquid the second the sun hung low in the sky.

Victor had guessed her game, and he began to haunt her during the daylight since he could no longer reach her in dreams. Unlike his prior efforts with direct attacks on her mindset, he now inflicted chatter—bored chatter—upon her. As if she was no longer even fun to toy with.

You are getting closer to me, dear Vhalla, Victor hummed across her consciousness.

"Don't call me that," she mumbled under her breath, swaying with Lightning's slow steps.

I can feel you, he continued. *Can you feel me?*

Each day, his assault became more relentless than the last. As the mountains rose higher around them, Vhalla's head slowly began to clear. She was certain it was the last stages of exhaustion and mental psychosis setting in, her body and mind finally throwing in the towel.

Does it not feel better, being closer to me? Closer to that other part of you you've been missing?

Come to me.

I have use of you. I had to kill you before—but now, now you are more. I can use you.

Each time she tried to fight against him, it only resulted in another mental assault. So Vhalla learned to keep quiet. She only had to endure a few days more. A few days that would feel like years.

Deep Sleep was a finite resource, and they finally ran out. Elecia didn't have the means to make more, and they were so close to the capital that it seemed unnecessary to spend precious time trying scrape together the ingredients. Without it, Vhalla was terrified to close her eyes. So she lay awake, fighting sleep, fighting thoughts of anything.

Vhalla, Victor whispered across her mind. Aldrik had long since fallen asleep, his back to her. *Do you want it to end?*

"It will end," she breathed. "With your death."

Still so confident? Victor's amusement reverberated across the edge of her mind. *Fine, then come to me.*

"I cannot kill you."

I lied.

"You did not; I know how Bonds work." Vhalla was not playing his game.

I will destroy the Bond.

Vhalla brought her hand to her mouth to clamp with a sob. Those words were sweeter than any she'd ever heard. It was a lie; she knew it was. But she wanted so desperately for it to be true.

"Why?" Her voice was barely audible to her own ears.

So I can kill you, he snarled.

That much she did believe.

Come to me, Vhalla. Set aside your army, and I will set aside mine.

She sat up, looking at Aldrik. His brow was furrowed, and his sleep did not look particularly restful. They had been married for little more than two months, and only one day of it had been happy. She wondered if he regretted taking her hand.

Come to me, Vhalla, the voice called.

"Just you and me?" She began to clip on her armor, painfully slow as to not wake her sleeping husband and Emperor.

Just us. Let us finish what was interrupted in the caves. Victor's voice held a promising tone.

Vhalla looked back to Aldrik. She ached in the spot where her heart used to be. But that woman was gone. She had been worn down and drugged away.

"One thing," Vhalla breathed. "If I come to you, you will kill me." She was hopeless before the monster she saw sitting on the throne in his memories. Vhalla knew it to be true.

That has been my plan from the beginning, Victor said simply, his words twisting a number of ways.

"If I come to you now, like this, spare Aldrik," Vhalla pleaded weakly.

Why would I spare the man who threatens my throne? Victor sounded amused.

"Because he will be of no threat once you break him with the horrible way in which you will kill me." Vhalla thought back to the Commons' screams. She would just be another voice pleading for an end.

Fine. Once his army is dead, his friends and family tortured before his eyes, and his home taken, I will put him on a little boat and let him row to the Crescent Continent and live there, Victor offered.

"So long as he lives." Vhalla reached out a hand, her fingertips hovering just over Aldrik's cheek. She didn't dare touch him.

Vhalla crawled out of the tent and started alone down the Great Southern Road. She took nothing but herself, Lightning, and her armor. All she had left behind was a few wet spots on the Emperor's pillow where the last of the woman he married had broken at the hands of a psychopath.

CHAPTER 30

RAIN. *OF COURSE* it would rain—it was the mountains in the summer. The fine mist that coated her cheeks stuck her hair to her forehead barely thirty minutes into her ride. Vhalla shivered in the saddle, gripping the wet leather of the horse's reins.

"I'm sorry, Lightning." She patted the horse's side, barely a dark shadow in the overcast moonlight. "I can't say I know what they'll do to you when I get there. But no matter how horrible it is, I won't be long after you."

Vhalla focused grimly on the road ahead. She put Aldrik behind her. *He will be safe there*, she knowingly lied to herself. The more distance she could put between her and him, the better he would be. Her emotions had become too wild and barely controllable in Victor's wake.

The trees served as silent sentinels to her lone march. She could barely remember what they had looked like the last time she had so peacefully travelled this road. It had been that long. She'd travelled it as a soldier on the run, and now this. It had been just two years since she'd met the prince. Two years that encompassed more events in her life than the seventeen before it. Vhalla was fast approaching twenty, but she doubted she'd live through that birthday.

Two years ago, her dreams had only been of sorcery and roses—of a garden that she doubted she'd ever see again. But there had been a madman in their midst. Someone who had known who she was and, one way or another, Vhalla's relatively peaceful life would've ended.

A twig snapped behind her. Vhalla's head shot up, and she turned, heart racing, just in time to see another horse dart from the trees in her direction.

She was faster, and Lightning surged into a full sprint when spurred by her heels and a snap of the reins. The other rider cut onto the road, giving quick pursuit. The hooves were like thunder in the quiet forest, and Vhalla tried to make out the rider through the misty rain and darkness.

"Vhalla!" Jax called. "Tonight is an awful night for a ride!"

She clenched her jaw. He, out of all people, would be the only one able to make jokes at a time like this. "Go back! Don't try to stop me!"

He determinedly closed the gap between them, and Vhalla could see he'd left his tent in haste. His long dark hair was heavy with water, and it flapped in chunks behind him. He wore nothing but chainmail, without even a shirt under, from the looks of it. Vhalla couldn't imagine the metal chill or pinching links as he bounded down the road for her.

"I want to ride with you! Isn't that my job?" He grinned madly.

Vhalla cursed under her breath. Why couldn't she have broken like him? She could've pushed her madness into being entirely different and detached from the world.

"Go back!" she shouted.

"Don't do this. You don't want to do this!"

He was pleading, she realized. He'd seen the growing insanity in her over the days, insanity that was now written as panic on her face. "Go, Jax!" Her cry had a whine to it. She didn't want him to force her hand. *She didn't want to fight her friend.*

"You know I can't—I won't do that!" he swore.

Vhalla's hand cut through the air. She telegraphed her move clearly, making the sweep of her arm as obvious as possible. She had never attacked one of her friends in malice or frustration, and she knew it would break her if she did so now.

Jax wasn't afraid to do what needed to be done. Fire crackled under Lightning's hooves. Short bursts, barely enough to burn the wet steed but more than enough to startle. The horse reared, trying to stomp out the flames that had already vanished. Vhalla was thrown off with a large crash of armor.

The hooves of Jax's horse stilled, and his boots clicked across the stone of the road. Vhalla rolled, pushing herself off the ground, fighting for her feet. She clenched both her fists, showing her Channel was open.

"Vhalla." Jax held out a hand. "Stop, this isn't you."

"You don't know me!" she screamed.

"I do!" he shouted back, his voice full and deep. "I've watched over you for more than a year. Don't act like I haven't been there to bear witness to most of the misfortune that has befallen you. Don't act like I can't sympathize with half of it!"

"Stay away." Vhalla took a step back, her breaths ragged. Her heart raced like a cornered animal, and a dangerous beat was starting against her eardrums.

"Vhalla, what do you think you can achieve alone? You have a whole army!" He threw his hands up in the air. "You went from nothing to an army. Hold on a little longer. Two days more, and we will all be there together. I will kill him for you if I must."

"You can't."

"Do you think Victor scares me?" Jax scoffed.

"He should!" She hated she was defending Victor's skill, but she wasn't about to have someone make light of the man who had succeeded in scrambling her brain for weeks.

"I will kill him even if it means my life. I vowed I would see you through this alive!"

As if she could have forgotten. They were all tied together so closely now. Knots in their lines of fate binding an Emperor, a library apprentice, a commoner Waterrunner, a noble Ci'Dan, a fallen lord, and a Northern princess. Her hand cut through the air, trying to push him away. Jax wasn't expecting the gale, and he was pushed off his feet, tumbling down the road.

"You can't kill him without killing me!" she shouted.

"What?" Jax struggled back to his feet, determined.

"If he dies, I die. If I die, he dies." Vhalla took a step back. Lightning had finally calmed down just a little further up the road. "Don't you get it? I-I'm trying to do you all a kindness! Aldrik won't make that decision, and he won't let me make it myself once he knows. If I go now, I can absolve you all of having to make that choice!"

"That's what this is?" Jax matched her retreat with advances. "A funeral march? You're going off to die like some wounded animal because you don't want to deal with finding an alternative?"

"I—" the words coated the inside of her mouth and tasted like bile. *Was that all this was—a coward's suicide?*

"Vhalla, come back, please," Jax dropped his voice, and it suddenly became gentle. "We can figure this out still. The sun isn't up yet. We'll call this a bad dream."

"My whole existence has become one bad dream!" She sent wind at him once more.

Jax was ready this time, and a burst of flame pushed against her wind. Vhalla was startled and was forced to blink water from her eyes at the sudden heat. He tackled her, head on, running through the flame. Chainmail clanged loudly on armor, and they rolled on the road. Vhalla struggled against him, throwing a punch.

The heartbeat was threatening to take over, and Vhalla didn't know how to regain control. She didn't want to kill Jax, and she knew the moment she gave Victor a hint of control, he would force her hand.

"Stop, Vhalla!" He was like a sea monster, long arms came out of nowhere every time she thought she'd wiggled free, pulling her down again and again.

"Let me go!"

"I won't!" Something new took over him—hurt. "What about Aldrik? Tell me! What will you have him do when he wakes and his bed is empty? What would you have me tell him? His love, the only woman—the only person—I have ever seen him truly devote himself to has gone to end her own life?"

"My life will put an end to this nightmare!" she screamed, even though his face was inches from hers.

"I don't believe you have to die for him to." He shook his head violently. "Did he tell you that? Or did you invent it on your own? Either way, it's horse shit."

Vhalla finally stopped fighting. He eased himself off of her and let her gain a seated position. He still held her by the wrists, ready to restrain her once more.

"This isn't just about Aldrik," raw emotion cluttered his frantic words. "What about the rest of us? What about Fritz? Elecia cares for you too now; you can see that, right? Oh, Mother, I know that woman has a crooked way of showing it. But she does, I promise you." Jax leaned forward, struggling to see her face. "We all believe in you two. We are all fighting for you. Do you know why?"

She shook her head. She didn't have the faintest idea.

"Because you two represent something, something more than you do individually. You are the impossible dreamers. The two who took on fate to be together. No one believed you could be anything. More than once, you both strove for more, for dreams that you should've never dreamed.

"So when you say you fight for peace, people believe it. Because you have cheated death and fate. Compared to that, finding peace will surely be easy."

Vhalla bit her lip. Her shoulders quivered, but she struggled to keep her tears in. Even if he was lying, it was a nice lie to believe.

"What about you?" she whispered.

"Pardon?" His grip went slack in surprise, but Vhalla didn't take the chance to run.

"What about you, Jax? You mention Fritz, and Elecia, and Aldrik . . . What about you?"

His face relaxed into something she'd never seen before. His eyes were heavy and sad, so wide Vhalla could see her reflection in the dark irises. He wrapped his arms around her shoulders and pulled her to him.

Vhalla was too startled to move. She had always initiated contact with Jax. He had never been this friendly with her, and, in a perfect role reversal, it was her turn not to move. She didn't have the foggiest idea of how to react.

"Well, let's see. You are the one Baldair told me to protect. You are the woman who gave me my freedom. Vhalla Solaris, I was never here for the Emperor. I'm here for *you*. You are my sovereign. And I will fight in your name until my last days because it is the only thing I have ever believed in other than Baldair's Golden Guard."

Her hands came to life, and Vhalla clung to him. The tears flooded from her, and she nearly howled with sobs. Her friend, her sworn guard, held her as she let out the pain she'd held in for weeks. He said nothing further; he let her mourn and unleash her cries to the sky.

Vhalla released it all. And when her throat was raw, her nose a waterfall, and her eyes burning, she finally stopped. Jax's arms loosened, and she pulled away, looking him in the eyes. His palm clasped around her neck, the other on her shoulder.

"Now, will you come back?"

"Don't let him get the better of me again," she whispered. Vhalla didn't think Jax could do anything, but just asking made her feel better.

"What can I do?" He clearly wanted to help but didn't know how.

Vhalla didn't have any idea either. "Treat me like a friend again?" She needed her friends. She needed them to be her friends, to trust and not fear her.

Jax seemed taken aback, but he recovered quickly. He gave her a nod and a tiny smile. They headed back for camp together, and, come the dawn, neither spoke of her early morning ride.

Chapter 31

HER HEART BEGAN to race the moment the capital city came into view. As the army ascended the road, they began to see the destruction Victor had wrought. Where previously there had been small towns leading up to the capital, now only stood ransacked and destroyed remains. Trees and foliage looked wilted and weak, and then she noticed they had taken on a greyish hue.

Vhalla realized the taint was infecting the very earth. The closer they got to the capital, the less vegetation grew. Everything was still and deathly silent.

The night prior, the majors had gone over the plan of attack, preparing the Imperial company's ascent. Unfortunately, there wasn't much strategy. An army of their size couldn't exactly sneak into the city, and Victor already knew they were coming. Once inside, they would divide into a two-pronged attack, half of the army taking the main roads, the other half marching in parallel a few blocks away. That way, if Victor trapped the main road, they had more chances to reach the castle, while still being close enough to assist each other.

But how to enter the city, that was the question that hovered in all the majors' minds. When they neared, only about an hour away, Vhalla gathered her magic and said a small prayer to the

Mother. She turned her eyes toward the overcast sky and swept her fingers through the air. Vhalla envisioned gusts of wind cutting through the clouds, pushing them away, dispersing them.

Vhalla assessed her work. She hoped it looked like a wing. But even more, she hoped Grahm was still alive to see her signal.

They proceeded with their march, and Vhalla maintained their signal in the sky. They began to hear a clamor rising from the capital. The horrid cry of a crystal beast tore through the sky, and far ahead, the drawbridge of the capital of the Solaris Empire began to open.

It had worked, and they had their war.

As soon as the bridge was down, as soon as they were within distance, the charge was called. There was no turning back now, and Vhalla's head seared from temple to temple. Victor was already trying to worm his way into her consciousness, to dissuade her from her attack.

Vhalla clenched her fists multiple times. This was it, the precipice of her destiny. She would lay it all down here. Her eyes swept to her left, meeting Aldrik's. They both looked terrible. Waterlogged, haggard, filthy, and exhausted. But flames were already lighting the air around his face. The wind was in her hair. They would burn and howl together.

Victor's tricks started just on the other side of the gate. A wall of crystals had been erected, cutting off all paths from the gate. Vhalla held out her hands, unleashing his power, the power of the crystals. She would let him in, but only to use his strength against him. The crystals darkened and fractured, collapsing under their own weight the second she rendered them useless.

Fritz, Elecia, and Sehra led a portion of the army down the main road. Vhalla, Aldrik, and Jax headed right. The majors wanted to see Vhalla and Aldrik split, to double the odds of one of their sovereigns making it through alive, but the couple had refused. Splitting them now would only hurt their chances.

Vhalla waved her arm through the air. Aldrik's magic rode the back of hers to create a curtain of flame suspended over them, blocking the ice and fire attacks from the sorcerers on the roofs above. Vhalla pulled on Lightning's reins.

"Archers, rooftops!" she cried.

Fighting had already broken out in the streets before they'd arrived. Vhalla saw blood staining the ground ahead. Spread lifelessly before sorcerers were men and women with silver wings painted on their breasts and backs.

Vhalla drew her sword and threw it. Directing it with her pointer finger, it sliced across sorcerers' throats, felling two before she summoned it back. Aldrik's fire burst forth at her left, and Vhalla brought her attention to where it burned, helping it with her winds.

The Imperial army made steady progress into the city, until the first monster descended upon them. The beast had a clear path, all talons and gaping jowls. Vhalla tried to suck the wind out from under it, but a searing pain from the back of her mind caused her magic to falter at the last moment.

She narrowly dodged, tumbling off Lightning. Gripping her head, she rolled to her feet and tried to find her sword. The monster had taken out Lightning, and half the army with him.

The horse had taken her to the end of the earth and back. Its death hit her in the chest, as hard as the death of any dear friend. Rage built in her throat. She didn't care if it was Victor's emotion or hers. She hoped it was both. She hoped she could feel his anger at knowing that her army was upon him. That they were not backing down, not now, not after they'd come so far.

Wincing, Vhalla drew herself to her feet as the monster banked high through the clouds. Sorcerers around her sent tongues of fire and spears of ice, but the magic failed to penetrate its leathery skin.

"Stay your magic!" Vhalla ordered. The soldiers faithfully turned their attention elsewhere. "Jax, guard me!"

Vhalla didn't even check to ensure he was. She trusted her guard and friend to be where she needed him. There was no room for fear or doubt in this battle. Her friends would do what they needed to do to survive, just as she would. The worry was etched in her heart, the closest to prayer she could afford.

She invited Victor's magic within her, and she felt it build. If he could make crystal monsters, she could destroy them. Vhalla unleashed his magic with a cry, and the monster exploded with a burst of light, shards of blackened crystal falling to earth like dark starlight.

She gasped for air, slumping. An arm was across her chest—strong, holding her up, supporting her. The magic had taken more out of her, using it more quickly than the last time. The army rushed around her, the battle raging on. A shield of fire sprung up, blocking an attack on the prone Empress.

"Thanks, Jax," she panted.

"Not quite." Vhalla looked up. *She hadn't been expecting Aldrik there.* His armor was scorched, scuffed, and bloody. "Are you all right?"

"I will be." She put on a brave front—there wasn't another choice.

Aldrik's arm lingered for one more brief moment. It couldn't have been more than a second, but it felt like an eternity. He spoke silent volumes. His heart sung to hers, and Vhalla's replied in kind. She knew he was there; they fought as one. No matter what happened, they stood here together.

Stable on her feet, Vhalla turned back, reentering the fray.

Victor had clearly prepared his soldiers for this attack. While the road they walked on was mostly un-trapped—Vhalla suspected Fritz, Elecia, and Sehra weren't having nearly as easy of a time—there was more than one large-scale assault from the false king.

Attack after attack, they pushed on. Vhalla had waved on more men and women from back lines to front than she could count. She was sending them to their deaths. They knew it, as they sprinted over the corpses of their comrades, but they pushed forward anyway. The whole army persisted with one goal in exact precision—*get to Victor, kill Victor.*

Victor's men were clever. Every crystal soldier could count for two of the Empire's army, taking advantage of magic and terrain. They jumped in and out of buildings. Stalled with walls of ice and fire. Groundbreakers ran from alleyways, slicing throats and continuing on without engaging, swords ringing clumsily against their hardened flesh.

Another monster soared overhead, so Vhalla repeated the process from earlier. She focused all her magic to strike the beast down from where it flew. As the crystal beast's corpse fell harmlessly to the ground, so did she.

Aldrik hoisted her up with both arms, wrapping her arm around his shoulders and carried her.

"Aldrik, we must—"

"You cannot stay on the front line." He pushed backward.

Vhalla hated the taste of retreat. "But you can."

"Vhalla—"

"Jax!" she called. Vhalla had no idea where the Westerner was, but he couldn't be far. Her assumption proved correct as she retreated into the center of the host. "Jax, I'm turning useless. But Aldrik isn't."

"I'll look after you." He knew what she was asking before she voiced her request.

They held up the rear guard as the fighting pushed into the night. When the moon was a third through the sky, Victor's men seemed to stop coming. Vhalla had destroyed one more crystal beast, but it took nearly everything she had to do so.

It was a stalemate, frustratingly quiet for both sides. The Imperial army held their line, Aldrik mindful not to give up their advance. Victor stopped sending men and monsters—or had no more to send.

Crystals littered the streets like dark shards of glass. Vhalla watched how they pulsed softly in the moonlight. Everyone had told her she could use crystal magic without it tainting her. Maybe that much was true. But it felt like it was tearing her apart every time she summoned it. Such unassuming stones, already fading and turning to dust, held so much weight.

"How do you feel?" Jax asked quietly, setting her down. They'd found a tavern, long abandoned, to regroup with the majors.

"How do I look?"

"Like death warmed up."

"Then assume how I feel to be ten times worse." Vhalla pressed her eyes closed, holding her head. Victor had been quiet; perhaps he was as exhausted as she.

Their table of majors was thinner than it had been the night before, reflective of this day's death toll. Aldrik had ordered them all to sit rather than stand.

He looked just as dead on his feet as she felt. Someone had struck his cheek, and a small chunk was missing from his ear, which indicated a sword had swung way too close to his face for her liking. But, otherwise, their Emperor was mostly in one piece. Vhalla breathed an internal sigh of relief, focusing on the plans before her.

Strokes of the pen on parchment began to carve out the remnants of their army. Compared to the host that had started at the city's entrance, only a small number—maybe a couple hundred—remained. *They would need a miracle, and another hundred or two soldiers to stand a chance.*

The door to the tavern was kicked open. All the majors turned, startled, half reaching for their weapons. Fritz stood in the doorframe, bloody, and holding their miracle.

CHAPTER 32

"ELECIA!" BY THE time Vhalla said the other woman's name, the healer was already on her feet. Elecia crossed the room and helped Fritz carry the man he was supporting to the table. Majors moved out of the way, freeing up a space where they could lay down Grahm. Vhalla looked at the Eastern man's body, Fritz at her side fidgeting.

Her eyes landed on the source of Fritz's stress. Grahm's hand was covered in tiny crystals jutting out from blackening skin. His fingers looked like they were in the late stages of frostbite. Spider-webbed veins connected each crystal, pulsing deathly taint between them, working their way up Grahm's arm.

"What happened?" she asked Fritz.

"We were beginning to establish a wall, a-a perimeter, so we didn't lose the ground we gained," Fritz started. "I saw more fighting. I thought it was another guerrilla force, the Wings, you know?" Her friend was clearly struggling to keep himself together. "But there were a lot of them. I went to investigate; I brought help with me because, you never know . . ."

Vhalla slipped her hand into Fritz's. She held him gently enough that it didn't distract him from his tale. But her fingers were firm, insistent that he wouldn't escape her. At any moment, her Southern friend looked like he could fall apart, and Vhalla would be there if he did.

"It was a group of Silver Wings, a large one. Not like the rest of them. They were trying to regroup as well, and Grahm was leading them."

There was a deep gash in Grahm's shoulder by his neck. A finger's width in almost any direction, and it likely would've been a fatal wound without a healer. Elecia's hands smeared with blood as she pressed them into the severed flesh, trying to force it to knit together.

"Elecia, can you fix him?" Fritz whispered.

"I'm trying," the woman didn't glance up, not removing her focus from the wound.

They were ignoring the inevitability of the crystals. Vhalla dropped to a knee, looking closely at Grahm's hand. He groaned softly, awareness returning with Elecia's ministrations. From her new vantage, Vhalla could see Elecia's eyes regularly darting to stones as well. The other woman was nervous about magically interacting with someone who was tainted.

"I have an idea." Vhalla caught Elecia's gaze. "But I want him to be physically stable before I try it."

"That sounds foreboding," Elecia mumbled.

Vhalla couldn't disagree. "I'm going to take control of the crystals and destroy them, like I do with the monsters and the gates."

"What will that do to him?" Fritz asked.

"I can't say for certain." Vhalla wasn't going to make it out to be something it wasn't. It was a last resort that could just as easily kill Grahm as save his life.

"Well, if you're going to do it, do it now." Elecia pulled her hands away. "While I have enough strength left in me to try to put him back together when you finish tearing him apart."

No one expected Elecia's sarcasm to be literal.

Vhalla raised her hand over Grahm's, blinking her eyes and shifting into her magic sight. Her magic was thin and struggling. Vhalla briefly wondered what would happen at the moment when she had the same amount of her own magic as she had crystal magic laced with Victor's. But she didn't give it thought. Her friend was before her and ailing. It wasn't the time for doubt.

Just like she did with the monsters, Vhalla connected herself to the crystals and willed their destruction. They exploded angrily off Grahm's hand. Black shards littered the ground along with chunks of Grahm's flesh.

All the majors took a step back to avoid being splattered with tainted blood.

The man lying on the bench cried out, roused back to awareness by the pain.

"Hold him down!" Elecia demanded.

Fritz was the first to respond. Sitting, he cupped Grahm's head in both of his, stroking his cheeks with his thumbs. "Grahm, it'll be all right."

Elecia hesitated only for a second before her hand thrust into the tainted flesh that had ripped open with the destruction of the crystals. Skin that was blackened and leathery turned into mush and goo in the instant the crystals had exploded. Elecia pulled her hand away, black flesh clinging to it like coagulated meat fat. She tried again in a different spot, the skin literally sliding over Grahm's bones.

Grahm twisted his head, trying to shake them off.

"Hold him down!" Elecia insisted, thinking quickly. She turned to the other person in the room she trusted implicitly. "Aldrik, I'm going to need your fire."

The Emperor gave his affirmation without question.

"Fritz, I need you to freeze him."

"What?" Fritz didn't follow.

"I need you to freeze him, slowly, don't shock him. I need his heart to slow; the less aware he is of what's happening and the slower his blood flow, the better," Elecia spoke slowly and clearly.

"He's another Waterrunner and—"

"And the taint has already passed his elbow. The damn things were like boils, and the infection is flooding the body!"

Vhalla stared in horror, wondering if she'd damned her friend. She swallowed, trying to follow Elecia's train of thought. Grahm was dead from the moment the taint set in. This was their only chance to save him.

She ran over to the tavern's bar, locating a long rag. On the way back she scooped up one of the major's swords.

"Wait, that's—"

The Empress silenced the major with a pointed glare. She didn't really give a damn that it was his. It could've been the Mother's for all Vhalla cared. The man realized it and silenced himself. Most of the majors took it as the cue to flee the room.

"Wait, you can't possibly mean to . . ." Fritz gaped in horror as Vhalla began to tourniquet Grahm's upper arm.

"This needs to go in his mouth to keep him from biting his tongue." Vhalla twisted up the other rag, placing it between Grahm's teeth.

"Isn't there—"

"Freeze him, hold him still, and say nothing else." Elecia's breathing was heavy, nerves beginning to take over. She was a good cleric, but this was going to be a test for the woman. "Vhalla, push over that bench, spread his arm across it."

Aldrik helped Vhalla accomplish Elecia's order. It had become the most makeshift operating table the any of them had ever seen, and it was all that stood between Grahm and certain death. Elecia drew the sword and adjusted her stance a few times, pushing the benches into just the right spots.

"Vhalla, hold his arm. Fritz his shoulders. Aldrik be ready with the fire," she commanded.

Vhalla gripped Grahm's wrist. Her fingers compressed against the rotted flesh and bones that squished and slid like pond scum on a rock. She ignored the chilling sensation and held the arm as straight as possible.

"Can't we rethink this?"

"Keep him subdued, Fritznangle!"

"But—"

"Fritz, trust Elecia!" Vhalla pleaded with her friend.

Fritz turned his head away as Elecia lined up her mark with the sword. Vhalla saw her plant her feet to the ground. She felt the tingle of magic through the air as the Groundbreaker made her arms as heavy as rocks in order to create as much momentum possible.

The blade *whizzed* through the air, and Fritz flinched as it connected with bone. Vhalla felt the crack reverberate through Grahm's arm. The man screamed into the rag in his mouth.

Elecia was undeterred. She freed the blade with a small jostle, and raised it again for a second swing. Marrow oozed from the wound, blood pooling on the benches and dripping to the floor.

It took two swings to sever Grahm's arm from his body.

"Aldrik, cauterize it, lightly," Elecia instructed. "I only want to help the clotting along, I may need to remove more later once I see what the taint or infection is doing."

"Remove more later?" Fritz swayed weakly.

"Hopefully when we have proper medical supplies," Elecia murmured.

Grahm moaned in agony as wisps of flame sealed his wound. But his pain seemed to be lessening due to Fritz's numbing of the spot, a makeshift sedative. Vhalla prayed that, when he woke, he would barely remember what occurred.

Elecia quickly bandaged the wound. But she didn't release

the tourniquet until the blood stopped seeping through the cloth. Fritz hadn't let go of Grahm; he stared in dumb shock at his lover's face.

"I'm going to go find something for him," Elecia announced. She swayed slightly. Vhalla knew the exhaustion was just as much mental as it was physical. "Some cleric in the rear guard must have something . . ."

"Will he be okay now?" Fritz whispered.

"I hope so." Vhalla cringed as she picked up the severed arm, enough meat left above the elbow for it to wag uncomfortably. She deposited it in the alleyway behind the tavern. Vhalla ran her hands over her pants legs all the way back, trying to remove the feeling of liquefied tainted flesh and a limp severed limb.

Grahm groaned softly. Vhalla quickly kicked away the bloody bench upon her return. It was bad enough what had happened to him. She didn't want him waking up and having to see the remnants.

"Grahm?" Fritz breathed.

"Fritz?" The Eastern man began to rouse.

"I'm here. I'm here with you," Fritz reassured.

"I need, I need to bring updates . . ." he murmured, almost delirious.

Shock did incredible things to the body, Vhalla reasoned.

"Hush, it's all right."

"No," Grahm refused Fritz's consoling, squinting his eyes open. "I need to tell the Emperor . . ."

"What?" Aldrik stepped into Grahm's field of vision so the patient wouldn't have to turn his head.

"Silver Wings," Grahm fought for every word. "My Emperor, they fight for you."

Vhalla stood, taking her place next to Aldrik. Grahm's eyes widened a fraction, as though he was struggling to see her.

"Lady Empress, it's true?"

"Grahm, thank you for your service," Vhalla soothed.

"It-it was our honor." He swallowed thickly. No doubt his mouth still had the cotton taste of the rag. "We have one hundred men and women who escaped the palace. They fought with me." Grahm looked up at Fritz. "Did they make it?"

"Most." Fritz nodded.

"Thank the Mother," Grahm's eyes pressed closed. "They'll know the paths, once you get in. There's another hundred or more, if they . . . fighting in the palace. They will help you. Victor's retreated - up. They'll help you get there . . . He's . . . There're more monsters. He's not done . . ."

"We understand. We do. Now rest." Fritz smoothed away hair from the man's forehead.

"Fritz . . ." Grahm stared up at his man, who was doing a better job of holding Graham than holding his own emotions together. "I'm glad I could see you again."

"Me, too."

"I love you," Grahm whispered.

"And I love you." Tears fell from Fritz's eyes. "Now, *don't die.*"

Elecia returned, crossing over to Grahm with intent, ending the conversation. She poured three vials down his throat that she swore would have nearly the same effect as Deep Sleep and helped Fritz carry Grahm up to the second floor of the tavern to be kept safe and hidden during the remainder of the battles.

Vhalla let out a heavy sigh. Aldrik's arms wrapped around her; she accepted his comfort and strength, stealing a moment alone with her husband. The room was quiet; even the night outside was still.

"What are we fighting for?" Vhalla closed her eyes for a moment, but all she saw was blood. Blood of her allies. Blood of her enemies. Enough blood to drown in ten times over. "What will be left when the wars are done?"

"That's what we're fighting for." He squeezed her gently. "Whatever, whomever, *is* left."

"Even if that's not us." Vhalla stepped away, not giving into the alluring comfort of retreat that his presence offered. There was still a war to win.

CHAPTER 33

VICTOR HAD LITTLE concern for the unspoken etiquette of war. Just as Grahm and his soldiers had forewarned, the false king had been preparing another wave of monsters and abominations. The lull was only long enough for him to plan that next attack.

They had barely enough time to brace themselves. But they did have some time, which was entirely thanks to Grahm and the Silver Wings.

The rush of battle seemed duller the second time around, and Vhalla struggled to move her feet with the same speed as she had before. Majors ran screaming into the early morning light, organizing what was left of the troops.

Vhalla followed, leading what was now her command. The defensive wall they'd built out of ice and earth had been destroyed. Vhalla sprinted in a direction opposite Aldrik, but Jax remained glued to her side. Jax was foolishly determined to live up to his prior oaths of dying for her life, if need be. Vhalla was equally determined to make sure it didn't come to pass. They weren't nearly as synced as she and Aldrik were, but it was better than any other soldier, and they were both fast learners.

Fritz remained behind with Grahm, a new reason to hold the line. Elecia's clerical opinion was uncertain; she couldn't be sure that he'd pull through, if the taint was even gone. The notion was one Vhalla refused to entertain.

Victor was terribly clever. His initial wave of soldiers carried crystals. Every one soldier that moved upon the Imperial army created two or three more enemy soldiers as they shoved small crystals into the corpses scattered throughout the battlefield. The crystals flared, and Vhalla could feel Victor's will summoning them back to a twisted form of life.

His magic twisted within her. She grabbed hold of the wriggling mass under her skin, pouring it into her hands. It resisted her some now, her exhausted state prevented her from being able to easily funnel it to her will. But the sorcery eventually sprung from her hands and rendered useless half of the crystal-reanimated soldiers.

Vhalla gripped her knees, winded a moment.

You wretched creature! Victor's voice raged faintly in the back of her mind.

"This works both ways," she panted. "If you're going to insist on invading my mind, then I'm going to use that against you."

The magic was a brutal and uncomfortable feeling. Each time she used it, it was harder than the last. It was like wrapping a noose around her own neck and tightening it one pull at a time. But this would be their final push; the castle gates were in sight, and Vhalla would give it all she had. And if that meant working herself to death, then she would die and hope to take Victor with her.

She moved through the field, willing her magic alongside his. They'd almost reached the castle when Victor finally gathered the strength to stop her, making her feel the same sharp feeling inside as that night in the tent.

"Jax!" she cried. He was at her side in an instant. "I need—need—" She inhaled sharply, the freezing pain blurring her vision. "Sehra."

The Westerner looked conflicted, assessing the field quickly. Deciding it was too unsafe to leave her where she was, he picked her up in his arms and bolted in the direction of the other half of the army. Vhalla watched Aldrik until he disappeared from her field of vision. The Emperor pushed on toward his palace.

"Princess Sehra!" Jax called. "Sehra!"

Vhalla began to shudder, and Jax's grip tightened on her. They had to move faster, but she was in too much pain, and her teeth wouldn't stop chattering long enough for her to tell him so. She closed her eyes, focusing on fighting the magic, on doing whatever she could. Vhalla felt the world slipping away as she began falling into the dark void known as death.

But, like before, light exploded within her, bright and brilliant. Vhalla's mind cleared, and awareness surged through her, momentarily free of Victor's weight.

Sehra was held tightly in Za's arms, the archer shaking her sovereign, trying to wake her.

"Sehra . . ." Vhalla sat. "Sehra!" she joined Za's call.

The princess opened her eyes weakly. "That was the last time . . ." she breathed weakly.

"I understand." Vhalla nodded. "We won't need it again."

"Sehra use too much of her power." Za began angrily. "Sehra in danger. She can no more—"

"I know, Za." Vhalla boldly rested a palm on the archer's shoulder. "Take her away, go, hide. If you can, flee."

When Vhalla expected Za to be relieved, her scowl only deepened.

"You think North listen to South command with no Sehra, no Za?" She shook her head. "North is proud. North finish our fight."

Vhalla stared in awe as Za stood and helped the exhausted Sehra to her feet. An explosion of fire shook the ground nearby, jolting them all back to the battle. Vhalla looked between the two Northerners and the exit of the alley they were currently hiding in.

"Stay alive, both of you," Vhalla demanded before returning to the battle at Jax's side.

With Victor's magic shut off, Vhalla could no longer disarm crystal traps or slay beasts from the sky. The army was forced to complete the final push to the castle gates using only traditional means—magic and steel. Vhalla and Jax returned to a thin, disorganized host. She scanned for majors, for any leadership, and found none. It had devolved into utter chaos.

"Jax," she spoke from the outside edge of the fray.

"Lady Empress?"

"This may be where we die." She faced the truth openly.

"No." He shook his head. "You've never done things the easy way, Vhalla. And death now would be the easy way out."

"You're insane," Vhalla laughed quietly and spurred her feet into a run.

She ran toward that dream that had lingered in her heart since the Night of Fire and Wind. A dream of peace, of freedom, of a tomorrow without fear. The streets were littered with bodies to be vaulted over or step upon. Bodies that could have been a friend. Or could have been a soldier she'd trained under. Or one she'd eaten with on the march. But she wouldn't grieve for them now. She wouldn't collapse before the overwhelming titan known as fear and worry. As long as one of their army lived, all their hearts beat as one. She'd want the same if it was her face-down in her own blood.

Soldiers locked in combat all around her, but Vhalla only had one focus. It stretched beyond the man in white and gold armor wielding flames—flames that didn't burn nearly as bright as they once had. Her eyes locked with her current foe—the locked gates of the palace.

"Those for Solaris, with me!" she screamed painfully.

"What's the plan?" Aldrik cried, seeing her running head-first through the chaos.

The only obvious one, Vhalla thought. She may no longer have Victor's magic, so there was only one option when it came to opening the crystal encrusted gates. It was dangerous and reckless, and it was something she'd avoided doing since the sandstorm in the West. Since Aldrik had cautioned her about throwing herself into her Channel.

But desperate times called for desperate measures.

"Hold your ground here!" she directed, keeping the soldiers away from the gates.

Wind already howled through the streets. It spun under her feet, nearly lifting her into the air with its force. She wanted to do this as brutally and forcefully as Victor had when he had wrenched the fragile peace that so many had died for under the previous Emperor's hands.

The wind rushed in her ears, but it was not enough. She needed every ounce of air the sky had left to give her. This was not a summer breeze or a mountain gale; she would be the wind, unstoppable and untamable.

And Vhalla let go.

She relinquished herself to the wind. The world faded away, and she lost sense of her corporal body. Muscles and bones popped and stretched with the force of the twister as her body was flung toward the doors, riding on the wind.

The air refused to let her be harmed while in its embrace so it was left with only one option—break down the gates before her, or smash her into them. They splintered. The crystals around them came crashing down, shattered with the brute force of her magic. Vhalla rolled across the ground, her magic failing the second she realized her mission had been accomplished.

Everything hurt. Everything was stretched past its limit, so far it couldn't even break. Her bones were too tired to even do that much.

She dug into the recesses of her magic and her will with determination. Vhalla raised her head, drawing herself to her knees. The doors to the ceremonial throne room began to open before her, no doubt thanks to the Wings. Far beyond, Vhalla could see a throne glittering with crystal, a place where she knew Victor had sat and sown horror.

It was a throne she would reclaim before the day was done.

CHAPTER 34

THEY PUSHED UPWARD through the palace, fighting against Victor's every resistance. The soldiers who could still conjure a flame or hold a sword reclaimed the palace, one floor at a time. Sorcerers seemed to materialize from the stonework itself to resist them. But the Imperial army continued, determined. They all hoped that, should they put an end to Victor, the rest would fall.

Aldrik led their center. Vhalla was at his right hand, Jax at hers. The teams were smaller now, and there was barely enough room in some hallways to run three side by side, much less fight.

Running with them were three men and women who she had neither met nor seen before, but she already trusted them implicitly. They had survived this far, and she had to assume it was for a reason.

The hallway they sprinted through opened up into a larger artery of the palace. Several sorcerers were waiting, and magic sparked on instinct. Aldrik and Jax were a well-made pair.

The Emperor stepped first, arcing fire between them and Victor's supporters. Jax sprinted, full-tilt, into the flames. By the time Aldrik's magic had vanished, Jax was searing one of the five to the bone. Vhalla was close on his tail but far enough behind to avoid being burned; she was ready the second the flames disappeared, ready to blow the face off one of the men.

"Keep on!" Jax shouted to her and Aldrik. "We'll handle this rabble."

They were close now, close to the pinnacle of the world. It was like they were spiraling upward into Victor's domain. Once beautiful statues had been toppled. Paintings had ink splattered overtop. Banners of Solaris hung in tatters, defiled. Crystals became more plentiful, as though the caverns had moved with Victor and taken root in the palace, determined to spread its taint across the world and to cast its lot in with the most likely man to help it do so.

They had been fighting for hours, days, weeks, *months*, but suddenly the two of them stood at the end of the hall leading to the Imperial quarters. The once beautiful golden doors hung at odd angles, completely encased in giant spears of crystal. This was where Victor had chosen to make his stand.

They both paused, catching their breath, staring at the magic that was tangible in the air. It was the last barrier between them and their impossible dream. But it was a barrier of a power far beyond explanation and the madman who harnessed it.

"I'm not going to insult you and tell you to turn back," she said, wishing her voice sounded a little stronger.

"Then I will do the same." Aldrik turned to her, and she looked at him. It was a sliver of quiet before the storm. "I'm not going to say goodbye."

"Then I will do the same," she parroted in turn.

Vhalla turned, and Aldrik caught her arm. He didn't have the strength he usually commanded when drawing her close, and Vhalla didn't quite leap toward him as she usually did, but their desperate kiss still held weight. It didn't feel like her first kiss; it was greater than that, more refined, heavier with all the words they couldn't say. Her lips tingled for that brief second, and Vhalla wondered if they'd both lied, if that had been goodbye.

The Emperor and Empress started down the hall that spelled certain doom, intent on reclaiming their home.

Vhalla unfurled the taut control she'd held over Victor's magic inside her. She slowly let it seep unhindered into her one final time. Sparks glittered on her fingers as she cleared a path through the crystal barricade to the central atrium of the Imperial quarters.

Victor sat bare-chested upon a throne of crystal. Stones embedded in his flesh pulsed in time with the crystals around him, their magic radiating outward. Victor had been right all along—the Crystal Caverns did, indeed, have a heart, and instead of killing it with the axe, he had claimed it and traded it for his own.

In a slightly different light, the crown shone weakly on his head. Her magic was dwindling from it slowly—perhaps another explanation for his weakening control over her—and that meant the taint was fighting more forcefully for his body.

They didn't come armed with anything other than their magic; they held no crystal weapons to aide them, but Vhalla knew this was their best chance to destroy the heart of the Crystal Caverns once and for all—while it was attached to flesh. Victor slowly raised his head from where his chin had fallen onto his chest, flashing a wild smile.

"Look who it is . . ." he rasped, his voice like stones grating together. "The prodigal Emperor and Empress, returning to reclaim their home. You've created quite the stir."

Aldrik was blank, impassive, immune to the taunts. Vhalla tried to follow his example.

"If you want power, come to me," he cooed. "You've had a taste, you little leech. Come to me and have it all."

Vhalla's shoulders quivered, and a muffled huffing noise

escaped before she could contain it. The next thing she knew she had thrown her head back in laughter. He had no principles or morals; it shouldn't be surprising that even now the man had no shame.

"Oh, Victor." Vhalla shook her head. "You underestimate just how much I need you to *die!*"

The gust of wind was among the strongest she'd ever produced, and Vhalla didn't even lift a finger to create it—Victor had no time to brace himself. He was slammed back into the crystals behind him, his head snapping against their smooth surface. Vhalla knew better than to think that would be all it took.

Victor leapt up before she had time to summon her magic for a second attack. Aldrik was ready, however, and fire blazed through the air. Vhalla watched as he winced, his fire flashing in color briefly as he drew from the magic of the crystals to level the playing field between him and the other two combatants.

The crystals on Victor's chest shone, and the fire moved over his skin harmlessly, as though repelled. Vhalla and Aldrik split, dodging in different directions as Victor launched into his first attack. They scrambled to their feet as the room tried to eat them whole. Gurgling and groaning, the walls shuddered to life. Thick layers of crystal rippled and rolled like waves at Victor's will. Vhalla turned, holding out a hand and deflecting a sharp crystal point with her fingers. But these stones held a deeper connection with the madman than any prior, and she couldn't control it for long.

Aldrik grunted, and Victor's laugh followed, drawing her attention from her own struggle. Her head whipped around, hair sticking to her sweaty cheeks as she saw him, armor caught on a glowing crystal point. Aldrik grit his teeth, clearly not wanting to grant Victor the satisfaction, but it was a battle he was losing.

With a scream of her husband's name, Vhalla cast aside

instinct for self-preservation and swung at Victor from a distance. One of the crystals upon his chest exploded with a satisfying pop and spray of dark blood. The man gave a welcome cry of agony.

Aldrik heard her unsaid words and pushed out his magic. A blaze encompassed Victor, drawing another satisfying scream. He backed off Aldrik, letting the Emperor free himself from the crystal point that had been trying to penetrate his plate.

Free of the flame, Victor moved. A short sword appeared in his palm, a sword made of ice so white it almost shone like metal. Vhalla tried to catch her breath, crossing over to the two men fighting, but Aldrik was closer to their enemy.

Fire burned brightly around Aldrik's body, keeping the edge off Victor's icy blade, but that was about all he could do. With crystal magic sustaining the sword against Aldrik's flames, the two men danced in fire and ice. Every move Aldrik made was toward Victor's face, and Victor moved to jab a spear of ice between Aldrik's plate. They had fought before. Each knew the other's tricks and favorite methods, resulting in a stalemate.

Vhalla shattered the even-footing with a kick to Victor's face. She'd been trying to throw the crown off his brow, but it was embedded into his body as much as the other crystals. Victor reeled, but Aldrik was forgotten as the false king spun and grabbed her, throwing her into the wall.

She gasped in both pain and surprise as a crystal jabbed the side of her head; a little lower and it would've taken off her ear. The crystal's magic overwhelmed her. It felt like it was trying to eat her whole.

Victor used the moment to turn back to Aldrik, gathering his strength. Dark veins pulsed outward from the crystals embedded into his skin. Pure magic zapped from his fingers straight into Aldrik's chest, sending the Emperor flying.

Vhalla screamed. She had to keep moving, *she had to*

fight. Her fingers closed tightly around a crystal point at her side. It seared beneath her fingers, as though it had its own consciousness and was rejecting her. Vhalla forced every ounce of her mental strength to command it to bend to her will. It resisted, but bend it did.

Hearing her footsteps nearing, Victor turned his attention from Aldrik. His sword of ice held up against her sword of crystal. Vhalla panted, and he bared his teeth at her.

Daniel. Her friend, he'd been brought into her life for a reason, and that reason had not been to be her lover. Vhalla's feet moved as he taught. They were light, as though she was still back in that tiny clearing between the houses he had made into his little patch of East. Vhalla parried, reposed, spun the weapon, and twirled with the wind.

Victor had never had the luxury of learning the sword from one of the greatest swordsmen alive—if the Golden Guard status meant anything—and it lived on in her training. Vhalla saw an opening and took it. The crystal sword embedded into his jaw, taking out a chunk.

Aldrik joined his magic with her assault. Startled, Victor couldn't shield himself as he had last time, and his flesh bubbled with horrible burns along one side. He lunged for her, giving Aldrik no choice but to call off his flames or incinerate them both.

Vhalla kicked him off her, tumbling overtop the sharp points of crystals. Grabbing one again, she repeated the process as before. But this time, she could only manage a dagger—her magic was weakening. *She didn't need much more.* They were close, and this fight would soon be over.

Straddling his chest, Vhalla held up the wicked sharp point. With both hands, she brought it down onto the man's face—and hit an invisible wall. Her muscles locked, and time felt like it froze. Vhalla tried to push the blade down further into Victor's mangled visage. But, try as she might, she couldn't strike the death blow.

He rasped through his shattered jaw and mangled lips. Victor was laughing at her. Because she realized it at the same time as he did—a simple rule about Bonds: one cannot kill the person they are Bonded to.

The truth that had drawn her to Aldrik, that had assured her all those months ago that there was more to the prince than met the eye, that he wasn't lying about his every intention with her, was now keeping her from her kill. She wanted to scream at the injustice of it all. Victor was hers, *hers* to kill. He had taken everything from her, and now he was going to take this, too.

"Do it," Aldrik encouraged. "End this."

"You do it, Aldrik." Vhalla eased away. It physically hurt to do so when she wanted so badly just to drive the dagger through Victor's eye again and again.

"He won't do it." Victor's eyes darted between them. The crystals in his skin were beginning to glow again, drawing strength from the magic in the room. "Not when he fought so hard to get you."

"What?" Aldrik hissed, instantly defensive by the subconscious notion of what Victor was implying.

"She didn't tell you? Well, let me say—"

His nose crunched as Vhalla screamed, cutting off Victor's sentence. She had leapt on him, flipping the dagger in her palm to smash the hilt against his nose, shattering it. Before the man had a chance to catch his breath, Vhalla brought the crystal onto his purpling flesh again. She hit him again and again, twenty-three times in total.

The skin of Victor's face changed from flesh-colored to a sickening grey, to a deep crimson. Hot spots speckled her face as his blood dotted her skin from every vicious bludgeon. She heaped her pain, her frustration, upon her target. And, just as she was to cross the threshold into what would be his death, her hands stopped again.

And Vhalla let out a raw scream of anguish. "Kill him, Aldrik!"

Aldrik didn't move. He hesitated, and she wanted to loathe him for that.

"I can't." Vhalla glared down at Victor. The man was somehow laughing through his chipped teeth and mangled torso. "I can't, so you have to do it!"

"If I die, she dies." Victor threw the verbal gauntlet.

"No more talking!" Vhalla shoved half the dagger, blunted side, down the man's throat.

"Is it true?" Aldrik demanded, the last of his hopeful ignorance cracking. Looking at the pain painted in blood on her face should've been evidence enough.

"He's the false king, you can't trust anything he says." Her voice broke from frustration and exhaustion. She wanted it ended. Victor was determined. Aldrik was hesitating. And she couldn't do it.

"If I kill him, will you die?" Aldrik rephrased the question.

"He must die!"

"Will you die, Vhalla?" Aldrik raised his voice to compete with hers.

"Kill him."

"Will. You. Die?" He'd crossed over to where she was still kneeling on Victor's chest.

Vhalla stared up at him, unmoving. She didn't blink; she didn't even breathe. There wasn't anything to say, and, in her speechlessness, he saw the truth.

"No," Aldrik breathed, shaking his head. "No, Vhalla." He looked back down to Victor. "We will chain him in Windwalker's chains. He'll keep the crown so he can live out the remainder of his miserable life. We can move him West, or into the darkest dungeons here. We can find a cell where he'll never see the light of day again."

Vhalla drew herself to her feet as he rambled. She unstrapped her plate, there was only one option left now.

"You didn't believe it," Vhalla reminded him. She didn't want Aldrik to force her hand in this way. "When we were Bonded, you didn't believe that if one of us died, both of us would."

"But there isn't enough research to say one way or the other."

"Exactly. So we never let it get in our way before." She remembered the sandstorm. Was she able to run head-first into certain danger because she'd believed she'd be magically stopped if it was going to kill him? Or because she never believed in mutual death? "It's time to conduct some research."

Aldrik opened his mouth to speak, but Victor had had enough time to recover, and he sent a wave of magic at both of them. Vhalla and Aldrik tumbled in different directions. The points of the crystals were far more agonizing with only her chainmail.

The Emperor engaged the false king. But Vhalla had a different battle to fight, one with herself. She pulled the fine chain Aldrik had made for her over her head, casting it aside. The clang of it falling to the floor distracted both men and neither seemed to be able to conceive what she was doing.

One more spear of crystal. Not a sword, not a dagger, just something with a wicked point. Aldrik's eyes widened in horror. Victor snarled with the same realization.

Vhalla's breath quickened. Did she have the strength to do this? Was she brave enough to really put an entire Empire before herself? It was time to find out.

They both moved, trying to stop her for different reasons. Vhalla clutched the crystal, white knuckled, and drove it through her abdomen. She grit her teeth, pain instant and agonizing.

"You bitch!" Victor roared.

"If you kill him, Aldrik, maybe I will die," she panted. "Maybe I won't. And you can help. But if you do not kill him, I will kill myself to try to take him with me, and you have no more Bonds to bring me back."

A surge of magic hit Vhalla square in the chest. She flew backwards, the bloodied crystal falling from her fingers. Her unprotected back was torn open by the stones. Vhalla wheezed with laughter, letting herself be reduced to a puddle of blood.

"The Bond says I can't kill you, Victor, but apparently it says nothing about letting myself die!" Vhalla laughed grimly. Unlike when Victor had been freezing her to death, Vhalla's senses felt heightened. Blood flowed freely from the gaping hole in her abdomen, coating her fingers that instinctually pressed against it. But she saw Victor clearly. She saw her husband. She would witness the end.

"I will encase you in crystal, you impossible cur, and you shall be mine forever!" Victor let out an animalistic sound of anguish, what was left of his face twisting into rage. He raised a hand and crystals encroached upon her. Vhalla struggled to keep them at bay, her magic finally faltering.

An explosion of fire distracted Victor from trapping Vhalla in place. She dismissed the remaining crystals with small explosions of black glass, which shredded her skin in the process. Vhalla saw Aldrik engaging Victor with all the fight he had left in him. Victor was pinned against the wall, Aldrik's hand clasped over his mouth.

"You do not speak that way to your Empress," Aldrik growled.

Fire licked around Aldrik's palm, and he unleashed his magical wrath upon the man who had killed his family and stolen his throne. What crystals remained on Victor's body began to shine, but his magic was weak and fading, just as Vhalla's was. She put her last remaining strength into rendering his magic useless, into exploding every crystal that marred his body.

Aldrik's flames burned hotter and hotter. Vhalla willed her magic into him. She willed the crystal's magic. She willed fate and love and everything that she held dear in the world into her Emperor's fire. It burned from Victor's nose, licked from his ears, boiled his eyes in their sockets before bursting through his skin with flames as brilliant as the crystal's magic.

She felt the moment it was over. Vhalla wheezed, struggling for air.

Victor's body went limp, pinned against the wall by Aldrik's hand. Aldrik slowly released, letting the charred remnants fall to the floor. When he turned, he looked at her with eyes brimming with tears, with fear.

It wasn't Victor's death that hit her, it was the fracturing of the crystal magic. All the crystals in the room darkened and splintered. Like a rug pulled out from underneath her, Vhalla felt her magical essence struggling to find something to grab to now that Victor's magic and the crystals were gone. Her body was the splintering fractures across their surfaces.

Vhalla gasped into the air, focusing on breathing, focusing on seeing the dawn she had fought so hard for.

CHAPTER 35

HER BODY WAS wracked with shudders and shakes. Vhalla clenched her teeth together out of fear that a violent convulsion would result in her accidently biting off her tongue. She rolled onto her side, trying to find her feet, trying to stand.

Whatever the nature of the Bond between her and the—now dead—Victor, there was more to it than she gave credit for. Moonlight streamed through the glass above her, shining through the refractions of dying crystals. *Perhaps that was it,* more than the Bond. Perhaps it was that she too had come to share in the heart of the crystals, and, as they died, she would, too. Or perhaps it was just the gaping wound in her stomach.

"Vhalla, Vhalla," he repeated her name, over and over again, as though all other words had vanished from his lexicon. Aldrik's arms enveloped her, hoisting her up, holding her to him.

"I'm sorry, Al-Al—"

"Hang on," a soft whine of agony weakened his words. "This isn't the end."

Vhalla reached up a hand and clutched the bloody and soot-covered plate that kept his chest from her. She lamented the metal's existence. She would give anything to rest her head one more time on him and hear his heartbeat and breaths. Her fingers clawed at the armor, as though she could scrape away the barrier.

"I had to." She finally found a grip on his armor and her mental capacity. "Please, don't resent me, my love, *I had to.*"

"I know, I know." Aldrik was sprinting down the hall. The sounds of glass shattering filled her ears. "We must get you to Elecia."

She sighed softly with a shake of her head. A cool numbness was tickling the edges of her fingers. It was lulling her into a gentle stasis. "I'm sorry that you will endure this—"

"I am enduring nothing!" he shouted, less at her than the world. Aldrik swallowed hard, and Vhalla watched the lump in his throat bob like the invisible knot he was trying to dislodge. "Don't you dare leave me, Vhalla Yarl Solaris. Not now."

Her eyes fluttered closed. *Vhalla Yarl Solaris*, she thought to herself. That was her name. So much had happened, but Vi was wrong. Vhalla hadn't traded her fate. This was simply another turn of the vortex. The first Empress Solaris had died a fate connected to the Crystal Caverns; the second would do the same.

Aldrik sprinted downward. The crystals no longer responded to their presence. They stayed dull and darkened as the two Imperials sprinted through the palace. Aldrik's fingers dug welts into her flesh.

His efforts were beautiful. He was beautiful. Even wounded, a chunk of his ear missing, that bump in his nose that had been set wrong—he was stunning to her. A shudder almost cast her from his arms, forcing the Emperor to slow.

"Aldrik—"

"Hush," he commanded tensely. "Don't talk, please, not one word. Save your strength."

He was on the move again, propelling them forward. His eyes remained glued to a distant horizon. Hope flickered through them, an ever elusive beacon in their world. Her vision blurred, and Vhalla finally began to panic.

She didn't want to lose him. Her magic was there, barely felt. But everything was disjointed. Nothing connected, forcing her into a limbo between life and death. Vhalla's eyes fluttered closed. Victor had taken everything from her. He could not win the world, so he would settle for taking her part of it in death.

"Vhalla, open your eyes." Aldrik intentionally jostled her in his arms. Her head lolled against his shoulder. "Open your eyes, damn it!"

She obliged, a small sliver of light returning to her. She tried to think of how much ground he could've covered with her, where they would be going. His chest heaved in contrast to the small swells of hers.

Imperial soldiers were ahead, a whole patrol of them. Aldrik's feet quickened with the dangerous fuel that Vhalla knew to be hope. Her chest ached, and not just because of the beginning stages of cardiac failure.

"Where is Elecia?" Aldrik barked, his voice thick and hoarse.

"M-my lord?" The soldier was aghast at the visage of their Emperor carrying their dying Empress.

"Lady Elecia Ci'Dan! Where did she set up her triage?" Aldrik's grip tightened even further.

Vhalla didn't have the strength to tell him he was hurting her. She would be gone soon; no matter how much she struggled, death was a siren, and she'd fully heard its call. She missed any reply, her eyes fluttering closed once more.

"We're almost there," Aldrik reassured frantically. "Elecia will fix you. I know she will."

The balmy summer hit her skin, and it was a breath of fresh air. Vhalla tried to place where she was in the palace. There were over a hundred gardens and a thousand possibilities. But chance didn't work randomly in her world. The moment her nose picked up the faint scent of roses, Vhalla knew the Gods didn't play games.

"Elecia's in the hall, just here," Aldrik said frantically. Vhalla realized he was talking to her. "She's coming. She'll be—"

The door to the greenhouse opened suddenly. "Let me see her," Elecia announced.

The woman's fingers were on Vhalla's face and neck. They ran down her body and back. They ghosted over her wound, unafraid of the gore, and paused at her breast over the fluttering beats of her heart.

Elecia pulled her hands away, and no one said anything for a small eternity. Vhalla cracked her eyes open, turning to the Western woman. She tried to smile. She tried to be strong. Nothing was about her anymore. It was about them, those who would inherit the world they'd fought so hard for.

"I don't know what to do," the healer confessed.

"I know," Vhalla whispered.

"You're going to die." Elecia fought for her clinical detachment, but a whimper of emotion betrayed the facade. "Aldrik, I'm sorry, I'm sorry I don't know—"

"Start with the wound, 'Cia. Please, please try," Aldrik spoke with utter desperation.

Elecia obliged, and Vhalla felt the other woman's magic pouring into her. She felt it seeking pathways that had been broken and strewn to the winds, unable to knit the broken flesh and muscle. Her magic had been too damaged by the crystals. It would have to be fixed before any other healing could be done.

The woman must have realized it in the same moment as Vhalla, because she stood suddenly. "I'm going to try to find Sehra!"

Elecia had bolted out the door before any of them could react. She left silence and death in her wake. Vhalla blinked intensely. She wouldn't leave now without saying goodbye.

"Aldrik." He was at her side in an instant. His long fingers scooped up hers, blood smearing across his gauntlets. "I'm so glad I saved you, back then."

"Don't say goodbye, *please*." He was close to breaking. He was fighting the obvious.

"I don't regret it. I don't." She could only hope he understood, that something she said would be enough for him to continue on without her.

She was crying, Vhalla realized. The shining points of light of her memories illuminated the dark and tumultuous road that had taken her to this moment. She didn't want to die. She didn't want to give up everything she'd fought for.

The door opened again, and both of their eyes looked at the lone figure. The princess floated over to the two Imperials, looking much more rested than the last time Vhalla had seen her. Two emerald eyes looked between Aldrik and Vhalla.

"Sehra," Aldrik pleaded. "Save her please, your magic, can it—"

"I understand," she whispered. The princess kneeled next to Vhalla. Her focus was only on the Empress. "You did well."

Vhalla was struggling to see. The princess faded, vacillating between her normal visage and something *different*. Hazy blurs and lines that didn't quite connect. Long fingers, almost like Aldrik's, cupped her cheek thoughtfully. The gesture was more forward than the princess had ever been.

"The crystals' magic is diminishing. They were never meant to be used as they were, manipulated for man's greed. They weren't left with that intent."

"What?" Aldrik asked Vhalla's question.

"You saw them." Sehra spoke to both of them, to no one. "They turn brittle and shatter under their own weight. They will be gone by dawn."

"Princess, we need to act quickly," Aldrik urged. "She's dying."

"I know," Sehra said without hesitation. "Vhalla Yarl, after all that you have been through, do you still want to be upon this earth?"

"How can you ask that?" Vhalla opened her eyes. "Of course, I do."

"*Of course*," Sehra repeated softly. "Very well. I will grant you the power of Yargen one more time. I will change this fate set before you."

The princess had a gently, almost motherly—familial— smile. She placed both hands on Vhalla's face. Her whole palm tingled, and Vhalla felt the same light she'd experienced every time before.

No, it wasn't the same. Sehra's power before had been like a battering ram, forcing its way into her. This was familiar, like it complemented her. It flowed through Vhalla's veins with palpable force. Her heart beat in time to it. Her flesh mended with it. Vhalla blinked, the red dawn flashing a moment in the woman's eyes.

Whatever Sehra did, it worked. And when she pulled her hands away, Vhalla's whole body felt warm, as though she'd been lying in the sun for hours. Her eyes fell back into focus, her breathing strengthened, her heartbeat regulated once more.

The princess stood tiredly, swaying slightly.

"Are you all right?" Aldrik took a step toward the young woman.

"I am, but time is short," she answered cryptically. "I'm no longer meant for this world."

Sehra started for the door. Aldrik looked between Vhalla and the Northern princess.

"Sehra, we can seek out another cleric."

"No need." Her hand paused on the door knob. Vhalla sat slowly, trying to make out the familiar glint in the woman's eyes.

"You did well, but things are only beginning now. The vortex still spins."

"Sehra!" Vhalla was on her feet, not realizing how quickly she could suddenly move, how strong she felt.

"If that is the name you choose." With those words, the woman vanished through the fogged glass of the door.

Vhalla looked to Aldrik. He was confused. *Which meant it hadn't been a dream or hallucination.* He'd heard those words. That had been real.

"Sehra!" Vhalla cried. She threw open the door. "Sehra!"

A cleric looked over from the gate leading into the Imperial hall, confused at the Empress's cries.

"Tell me," Vhalla called. "Have you seen the Northern Princess Sehra?"

"I haven't seen the lady for hours," he answered uncertainly.

"Did you miss her?" Vhalla walked over quickly, Aldrik on her heels. "Could you not have seen her?"

"I have been here since the Emperor took you-you . . . Shouldn't you be resting?"

"Just now, someone left." Aldrik looked through the garden.

"My lord, lady, I-I . . ." The man was clearly at a loss for words, incapable of giving them the answers they wanted. "I suppose, it's possible, that I missed someone."

"Vhalla?" Elecia's voice called. Sehra, Za, Jax, and Fritz were in tow. The group that was to be Vhalla's mourning party. "You should lie down!"

The Western noble crossed to her in a few hasty steps. Her hands were on Vhalla, but she barely felt them. Vhalla stared at Aldrik, and he met her eyes with equal confuson. There was no explanation that she could give him. Trying to explain the full details of her last, tragic encounter with Vi would be impossible now.

Magic glowing around crystals that had looked like *feathers*.

Fire that had saved her life by burning *wheat.*
And a final encounter in a garden of *roses.*
If that is the name you choose.

It was a series of dreams connected by an impossibility. Something beyond her world. A force greater than everything Vhalla had ever known. Something that would fade with time into a vague dream-like memory.

"Vhalla." Elecia forcefully grabbed Vhalla's face, pulling it back toward her. "What did you do? What did you take?"

"I didn't do anything."

"Then how do you explain this?" Elecia grabbed the front of Vhalla's shirt and pulled it up without concern for propriety. There, on Vhalla's stomach, was soft pink flesh where a mortal wound had been moments before. Elecia turned to Aldrik. "You were with her."

"It-it must be something you did," Aldrik inserted, grasping at any explanation.

"I didn't do anything."

Vhalla's eyes met the princess's. It was as though the Northern woman somehow knew. Her mouth curved in a telling smile, all the information the Empress would ever be able to worm from her.

"Maybe there was a cleric. We may have been misinformed," Aldrik mumbled. He turned back to Elecia with conviction. "Elecia, is Vhalla—"

"She's amazing!" Elecia had eyes as wide as a child in a pastry shop. "I must find who did this. They may be the best cleric in the world. She should be dead; there's no reason for her to be alive and healthier than ever. I must find out what they did!"

Elecia dashed off, asking the same cleric Vhalla had just spoken to. She moved down the hall, one person to the next. *But she wasn't going to find anyone,* Vhalla simply knew it to be fact. There was never anyone to find after.

"So, you're not actually dying?" Jax leaned against the iron gate with a dramatic sigh. "And here I had the best farewell speech planned."

"I guess it has to wait." Vhalla gave him a small smile.

"Good, I couldn't handle any more death." Fritz threw his arms around her shoulders, and Vhalla clutched him tightly. "Thank the Mother."

Perhaps they had more reason than they all knew to thank the Mother, Vhalla thought to herself, briefly. One impossible and unlikely explanation of what had happened was just as good as any other.

"Grahm?" she whispered into her friend's ear.

He just shook his head. Vhalla couldn't translate his shining tears. Were they joy? Were they telling her not to worry now? Or were they world-crushing sorrow?

Whatever it was, Vhalla would be at his side to shoulder those emotions as well.

"My lady." Aldrik's voice was heavy with something that she couldn't quite decipher.

She turned back to her lord. He held her gaze with every bit of adoration the world had been capable of producing. Vhalla's arms slid from around her friend's.

Vhalla turned to stand right before the Emperor. The man who she'd met as the Fire Lord, the aloof and distant prince. The man she'd fallen in love with. The man who'd been constant while she'd grown—side by side and even when apart.

They'd been pushed to the brink and pulled back again. Throughout it all, they'd managed to keep a few friends alive, but had lost so many along the way.

"What do we do now?" she breathed.

"Now?" He took a step toward her, crossing her personal space. Aldrik hooked her chin, guiding it upward. "Now, we rule, we live, and by the Mother, we get a bit of time to love."

"Do you promise?" Vhalla's hands curled around his armor. "More than anything, this I promise." The corner of his mouth pulled up into a one-sided grin.

He couldn't look at her like that. Vhalla tugged him and kissed him before friend and subject alike as dawn broke upon the Solaris Empire.

EPILOGUE

WINTER FELL HEAVY in the mountains. Snow painted a thick white carpet across the barren earth, save for the hoof-prints and wheel ruts left behind the carriage. It was a large and unnecessarily lavish contraption, even by her standards; it creaked and moaned as it bumbled up the rocky mountain roads. A wheel snagged momentarily in a particularly large divot, which sent everything within the cabin lurching, a curly-haired Western woman included.

"Watch where you are driving!" Elecia stuck her head out the window, instantly regretting the decision as wind whipped about her face, blowing snow into her eyes.

"Apologies m'lady! It's difficult to see with all this snow!" the driver called back.

Elecia sat back down in a huff, crossing her arms over her chest. *An Imperial summons.* It had finally come to that. Her cousin and that crazy Eastern woman he had taken for a wife had been all too determined for months to get Elecia back South.

She plucked the letter from where it had slipped onto the floor. The words were hard to read amidst the jostling, so she quickly folded it, stashing it into the small leather purse at her side. Resting her elbow on the small shelf built upon the

tiny door of the carriage, Elecia looked out at the winter world surrounding her. If they were going to be so stubborn, then she would dig her heels in as far as she could.

"I hate snow," Elecia muttered to herself.

After the battle, Elecia had eventually returned to the West. She had stayed through the last Southern winter to help heal the remaining wounded soldiers and, upon Aldrik's request, to help reestablish a clerical program in the palace. Elecia had, of course, bemoaned her sacrifice the entire time she remained there. But she kept it to herself that she actually had enjoyed having full control of how she thought clerics should be trained. When she left things were running smoothly in the capable hands of a particularly talented healer named Luzbelle.

It hadn't all been smooth. Dissenters were still rampant through the winter and Jax, who had been made head of the guard, was busy trying to get the city—and Empire—back under control. Aldrik was often busy with Jax in that respect, and many nights Elecia had found the two men deep in argument over how best to ensure the continent was once more safe and loyal. It had pleased her to see that, even as things returned to normal, her cousin still avoided the bottle. She saw how he looked at it on long days, but Aldrik never touched it. Even when Jax gave in and sipped from his own glass.

The last she heard, Jax was being sent off to the East to help rebuild there. It was an equally personal mission as he went hunting for Daniel. But their last correspondence had painted a bleak picture on that front. It made her contemplate how he was doing on many an occasion. She wondered if he was back in the South, or if he had just decided to take up residence in Hastan. Elecia wondered, but she had a pretty good idea already.

Eventually, as what often occurred, people tired of fighting. The crystals had vanished, remaining as mysterious as they'd ever been. They had fractured and broken down, shattering under their own weight before turning to dust. It was as though all the magic had been exhausted, and Elecia couldn't fathom how no matter *how* hard she tried.

The caverns had been crystal-free and filled with dust when Vhalla and Aldrik had sent Groundbreakers to check. Even still, they left nothing to chance. The Groundbreakers had collapsed the mountainside. One of their first Imperial decrees was striking the infamous place from all maps and records.

She hummed to herself, and a little smile crept upon Elecia's face. She was looking forward to seeing them all once more. She allowed herself to enjoy life and be excited now. The last thing she wanted any of them to see was her enthusiasm at the idea of a reunion. Mother forbid they got the idea that she would stay longer than necessary. *She had an image to upkeep.*

However, the luggage strapped to the back of her carriage may betray her. Even her father had questioned the quantity of possessions she had brought. Elecia scolded him for thinking a woman could need anything less. He said little else, his focus fraying with her mother leaving for the North.

Things had actually progressed smoothly on that front. Last Elecia heard, Vhalla and Aldrik were struggling with breaking the news of the deal they'd struck with Sehra to their advisors and quickly recovering Senate. But the princess seemed ever patient, poised, and unworried. She was not a scheming ruler waiting at Vhalla's bedside for a child. It reassured Elecia and her mother, who was the newly appointed ambassador. Despite the turmoil, things were moving toward peace.

Elecia stretched her legs, glancing out the window. She may have been able to walk to the capital faster.

The carriage door swung open as the wheels ground to a halt. Elecia hardly acknowledged the man who had driven her halfway across the continent. *He had been so-so at best,* she mused as she drew her cloak about her. It was a wonderful garment that had been specially made at her request, lined with thick fur, an inner layer of wool, and an outer layer of rich red velvet to keep out the chill—function and fashion. It kept her warm, she determined as she stepped off the metal rung onto the snow-covered ground of the stables.

Rebuilding had progressed nicely. The new stables were erected, and the decorative wood overlays looked to have been receiving their first coats of paint and gilding when the wet part of winter had set in and stalled work. She thought the wings over a certain horse's stable were a bit much. But Aldrik always had a flair for the dramatic and overt symbolism when it came to the woman. *As if he really needed to mark his territory*; the woman only had eyes for him. The irony had never been lost on Elecia when her cousin was so secretive on everything else.

"Elecia!" a familiar voice called.

Fritz raced over to her from the palace stairs, darting from a side door. His hair had grown out, and part was pulled back behind his head in a limp ponytail. Elecia tilted her head. Somehow, the weight pulled out the wave and frizz and made it more presentable. It matched the formal clothes they had thrown him into, more befitting of his station than the shaggy cut he wore prior.

"It's been awhile." Elecia smiled. She had decided forever ago that Fritz was worthy of her smiles. *But only if too many people weren't looking.*

"Too!" He threw his arms around her, and, were it not for Elecia planting her feet to the ground with a small tingle of magic a moment before he reached her, she would've toppled into the wet snow. "Long!"

"You are making a scene." She patted his back nicely before shoving him away with both hands. He could be as bad as an Easterner with his affection. A habit he'd no doubt learned from a certain someone. "Now, let me look at you."

"Are you coming to see Vhal? You must be, right? I hear she's refused all other clerics. Wait 'til you see her! She's—" Fritz was practically bouncing up and down.

"Yes, yes. I'm here to see our stubborn little Empress," Elecia cut him off before he got carried away. With a small amount of amusement, she reached up and looked at the broken moon pin he had affixed to his chest. "Don't you look official, Lord Charem?"

"Stop it." Fritz pulled away with a laugh. He had been the hardest to convince to accept his new role in Aldrik and Vhalla's world order. With Victor dead, a new Minister of Sorcery was needed. Once Vhalla got the idea in her head of Fritz filling the role, no one could persuade her differently. *The woman was bound to have at least one or two good ideas.*

"How have you been settling into it?" Elecia asked, folding her hands behind her back. Aldrik always looked so regal when he did so. She was the cousin of the Emperor and the Lady of the West in training; she had every right to look regal.

"Some bumps, here and there." Fritz scratched the back of his head as they walked for the palace, Elecia's baggage being unloaded behind them. "Not everyone agreed with Vhal on my appointment."

"Power hungry mongrels, Fritz." Elecia shook her head, sending the snow scattering onto the stone steps leading into the palace. "No matter what, there were going to be people clamoring for prestige in the aftermath."

"That's what Aldrik said." Fritz sent snow scattering off his own shoulders.

"Aldrik." Elecia glanced down, adjusting her cloak. It served to hide a small grin. It had always grated her cousin that a common born Southerner seemed to have little qualms addressing him by his first name without ever receiving express permission. Naturally, Elecia saw no point in correcting Fritz. Someone had to give Aldrik a hard time when she wasn't around. "How is my dear cousin?"

"Slowly going crazy." Fritz laughed. "With Vhalla as she is."

"Lovely," Elecia rolled her eyes. *Why did men seek to complicate the littlest things when it came to the nature of women?*

They ascended the stairs together until they reached halfway to the Imperial quarters. Fritz told her how they had decided to postpone the Festival of the Sun this year. That there was too much left to rebuild to be putting on a lavish festival. Elecia hummed over that; it wouldn't have been her choice.

She understood why last year's Festival of the Sun had been cancelled. It would have come only months after Victor's ultimate demise. But this year, this year she felt the people could use a touch of normalcy in their lives. It was one of the many times that Elecia wondered what kind of Empress she would have been if given the chance.

An Eastern man waited in the hall. His palm was on the stone of a windowsill, and, with a small smile, he watched the snow fall outside. He turned upon hearing them approach.

"Grahm," Elecia held out her hand.

"Lady Ci'Dan." Grahm took her hand and shook it warmly. It had taken some time to convince Elecia that Grahm was worthy of the Southerner whom she had claimed as her own—but he won her over eventually. "It is good to see you in the palace once more. How are you?"

The man's work with the Silver Wings had made him the figurehead of the resistance, someone people looked to. Elecia's tolerance of him warmed to a quiet appreciation as time dragged on. And the effect he had on Fritz was heartwarming. If Aldrik and Vhalla weren't bad, these two were almost enough to make her feel lonely.

Elecia's eyes glossed over the knot in Grahm's sleeve. She'd managed to salvage that mess of an amputation following the final battle of the war. The amputation, the crystals going dormant, or both had saved Grahm's life. Though, Fritz still wrote her time to time asking about the dreams that still afflicted his now engaged, fearful of the taint. Elecia reassured him; there were so many reasons for them all to have nightmares.

"I am in the South in the winter; how well do you think I am?" Elecia bemoaned once more, drawing her cloak tighter about her for effect.

"Shall I have a Firebearer appointed to your chambers again to ensure they are properly warmed before bed?" Grahm asked.

With that offer, Elecia knew instantly who was the real Minister of Sorcery. "You thought that would even be a question?" She sniffed at the cold air about her.

"It will be my pleasure." Grahm smiled.

"Join us for dinner?" Fritz asked, tugging on her hand like a little brother.

"If the Imperial family does not demand me." Elecia nodded.

"I haven't seen Vhal in forever!" Fritz whined. "If they demand you, then bring me with you!"

"It's only been three days." Grahm chuckled, adjusting the knot at the bottom of a limp sleeve.

"Forever!" Fritz repeated, exasperated.

His friendship with the Eastern woman had intrigued Elecia at the beginning. It took some time before she realized what drew people to Vhalla Yarl. As much as she tried otherwise, she, too, was eventually ensnared by the woman's determination and general optimism. Elecia would likely die before she let the Empress know. Someone had to make sure their Windwalker did not get haughty.

"She's busy with the library," Grahm reminded Fritz.

"Oh, who was appointed Master of Tome?" Elecia asked. It had not been decided when she left. The last master had not made it through the war, and the news had hit Vhalla hard.

"Vhal's old friend, I think her name is . . ." Fritz chewed it over. "Roan, it's Roan."

Elecia remembered Vhalla going through multiple conversations with the woman. They'd seemed tense. She hadn't understood at the time; anyone would be ecstatic to be elevated beyond their status. But the Empress had refused to speak on it, handling it entirely between her and the Southern woman. *Well, whatever it was had clearly been worked out.*

Time was what they all needed. People moved away as soon as they were free to do so. For the first months after the end of the war, the capital felt like a town of facades, beautiful outside but empty on the inside.

Too many people had seen too much and experienced such horrors that the streets would never be the same again. It led to a decline in the normally steep price of capital homes, and Aldrik had been smart enough to raise taxes before people took advantage of the low prices and started buying. Thus, the crown's coffers were replenishing.

Even now, the castle seemed understaffed to Elecia. After saying goodbye to Fritz and Grahm, it was too long before she saw another staff or servant. Time would heal this, too, of that she was certain.

Elecia had not been immune. She'd had to leave and return for the West. It was all too much to still be in the place where there had been so much blood and death. She needed to see her family and simply relax, but she hadn't told anyone else that. The last thing she wanted people to think was that she was weak. Others would be like her. Once they breathed, they would come home.

The Imperial halls were almost back to normal. Once all the crystal debris had been cleared, they had put a low priority—comparative to all which needed to be done—on restoring the artistic nature of the palace. She was surprised at how far they had come in one year. As she rounded the staircase up the main atrium that housed the Emperor and Empress, she was impressed at how normal it all seemed.

She paused briefly and looked down the hall that she knew led to Aldrik and Baldair's old rooms. What were they being used for now? Perhaps Vhalla's father had been put up in one. It seemed a shame to let them sit empty. Though, the Imperial living area was so large and room-filled that there was almost always going to be something that stood vacant.

The door to the Emperor and Empress's chambers was a large portal at the highest point in the atrium. It was an arched double doorway cast entirely in gold. *Aldrik's father had been so gaudy in his choices for decor.* She gave the knocker a solid rap, wondering if they had truly not heard of her arrival yet.

A minute dragged by, and Elecia began to feel offended by lack of greeting.

"They're not there," a male voice echoed up from halfway down the stairs—through the entire hollow of the room.

Elecia stilled, turning slowly. She didn't allow for one crack in her usual demeanor. She pretended to ignore the tingle on her skin as she turned to look at the frustratingly stunning specimen of a man. Jax gave her an easy smile in reply.

"Would you like me to escort you to them, Lady Ci'Dan?" He ascended a few more stairs, holding out a hand.

She noticed immediately the golden bracer that adorned his wrist. Elecia wondered if he'd managed to start the Golden Guard once more in Baldair's honor, if he'd created a new charter dedicated to the defense of the whole Imperial family. But she didn't ask. Her tongue had turned to lead in her mouth.

"That would be acceptable." Elecia nodded and took his hand as casually as possible.

When they reached the bottom of the stairs, her hand shifted safely to the crook of his elbow. They continued through the palace in silence. Elecia's stomach felt awkward. *Were they going to talk about last winter at all?*

"How are you, 'Cia?" Jax's voice shifted from the laughing playboy to the dangerously broken man she knew lived beneath.

Elecia had grown up in the remnants of Western royalty. From the moment Aldrik and Jax had taken a magical shining to each other after Baldair's "adoption" of the man, he had been in her life anytime she was near the royal family. He was one of the few people left alive who she would tolerate using her childhood nickname, and it was partly because he knew she would flay him if he used it publicaly.

"I'm well," Elecia replied softly. "How are you?"

"Well enough. The guard here is taking shape nicely once more," he answered casually.

Elecia glanced up at him. He had taken to wearing his hair loose and down over his shoulders after she had commented once on how it looked nice. She was surprised to see he still did and prayed to the Mother that he did not cite her as the reason for the change in style.

"That's good. It is nice to know that one even as incompetent as yourself can put together a bunch of men and women with swords," Elecia hummed.

"I should keep you around more often. Here I was allowing myself to feel proud of my work." Jax laughed. "You'll never let me get a big head, will you?"

"It shall be my duty to bear," she replied. "How was the East?"

"Fine."

A one word response; *how she hated those.* Elecia bit her cheeks and kept her questions to herself. The last thing she wanted to seem was eager or worried about what non-work related activities he might have participated in with any men or women.

From the moment they arrived at the garden, Elecia's eyes

were glued on the fantastic glass gazebo that she had been in awe over since her grandfather had told her why it was built. Its walls were steamed from the heat of the inside reacting to the thick snow falling around it. Elecia could only make out the green blurs that she knew to be rose bushes.

"Will you tell them for me that lunch will be ready soon?"

"Why don't you tell them yourself?" Elecia paused, still under cover from the snow.

"I'm a guard; I should do so." Jax grinned, crossing his arms over his chest and leaning against the iron of one side of the gate.

"You just don't want to get cold and wet." Elecia rolled her eyes before trudging into the snow. She mentally ordered herself not to glance at the pair of eyes she felt on her back as she reached the door of the glass structure.

Warmth hit her the moment she eased open the door and, once she was inside, Elecia shrugged off her cloak. Aldrik was very diligent about the temperature, and she noticed the roses were preparing themselves for another bloom as a result. It wasn't until she rounded the central pillar she was even certain she was not alone, given that not one sound could be heard.

Aldrik sat with his arm draped around the woman who napped upon his shoulder. He was dressed in a regal white and gold ensemble, fitting of his station. Elecia had never told Vhalla, but she had always been thankful for whatever the woman had done to make Aldrik show the world that he was their ruler.

As striking as black looked on him, he needed to dress to his role. His eyes looked up from the book that was in his lap, and a smile crept upon his lips. Her cousin was handsome with his small smiles. Even Elecia could not deny that.

"My love." Aldrik rubbed the sleeping woman's shoulder lightly. "Elecia is here."

Vhalla groaned softly, blinking her eyes open. She wore a long golden gown that creatively draped her in Southern classical design. Even the blue ribbon that was just under her growing bust was a nice touch. But no trick of cloth could be used to hide or diminish the massive swell of the Empress's stomach.

"Elecia!" Vhalla struggled to sit up. A palm instinctually rested on the curve of her belly. Elecia wondered what made all pregnant women, regardless of age, class, or location, do so. "You finally came! It is so good to see you!"

"Sit, foolish woman," Elecia demanded as Vhalla tried to stand to greet her. Aldrik did not even make an effort, his arm fastened to Vhalla's shoulders.

"I missed you, too," Vhalla laughed.

"All right, let me see what my cousin has inflicted upon you." Elecia crossed over to the Empress.

Aldrik glanced away. Men—at least the good ones—always had a touch of guilt for what they were going to force their women to endure on their children's behalf. *As they should*, Elecia believed. It was part of the reason why she insisted every man be present for the birth of their child. Not just for support and to see their offspring, but to ensure they understood what it was that their loved ones went through. It was also a direct way to point out the risk it held for mother and child. The truth was that a birthing room could as easily be the last moments of life rather than the first.

"She hasn't allowed any clerics to touch her—"Aldrik began.

"I didn't trust them, and I wanted the best," Vhalla proclaimed as though the fact were obvious.

"So you said in your letter." Elecia placed her palms on her hips, looking down at the Empress. "Really, Vhalla, it's dangerous for a woman to go so long without a cleric taking a look."

"It hasn't been that long." Vhalla rolled her eyes.

"When did she start to show?" Elecia turned to the dark-haired man. Hardly anything about him had changed since she had seen him last. It was something Elecia appreciated. Aldrik was consistent. He'd even worn his hair the same length as long as she had known him.

"Perhaps . . ." Aldrik was lost in thought. His gaze was fixed on Vhalla's stomach as though it would tell him. "Three months ago?"

"Three months?" Elecia blinked. "You're further than I thought then. A spring birth, I'd estimate."

"You shouldn't have taken so long." Vhalla grinned up at her, and Elecia only offered an unlady-like snort in response. It was adorable when the woman thought she could return Elecia's humor in kind.

"I was busy." Elecia knelt down before the Empress.

"Were you?" Vhalla asked with an annoying little smile.

"Are you well?" Aldrik inquired.

"I am, cousin." Elecia nodded with a smile just for him and completely ignored Vhalla's question. "And you both?"

"We could not be happier," Aldrik proclaimed boldly, his fingers wrapping around Vhalla's still resting on the swell of her stomach.

Elecia shook her head with a small smile as the two shared a look, and she was forgotten for a moment. She wasn't going to be the one to mention the Northern princess's deal and cast a shadow over that look he was giving his wife.

"That's beautiful, but she has not been properly looked at yet. Let me see if you truly have cause to be happy," Elecia cautioned, reaching forward and placing her hands upon the swollen abdomen of the other woman.

"Is there a risk?" Aldrik leaned forward. "Is something wrong?"

"I don't know yet." Elecia shook her head. "If she's progressed this far without problem, then you should be well on your way to a healthy child. But we can't be certain until I've taken a look at her, and more until the babe is here."

"Right." Aldrik sat back. Vhalla gave him a little grin. Apparently, the worried questioning was not new, and it wasn't about to stop. "Her feet are swollen, and the small of her back aches."

"So rub them." Elecia rolled her eyes.

"Can it be made better?" Aldrik asked. "Perhaps some potion or—"

"Aldrik," Vhalla stopped him with a squeeze of her hand. "I'm fine."

Elecia saw the look her cousin was being given by his wife and returned her attention to the work at hand. She remembered how Aldrik had reacted to the miscarriage at the Crossroads. Clearly, women's matters still troubled him deeply.

Closing her eyes, Elecia shifted her focus, delicately sending waves of magic through the veins in Vhalla's body. Elecia checked the responses echoing back to her. If the response was slow or did not come, something was likely broken. If it was cold, that could mean there was a problem of a different sort. If it was too warm, it normally indicated sickness or infection. But everything returned to her palms with ease.

"You feel good, Vhalla," Elecia encouraged, more for her cousin's sake than anyone else's. "Let me check the child also."

Elecia probed gently, connecting through mother to what was carried within the womb. She paused, furrowing her brow and shutting her eyes once more. Listening closely, she tried to make sense of the response that echoed in her ears.

"Elecia, what is it? What's wrong?" Aldrik asked hastily at her expression.

"Quiet," Elecia ordered without opening her eyes. Vhalla's heartbeat was clear and strong. However, underneath that was not one *but two* additional heartbeats.

Elecia pulled her hands away slowly, opening her eyes. *Three total heartbeats*. It was small wonder Vhalla was so large so early.

"So!" Elecia stood quickly. "Do you want a boy or a girl?"

"The baby is well? Do you know that already?" Aldrik looked with eager interest.

"Who do you think I am?" Elecia laughed. Had they not called her out from the West just for the care she could give? Though, now that she knew the truth of the Empress's pregnancy, Elecia was thankful for it. There was a hard road ahead before these babies could be brought screaming into the world.

"It's a boy," Vhalla said definitively. "I've never had an appetite like this." She rubbed a palm on her stomach, and Elecia withheld comment on why she thought that fact to be true. "Clearly it must be a boy to demand so much food of me."

"Not all women are like you and have trouble eating. You carry a girl, I can feel it." Aldrik kissed her temple.

"You can feel it?" Vhalla laughed, smiling brightly at her husband. "I carry *him* in me, I know what I feel."

Elecia smirked. Both of them looked back to her expectantly. She turned for the door and began shrugging her cloak back on.

"I'm hungry. Maybe I'll tell you what they are over lunch," Elecia announced. The information was far too satisfying to give it all up at once.

There was a long silence. Elecia looked over from the ties on her cloak to see them frozen in place. Aldrik's hand was still on Vhalla's back, the other wrapped around hers as he helped her up. The Empress blinked at Elecia, total shock in her eyes.

"Elecia," Aldrik finally forced on both of their behalves. "*They?*"

Elecia shook her head with a laugh. He was truly going to be in for trouble. She began to wonder what kind of father Aldrik would be. She thought she had a far better idea already of the mother before her, but Aldrik was an amusing mystery yet. Far removed from the man he once was, Elecia had faith that he would surprise them all.

"Good luck, both of you. You'll need it for both of them." Elecia glanced back to Vhalla's swollen stomach.

She did not say it aloud, but she already looked forward to meeting *the children of fire and wind.*

THE GOLDEN GUARD TRILOGY

AIR AWAKENS PREQUELS

Book One—The Crown's Dog

A coastal summer is turned upside down by a violent murder, and a quest for lost pirate treasure turns into a hunt for the killer.

Jax Wendyll is the crown's dog. As punishment for the unspeakable crimes that tourment him to this day, his life has been conscripted to the Empire Solaris. However, in an Empire afflicted by peace, his duties are relegated to unquestioningly aiding the antics of the youngest prince, Baldair.

Erion Le'Dan, a nobleman's son, expects a quiet summer visit to the Imperial Palace, his only agenda to visit with his unlikely friends. But Jax's discovery the legendary pirate Adela Lagmir's old workroom inspires a hunt for her long lost treasure.

The pursuit of Adela's truth takes the three men to the Imperial summer manor, built along the old pirate mainstays. When Adela's trident is branded into a murdered servant, Prince Baldair's summer amusement of treasure-hunting becomes a hunt to find the killer. But, as mysteries compound, the ghosts of Jax's past may not be the only things haunting them.

The ALCHEMISTS of L⊗OM

A new fantasy epic from author Elise Kova

COMING IN JANUARY 2017

Her vengeance. His vision.

Ari lost everything she once loved when the Five Guilds' resistance fell to the Dragon King. Now, she uses her unparalleled gift for clockwork machinery in tandem with notoriously unscrupulous morals to contribute to a thriving underground organ market. There isn't a place on Loom that is secure from the engineer turned thief, and her magical talents are sold to the highest bidder as long as the job defies their Dragon oppressors.

Cvareh would do anything to see his sister usurp the Dragon King and sit on the throne. His family's house has endured the shame of being the lowest rung in the Dragons' society for far too long. The Alchemist Guild, down on Loom, may just hold the key to putting his kin in power, if Cvareh can get to them before the Dragon King's assassins.

When Ari stumbles upon a wounded Cvareh, she sees an opportunity to slaughter an enemy and make a profit off his corpse. But the Dragon sees an opportunity to navigate Loom with the best person to get him where he wants to go. He offers her the one thing Ari can't refuse:

A wish of her greatest desire, if she brings him to
the Alchemists of Loom.

ACKNOWLEDGEMENTS

MY DEAR READER—without you, this would be nothing. Every word I write now and forevermore is my love letter to you. Every key stroke is done with thanks that you let me take you on these journeys into fantastical worlds. Thank you for following me, for reading this tale, and, hopefully, for letting me take you on many more adventures in the future. I may not know your name, but that makes you no less precious to me.

Merilliza Chan—you will always have a place in my heart as the first cover designer I worked with. You're as beautiful a person inside as your art is outside. I wish you all the success in the world and every dream you have to be a reality.

Monica Wanat—thank you for dutifully looking over more than 500,000 of my words. I learned a lot in our time together and I'm very grateful you were willing to edit for a newbie author such as myself.

Nick—I could write an entire book on what you mean to me as a friend and it wouldn't be enough. So I'll settle for a sentence and the faith that you know how desperately I need our hour long phone calls to talk me off mental ledges and talk out all my wild story ideas.

Katie—every time we're together, I just think, "How lucky we are to be alive right now." (Yes, I just immortalized our Hamilton obsession and there's nothing you can do about it) You remind me to have fun, to let go, to not be so tunnel-visioned on the future that I forget the present. Thank you for being the best friend a girl could ever ask for.

Mer—I love you sister. But you knew that already. You never let me forget what I'm capable of, you never let me give up, and you're never afraid to tell me what I need to hear. Beyond that, you're my "octurnal twin" and there's no one else I'd rather be up until three A.M., eating cookie dough ice cream, and having Taylor Swift dance parties with.

Mom and Dad—you two are my biggest cheerleaders and largest supporters. Thank you for always being there to help me, for every bookmark you passed out, for every manuscript you've read. You both inspire me to be the best I can be both as an author and as a person. Every day, I consider myself lucky that you both are my parents.

Aunt Susan—I look forward to both your comments on and edits of my manuscripts. Thank you for your time and your support. You took a huge weight off my shoulders and I am deeply appreciative.

Betsy—thank you for not just supporting me in the literary world, but in life. You're wonderful and I'm so lucky to have you as official family now.

Susan Dennard, author of *Truthwitch*—you, you beautiful person you, what am I supposed to say? You're the awesomeist of awesomes? You're as kind as your writing is superb? I'm so glad we met and bewildered—I mean overjoyed—that you're not scared off by my crazy. Thank you for being an ear, offering advice, and just being a good friend.

Danielle L. Jensen, author of the *Malediction Trilogy*—I'm surprised Twitter hasn't kicked us off for the gigabits of space our message history must be taking up. Even though we've yet to meet (as of when I'm writing this) I already feel like you're a girlfriend I've had for years, the type of friend who you sit on the couch with in your PJs and order pizza after a long week. Thank you for that.

Michelle Madow, author of *Elementals*—look at how far we've come! You helped me right at the start and have been in my corner since. I deeply appreciate all the insights you've given me along the way.

Rob and the Gatekeeper Press Team—I couldn't have done this without you. I'm so glad I found you all right at the start of my publishing journey. I couldn't imagine my stress levels if I hadn't had you to help manage things. I appreciate your insights, professionalism, and dependability.

Jamie—I feel like you are my book blog consultant. You know so much about the bookish world and I can't tell you how valuable your thoughts have been to me. But, beyond that, you're a great person and an even better friend. I appreciate everything you give to me more than you know. I don't say it enough, but thank you.

Dani—my "real Vhalla Yarl", thank you for always being there when I need and ear. I feel like we're truly kindred spirits and I can't wait to give you a big hug in person! Your help on these manuscripts has been essential to getting them where they need to be.

Iris—I'm so glad I met you at the start of my career. You're a lovely person and have been a great friend to me through the ups and downs of all of this.

Lauren & Sabrina—your enthusiasm and willingness to give advice has truly helped me throughout this process. I know whenever I've had a hard day I can talk to you two and I'll be met with love and positivity. Thank you both for being such great Twitter buddies.

My Tower Guard—I'm struggling to write this, because

nothing I write seems like enough for you. Every single guard member has been essential in helping me through this process. When I need something, you've risen to task. When I was down, you were there to pick me back up. When I questioned, you reminded me of why I'm doing this without even trying. Thank you to each and every one of you. I hope that we can go on many more adventures together.

ABOUT THE AUTHOR

ELISE KOVA has always had a profound love of fantastical worlds. Somehow, she managed to focus on the real world long enough to graduate with a Master's in Business Administration before crawling back under her favorite writing blanket to conceptualize her next magic system. She currently lives in St. Petersburg, Florida, and when she is not writing can be found playing video games, watching anime, or talking with readers on social media.

Visit her on the Web at www.elisekova.com
Twitter (@EliseKova)
Facebook.com/AuthorEliseKova
Instagram (@Elise.Kova)

Subscribe to her monthly newsletter
on books and writing at www.elisekova.com/subscribe

CPSIA information can be obtained
at www.ICGtesting.com
Printed in the USA
FFHW01n1250210818
47975708-51666FF